Virgi...r. Her
much-loved novel..*mphony*,
Music in the Night and *Olivia*. Virginia Andrews' novels have
sold more than eighty million copies and have been translated
into twenty-two foreign languages.

VIRGINIA ANDREWS®

HEART SONG

POCKET
BOOKS

LONDON • SYDNEY • NEW YORK • TORONTO

First published in Great Britain by Simon & Schuster UK Ltd, 1997
This edition published by Pocket Books, 2004
An imprint of Simon & Schuster UK Ltd
A Viacom Company

1 3 5 7 9 10 8 6 4 2

Simon & Schuster UK Ltd
Africa House
64–78 Kingsway
London WC2B 6AH

www.simonsays.co.uk

Simon & Schuster Australia
Sydney

A CIP catalogue record for this book is available from the British Library

ISBN 0-7434-9514-4

Printed and bound in Great Britain by
Bookmarque Ltd, Croydon, Surrey

HEART SONG

Prologue

As a little girl, I'd spend hours looking out our trailer window, dreaming of the life I'd have when I grew older. I dreamed of all the friends I'd make, the parties I'd attend, the special boyfriends I'd bring home to meet Mommy and Daddy. Oh, if I'd only known that the coming years would bring more sadness and pain than I could ever imagine. If only I'd wished harder, dreamed longer, maybe my life would be different, maybe I wouldn't be sitting on this beach so lonely and confused.

Instead of parties and friends to occupy my time, I spend many of my days here, staring out at the ocean, thinking about Mommy and my step-daddy, about how they're gone now, dead and buried, leaving me all alone, an orphan. Of course, I'm not completely alone. I have my new family, the Logans: Grandma Olivia, Grandpa Samuel, Grandma Belinda, Uncle Jacob, Aunt Sara, and Cary, too, but they all have their own reasons for making me feel unwelcome, unwanted. After all, they hadn't asked me to come

1

live with them. In fact, in all my sixteen years they hadn't asked for me at all.

When Mommy first brought me to Provincetown after my step-daddy died, I couldn't believe she was going to leave me with strangers. I didn't know them, and, family or not, they made it clear they didn't want to know me. They couldn't get past the fact that I was Haille's child and the Logans had nothing but hate and contempt for my mother. I begged Mommy to take me with her, not to leave me grieving all alone. I had just lost the only daddy I had ever known, and now she was leaving too! But nothing I did or said would make her stay; she was determined to become a famous actress or model and she said I would just stand in her way.

At first I believed Mommy would come back for me. Surely she would miss me as much as I missed her. Didn't she cry herself to sleep each night as I did, missing Daddy, missing our old life back in Sewell, West Virginia? But no, Mommy was too self-absorbed to miss me or think of me or even to remember to call when she said she would. I finally realized that I was stuck in Provincetown for good. Oh how I hated Mommy for being so selfish, for running off with her lover Archie Marlin and leaving me with this family who hated me, hated her, and wanted me to be someone I wasn't. It seemed the only way I fit into the Logans' life was if I replaced my cousin Laura, Cary's twin who had died in a boating accident.

But I didn't want to be Laura, I wanted to be me! But who am I? When Daddy died and I learned he was really my step-daddy, I was left with a million questions. Who was my real Daddy? Did he think of me? Did he even know I existed? I thought I could find some answers with the Logans, but they refused to discuss my search for my father and became more secretive with each question I asked. Cary was the only one who would help me, and together we learned

2

that Kenneth Childs, a local artist and friend of the family, was once in love with Mommy and could possibly be my father.

I hadn't had long to rejoice in my news when word came that Mommy had been killed in a car accident in California. Was I never to be happy again? It seemed that whenever anything good happened to me it was always followed by some horrible tragedy. What could be worse than losing Mommy? I thought a part of me died with Daddy, but it wasn't until Mommy was gone too that I realized how truly alone I was. If only I could find my real father I knew he would make things different. Better. I would have a whole new life with him, a life where I was loved and cared for, a life like the one I remembered in West Virginia. Kenneth Childs just had to be my real daddy. He had to be.

1

Curiosity Killed the Cat

"*I*'m leaving, Aunt Sara!" I shouted toward the kitchen as I hurried to the front door after hearing Kenneth Childs blow the horn of his jeep. Cary had introduced me to Kenneth at the beginning of the summer, and it wasn't long after that Kenneth hired me to be his assistant. Kenneth was mostly a loner and a bit of a slob, so I helped him around the house, cooking, cleaning, generally keeping him organized, as well as helping him around his art studio. As I cleaned and swept and dusted I waited, waited for him to open up to me, to tell me if I was his daughter.

When Grandma Olivia revealed that my true grandmother was really her sister Belinda, I realized that Uncle Jacob and Aunt Sara were not actually my uncle and aunt; they were my cousins, as were Cary and May. But because Jacob was my step-father's brother, I continued to call him Uncle and call Sara, Aunt Sara. Cary was happier knowing we weren't as closely blood related as we both originally thought. Ironically, this made him behave more shyly toward me, as though now that a true relationship was not

5

forbidden as some unforgivable sin, he wasn't sure how to proceed.

I put these thoughts of Cary and our blossoming friendship behind me as I grabbed my gear and headed outside to meet Kenneth.

As usual, Kenneth's dog, Ulysses, was sitting in the rear of the jeep. His pink tongue was out, and he was panting, looking as if he were smiling in anticipation of my arrival. His ebony coat had streaks of gray running through it, especially around his snout. During one of Kenneth's rare warm moments, he told me Ulysses had become sprier since I had begun to look after him. "Despite his age," Kenneth added, for Ulysses was nearly a hundred in human years.

So far, that remark about Ulysses was the closest Kenneth had come to giving me a compliment. He had merely grunted his approval when he saw how well I had cleaned and organized his home, and he simply nodded when I did the same in the studio. Most of the time, he was so absorbed in his work, we barely spoke. He made it clear from the beginning that he wouldn't tolerate any interruptions to his concentration, so once he stepped into that studio and began something, I had to move like a ghost.

"An artist has to step out of the real world and dwell in the world of his own creation if he is to succeed," he explained. "It takes a while to get there, and when he's jarred out of it, for whatever reason, it's like starting all over again each time he goes back to what he was doing. Understand?"

I nodded and he seemed satisfied.

"Morning," he said as I stepped up and into the jeep.

"Good morning."

I had my hair brushed back and tied with one of Laura's mauve silk ribbons and I was wearing what was to become my summer uniform: a sweatshirt and dungarees and a pair of sneakers without socks. The sweatshirt was navy blue with Provincetown printed on it in faded white lettering and it, too, had been Laura's.

When I had first arrived in Provincetown to live with Uncle Jacob and Aunt Sara, I felt funny wearing Laura's things. I saw how much it bothered Cary, but if I refused to wear anything Aunt Sara suggested I wear, she became very hurt. Now, Cary accepted it and I . . . I had the feeling Laura would want me to wear her clothes, even though I had never met her and knew her only from what I heard and the pictures of her I had seen.

Ulysses leaned forward for my hug and licked my face.

"Good morning, Ulysses." I laughed. "Don't eat me for breakfast."

"I think it's going to be overcast all day today. Might even rain," Kenneth said as he turned the jeep around and we bounced over the road.

For New Englanders, especially Cape Codders, I thought, the weather was the safest topic to discuss. Everyone had something to say about it, and it usually had nothing to do with politics or religion, although I had heard Judge Childs at one of Grandma Olivia's formal luncheons recently blame the Democrats for too much rain last year.

"I don't mind the thunderstorms. We had them in West Virginia, but I wouldn't want to be in a hurricane," I said.

"No. I've been in a few and they're not pleasant."

We turned onto the highway and headed out toward the Point, where Kenneth lived and had his studio. Although the jeep rode well enough, it looked as weathered and worn as an old pair of shoes, the sort you hated to give up because they were so comfortable. Despite his success as an artist, Kenneth had few of the trappings of wealth. He just didn't look as if he belonged in a shiny new luxury automobile. It would

7

be impractical for him to drive it over the beach road to his home anyway.

I had been working for him only a little more than a week, but I already knew that he didn't spend much time relaxing by the ocean. Occasionally, he went for a walk to think through something artistic that confused him, and it was mainly from those walks and the driving he did in the open jeep that he got his bronze color. His darkened complexion brought out the hazel specks in his otherwise often dark brown eyes, especially during the morning hours, when he looked so bright and alert.

As usual, he wore a pair of leather sandals, ragged jeans, and one of his faded blue T-shirts. This one had some small holes down the right side. With his full beard looking a bit more straggly than usual, he could easily pass for a homeless man, I thought. However, he did keep his dark brown hair neatly tied in a pony tail. Most of the time, he simply had it tied with a short piece of string. Today he had it bound with a thick rubber band. He had a small gold dot of an earring in his right lobe, and wore a shiny piece of black driftwood shaped in a half moon tied around his neck with a string of tiny sea shells.

He drove quietly, his eyes fixed on the road, his face so still, it reminded me of the faces on his statues. There was just the slightest twitch in the muscles of his jaw. I thought he had the type of face that would make any woman's heart flutter when he looked her way, or even when he didn't.

Despite the cloudy sky, the air was warm. Provincetown was crowded with summer tourists. There was much more automobile traffic than usual, and even at this early hour, there were people walking along the streets. Kenneth didn't rage about the invasion of outsiders as did so many other Cape Codders I had met. He spent so little of his time in town, he didn't seem to notice or care. And then, of course, there was the prospect of his works being sold faster when the tourists arrived. Their dollars were just as good as local dollars he told me when I mentioned Uncle Jacob's attitude.

"Did you see anything in the marble block yet?" I asked as we approached the beach road that wound around and over the dunes to his home and studio.

He glanced at me quickly, looked forward, and then shook his head.

"Nope," he said. "Nothing."

"How can you be sure it will come?" I asked. It took him so long to respond, I thought he wasn't going to answer.

"It always has before," he finally said.

The first day he brought me to the studio to work for him, I saw he had a six-foot-tall by nearly four-foot-wide block of marble. He told me it had been delivered the week before.

"It's just like a blank canvas," he explained. When I said I didn't understand, he approached it, put his hand on the stone, and lowered his head as if in prayer. Then, he walked around the piece as he began his lecture.

"The ancient Greeks believed the artistic work was already in the stone. The artist's job is to free it, to bring it out."

"It's in the stone?"

"Yes," he said, almost smiling at my incredulity. "This is what is meant by the artist's vision. In time it will appear to me."

I stared at the marble, looking for some hint, some small indication of a shape within, but I saw nothing. At the time I wondered how long it would be before he saw something. According to him it had been over two weeks and he still hadn't, but he didn't seem upset or nervous about it. He had a patience, a calmness, I had already come to admire.

Although I had been trying to ask him casually

9

about himself all week, I still knew very little about him. He never volunteered any information and getting him to answer my questions was like pulling porcupine quills out of a hound dog.

The house and studio came into view.

"Were you always artistic?" I asked. "Even as a child?"

"Yes," he said. We pulled up to the house and he turned off the engine. Then he reached back for a bag of groceries he had bought before picking me up.

"Did my mother ever see anything you created?" I asked quickly. He didn't pause. He opened the door, the groceries under his arm.

"Everyone I know has seen something I did one time or another," he said and headed for the house. I watched him in frustration as he walked away from my questions. I keep giving him opportunities to open up a conversation about the past, I thought, and every time, he shuts the door in my face. No matter how hard I struggled to find a common ground, a topic of conversation that would lead us to talk about the past and maybe produce the revelations I expected, Kenneth either ignored me or changed the subject. So far, he had succeeded in keeping himself shut up in his work and his private thoughts.

I got out of the jeep, Ulysses following behind me. Kenneth paused at the door.

"Just put all this away and then come to the studio. I want you to prepare some clay. I've decided to do those vases for the Bakerfields to kill time while I wait for my vision. They've been after me for months and they have so much money, it's obscene. Might as well help them lessen the burden of their wealth," he added dryly and entered the house.

Were all artists as disdainful of their customers? I wondered. He acted as if he were doing everyone who liked his art work a favor, instead of being grateful for all the attention he was receiving. Hundreds, probably thousands of artists would die to be in his shoes, I thought.

I was beginning to wonder if I even liked the man who could be my father, much less ever come to love him. Was it possible for me to love him anyway? Is blood enough to bind two people? Surely love had to come from other things, the most important of which was trust. Trust was coming hard to me these days, as one by one everyone and everything I'd come to believe in had let me down.

When I decided to take the job and work for Kenneth, I hoped that just being around him, seeing how and where he lived, would make it possible for me to understand him, but Kenneth's house, furniture, clothing, and possessions were as inscrutable as everything else in his life. The day Cary first brought me to the house, I ventured up to the front windows and peered in. Cary had described Kenneth's furniture as something from a thrift store. When I looked in, I realized he hadn't been exaggerating.

I did the best I could with the thinned and frayed rugs and the worn easy chair, settee, and scratched wooden tables, however polishing and cleaning only seemed to bring out their age and damage. But the house did need a good once-over. I found cobwebs in almost all the corners and sand tracked in everywhere. The windows were clouded with salt and dust and the kitchen was a disaster. The stove was caked with grime, the stove top stained. It took me most of my first week just to get the kitchen clean enough to use. Again, I wondered if all artists were like Kenneth Childs, and if they were, why would anyone really want to be one?

His bedroom wasn't any different from the rest of the house. I could have planted flowers in the dirt under the bed and behind the dresser. I swept and washed the wooden floors. I took all of his clothes out of the closet and organized them, after I had washed

11

and ironed most of them. I emptied the dresser drawers and arranged everything in an orderly fashion and then I washed the windows and polished everything I could.

At first I really thought he was absentminded. He didn't seem to notice any difference, or if he did, he behaved as if he expected it. I had to fish for approval.

"Is the housework all right?" I finally asked. That was when he gave me his grunt.

Kenneth's lack of appreciation for my work made me furious, and I left to walk Ulysses on the beach and blow off some steam. In many ways Kenneth was as selfish and self-absorbed as my mother. He was so oblivious to others around him that I thought I could probably up and quit and it would take him three or four days to notice that I wasn't coming around anymore. But I couldn't just give up and go home. Kenneth could hold all the answers I'd been searching for. If only he'd just notice something other than his damn art. He wasn't like my step-daddy, who took the time to praise the little things I'd done around our little trailer, even things I thought were too insignificant to notice. It seemed as if nothing mattered to Kenneth but his art, and if I didn't fit neatly into the world he'd created around his talent, then I would surely be left out of his life, no matter whether I was his daughter or not.

In my short time with Kenneth I'd found that walking along the beach had a soothing effect on me. The rhythm of the waves, the sheen on the surface, the vastness of the horizon put everything in perspective and made me realize I needed to be patient, to wait calmly for answers. If Kenneth were truly my father, he would let me know in his own time, in his own way. No matter how long it took, I would wait for him to tell me the truth; it was coming as surely as the next wave would wash upon the shore.

So I swallowed my pride and returned to keep

Kenneth's house in order, prepare his meals, and help with his artistic materials. Occasionally, he left me alone in his studio, and when he did, I wandered about gazing at some of his drawings and sculptures, always looking for some clue, something that would tell me more about him. And maybe, just maybe, about myself.

The studio itself was mainly just a large room. On one side were tables and a kiln, and on the tables were his tools and materials, which I had recently reorganized. There was a beat-up tweed settee in the far corner with a driftwood table in front of it. When someone sat on the settee, a cloud of dust rose from the cushions, so I spent a lot of time vacuuming it.

The only truly curious thing in the studio was a door set into the back wall that Kenneth kept locked with a combination lock. I assumed it was where he kept his hazardous chemicals and asked him if he wanted me to do any cleaning in there. He virtually barked at my question. "No. Leave that room alone."

But I couldn't help thinking about it. Why was it necessary for him to keep that door locked? He didn't even lock his house, nor did he bother to lock the door to the studio. One afternoon, when I was alone in the studio, I tried to peek through the locked door, but it was too dark behind it to see anything. I told Cary about it and he was intrigued, too.

Today, I spent most of the morning working with Kenneth in his studio, watching him shape and mold the vases. The first few times I had been in the studio while he worked, he simply acted as if I weren't even there. Of course, after hearing his warning about it, I didn't make a sound, but twice, and now a third time, he talked while he worked, but it was always about art.

"Yes, I've been artistic for as long as I can remember," he said, returning to the conversation we'd started that morning, "but I'm primarily a sculptor now. Sculpture is probably the oldest art form and has undergone only minor variations. Real sculpting, that is," he added glancing at me. I sat on a wooden stool and watched and listened. "I don't go for this new, radical stuff, welding, using neon tubes. A gimmick is not art. An artist has to be authentic. That's the most important thing. An artist must always be true and as pure and simple in his impulse as he or she can be," he lectured.

He stepped back and looked at the vase he was shaping. It was different from any I had ever seen. It was almost shaped like an S.

"I don't recall seeing any of your works in Grandma Olivia's house," I said. "How come she doesn't have anything? She's such good friends with your father and he's so proud of you."

Kenneth paused and stiffened as if I had lashed him with a whip. He never talked about his father, nor, as far as I could tell, did they ever spend time with each other. Without answering my question, he turned back to his work.

"By using soft, yielding materials like this," he explained, "a sculptor can capture and record fleeting impressions much the way a painter does in a quick sketch."

"It's very interesting," I said.

"Everything I do is different. I don't believe true art can be mass produced. It's a contradiction to reproduce it. If it's art, it is by definition one of a kind."

"But then how would people who can't afford them ever have nice things? Not everyone can afford an original."

"Let them go to museums," he replied. Then he paused and glanced at me. "I've given things away to people who can't afford to buy them if I believed they really appreciated the art. Lawyers do pro bono work; so can artists," he added. "This town is full of

14

business people disguised as artists. If you're in it for the money, you're a hypocrite," he added bitterly.

"But everyone needs money to eat, to live," I protested.

"That just follows," he said. "You don't make it a priority. The art, that's the priority." He paused and really looked at me. "Don't you feel that way about your music?"

"I'm not really that good," I said.

He turned away with a shrug.

"If you say you're not, you're not," he muttered. "You have to believe in yourself if you want anyone else to believe in you," he added. The hardness of his words brought tears to my eyes. I felt a lump grow in my throat and had to look away for a moment, but he didn't notice, or if he did, he chose not to pay attention.

"I'm actually working up an appetite," he said. "Why don't you go think about lunch."

I nodded and slipped off the stool. I looked back once before leaving the studio. He was working on his vase, seemingly oblivious to the questions his words brought to my mind. Would I ever find something to believe in so strongly? Kenneth had his art, Momma'd had her acting, even Uncle Jacob had his fishing business. But does believing in yourself mean you become so distanced from others that no one can believe in you?

It was the first, but far from the last time the thought occurred to me that Kenneth Childs hid behind his art, used it like a shield or a fortress to keep anyone and everyone away from touching him. Why? I wondered, and understood that when I found the answer to that, I would find the answer to everything there was between us.

Sometimes Kenneth chose to eat his lunch in his studio, staring at his work in progress and thinking as

15

he ate. If he did that, I ate my lunch on the beach with Ulysses at my side. But it was when Kenneth and I ate lunch together in the kitchen that he was the friendliest and the warmest. At these times I had the feeling he was trying to relax with me, ease himself into more personal conversations, almost the way someone might lower himself into a hot bath.

This particular afternoon, we ate together in the kitchen. I made us cheese and turkey sandwiches on Portuguese bread and some fresh lemonade.

"How do you like going to school here?" he asked.

"It's all right. I've had good teachers. Mama Arlene used to tell me school was like anything else—it's as good as you make it, as you want it to be."

"Who are this Mama Arlene and Papa George you've mentioned? I don't recall any Logan relatives by those names," he said. When he grimaced, the lines at the corners of his eyes deepened and cut through his temples, almost as if someone had taken a pencil and drawn them.

As I explained who they were, he ate, listened, and nodded.

"Despite what I have learned about my family, I still think of them as my grandparents," I concluded.

"But Papa George died and Mama Arlene moved away from Sewell?"

"Yes. I visited his grave when I visited my stepdaddy's."

He stared at me intently and then looked out the window. I thought he would grow interested in something else, the glide of a tern, the shape of a cloud, and drift off in his own thoughts as he so often did. But instead he turned back to me.

"What exactly have you learned about your own family?" he asked. My heart began to thump. Was this it? Was this the moment I had been waiting for?

"First, I was surprised to discover Mommy had

been brought up with my step-daddy, the two of them living as brother and sister. Neither of them had ever told me that."

He nodded.

"Yes," he said, "they were like brother and sister. Brothers and sister I should say, for Jacob was there, too. When I was little and I used to play with them, I didn't realize Haille had been adopted by the Logans. As far as I knew, she had always been there, part of that family. And then one day, I think I was about nine or ten, something like that, Jacob told me. He just blurted it out like kids do. He said something like. . . . Haille's not really our sister. She's a waif."

Kenneth laughed to himself and I didn't move or utter a sound for fear he would stop and I'd never learn anything about my past. He continued, "At the time I thought he said 'wave.' But he said it again, and finally I asked my father what that meant and he explained that the Logans adopted her, but I didn't learn who her mother was until much, much later. No one has a better lock on the door to their closet of skeletons than the Logans, especially Olivia Logan."

"How did my mother feel about being an orphan?"

"I think it bothered her only because Olivia made a point of reminding her," he said.

"Maybe that's why . . ."

"Why what?"

"She was so wild," I said reluctantly. I hated saying anything bad about her, especially since she was no longer here to defend herself. "She was just rebelling."

Kenneth didn't agree or disagree. He just glanced out the window again then said, "I like Olivia. She and I have a healthy respect for one another when we see each other, but she is like the dowager queen of Provincetown. There's no one with bluer blood. Haille was never impressed with all that. In a sense you're right. The truth is I think she hated not knowing where she came from, hated who Olivia wanted her to be."

"No one likes not knowing who their parents are," I said. "No one wants to be an orphan."

He turned to me again, and again I held my breath.

"Sometimes, you're better off not knowing," he finally replied.

"How can you be better off not knowing?"

"It's like you have a clean slate, no one's sins to overcome or forget. You can be yourself, and anyone who can be an individual these days is lucky, especially if he can make a living at the same time. Speaking of which, I've got to go into town to get some supplies," he added and stood. "Got to earn money. I'll be back in a few hours."

I sat there fuming, feeling as if I had hit another wall of silence about my past. How could he be so cold about it? If he was my father, why didn't he just admit it? Was he afraid I would ask to move in with him? Was he afraid he would have to provide for me?

Maybe, just as he said, I was better off not knowing. I could create my father out of my own imagination and make him perfect. He would have no skeletons in his closet and no sins to weigh on both of us. He would be like some mythical god, who sailed in on a cloud of sea mist and strolled confidently into Provincetown and when he saw Mommy and she saw him they fell in love instantly and spent warm nights on the beach. One day, he was just gone and then I was born.

Now that I was here, one day or one night I would be on the beach and my mythical father would appear and tell me everything was all right. I wasn't an orphan and I had a destiny.

Dreams, I thought. They're the riches of a poor person, stashed in treasure chests buried deeply in the imagination. But are dreams enough?

18

I cleaned up and took Ulysses for his afternoon walk. The clouds had broken up and the sky had become a quilt with deep, large patches of blue. The breeze was still strong, making my hair dance around my face. The breakers were high and sparkling, and once again I turned to the sea for answers.

I was so lost in my own thoughts and the surf was so loud, I didn't hear the horn or the shouts until I turned to look back at the house and saw that Cary had driven up in his truck and was waving wildly from the top of a dune. I waved back and started toward him.

"What are you doing here?"

"The water is too rough today. My father decided to come in early, so I thought I'd take a ride over to see how you were doing. Where's Kenneth?"

"He went on an errand he said would take him a few hours," I replied.

Cary knelt and patted Ulysses, but kept his eyes on me.

"Has he said anything?"

"Very little. I thought he was going to say something at lunch today, but—"

"But?"

"He said some people are better off not knowing who their parents are."

"He said that?"

I nodded.

"Strange."

"Something's making him very bitter. I wish I could get him to tell me more."

"I guess he will, in time."

"I'm afraid I might be old and gray by then," I wailed.

Cary laughed and stood up, reaching out to help me climb up the knoll.

"Somehow I can't imagine you old and gray." He continued to hold my hand even though I was beside him. His eyes washed over my face. "The sun's bringing out your freckles," he said. When I started to moan, he quickly added, "but that's cute."

"Cute? I'm too old to be cute," I snapped, pulling my hand from his as I started for the house.

"Hey," he called, but I just kept walking. Suddenly I felt like screaming at everyone and everything. "I'm sorry," he said catching up. "I didn't mean—"

"It's all right," I said. "It's just that I'm so sick of everyone treating me like a child."

"Huh?"

I walked slower, my arms crossed under my breasts. The blood that had rushed into my cheeks warmed my face. I couldn't explain why I was suddenly so angry. Maybe I wasn't angry; maybe I was just afraid, afraid that no one would ever take me and my questions seriously. Cary seized my arm at the elbow and I spun around.

"If you want," he said, "I'll just confront him. I'll just come right out and ask him. I'm not afraid of him," he bragged.

"If he won't tell me anything, what makes you think he would tell you?"

"Then maybe you shouldn't work here anymore," he said.

"Maybe I shouldn't. Maybe I shouldn't have let you talk me into coming back to the Cape in the first place."

I had run away when Grandma Olivia told me about Mommy being raised a Logan. I had gone back to Sewell, but that was when I found out Papa George had died and Mama Arlene had gone to live with her sister in North Carolina. I had no one in Sewell, either, except my best friend Alice Morgan. But I couldn't live with her. Her mother couldn't understand how a daughter of hers would befriend someone raised in a trailer park.

"Of course you should have come back. This is where you belong," Cary insisted. "People care about you here."

"People care about me? I've got a grandmother who wishes I would wash out to sea so I don't embarrass her; an uncle, your father, who thinks I'm the daughter of Satan; a man who could be my father but is unwilling to tell me——"

"I care about you," he said. "A lot."

I tried to hold on to my anger but instead I took a deep breath and let my shoulders sag. I believed Cary, but somehow it wasn't the same. I needed someone to love me the way my daddy did. Of course this thought made me feel guilty, as if I were trying to replace him in my heart. But wasn't that exactly what I was doing?

"It's all just confusing," I said. "Confusing and frustrating."

He nodded.

"Well, you've been here a while. You clean his house, see his things. Are there any hints, clues? Pictures, letters?"

"Nothing I've seen." And then I remembered. "There's only one place I haven't looked."

"Where's that?"

"Remember I told you about that door he has locked in the studio?"

"Oh, yeah. Let me look at it," he said. My heart began to pound.

"Kenneth doesn't like anyone going into his studio when he's away."

"He keeps it unlocked, doesn't he?"

"Yes, but——"

"We won't touch anything. Let me just look," he said.

I looked toward the dune road and thought about Cary's plan. Kenneth had said he would be away for hours.

"Okay," I said, "but don't touch any of his things in the studio. Even though it's usually a mess, he would know if something had been moved an inch."

"Fine," Cary said.

We walked to the studio, pausing momentarily to look into the fish pond.

"When did he add the turtle?" Cary asked.

"I don't know. Maybe last weekend. He calls him Shell."

Cary laughed and we went into the studio. He saw the block of marble and asked about it immediately. I explained the artistic vision just the way Kenneth had explained it to me, but Cary squeezed his eyebrows toward each other, smirked, and asked, "How can you see anything in a block of marble?"

"You can if you have an artist's eyes," I said. He shrugged again and then went to the closet door. For a few minutes, he studied the lock and the hasp.

"Just a combination lock, but it would take forever to figure out the combination. However . . ."

"However what?" I asked coming up beside him.

"This hasp is attached with only these four screws. It would be easy to unscrew them, take off the hasp, leave the lock in place, and open the door. I could do it in five minutes," he claimed. I started to shake my head. "And I can put it back just the way it is so no one would notice. It's easier than finding seaweed on the beach."

"No," I said, turning away. He seized my wrist.

"You haven't gotten him to say anything important and you haven't found anything that would give you any clues."

"He wouldn't have put a lock on it if it wasn't very private," I said.

"You have a right to know about yourself. No one has a right to keep that under lock and key, do they? Well?" he pursued.

I thought a moment.

22

"You can put it back just the way it is?"

"Easily." He reached into his pocket and produced his Swiss Army pocket knife to show me the small screwdriver. "Okay?" he asked.

I looked at the lock again. Maybe there was nothing behind this door. Maybe it was just filled with some of his vases or statues, but Cary was right. I would always wonder.

"Okay," I said. He smiled and put the screwdriver to work. In minutes, just as he had predicted, the hasp came free of the wall and with it, the lock. He folded his knife and turned the handle.

"Ready?"

I took a deep breath and nodded. He opened the door. It was a deeper closet than I had anticipated. Apparently, no one had been in it for a long time. There were cobwebs across the doorway. Cary cleared them out of our way and we stepped into the closet. We saw an easel on the right, a carton filled with brushes, and another carton filled with carving tools beside it. There was an artist's smock hanging from a hook on the wall above the cartons.

"Nothing unusual," I said, my voice tinged with disappointment.

"Isn't there a light in here?" Cary asked as he groped through the air for a pull chain. He found a string and pulled it to turn on a single, naked bulb dangling from the ceiling. The illumination washed away the shadows and revealed a pile of canvases under a white sheet. The sheet was caked with dust. Cary curiously lifted one edge and gazed under it, but I had been hoping we would find a box of letters from Mommy or a diary, something I could read to discover information.

"It just looks like some pictures of someone, but I can't tell anything. I'll hold this up. You pull one out," he instructed.

"We shouldn't, Cary. He's going to know."

23

"We'll just put it back the way we found it," he said. "Go on," he urged. "Aren't you curious?"

I was, but I was also afraid. Ulysses stood in the doorway behind us, watching, and to me it was as if he were wondering why I had betrayed his master.

"Let's just back out of here and put the hasp back in place, Cary."

"We're in here already; we might as well look at everything," he insisted and held the sheet up with one hand while he worked the first canvas off the top of the pile. As it came out, I stepped closer.

First, we saw a pair of legs and then, as more and more of the canvas was revealed, we saw it was a naked woman sprawled on a beach blanket. The picture was done in a most realistic style; it was practically a photograph. Cary got so excited, he dropped the sheet entirely and used both hands to lift the canvas and place it on the floor.

We both stared down, neither of us able to speak, for we both recognized the woman. She couldn't be mistaken. It was Mommy, and the picture was done when she was much younger, perhaps in her late teens.

"Wow," Cary said.

"Put it back, Cary," I urged, my throat quickly closing. Instead, he reached in and pulled out the next canvas. This, too, was of Mommy, only in this one, she was standing, completely naked, gazing at the ocean. It had been drawn and painted very precisely. I recalled the small birthmark just below her left hip.

Cary said nothing as he continued to look at the other paintings.

"They're all of her," he said. "Different poses, different places. Here's one on a boat. She could have been a Playboy centerfold."

"Put it all back!" I cried, tears burning my eyes. I turned away. Suddenly, the small room had become stifling and I couldn't breathe. I rushed out and threw myself onto the settee. Cary put everything back the way it was and shut off the closet light.

"Are you all right?" he asked.

"No," I wailed. My tears were freely carving wet lines down my cheeks.

Cary hurried to replace the hasp on the door, and after he had tightened the last screw, he came to me. I raised my eyes and wiped the tears away, a pit of bitterness growing inside me.

"You were right. Those paintings are so explicit they belong in one of those magazines. No wonder he's keeping them behind a locked door."

"Well, no one ever said your mother was shy," Cary offered with a smile.

"Thanks for reminding me," I spit back. I got up and charged out of the studio, my arms folded, my head down. Cary hurried behind, but I kept walking. Ulysses trotted alongside.

"I'm sorry. I just don't know what to say. I was just as surprised as you were."

I stopped by his truck and stared out at the sea.

"Obviously, they were very close when they were younger, for her to have done that. That must mean something," Cary continued.

"Maybe," I said. "Maybe she was just being his model. She never told me anything so I can only guess."

"Just come out and ask Kenneth," Cary suggested.

"And tell him what? That I went spying in his closet?"

"Well . . ."

"I don't want him to hate me," I said. "He'd never tell me anything then." I spun on Cary. "I don't want anyone to know about this."

"Sure," he said quickly. "Who would I tell, anyway?"

"It's not that you would tell anyone. It just might slip out one day."

"It won't," he promised.

"It would be better if you weren't here when he returns," I said nervously, checking the road into town for signs of Kenneth's jeep.

"Okay. We can talk about it all later, if you want."

I nodded. Quickly, before I realized what he was going to do, Cary reached out and put his arms around me to draw me closer and hug me.

"Everything will be all right," he promised. Then he got into his truck and started the engine. He smiled and waved as he backed it up and drove away. Ulysses and I stood watching the truck bounce over the dune road until it disappeared from sight.

I returned to the house to do some cleaning, and nearly an hour and a half later, I heard the sound of Kenneth's jeep and the quick honking of its horn. Curious, I came out of the house, dust rag still in hand, and watched as Kenneth drove his jeep faster than usual down the dune toward the house. He shut off the engine and leaped over the driver's-side door without even bothering to open it. From where I stood I could see that he had a small package under his arm. I had never seen him so excited.

"I've got it!" he cried, his face beaming.

"What is it?" I asked nodding at the package.

"Not this," he said. "This is just a new tool I needed," he added quickly and took my hand. "Come, quickly!"

"Where?" I asked, starting to laugh at his newfound enthusiasm.

He pulled me along, around the corner of the house and back toward the studio. He thrust open the door but stopped after we entered. We were facing the block of marble. He stood in the doorway, still holding my hand and staring at the marble block. Then he nodded and said, "Yes, yes, yes." He looked at me, nodded again, and looked at the marble.

"What is it?" I asked, now holding my breath.

26

"The vision. It finally came to me. It happened as I was on my way back home. I was thinking about you."

"Me?"

"And then I looked toward the ocean and it just burst before me, the whole finished work."

"But why me?"

"Because you're the center of this work," he said, nodding at the marble.

"I am?"

"Sit," he ordered, and pulled me toward the settee. I did as he instructed and watched him pace around the block, as I'd seen him do a hundred times before. Except this time there was a peculiar light shining in his eyes.

"Out of a wave emerges this beautiful young woman. I want to catch that transition, that birth from the water, which I will call, The Birth of Neptune's Daughter!" he exclaimed, whirling about to face me.

I had never seen Kenneth's face filled with more excitement. His eyes were positively luminous. He seemed so full of energy, I thought he might just burst before my eyes. The veins strained in his neck and around his temples.

"It's almost as if the muses, the gods and goddesses of art, sent you here," he declared.

I smiled. At last he was looking at me, talking to me, not at me, not through me, or above me. He stepped forward and took my hands into his, pulling me to my feet again.

"Kenneth are you sure?"

"Just stand there," he said bringing me to the marble block. He placed me where he wanted me and then stepped back and stared so intently at me, I couldn't help blushing. He nodded. "Yes, yes," he said. "This is it."

"I don't think I completely understand," I said.

"You will. First, I'll draw the picture and then I'll

27

figure out a method, materials I want to use to make a mockup. You'll be more than just the model. You'll be my assistant. I'll show you how to start on the block and you'll do some of the preliminary work. Artistic assistants often help with the rough cutting and chiseling."

"Model?" I said.

"Of course. It's you I see emerging. Think about it. You came back here to start a whole new life. It is as if you were emerging from the sea. You've been reborn."

He was so excited he could hardly contain his words.

"I'll explain more to you as we go along, but this work is more than just a classical piece about the god of the sea; it's about the birth of femininity, of a woman, the depiction of a young girl's transition into maturity, blossoming, blooming, exploding in her sexuality. Just the way you are right now," he added.

I didn't think it was possible for me to turn any more crimson than I had, but my skin felt as if it were on fire.

"Me?" I said again, horrified at the thought that Kenneth could see all those emotions brewing inside me.

"Of course you. This might very well be the most important work of my whole life, the pinnacle of my career," he said. He grew serious as he stepped closer. "You'll do this with me, won't you? You're not too shy or afraid?"

"I—"

"I'll take my time with you and I'll show you everything you need to know every step of the way." He took my hands into his again. "We're going to do this together. You'll be part of something very significant, Melody."

I nodded, slowly, still in a daze, bowled over by his exhilaration.

"We'll start tomorrow," he said. "First, I want to

spend some time thinking, envisioning. I want to go down to the sea and stare at the waves until I get the shape and the movement I need. In the morning, I'll show you how to use the tools for the rough cut. You can practice on another piece first, okay?"

"I guess," I said. He laughed and slapped his hands together. Then he went back to the marble block and put his hands on it as if he drew some sort of energy and power from it. He stood there with his eyes closed and whispered loudly.

"Yes, yes. I can feel it. This is the vision I've been waiting for."

I guess I was wide eyed, for when he looked at me again, he laughed.

"I'm scaring you, huh?"

"No, I'm just surprised," I said. "Is this what happens to all artists when they get an idea?"

He laughed.

"I don't know about other artists; I know only about myself." He approached me and again took my hands into his as he fixed his intense eyes on me. "Are you afraid you can't be a model?"

"I've never done anything like that."

"We'll go about it slowly. I won't rush you into anything until you're comfortable because if you're not comfortable, you'll be sending out the wrong emotions and I won't be able to create what's in my mind and what's in the marble," he said. "But once we start," he added, smiling, "you'll see it's nothing to be afraid of or ashamed of. You'll feel the power of your own intrinsic beauty and you'll flourish."

His words exhilarated me and I wondered if this was what he had said to my mother? Was this the way he had gotten her to model? Or was there something else between them, the love I suspected? Perhaps what Kenneth really had discovered was his way, his path to follow to tell me about himself and about me and all that had occurred.

I couldn't deny that the idea made me tremble. He must have felt my hands shaking. He squeezed a bit tighter and held his gaze on me firmly as he continued.

"Few people really understand the artistic vision," he said. "Or appreciate it. Somehow, I think you do."

"Why?" I asked, curious to know what he had seen in me.

"It's just a feeling I have, an instinct, and my instincts have always been accurate, especially when it comes to people," he added, his eyes darkening to tell me some of those accurate instinctive readings were unpleasant.

But what was he really telling me with these words and those eyes? Was he saying I would appreciate the artist's instinct because I had inherited it from him?

"For now," he continued, "I think it would be best if you didn't mention this to anyone else, especially your uncle Jacob and the rest of the Logans. Their thinking, like too many others', I'm afraid, is quite narrow. They just wouldn't understand. Can you do that? Can you keep a secret for a while?"

"I'm used to secrets," I said pointedly, but he just smiled and nodded.

"Good." He turned back to the marble. "I know I haven't been this excited in years," he said. And then he looked at me again, "And I know now it's because of you."

I looked at the block of marble and just like him, I suddenly saw that it was more than stone.

It was possibly the way to my father and to the truth, and to the happiness I hoped lay just behind it.

I couldn't wait to begin.

2

&

A Model's Life

All the way back to Uncle Jacob's house, Kenneth talked continuously about his new art project, barely pausing to take a breath between sentences. He described the mythological background, the idea of creating Neptune's daughter, how art helps us to understand problems in the modern world and why he believed the artist was the only true prophet. Sitting in his jeep as we drove along, I felt as if I were sitting in a college classroom. He made it all sound so interesting. I noticed when he spoke about the things that were close to his heart, his whole face brightened; he seemed to rise out of his visions and ideas and become more vibrant. I was too shy to say it, but often, when I played my fiddle and closed my eyes, I felt just the way he felt now. Maybe that was the link that would bind us together, I thought, our mutual artistic loves.

"I'll see you bright and early in the morning," he declared when we stopped at the house. "Tomorrow, we'll begin."

"Okay."

31

He grabbed my elbow as I started to open the door.

"And remember what I said. Let this just be something between us for now, okay?" His eyes were full of warning.

I nodded and stepped out of the jeep, feeling his eerie gaze on my back.

"Don't do anything different with your hair. It's perfect as it is," he said. I started to smile. "It's the way I saw her in my vision. Bye," he said and drove off.

What did he mean? It's the way he saw *her* in his vision? Was he looking at me, as I had thought, or was he seeing some mythical creature, some figment of his imagination, or even a young girl from his past, created out of memories? Wasn't I the most important thing in his life right now? Or was it Mommy taking away my happiness from beyond the grave? I was more confused than ever when I turned and walked into the house.

Uncle Jacob was coming down the stairs as I entered. He looked as if he had been taking a nap. His hair was disheveled, his face was full of crinkles, and his eyes were glassy. The shadows on his unshaven chin resembled bruises. The sleeves of his shirt were rolled to his elbows and he wore his fur-lined slippers over his bare feet. He paused on the steps and stiffened when I gazed up at him.

"He ought to bring you home a little earlier so you can help Sara with dinner," he said.

"I'm sorry. I'll tell him."

Uncle Jacob grunted.

"So, what's he been up to?" he asked. "Did he come forth and confess his sins yet?"

"I don't know about any sins."

He smirked with skepticism.

"When's he supposed to pay you?"

"Every two weeks is what he told us when he first came to the house," I reminded him.

"Remember to put half in the kitchen pot," he countered and continued down the steps toward the living room.

"Is that you, dear?" I heard Aunt Sara call from the kitchen doorway, where she stood wiping her hands on her apron. She came forward, looking very excited.

"Hi, Aunt Sara."

"I have some news for you." She stepped forward and in a loud whisper asked, "Did Jacob tell you?"

I shook my head.

"Olivia called this afternoon to invite you to lunch on Saturday. Just you!" she exclaimed girlishly.

"Just me? Why?"

"I don't know dear, but isn't that nice? She's sending Raymond with the car to pick you up at twelve sharp. You'll wear something nice, one of those sun dresses. Maybe the one with the yellow tear drops and the white collar?"

I really hadn't gone through Laura's entire wardrobe and didn't recall the dress, but I nodded anyway because Aunt Sara acted as though I had worn it.

"I'll just go wash up and then come down to help you, Aunt Sara."

"Everything's done," she said. "Don't hurry. Rest. You're a working girl now." Her smile froze. "Laura always wanted to be working, but Jacob didn't want her to do anything involving tourists. She liked Kenneth, especially his paintings and statues. She would have wanted to work for him, too," she added, sighing deeply as she returned to the kitchen.

I gazed into the living room and saw Uncle Jacob sitting in his chair, staring out at me. He had the strangest look on his face, a dreamy, far-off expression, softer than I had ever seen. He realized he was staring and quickly dropped his gaze to the newspaper in his lap. I hurried up the steps to my room and saw that the ladder to Cary's attic hideaway was down. That meant he was up there working on his models. I was only in my room for a few moments when May appeared at my door. Most evenings she would come to my bedroom to excitedly relay the events of her day.

May continued attending her special school during the summer and had only a short ten-day break before the start of the regular school year. Her summer day was abbreviated, but she would rather have had the summers off just like the kids who attended the regular public school. Ever since I started working for Kenneth she had been begging me to take her to see his studio. Uncle Jacob had forbidden it up until now, telling her she couldn't miss a day of her school just to waste time watching me clean someone else's house and make someone else his lunch. But with Cary on the fishing boat and me away most of the day, she had to spend more time alone than ever. She was starved for conversation and attention by the time Cary and I returned from work each day.

As usual, May's hands went a mile a minute, signing questions, telling me about things she had done, and expressing her desire to accompany me to Kenneth's studio.

I promised I would ask Uncle Jacob again, but she didn't look hopeful. In fact she looked downright sad. May was smaller than most girls her age, and it seemed to me that she was even paler and thinner these days. I thought she resembled a flower without enough rain and sunshine, withering under dark, oppressive clouds. In her large, shadowed hazel eyes lingered more dark sufferings than a child her age should know, I thought. She lived in a silent world, hearing only her own thoughts, craving smiles, wondering about the sound of laughter.

It occurred to me that May didn't even know what

it was like to hear someone cry. Of course, from the looks on people's faces, she knew happiness from sadness, anger from approval, but for me, someone who loved to make music and listen to it, the idea of being deaf seemed overwhelming. The eternal silence would drive me mad, I thought, and wondered what made May so strong. Sometimes her strength worked against her, and people forgot that she still needed little joys in her life. How could Uncle Jacob refuse her anything? He must have beach sand in his veins instead of blood, and a heart made from an old barnacle.

I told May about the things I had done all day, though I didn't reveal that Cary had visited. I was sure she would be upset that he hadn't offered to take her along. As I described my walks along the beach with Ulysses and even the cleaning I did in Kenneth's house, May stood looking at my hands as though I were drawing the most wonderful pictures of fun. Her eyes were wide and she nodded and smiled to keep me going. She laughed aloud when I described how Ulysses hid under Kenneth's jeep whenever the sky filled with thunder and lightning. When she asked me about Kenneth's paintings and statues, I looked away in shame, thinking about Mommy in Kenneth's secret paintings.

For the first time I realized that Mommy had lived a whole other life here. She had made friends she had never mentioned, especially boyfriends. How could she keep secret growing up at that big, wonderful house, living on the beach with the sailing and the swimming and all the parties? How could she drive those memories down so deeply that she never even slipped and mentioned something nice to me? Didn't she have any happiness here? Wasn't there anything that she had longed to see again, to hear again? The smell of the ocean was so strong, it soaked into your very being. I was sure of that because it already seemed to be part of me. How hateful and traumatic her flight from Provincetown must have been for her to keep so many secrets, I thought.

May tapped me on the shoulder. I had become so absorbed with my musings, I forgot that she was standing there. I smiled at her and then began to describe the vase Kenneth was creating. She nodded, thought about something for a minute, and then asked me to wait right there in the room until she returned. She hurried out and I went to the closet to search for the dress Aunt Sara had described. I found it hanging all the way in the back of the closet. She was right: it was a happy, bright dress, perfect for an afternoon. Moments later, May returned with a drawing pad in her hands. She hesitated, her eyes filled with trepidation, and then handed it to me.

Curious, I sat on the bed and lifted the cover. What I found amazed me. In the pad were excellent India-ink drawings, many of which were of me. There were pictures of me standing on the beach, pictures of me in the kitchen, and pictures of me holding May's hand and walking with her down the street toward town.

I quickly signed how wonderful I thought her pictures were, and then she shook her head.

"What?" I asked, even more curious. She took the pad from me and flipped the pages to the end to show me the inside of the back cover. I gazed down at it and felt my blood freeze in my veins.

"I don't understand," I signed. "Aren't these your drawings?"

She shook her head and I looked at the words scribbled on the inside back pages again.

"But—"

I flipped through the pad, gazing more closely at the drawings I thought were drawings of me. I guess it was just that I assumed it was I who had been depicted. How strange . . . eerie. This pad had belonged to

Laura. She had been the artist and she had drawn pictures of herself and pictures of herself with May.

Somehow, maybe because of the way Aunt Sara treated me and spoke to me, or because I was living in her room and wearing her things, I had mistaken Laura for myself in these drawings. At this moment I could appreciate and understand what Aunt Sara was experiencing when she looked at me with sad eyes that told me I reminded her of Laura.

"Do you draw, too?" I asked May. She shook her head and asked me if I wanted to show the pictures to Kenneth.

"Yes, maybe I will," I signed, which pleased her. I perused the rest of the pad and found a picture of Cary that intrigued me. In it he was standing on the beach, holding his hands out while sand was falling through his fingers. It was as if he were saying that something he thought was important really had no meaning.

Just then, as if on cue, I heard Cary coming down the ladder. May saw the direction my eyes had taken and turned in anticipation, too.

"Hi," he said. "How did the rest of the day go?"

"Fine."

"But nothing . . ."

"No."

"What do you have there?" he asked stepping through the doorway.

"May brought me these pictures Laura drew and gave her. She wants me to show them to Kenneth."

He saw that I had turned to the page containing the picture of him.

"I gave May that pad the week Laura died," he said, his dark eyes gone bleak, "so she would have something to cherish, but it's not the sort of thing I wanted to show everyone. I don't mind your seeing it, but Laura was very choosy about whom she would show

37

those drawings. Nobody in school saw them, not even her art teacher, and if she wanted Kenneth to see them, I'm sure she would have shown them to him herself."

"Okay," I said, trying to hide my nervous laughter.

"What's funny?"

"I thought May had done them and was bringing them to me to show her own work." I answered, though I didn't add that I thought they were pictures of me.

He signed to May, telling her she should keep the pad in her own room where it belonged. She looked disappointed, but took the pad back when I handed it to her.

"Did you deliberately pose for any of them?" I asked. It was more than just curiosity. I wanted to know what he felt like modeling for someone, but he wasn't willing to talk about it.

"For a few," he admitted. "I'm starving," he quickly added to change the subject. "Is dinner ready?"

"I think so. Did you hear about my invitation to Grandma Olivia's?"

"As soon as I walked in the door. It was the first thing Ma told me," he said.

"Why just me?"

He shrugged.

"She wants to get to know you better?"

I smiled skeptically.

"Maybe Grandma's easing up. Old age," he added with a grin.

We all went down to dinner, where I helped serve. I noticed throughout the meal that Uncle Jacob was staring at me from time to time. Finally, before we were finished, he stopped chewing, drank some water, and leaned back.

"You mean to tell me," he said as if we were still in the middle of our earlier conversation, "you've been there over a week and he hasn't mentioned nothin' about Haille?"

Cary shifted his eyes to me quickly.

"He spoke of her," I said, "but he didn't say they had been romantically involved."

"Romantically involved?" Uncle Jacob said with a laugh. He shook his head. "Romantically involved for Haille meant sneaking behind some boat house."

"Jacob!" Aunt Sara said. "Shame on you speaking of the dead that way, and especially in front of young people."

"I'm sure they've heard a lot worse," he said, glancing at me and then at Aunt Sara. "I'm just sayin' how it was."

"There's a time and place for such talk and you know it's not at the dinner table, Jacob Logan," she insisted.

He turned a little crimson at the reprimand. The tension was so thick, it felt as if we were sitting in a roomful of cobwebs. Yet I thought I knew the underlying purpose to all these questions about Kenneth and me.

"I'm sorry I'm a burden to you, Uncle Jacob," I said. "I know you would like Kenneth Childs or someone to admit to being my father so he would have to look after me," I said firmly.

"Well that isn't my whole reason, but it would be the right thing to do, wouldn't it?" He looked across the table at Aunt Sara. "The Bible tells us to suffer the children. It means our own, Sara."

"She is our own," Aunt Sara said. "God brought her for a purpose, Jacob," she retorted with more grit than I had seen or heard in her voice since first coming to their home. She looked as if she would heave a plate at him if he uttered one syllable of disagreement.

Uncle Jacob just grunted and mumbled about being finished. He left the table.

I helped clean up and while I washed the silverware and dishes, Aunt Sara told me not to mind anything Uncle Jacob said.

"What he says today, he regrets tomorrow," she told me. "He's always been like that. That man has swallowed more of his own sour words than anyone I know. It's a wonder he doesn't walk around all day with a bellyache."

"He's not completely wrong, Aunt Sara. People shouldn't have children and then leave them for someone else to look after. Even though you've been more of a mother to me than my own mother, she shouldn't have just dumped me here," I added. Aunt Sara's eyes filled with tears. She turned to hug me.

"You poor child. You never think of yourself as being dumped here, understand? And don't you ever think of yourself. as being an orphan, Melody. Not while I have a breath left in my body, hear? We've both got holes in our hearts and we're plugging them up for each other," she said and kissed my forehead. I hugged her back and thanked her before going upstairs. Cary poked his head through the attic trapdoor as soon as I reached the landing.

"Want to see the model I just finished?" he asked.

"I promised May I'd play Monopoly with her."

"So, you will," he said. I looked toward May's doorway and then hurried up the ladder into the attic.

The attic hideaway wasn't much bigger than my room. The biggest piece of furniture up there was the table on which Cary worked meticulously on his model ships. Above the table were shelves filled with the models he had completed over the years. There were also a small sofa and some boxes and sea chests sharing the space.

Cary knew a great deal about ship building from studying the historical models he had completed. There were Egyptian, Greek, and Roman models, even Chinese junks. He had clipper ships and battle ships, steamships, tankers, and luxury liners, including a replica of the *Titanic*. His newest model was a nuclear submarine.

"Look," he said drawing me closer. Carefully, like a surgeon operating on a human heart, he snapped off one side of the submarine and showed me the interior. I couldn't believe the details, even down to tiny lights.

"It's beautiful, Cary. All of your work is tremendous. I wish you would let more people see it."

"I don't do it for people. I do it for myself," he said sharply. "It's almost like . . . like why Kenneth painted those portraits of your mother."

The smile left my face and I thought again about Kenneth's proposal for me to become his model. I wondered if I could confide in Cary, or if he would get so upset about it, he would do something to stop me. In my mind I still saw the whole thing as Kenneth's way to reveal his deep secrets and perhaps bring me truly home. I wasn't willing to risk losing that just yet. The other thoughts, of me being like my mother and posing just like a model in a sleazy magazine, I pushed to the back of my mind.

"A real artist like Kenneth doesn't look at someone the same way," I offered, but turned as I spoke so I could gaze out the small window toward the ocean in the distance. The moonlight cut a pathway over the silvery surface. "He sees something else."

"What?" Cary pursued.

"He sees beauty; he sees deep meaning."

"That's hogwash. A man sees one thing when he looks at a naked woman."

"Cary Logan, that's not true!" I snapped, turning sharply on him. "Does a doctor see one thing when he looks at a woman patient?"

"Well no, I guess not," he admitted.

41

"Then it all depends on his purpose for looking, doesn't it?" I asked sharply, not knowing whom I needed to convince more, Cary or myself.

Cary shook his head.

"I'm sorry, Melody. I can't imagine looking at you with your clothes off and thinking about anything else but you. My hand would shake so much, the paint-brush would go all over the page," he added smiling. The way he looked at me made me blush all over. It was as if I were really naked and standing in front of him.

"That's because you're not an artist," I insisted. "They have more control of themselves."

"I guess so," he said. Then he laughed. "I don't think I'd want to be an artist if that's what happens to them."

I stamped my foot in frustration.

"You're just like any other boy, Cary Logan." I started toward the door, but he reached out and grabbed my wrist.

"Whoa. Set anchor for a minute, will ya. I'm just teasing you a little. I thought you believed we were all too serious in this house. Didn't you tell me that once?"

I hesitated, the smoke I imagined coming out of my ears, disappearing.

"Yes, I did, and I still say it."

"So?"

"That doesn't mean you should tease me like that," I said. "Don't joke about anything when it comes to Kenneth. You of all people know how sensitive I am about it all."

"Okay." He let go of my wrist and raised his hand. "I promise."

I relaxed.

"I better get down to May."

"Okay. But you didn't tell me anything. What happened when he returned?"

42

"He was all excited," I said. "He had an idea for his block of marble."

"You mean he saw the shape in the stone finally?"

"Yes."

"What's the shape?"

"He calls it Neptune's daughter. I'll know more tomorrow and the day after. He's going to draw it first."

"Artists really are strange," Cary said shaking his head.

"You better stop saying things like that, Cary Logan. You're an artist, too. All this is creative," I said sweeping my hand toward the shelves of models.

"It's just something I do to take up time, but it's really what I'd like to do someday—build ships. I want to build custom sailboats for people. You know I'd rather do that than anything," he admitted.

"Did you do what I said? Did you tell your father?"

"Yeah." He dropped his gaze and turned away.

"He disapproves, of course," I concluded, "but did he see how much you wanted to do it?"

"We've been fishermen forever in this family. He has this religious belief in tradition."

"What you want to do still has to do with the sea, doesn't it?"

"It's not the same thing to him," he said.

"Well, it's not fair. It's not his life, it's yours. You've got to do what you want to do," I asserted.

Cary nodded, but smiled.

"Sure. Only one small thing. It takes money."

"Well, I'm getting a lot of money someday. You remember what Grandma Olivia told me about my inheritance. And when I get it, I'm giving you what you need to start your business."

"You are?"

"Yes," I said firmly. "Uncle Jacob will probably hate me a little more, if that's possible, but I don't care," I said. Cary beamed.

43

"For someone who has had such a hard time of it, you're the most generous, sweetest person, I know," he said as he stood up from his desk. Because of the size of the room, we were only inches apart. He took my hand in his.

"I'm glad you're not my uncle Chester's daughter, Melody. I'm glad you're only a distant cousin, at most. No one can condemn me for feeling more for you," he confessed. I saw that it took all his courage, but these were words that had been hanging between us for months now. I knew that having feelings for your cousin, even a distant one, was supposed to be wrong, but neither Cary nor I could hold back our hearts.

I didn't speak. Our eyes seemed incapable of moving away from each other's faces. Slowly, almost as slowly as the turning of the earth, our mouths moved toward each other until our lips grazed and then gently pressed together. His left hand moved to my shoulder and his right to my waist. My hands remained at my sides.

I was both surprised and a little frightened by the small bursts of heat I felt coursing through my body. It was as if warm massaging fingers moved under my clothing, tracing down between my breasts, over my stomach. He slipped his lips off mine and kissed my cheek as his right hand began to move up my side, over my ribs. I raised my hand quickly and caught his just as it touched my breast. We stood there, gazing into each other's eyes, neither moving, neither speaking, each feeling as if we had opened some door to a forbidden room. It was the moment when we would decide to go further or softly close the door again between us.

"I can't help myself," he simply admitted. Was I to say the same thing or was I to bear the responsibility of stopping something that we both knew would bring more problems into this already unstable family? If I lifted my hand from his, I would be pulling him into that room. I wanted to, but I also wanted to be confident that it was right. My heart was thumping so hard, I thought I would lose my breath. His lips had tasted sweet and the warmth that trickled down my spine and through my body was a delightful feeling. Nothing about our kiss was unpleasant to me.

The moonlight reflecting off the ocean lit the world outside the small window. It was as if a giant candle had been lit on a birthday cake to celebrate this birth of love, if it truly was love. What was that special *yes* that followed the surge of excitement in your body? How did you know when the kiss that tingled was a greater kiss than any other? Where were the bells, the trumpets, the voices of angels that were supposed to sound when true love appeared?

These thoughts zipped through my mind with lightning speed. Meanwhile, Cary's courage grew. His kisses became more intense, firmer, and his other hand moved up to caress my shoulders. I felt my resistance soften as I kissed him back and let him turn my body neatly into his. He started to move me with him toward the sofa. What would happen? What would we do? I wanted to go along almost out of a curiosity about myself, to see what I was capable of wanting, of doing.

But just as we reached the side of the sofa and were about to lower ourselves to it, we heard May's cry at the bottom of the ladder.

Cary moaned his great disappointment and his body tightened with frustration.

May called again for me. She had gone into my room looking for me and then realized I was upstairs. We heard her start up the ladder. Quickly, we parted and I straightened my hair. There was no way I could quickly diminish the flush in my face, but I was sure May wouldn't understand. She poked her head through the attic doorway.

45

Cary quickly signed his anger. She looked confused, hurt.

"Don't Cary. I promised her I would play with her."

He turned away and took a deep breath. I put my hand on his shoulder and he looked at me.

"She's all alone much of the day, shut up in a soundless world. We're all she really has right now," I said.

He nodded, looking ashamed. Then he shook his head and lifted his eyes to me.

"You're just like Laura. You bring out the good in all of us," he said.

I know he meant it to be a big compliment, but it left me cold. When would he stop comparing me to his dead twin sister? Did he have these feelings for her as well? Did everyone see me as someone else? Was that to be my fate? Kenneth saw me as some mythical goddess, Aunt Sara saw me as her lost daughter, and even May must have seen some of Laura in me to have brought me those drawings earlier. Perhaps I wouldn't be able to be my own person until I found out who my real father was and everyone knew where I had come from and to whom I really belonged.

All the threads of lies I had started to unravel had to lead me to the threads of truth.

Instead of shouting out that I did not *want* to be like Laura, I kept my anguish inside and signed to May that I would follow her down the ladder. When I looked up as I reached the bottom, I saw Cary gazing down at me. The disappointment that lingered in his eyes made him look as distant and as forbidden as love itself is for one still searching for her own name.

Kenneth's excitement over his new artistic vision hadn't diminished one bit by the time he arrived to pick me up the next morning. Even Ulysses seemed to be affected by the change in Kenneth's mood and

46

demeanor. He was more energetic; his tail wagged like a windshield wiper in a rain storm and he barked as soon as I appeared in the doorway. I laughed and hurried to the jeep. Almost before I closed the door, Kenneth put the vehicle in gear and whipped it around to accelerate and head back to the studio.

"I couldn't sleep last night," he said. He didn't look fatigued or drowsy to me, however. "I got up twice and went into the studio to look at the block. That statue wants to burst out of there. An artist literally frees the art, releases it into the world. It's chained to darkness by the ignorance and blindness of people. The artist comes like someone carrying a candle in the night and peels away the shadows."

He paused and looked at me.

"You think I'm babbling away, don't you?"

"No," I said quickly. Actually, I was afraid he would stop. The exhilaration in his voice was contagious.

He was quiet a moment as he drove. Then he nodded.

"Maybe you can understand."

"My mother wasn't artistic," I said. "Was she?"

He smiled at me.

"Well, in her own way, maybe. Haille always liked beautiful things. I used to tease her and say beauty's only skin deep, and she would reply, so who wants to go deeper?" He laughed. "Maybe she was right." He turned onto the dune road.

"Did you spend a lot of time with her?"

"Not a lot. Some," he replied. Then, as if he realized he was telling me things that might lead to more questions, he stiffened. "What would you say to working on Saturday, too?"

"I can't this Saturday. I've been invited to Grandma Olivia's for lunch."

"Oh?" He shook his head. "And no one refuses an invitation from Olivia Logan," he added.

47

"Why should I refuse?"

"You shouldn't if you want to go. Well, maybe the following Saturday. Just like any other employee anywhere, you'll get time and a half for coming," he said as we came to a stop by his house.

"If I come it's not for the money," I said firmly. I felt my eyelids narrow into slits of anger and he saw it, too. It brought a smile to his face.

"You're more like your mother than you know," he said.

"How come you know so much about her if you only spent *some* time with her?" I countered.

"It's not how long you're with someone, it's the quality of the time," he replied. "Come on, let's get started."

He reached back for the daily groceries he had purchased before picking me up and I followed him to the house. The kitchen was a mess from breakfast, but he wanted to get started on our project right away. After he put away the groceries we went directly to the studio, where he had an easel set up across from the block of marble and a large artist's pad open on it.

"I want to play around with some lines for a while this morning, sort of experiment with shapes, sizes, relationships. All you have to do is stand there as quietly and as still as you can," he added, pointing to the marble.

"Just stand?"

"Stand. I'll give you instructions as we go along."

Ulysses folded his body at Kenneth's feet as I positioned myself in front of the marble. I felt a little silly just staring back at him as he stared at me. My stomach was nervous, too. It made me self-conscious to have him look at me so intently, and for so long, and we'd only just begun. I shifted my weight from one leg to the other and waited.

"Look off to the left. Good. Now lift your chin just a little. A little more. Good. No, don't fold your arms.

48

Just try to stand with them down at your sides for a while. Okay," he said and worked his pencil quickly over the page. In no time at all my neck began to feel stiff.

"You're not relaxing," Kenneth said. "If you don't relax, you'll get tired faster and need more breaks. But don't worry," he added quickly. "In time you'll get used to it and you'll ease up."

"Do you work with models often?" I asked. He didn't reply for a while.

"Very rarely," he finally said. "Usually, if I need a face or a figure, I take a mental picture and commit it to memory."

"Then why can't you do the same now?"

"This is different. This is very special, and I told you," he said, not without a note of impatience, "the work requires a sense of transition, movement, change. I'm trying to capture a metamorphosis."

"Have you ever done anything like this before?"

"You'll have to stop asking me questions," he said. "You're breaking my concentration."

I pressed my lips together and closed my eyes.

"Don't close your eyes," he said immediately. I opened them a bit wider than usual and he groaned with impatience. "Relax. Please. Try to relax."

"It's not easy," I complained. "Now I know why people are paid a lot of money to do this."

He laughed. "Who said they are?"

"Aren't they?"

"You're tricking me into talking, Melody. Every time I answer one of your questions or you force me to respond, I stop thinking artistically. An artist has to lose himself in the work, not really see the person as a person anymore, but as the object of his art, and that takes very intense concentration."

I thought about Mommy in his paintings and wondered if that was precisely what had happened with her or if was Cary right. Did Kenneth look at her

49

not as his subject but as a woman he desired? If Cary was right, what did that mean about the way Kenneth was looking at me?

Kenneth told me to turn toward him and he studied me for a while. Then he asked me to look more to my right. He flipped his pages and worked and flipped some more pages. Finally, he slapped his pencil on the easel and stepped back.

"Something's not right," he said.

"Am I doing something wrong?"

"No, it's not you. It's me." He thought a moment. "I'm going down to the sea. You can work in the house until I return," he said and marched out of the studio.

I went into the house and cleaned up the kitchen. Kenneth still hadn't returned by the time I finished, so I went to his bedroom. It looked as if he had been wrestling with someone in his bed. The blanket was twisted, the sheet was pulled up and nearly half off, and one of his pillows was on the floor. Clothes were scattered about as if he had thrown them against the walls. I scooped everything up, deciding what needed to be washed and ironed and what needed to be just folded and put in the closet or the dresser. When I couldn't find a second sock, I got on my hands and knees and looked under the bed. Something else attracted my attention. It looked like a photograph. I knew it hadn't been there the week before when I cleaned, so Kenneth must have dropped it recently.

I strained and reached under until my fingers found it and I could bring it out. Then I turned, sat with my back against the bed frame, and looked at the picture. It was a picture of Mommy and me when I was no more than two or three. It had been taken in front of our trailer home in Sewell and it was badly faded, the black and white had turned brown. I turned it over and saw the writing was nearly faded, too, but I could make out most of the words and figure out the rest.

I thought you'd like this picture. Her name is Melody. I'm sorry.

Sorry? Why was she sorry? Surely, she wasn't sorry simply because she had named me Melody. Should I just confront Kenneth with the picture and ask him about it right now? I wondered.

I stood up, holding the picture close to my heart. I went to the window and looked out at the beach. I could barely see Kenneth, sitting a little below a sand hill, gazing at the waves.

I've waited long enough for answers, I thought. I want to know the truth. Armed with the photograph and my own resolve, I marched out of the house and over the sand toward Kenneth. Ulysses was at his side, and his tail began wagging as soon as I appeared. Kenneth didn't turn, didn't move. He looked as if he had turned to stone himself.

"Can I talk to you?" I asked.

"Can't it wait?" he replied.

"No," I said adamantly. His shoulders sagged a bit with his annoyance and he turned.

"What's so important?" he moaned. "I can't keep having my concentration broken. This entire thing is an ongoing process. It develops in small stages, but the creative period has to remain smooth, fluid. I thought you understood."

"I don't understand a lot of things," I said sharply. He raised his eyebrows. I extended my arm toward him, the picture in my hand. "I found this when I was cleaning up your room. It was under the bed. It wasn't there the other day."

He looked at the picture and then took it from my hand.

"I wondered where this went," he said. "I was looking at it last night."

"Why do you have it and what does it mean?" I demanded.

51

"What do you mean what does it mean? It is what it is. A picture of you with Haille. She sent it to me years ago."

"Why?"

"Why? I told you. We were friends once."

"Just friends?"

"Good friends," he said.

"Why does she say 'I'm sorry'?"

He shook his head.

"You know most of this. She got pregnant and ran off with Chester. I guess she thought I was disappointed in her so she wrote, I'm sorry. What's the mystery?"

"Were you disappointed in her?"

"Yes," he said looking at the picture. "I had higher hopes for her. I wasn't surprised that she eventually had problems with Olivia and Samuel, but I had higher hopes. Okay?"

Tears burned under my eyelids, but I pressed my lips together and held my breath. He put the picture in his pocket and turned back to the sea.

"Why drag up the ugly past now?" he muttered.

"That's what Grandma Olivia says," I retorted harshly.

"This time she's right. Nothing can be changed and all it does is make people unhappy."

"Except I'm the one who doesn't know what she has to know. I don't know who my real father is," I said. He was quiet. "Do you know?"

"Look," he said, "this can't be a pleasant subject for you. I don't think I should be the one to say anything. If you want answers to those questions, ask your relatives. Once, I knew your mother. She was a beautiful young woman. We had a good relationship for a while and then her lifestyle got between us and she went her way and I went mine. I don't condemn her, blame her, look down on her. I don't judge people."

"You're not answering my questions," I pursued. He shook his head.

"I don't know the answer," he snapped. "There were a lot of rumors, nasty rumors, and the next thing I heard was she and Chester had run off."

The tears were streaming down my cheeks now. I turned away from him.

"You're not telling me what you really know," I fired back and stomped down the sand hill to the beach. I folded my arms and walked along, just out of reach of the waves. Moments later I felt his hand on my shoulder.

"Why do you want me to tell you unpleasant things?" he asked when I turned.

"I'm old enough to hear the bad with the good, Kenneth," I said, full of fire and determination. He nodded.

"Okay. You want the bad with the good? The bad is that your mother was very promiscuous. She slept around a lot; she was very wild. Some guy would come riding through here on a motorcycle and minutes later, your mother was sitting behind him speeding down the Cape highway for some rendezvous on a beach blanket. Then the guy was gone. She dirtied her reputation just to put a blot on the perfect Logan name, I think. She was angry at everyone in the family for one reason or another.

"She would come to see me often and confide in me and I would give her the best advice I could. Sometimes, I thought she had followed my advice, and then she would disappoint me. It happened more times than I care to remember. I got angry with her and I told her to stay away from me. She was driving me mad. Then she got into trouble, had that awful argument with Olivia and Samuel, and ran off with Chester, who was always head over heels in love with her anyway.

"She had him wrapped around her finger and she

53

could get him to do anything she wanted anytime she wanted. I can't even begin to imagine how many times he rescued her from a bad scene, picked her up when she was dead drunk or stoned or just worn out from a night of wildness. He would forgive her anything if she would just talk to him or let him help her. So, she ran off with him. You told me you knew what happened afterward. You know how your uncle Jacob feels about it all, and you know Olivia's views."

"You let her go, too?" I asked softly. "You gave up on her?"

"I tried my best at first. You can't even begin to imagine the frustration I experienced. Haille could make a promise that sounded as if it were chipped in cement—or marble, I should say." He smiled. "She could make the worst agnostic a believer, melt a hard heart in seconds, charm a fish out of water. And then she would break that promise and laugh and just promise again, and you know what, everyone, especially men, wanted to believe her so much, they refused to see her for what she was. Only, finally I saw the truth. What else do you want me to tell you?"

"I want to know who my father is," I said.

"I can't tell you that."

"Because you don't know?"

"Let's just leave it, Melody. Have this conversation with someone else. Go back to Olivia," he pleaded. "I like you," he said. "You're a very intelligent, sensitive young woman, and as you were probably told, I don't have many acquaintances, so I don't throw those compliments around lightly. I would really like for us to be friends. I hope you'll stay with me and help me create the Birth of Neptune's Daughter," he added, turning to walk away. Ulysses trotted at his heels.

The rhythmic chant of the waves sounded behind me and sea spray hit my cheeks. Terns circled and swooped over the waves. The breeze tickled my neck.

Some of what he had told me was the truth, but I

knew in my heart that there was more. The secret he kept was burning at him. It was as if he had been branded with the knowledge and knew that every time he was forced to talk about the past, he suffered the agony of remembering.

How strange, I thought as he walked away with his head down. He had a lean, tall figure. His face was bearded, browned by the sea, sun, and wind, and his eyes were full of wisdom and insight beyond his years. I should have felt angrier at him, disappointed, and yet, at this moment, for reasons I was yet to understand, I felt more sorry for him than I did for myself.

And I was the one left standing in the darkness. I was the one who still felt incomplete, lost, drifting in the ocean breeze. I felt like a lone leaf that had fallen from the branch and longed to return if only someone, something showed it the way.

I followed behind Kenneth. He sat again by the sand hill and stared at the waves. I sat beside him and looked out at the turbulent sea.

"I'm looking for just the right one," he said. "Just the right shape, the right image. If I look long enough, the sea will unveil it. Truth requires patience," he said.

I wondered if he were giving me advice. I wondered if he were asking me to be patient.

Just like the sea, he had something more to offer. It was only a matter of time, time to strengthen me so I could handle the truth.

I finally decided.

I liked him. And I would trust Kenneth Childs whether he was my father or not.

3

❧

Don't Look Back

I couldn't help feeling nervous before I went to Grandma Olivia's for lunch on Saturday. I was always jittery whenever I was around her, but it seemed to me she made everyone stand or sit on pins and needles. The only one who appeared at all at ease in her presence was Judge Childs. Even Grandpa Samuel looked uncomfortable most of the time. I winced at the way she dished out biting criticism of him and the things he did. She talked down to him as if he were an insignificant or unintelligent person. I wondered why he tolerated it, and I couldn't imagine the two of them, younger, falling in love.

Nowadays, Grandpa Samuel wore his marriage as if it were a shoe two sizes too small. From what Cary told me and from what I had observed on other occasions, Grandpa Samuel spent as much time as he could away from home, even though he was retired. He played cards with his old friends a few nights a week, never turning down an opportunity to go somewhere in the evening if and when he was invited. Cary said Grandpa regretted retirement and had only stopped working because Grandma Olivia thought it looked as if they needed money if he continued to go to work year after year. During the day he was often down at the docks talking with fishermen and boatmen.

But Grandma Olivia would never permit him to miss one of her formal luncheons on Saturday. Usually, from what I understood, she invited someone of importance from Provincetown or the surrounding area. Political candidates, wealthy business people, even from as far away as Boston, were honored by her invitations and attended.

Grandma Olivia's driver Raymond was a man in his mid sixties, and what people in Provincetown called a Brava, half Negro, half Portuguese. He was one of Roy Patterson's uncles. Roy worked for Uncle Jacob and Roy's daughter Theresa was in my class at school. Everyone knew everyone else here, whether they socialized with each other or not.

Raymond came for me in Grandma and Grandpa Logan's vintage Rolls Royce. It was a partly cloudy day with just enough of a breeze to lift the sand and send it across the road in waves to salt the pavement. The sea air was crisp and fresh like the morning after the first snow in West Virginia. The clouds were the soft, marshmallow type, puffy, large, lazily drifting across the blue. It was a perfect day for an afternoon social affair.

I should have felt like some little princess in the back of the Rolls, sitting on the spotless leather, having a driver open and close doors for me and drive me up to the Logan compound, as it was known. Cary had long since left to work with Uncle Jacob by the time the limousine arrived. I was glad, because I knew he would tease me about it. Uncle Jacob only took Sundays off, and sometimes, not even the entire day. I felt sorry for May, who stood in the doorway watching me get into the limousine. She looked like a sad little rag doll gently waving good-bye. Why couldn't Grandma Olivia have invited her? I wondered. I asked Aunt Sara before I left.

"I don't know, dear," she replied. "Maybe she just wants to spend more time with you or introduce you to important people. But don't worry about May. She'll be fine with me. I'm going to take her in to town for lunch and some shopping."

Still, I thought it was a bitter pill for a little girl to have to swallow. How could a grandmother be so insensitive, especially to a grandchild like May who needed extra care and affection? It put tears in my eyes and washed away any joy or excitement I could have felt going to the luncheon in this plush automobile.

When I arrived, I found only Grandma Olivia, Grandpa Samuel, and Judge Childs sitting on the rear patio. As usual, whenever Grandma Olivia had company, she had servants. A maid was offering them hors d'oeuvres and glasses of champagne. They all turned as I stepped through the doorway.

Even seated, Grandma Olivia had a way of rising beyond her actual height. She stood only a little more than five foot four in her stocking feet, but because of the manner in which she carried herself and the way she sat regally in chairs and somehow managed to gaze down at people (even those who stood a foot taller), she presented a firmer, stronger appearance. As usual, her snow white hair was pulled back in a bun as severely as Aunt Sara's, with a pearl studded comb at the crown. Sometime after I had first met Grandma Olivia, I realized the reason Aunt Sara wore her hair that way was because it was the way Grandma Olivia wore hers. Whether she did it simply to please Uncle Jacob or because she believed everything Grandma Olivia did was, as Mama Arlene would say, "The cat's meow," I don't know, but she did it.

The tiny age spots clustered at Grandma Olivia's

hair line and on her cheeks looked more like freckles in the sunlight. Today, she wore a little blush on her cheeks. It was about the only makeup I ever saw on her. She had small features, her mouth just the width of her chin. Under her jaw, her skin hung loosely like a hen's, but her collarbone stood out prominently beneath her nearly transparent complexion. Tiny veins crisscrossed her temples. I was sure that when she gazed at herself in the mirror and saw the illusory azure fluid running through her, she was further convinced she was a true blue-blood.

Today she wore an ivory cotton dress with frilled sleeves and a frilled hem. It had tiny pearls sewn onto the collar and down between her breasts. She had an elegant gold bracelet spotted with diamonds on her right wrist and a small gold watch she must have worn just for show. The hands and numbers were so tiny I couldn't imagine how she could read the time.

Despite her temperament, Grandma Olivia's skin was smoother than the skin of most women her age, her perpetual frowns had not put any wrinkles in her face. Her hands were graceful, the knuckles a bit bony with some age spots across them, but the skin wasn't crinkled. I was willing to bet she had never washed a dish or ironed an article of clothing in her life.

Grandpa Samuel looked dapper in his light blue sports jacket and matching slacks. He wore a pair of polished white loafers and bright blue socks. Grandpa Samuel's hair was mostly gray, but he still had a remarkably full and healthy looking head of it. It was trimmed neatly at the ears and sides with the top brushed back. There was a trace of a wave running through it. His green eyes brightened at the sight of me and he relaxed his lips into a soft smile.

Judge Childs held a cigar in his right hand, a glass of champagne in his left, his big diamond pinky ring glittering in the sunlight. Ever since I had begun thinking that Kenneth Childs might be my real father,

I looked at the judge with a great deal more interest each time I saw him. After all, I thought, this man could be my grandfather.

The judge was a distinguished looking, elderly man with gray hair still showing some of its original light brown color. He wore it neatly trimmed and parted on the right side. He dressed more conservatively than Grandpa Samuel, wearing a charcoal jacket and pants, a bow tie, and black shoes and socks. I had seen pictures of Kenneth's mother in Kenneth's home. She was a very attractive woman with dark brown hair, but there was no question in my mind that Kenneth took after his father and had the same shape nose and chin. Kenneth's eyes were a darker brown, but the judge's eyes always seemed to darken when he gazed at me.

"Well, the guest of honor has arrived," the judge said. Both he and Grandpa Samuel rose, each bowing slightly. It brought a smile to my lips. I felt as if I had walked into a scene from *Gone with the Wind*.

I looked at Grandma Olivia and then at the rear of the house. There were no other guests, no elaborate setup of tables, tents, and chairs. Was I really the guest of honor?

"Good afternoon, Grandma Olivia," I said.

"I always liked that dress on Laura," she replied instead of greeting me. The way she said it made me feel as if I was a poor relation dressed in a hand-me-down.

"You look very nice, Melody," Grandpa Samuel said, nodding. "Come sit here," he said, patting the cushioned lawn chair beside him.

"Just like Samuel to want to sit next to the pretty lady," the judge said.

"You're just jealous because I invited her first," Grandpa said.

"Don't the two of you start acting like idiotic school boys," Grandma Olivia warned. "Sit where

60

you want," she told me. I sat next to Grandpa Samuel, who beamed a smile back at the judge.

"Now here's a young woman with some taste," he said, making the judge laugh.

The maid brought the tray of hors d'oeuvres to me and I choose one and took a napkin. It was shrimp in a pastry shell and it was absolutely delicious.

"Please get her some lemonade," Grandma Olivia told the maid. She nodded and hurried out.

"What's going on at Jacob's house?" Grandpa Samuel asked.

"Cary and Uncle Jacob are working. May and Aunt Sara are going to town."

"I hate going to town during the season," Grandma Olivia remarked. "It's too crowded on those narrow streets with all those tourists gawking into store windows. I don't know why she drags that disabled child all about like that," she added looking at me as if I had the answer. I did.

"Aunt Sara is just trying to keep May occupied," I said pointedly. "She was all alone when I left."

"Yes," Grandpa said nodding. "I guess you could have invited Sara and the child, Olivia," he told her.

"Don't tell me who to invite and who not to, Samuel Logan," she snapped. He stared at her a moment, his eyes cold and sharp but quickly warming as he folded his face into a smile again.

"Did you hear that whip snap, Judge?"

When the judge didn't respond immediately, I gazed at him and saw he was staring intently at me.

"What's that? A whip? Oh, yes, yes," he said laughing. "Well, I warned you, Samuel. Years and years ago, I warned you about the Gordons."

"You have that backwards," Grandma Olivia said. "Everyone in Provincetown warned me about the Logans."

The judge roared and sipped some champagne. He and Grandma Olivia exchanged furtive glances.

"I understand you are working for Kenneth," Grandma Olivia said, turning back to me. "How has that been going?"

"It's been fine, thank you."

"My son hasn't been too hard a boss then?" the judge asked quickly. "You're not bored out there in no-man's-land?"

"No. Actually, I'm learning a great deal about art."

"You're artistic too?" he followed.

"No, sir."

"She's musically inclined. Didn't you hear her play at the variety show?" Grandpa Samuel asked.

"Oh, I know she's musically inclined, but some people have a variety of talents."

"And some have none," Grandma Olivia inserted, her eyes fixed on Grandpa Samuel. "Except when it comes to putting their foot in their mouth." Grandpa Samuel looked uncomfortable and shifted his weight in his chair. Then he cleared his throat.

I didn't like the nasty tone of voice Grandma Olivia used, but I couldn't help being in awe of her strength and power. From what well did she draw it? I wondered. Where did she get such confidence, such self-assurance? I didn't like her, but I couldn't help wanting to learn something from her. She was living proof that women could be tough and strong when need be, and someday, someday soon, I too would need to find that strength.

"What's Kenneth have you doing there?" the judge asked.

"I help straighten up his home, make lunch, prepare his supplies, keep his studio in order, do odd jobs, take care of Ulysses. He showed me how to prepare the clay he uses for vases and small statues."

"Whatever he pays you to straighten up that home of his it can't be enough. He barely makes enough on that art work of his to feed the dog," the judge quipped.

"He doesn't believe an artist should be obsessed with making money," I offered and immediately regretted it, because they all looked at me as if I had said something blasphemous.

"Apparently, you've gotten to know him well already," the judge said after a moment of deep silence.

"No, not really," I replied. "We're just getting to know each other."

"Did he tell you he used to practically live here?" Grandpa Samuel asked with a wide smile. "I had to wash him off the welcome mat most of the time."

"Samuel, please," Grandma Olivia said. "He didn't live here."

"Well, he was here enough, wasn't he, Nelson?" Grandpa Samuel asked the judge.

"When Kenneth was younger, I had less of a fix on him than I have now," the judge said mournfully. Everyone sipped their champagne, but the judge and Grandma Olivia gave each other that sideways glance again. I took the lemonade from the maid, thanked her, and took a sip. I still wasn't sure why I had been invited to this luncheon, but I knew from everything I had been told and everything I had observed that Grandma Olivia didn't do anything unless it had a purpose.

"I hope you're hungry," Grandpa Samuel said. "We've got a small feast. Cold lobster, some of those wonderful fried potatoes I shouldn't eat, hickory-smoked ham."

"From the way he talks, you'd think that's all he cares about these days is food," Grandma Olivia said with a sigh. "I guess we had better get to it before he chews the arm off the chair." She started to rise.

"That is all he cares about," the judge quipped, and stood. Grandpa Samuel held out his arm for me to take and we followed the judge and Grandma Olivia into the house to the dining room, where the luncheon had been set out in smorgasbord style. The maid

63

stood beside the table, waiting to hand us each a plate. Grandma Olivia went first and the judge stepped back for me to follow. The lobster meat had been shelled and dressed on a platter. Beside the potatoes Grandpa Samuel favored, there was a variety of vegetables, cranberry sauce and apple sauce. The hickory-smoked ham looked delicious.

Aunt Sara had warned me not to fill up my plate at Grandma Olivia's luncheons. That was something Grandma Olivia believed real ladies didn't do. It was proper to have something else afterward, a second helping of ham or vegetables, but not to fill the plate again. I saw how she watched out of the corner of her eye as I moved behind her, and I took a lot less than I wanted. The judge and Grandpa Samuel loaded their plates to the brim. We sat at the dining room table.

"As usual, wonderful, Olivia," the judge said. She nodded slightly, as one who expected compliments would nod.

"You seem to have adjusted well to your new home," Grandpa Samuel said to me.

"What choice did she have?" Grandma Olivia snapped. "What you have to do, you do."

"Well, sometimes you can be lucky and you can like the things you have to do, too," he offered, without any hint of contradiction in his voice. He winked at me and we ate in silence until the judge and Grandma Olivia exchanged another one of those quiet looks filled with question marks.

"What do you do while Kenneth works in his studio?" Grandma Olivia asked.

"Sometimes I use the time to clean the house or walk Ulysses and sometimes I watch Kenneth work. He doesn't mind as long as I don't break his concentration," I added. "Once, he asked me to play my fiddle while he worked."

"He's not very talkative then?" she asked.

"When he talks about his art, he is," I said. I tilted

64

my head, wondering why, if Kenneth had practically grown up here and this was his father who was sitting across from me, they were asking all these questions about him? They all acted as if they barely knew him and they should have known him far better than I did.

"Is that all he talks about?" the judge asked me insistently. He seemed impatient.

"Let the girl eat," Grandpa Samuel said. Grandma Olivia shot darts at him from her eyes, causing him to shake his head and return his concentration to his food.

I swallowed what I was chewing and replied.

"No. Sometimes he talks about the past," I said. The judge's eyes widened and Grandma Olivia held her fork frozen between the plate and her mouth.

"Oh? And exactly what has he told you about the past?" the judge followed.

"Just a little bit about what it was like to grow up here in Provincetown," I said.

Grandma Olivia put her fork down and looked at the judge, shaking her head in the slightest, but just discernable way. The judge returned to his food and the topic of conversation changed to what would happen to the country's economy if the Republicans didn't win control of the Senate.

After we had eaten, Grandma Olivia proposed something that made my eyes bulge with surprise.

"While you two idiots go have your cigars, Melody and I will walk out to the gazebo and have a private talk," she said. "Come along," she told me as she rose from the table.

"We'll be there shortly," Grandpa Samuel said.

"Don't rush your filthy habit on my account," she replied. The judge laughed and Grandpa shrugged. I followed Grandma Olivia out of the house and down the back steps. She paused and waited for me to walk alongside her.

"Did you enjoy the lunch?"

"Oh yes. Thank you. Everything was wonderful."

"Later, we'll have some tea and some petit fours. Tell me more about this summer job of yours," she said and continued down the pathway toward the gazebo.

Why was my working for Kenneth such an important topic? What did they expect me to tell them?

"There's not much more to say about it, Grandma Olivia. I enjoy watching Kenneth work. He lives in an interesting place, so close to the sea, to nature. I enjoy my walks along—"

"When he talked to you about the past," she interrupted, not satisfied with my response, "he didn't mention anything about his father?" When I didn't respond immediately, she stopped and looked at me. "Well?"

"He doesn't like talking about his father very much," I offered, but I saw that wasn't enough. She grimaced as if she had bitten into a sour apple, and then turned to step into the gazebo. I followed her inside and sat across from her on a pristine white garden bench.

"What did you want to talk about?" I finally asked. Surely my summer job wasn't the topic; it was obvious by now that I had been brought here for some sort of cross-examination.

"I think you're a lot smarter than your mother was at your age," she began. "Your mother's interests were quite simple to begin with, and her curiosity about anything more than boys was limited."

"I don't think it's fair to talk about her this way. She's not alive. She can't dispute anything," I countered. Standing up to her brought tears to sting my eyes. I took a deep breath and then looked away.

"Nonsense. If we couldn't talk about anyone who was dead, a great many mistakes would be made. It would also be a mistake for you not to tell me what, if anything, Kenneth Childs said about his father."

I turned back to her.

"Why is that so important to you?" I asked.

"Don't you dare ask me questions in response to questions I ask you," she admonished.

"All I know is that they don't talk much to each other, but I don't know why."

She raised her eyebrows.

"He didn't say?" she asked cautiously.

"No, not really."

"What's that mean, not really? Either he did or he didn't," she said, leaning impatiently forward in her seat.

"He didn't," I replied, the tears welling again in my eyes.

"I see," she said, continuing to scrutinize me. I felt as if I were sitting under a bright light in a police station.

"Is this why you invited me to luncheon, to interrogate me about what Kenneth said about his own father?" I demanded to know, despite her strict warning about questioning her.

"Don't be impudent," she snapped.

"I think it's pretty sad if the only way the judge can find out about his own son is through someone spying on him," I added.

"Don't you dare say anything like that to the judge," she chastised. "No one said anything about you spying on anyone," she added, but I glared back at her.

"You could have invited Kenneth to this luncheon," I suggested, "and asked him the same questions."

She glared at me and shook her head.

"Obviously, my son did not impart any of the good manners to you that I taught him, or if he did, your mother ruined them," she said.

"How can you still hate her even though she's dead?" I asked. Finally, I had said something that

67

made her turn away. She gazed toward the ocean, a blank look coming over her face.

"I don't hate her. I disapproved of her and I actually ended up feeling sorry for her, pitying her and Chester. To permit himself to believe such a terrible thing about his own father, just to have her as his wife. To think that my husband would seduce a young girl and embarrass me." She shook her head. "Well, that's all over now. Terrible words and ideas are like the tide. Once they go out, you can never pull them back. You can't unring a bell." She sighed. "So there's no point in discussing it now."

"Yes there is," I said boldly.

She turned to me. If her eyes were daggers, I'd have a hundred holes in me, I thought.

"What did you say?"

"I want to know the truth," I said. "Is Kenneth Childs my father? Is that why you have been questioning me about him?"

She started to smile.

"Is that what he told you?"

"He hasn't told me anything."

Her smile faded.

"I'm sure if there is one thing I don't know and don't care to know it's which of Haille's many men friends sired you. It would be easier to find the father of some shark in the ocean," she added with a wave of her hand toward the sea.

"Perhaps my real grandmother would know," I said, and Grandma Olivia burst out laughing.

"Belinda? Know anything that goes on around her? Please."

"I'd like to meet her. I would," I insisted.

She stopped laughing.

"Don't be silly. She wouldn't have the slightest idea who you were or be able to make sense out of anything you said or asked her," Grandma Olivia said. "It would be a pointless visit."

"Still, I'd like to do it. Isn't she permitted to have any visitors?"

"She can have visitors, but I can't think of anything that would be more of a waste of time than visiting Belinda Gordon."

"I have the time to waste," I said. "Did my mother ever visit her?"

"Not once," Grandma Olivia replied and smirked. "And let me tell you, it wasn't because I forbade her either."

"Then that's all the more reason for me to go," I said firmly. She raised her eyebrows again and widened her eyes as she nodded.

"Maybe I'm wrong," she said. "Maybe I should have taken an interest in who your father was. Whoever he was, he must have had some backbone."

If ever I was to receive a backhanded compliment, I thought, this was it.

"Okay," she said after another moment. "You're so determined to meet your real grandmother," she added, pronouncing real as if it were a dirty word, "I'll even have Raymond drive you up there."

"Thank you," I said quickly. "When?"

"Tomorrow. Sunday is visitors' day. He'll pick you up at ten A.M. They like the patients to have visitors in the morning," she said.

"Haven't you ever visited her?" I asked.

"Of course not."

"But she's your sister," I said. She looked as if she had a rod of steel down her back.

"I did more for her than she would have ever done for me," she retorted, "especially under the circumstances."

"What circumstances?"

"Please. I don't want to have to till that soil again. Just make your dutiful visit and get it over with," she added with another wave of her hand. Ideas or words she disapproved of or disliked were like flies for her to

69

swat away from sight. No one could ever be more infuriating, I thought.

"It's not a dutiful visit. I really would like to meet her."

"You're going to be quite disappointed," she warned, almost gleefully.

"I've been disappointed many times before," I said. She sent fire from her eyes again and then calmed down when we heard the judge and Grandpa Samuel as they emerged from the house and started toward us. Grandma Olivia sat forward.

"Don't mention this conversation to anyone else," she ordered. "And especially say nothing to Kenneth. I don't expect your loyalty, but I do expect your obedience," she said. "And I'm sure you know," she added, leaning closer toward me, her eyes filled with warning, "what is at stake should you disappoint me."

The threat hovered over me like a storm cloud and then the judge and Grandpa Samuel stepped into the gazebo.

"Well now, did you two have a good womanly chat?" Grandpa Samuel kidded.

"I assure you, Samuel, our conversation was miles above the one you two jabbered through cigar smoke," she replied.

"Now, now, Olivia, no sexism," the judge chided. He and Grandma Olivia exchanged a quick look and I saw the question in his face. She shook her head slightly and I thought he looked relieved. Then he smiled at me.

"Well now," he said, sitting on the bench adjacent to me, "let's hear some more about my son's new art project."

"I think it would be easier if you came out and spoke to him about it yourself, Judge Childs," I said. "I don't mean to seem secretive about it," I quickly

70

added. "It's just that I don't want to describe it incorrectly."

He held his smile a moment and then nodded.

"Of course," he said. "That's just what I intend to do. One of these days," he said. "One of these days."

Grandma Olivia had the maid serve us our tea and small cakes in the gazebo. The conversation drifted to political subjects again and I was practically ignored until the judge announced he had to leave. When he rose, he turned to me.

"It's been delightful spending the afternoon with you, Melody. Perhaps one day you'll visit me at my beach house. Do you play chess?"

"No, sir."

"Fine. I'll teach you. In no time you'll be able to beat your grandfather Samuel."

"I'm sure she has better things to do than waste her time with senile old men," Grandma Olivia said scowling.

"Maybe," the judge said and winked. "Say hello to my son for me. Olivia." He bowed.

"I'll walk you out," she said and rose.

I suddenly realized it was the first time Grandpa Samuel and I had ever been alone. He quietly watched Grandma Olivia and the judge and then he turned to me.

"You mustn't be too quick to pass judgment on Olivia," he said, obviously noticing the disapproving look on my face. "She appears to be a very hard woman, but she has had more than her share of burdens to bear."

His sympathy for her took me completely by surprise.

"What burdens?"

"You know a little about the difficulties we had with her sister."

"My grandmother," I said.

"Yes, your grandmother." He shook his head sadly.

"Their father was a difficult man, according to what Olivia tells me. He made many demands on Olivia and tried to set a strict atmosphere. Belinda rebelled and became promiscuous; Olivia stood up to him and I suppose that was how she developed such a strong backbone."

"She's always snapping at you," I said. He shrugged.

"It's her manner. We get along better than many couples married as long as we've been married. Don't worry," he added with a smile. "I'm not as browbeaten as most people think. But that will be our little secret, okay? Now, I want you to come to me if ever you have any problems, especially with my son Jacob. I know he can be sterner than a constipated minister at times. You're a good girl, a talented and smart young woman. You'll be fine. I'm sure.

"We all have to find ways to rise above our bad luck from time to time," he added with a deep sigh.

"I'm going to visit my grandmother Belinda tomorrow," I said.

"Oh?" He looked toward the house. "Does Olivia know?"

"She's arranging for Raymond to take me."

"Really? Well, that's very nice. You know of course that Belinda is not quite all there these days."

"I don't know anything about her. That's why I'm going."

He nodded and then leaned toward me to whisper.

"She has a tendency to fantasize about people she knew. Don't believe most of it. Just come and ask me if you want to know if anything she says is true. Okay?" I nodded. "Don't tell Olivia. Just come to me," he added and sat back quickly when Grandma Olivia emerged from the house again. He smiled and winked.

All these people living side by side and keeping

72

secrets from each other, I thought. It had to mean something terrible. How much of it, I wondered, had to do with me?

Cary was home by the time the limousine brought me back. From the way he emerged from the house the minute I stepped out of the Rolls, it was obvious he had been waiting and watching at the window.

"How was lunch?" he asked as I drew closer.

"At least the food was good," I said and he rolled his eyes.

"Uh-oh. I don't like the sound of that."

"I'm going to change out of this hand-me-down, as Grandma Olivia characterized it," I said.

"Then let's go for a walk to the cranberry bog."

"Okay. Where's May?"

"She and mother aren't back from wherever they went," he said.

I hurried upstairs and changed into a pair of jeans and a comfortable sweatshirt. Uncle Jacob was apparently taking a nap. The bedroom door was closed. I walked softly down the stairs and out into the front yard, where I found Cary tossing rocks across the road. The late afternoon sun had fallen behind a long stream of clouds, turning the ocean a metallic blue, making the breakers glitter like mirrors.

"Ready?" he asked.

"Ready."

We started across the beach. As we walked, I told Cary about the afternoon and how I had been cross-examined about Kenneth.

"It made me feel like Grandma Olivia's little spy. Do you know why Kenneth and his father don't get along?"

"Probably because he failed to follow in his father's footsteps and become a lawyer. Look at all the money they wasted sending him to law school," Cary surmised.

"It's something more than that," I said. Then I told him I was going to visit Grandma Belinda.

"Grandma Olivia's sending the car?"

I nodded. I told him what Grandpa Samuel had said to me about coming to him with any stories Grandma Belinda might babble. Cary thought about this for a few minutes.

"I don't know. I don't think any of it means anything," he concluded. "Grandpa Samuel is probably just trying to let you know he's not hard and bitter like his wife."

We sat at the top of the hill and gazed at the bog.

"It's gonna be a good crop. We need it," he said. "The lobster-fishing business stinks these days." He played a blade of crabgrass over his lips and stole a quick glance at me. "About last night, before May came," he said.

"Yes?" My heart began to thud in my chest, as if we'd just finished jogging the entire way to the bog.

"I hope you're not mad."

"Why should I be mad?"

He smiled.

"I thought you might think I had invited you up just so something like that would happen."

"Didn't you?" I asked, and he blushed.

"No."

"Really?" I teased. His face went from red to cherry-blossom white, especially around his lips.

"No! I'm not like Adam Jackson. I don't trick girls into believing one thing and then trap them or something," he said, his voice cracking with indignation.

"Okay. Then, it just happened."

"Yes," he said firmly.

"Think it will happen again?" I asked hesitantly, not sure myself how I felt about our new relationship.

He turned, surprised.

"I don't know."

74

"Do you want it to?" I pursued.

"Do you?" he countered.

"Maybe," I said, thinking that at least with Cary I could be myself, that he wouldn't take my confusion as a sign of weakness.

He stared at me and then he began to lean toward me, his lips slightly parted and wet. I inched toward him and we kissed, softly, quickly. I immediately turned onto my stomach and lowered my chin to my arms as I gazed at the bog. He turned on his back beside me and neither of us spoke for quite a while.

"I came right out and asked Kenneth if he knew who my father was," I said finally, breaking the uncomfortable silence.

"You did? What did he say?"

"First, he said he didn't know. Then he said he couldn't tell me." I turned on my back. Cary braced himself on his arm and gazed down into my face.

"What's that supposed to mean?"

"I don't know. I think it means he knows but he doesn't want me to be hurt, or maybe it means he can't face the truth himself. Oh Cary," I said, nearly in tears. "I just know there's something terrible left to discover, even more terrible than the things I've already learned."

"Then maybe you should stop asking questions," he suggested. "It's like when you didn't want me to open the door to that closet in the studio. You were probably right. Some doors are better left locked."

"I didn't want it unlocked, but once it was, I wanted to go in and look, and I didn't want you to pull out those pictures, but once you had, I looked too."

He nodded and then swallowed hard and looked away.

"What?"

"You're like Lot's wife in the Bible."

"I forget who she was."

"Lot told her not to turn around and look because if she did, she would turn into a pillar of salt."

"And?"

"She looked," he said, and it was as if thunder had clapped across the sky. The heat that moment before had been flooding my body disappeared instantly, leaving a cold, hard ball of fear in the pit of my stomach.

Maybe he was right.

Maybe I should stop asking questions.

4
∽

To Grandmother's House I Go

Raymond arrived at the house promptly at ten A.M. I was very nervous and babbled a bit, asking him a million questions, but, just as he was when he picked me up to go to the luncheon, Raymond was not talkative. He actually seemed frightened of questions. I assumed he was afraid of Grandma Olivia and of losing his job, but most of the New Englanders I had met had their lips glued most of the time, especially around people they considered outsiders. Sometimes, the way some of them talked about people who didn't come from here made me think I was walking around with a third eye in my forehead.

Cary tried to explain it by telling me that people who lived off the sea tended to distrust landlubbers, thinking of them as softer, spoiled, unappreciative, taking the fish on the plate for granted.

"How far is the rest home, Raymond?" I asked when we started off.

"Not far."

"Have you been there before?" I asked, and he

turned and looked at me as if to see if I were asking a serious question.

"Aye," he replied.

"To take my grandmother to see Belinda?" I asked. Maybe Grandma Olivia had lied to me.

"No."

"Do you have a relative there?" I persisted.

"No," he said, but he didn't continue.

No wonder they all loved clams so much here on the Cape, I thought. This family and all the people associated with them couldn't be within a tighter shell.

It had rained earlier and I thought it was going to be a dark, dreary day, one of those days when the sea breeze was so chilly you wanted to wear a sweater, even in the summer. But just before Raymond arrived, the blanket of charcoal gray clouds developed a seam of blue that widened and widened until the clouds began to melt away like snow in spring sunshine. The warm rays made me squint when I gazed at the scenery, but at least I felt a little better.

I had woken this particular morning with a stomach so tight I could barely swallow water. I floundered about the bedroom, sifting through the clothes in my closet, trying to decide what would be appropriate to wear, not only to a rest home, but to meet my real grandmother for the first time ever. I didn't want to get too dressed up and look formal, but I didn't want to look underdressed, as if I didn't place great importance on this visit.

Because of the gloomy looking day I found when I first looked out the window in the morning, I chose a light blue cotton cardigan with a matching tank top and a silky rayon posy print skirt. The hem rested a little less than an inch above my knees. It was another one of Laura's outfits I had tried on but not worn. I brushed out my hair and put on some lipstick, even though Uncle Jacob had told me on more than one occasion that a young woman shouldn't be wearing lipstick during the day. I didn't know from what well of information he drew these rules, but I began to feel more pity for my dead cousin Laura, imagining what she had gone through, although Uncle Jacob never missed an opportunity to tell me how obedient and respectful she was. Intimidated and terrified was more like it, I thought.

He gave me a disapproving look when I went down to breakfast.

"How do you eat with lipstick painted on your mouth?" he asked.

"It's not a problem," I said softly. Aunt Sara looked away and busied herself with something to avoid the discussion.

"Disgusting habits some young women have these days," Uncle Jacob muttered. I felt the blood rush into my face.

"Men are more disgusting when they puff on pipes, cigars, and cigarettes, filling their mouths with nicotine and tar and turning their teeth yellow and giving themselves breath like a dragon," I countered. Cary laughed. Uncle Jacob turned purple with anger, but swallowed his words and went back to his food instead.

Naturally, May was full of questions about why I was dressed up and where I was going. I did my best to explain, but she couldn't understand why I kept referring to Belinda as Grandma Belinda. Cary promised her he would spend the morning with her and help her understand.

I expected to be back before lunch and Cary had proposed that he, May, and I go to town. I agreed, even though it was hard to think past my meeting with my grandmother. I hoped it would go well and I would return feeling I had someone I could really call family, but the trepidation that had seeped into my body all night was now making my legs tremble and my heart kept thumping harder and faster than normal all the way to the rest home.

We rode for nearly a half an hour before Raymond turned up a side road into more wooded country. It was heavy with pine, wild apple, and scrub oak. At a clearing on our right, I saw a flock of song sparrows circle and then soar to the right over the tops of the trees before they parted. It was another ten minutes before the rest home came into view. Whoever had planned its location obviously wanted it away from the more populated areas. I wondered if the owners were thinking how much people like to keep their sick and elderly out of sight and out of mind.

As we drove on in silence, I couldn't keep from wondering who came to visit Grandma Belinda if Grandma Olivia didn't? There was no one else in her family that I knew. What was it like to be housed, institutionalized, in a world without friends and relatives, dependent entirely on the kindness of strangers? Did she feel helpless, forgotten and discarded? Did this keep her from ever trying to get well?

Knowing this family, I thought, she might be better off where she is.

The rest home wasn't in an unpleasant setting. The ocean was behind it with the sun now glimmering on its silvery-gray surface. The front of the building faced a long, rolling lawn with benches, a rock garden, and some fountains. It looked peaceful, clean, and well maintained. It was obviously a rest home for the wealthier sick and elderly.

The building itself had three stories, with a steeply pitched gabled roof. It had a front porch the width of the building with a short set of cement steps. The wooden wall cladding was done in a Wedgwood blue and the shutters on the windows were bone white. As we pulled up the drive, I saw there were two elderly gentlemen sitting on the porch, rocking and gazing at us with some interest. The driveway pitched to the right and the parking area was just adjacent to the building. I could see that behind the large house there was a more elaborate garden, more benches and seating areas, and a gazebo twice the size of Grandma Olivia's. There were some full red maple trees, more scrub oak and pine, and the pathways were lined with trimmed bushes.

After he shut off the engine, Raymond stepped out and came around to open my door. I got out slowly.

"The front entrance is right there," he said nodding. "I'll wait in the car."

"The whole time?"

"I don't mind," he said and returned to his seat, pulled his cap down over his eyes, and settled in for a nap. I walked over the flagstone walkway and started up the stairs. One of the elderly men smiled at me; the other continued to look in the direction from which we had come, as if he expected to see more cars. The man who smiled, nodded.

"Hello," I said.

"You bring the paper?" he asked.

"Pardon?"

"Today's paper. You bring the paper?"

"No. I'm sorry. I'm here visiting Belinda Gordon."

"Where's the paper?" the other elderly man asked him, holding his hand behind his right ear.

"She ain't got it," he said.

"What?"

"She ain't got it," he shouted.

"What's today, a holiday?" the second man asked. I smiled at them nervously and entered the home.

The lobby was bright and homey with light blue curtains and a blond oak floor. The walls had large paintings depicting rustic country scenes and ocean scenes in rainbow colors, some with fishermen, some simply with sailboats painted against the twilight sky. The cushioned chairs and settees were all done in a light blue floral pattern. There were small wooden

81

tables, book and magazine racks, with rocking chairs in front of the large, brick fireplace. Light, classical music was being piped in through two small wall-mounted speakers.

A little more than a dozen residents were seated in the lobby, a few reading magazines, some talking, two playing checkers, and some just sitting and staring at nothing. Two women in nurses' uniforms circulated around the lobby, seeing to the needs of the residents. Everyone was well dressed and appeared well looked after. Those who seemed aware of what was happening around them gazed up at me with anticipation as I entered. Almost all looked as if they hoped I was there to visit them. I could practically feel the loneliness.

A tall, thin woman with dark hair and a narrow face that held her dark eyes close to each other came strutting out of the corridor to the right. She wore a dark gray cotton suit that looked tailored to her lean figure. Her high heels clicked sharply on the wooden floor. It reminded me of the tap, tap, tap of a woodpecker. She wore her chestnut brown hair cut short, barely below her ears, where she wore tiny opal earrings. Her nose was long and a bit pointed and her mouth turned down at the corners. She didn't smile when she approached.

"Can I help you?" she asked.

"I'm Melody Logan, here to see Belinda Gordon."

"Oh yes. Mrs. Logan called to say you would be coming. I'm Mrs. Greene. Miss Gordon is in recreation. You haven't brought her any candy, have you? We try to limit the sugar intake. Many of our residents are diabetic, but they don't watch themselves and they offer each other candy."

"No ma'am," I said. "I've brought nothing but myself."

"Fine," she said nodding. "Right this way, please."

I looked back at the people lounging in the lobby.

Everyone looked frozen. One of the men playing checkers was holding his hand in midair, a checker piece between his fingers, and one thin lady in a rocker had stopped it in its forward motion and sat with her mouth wide open, leaning and staring at me. She looked as if she might break into tears any moment.

"This way," Mrs. Greene said, pausing in the doorway to the corridor. I hurried to catch up.

"How is Miss Gordon?" I asked.

"Actually, she's doing very well. Being on a healthy diet with proper exercise has given her a new lease on life and has added years. She happens to be one of the residents of whom I am very proud. Are you a friend of the family?" she inquired as we turned down another corridor toward a double door.

"I happen to be her granddaughter," I said as matter-of-factly as I could. She stopped walking.

"Granddaughter?" Her smile was like a stretching of her thin lips to the point where they looked like rubber bands about to snap. "But my understanding is Belinda Gordon had no children."

I shrugged. "That's who I am," I said. She squeezed her eyebrows toward each other and then shook her head, clicking her tongue as she continued toward the double doors.

"I would have thought Mrs. Logan would have mentioned that," she muttered.

"She must have just forgotten," I said. She looked at me sideways as she opened the double doors to a room filled with game tables, a television set, and imitation leather settees and easy chairs. There were at least another dozen residents here. They looked younger, more alert and healthier than the elderly people in the lobby.

I paused as the realization hit me: I didn't know what my own grandmother looked like! The only pictures I had seen of her in Grandma Olivia's basement were pictures of her when she was much, much younger.

Mrs. Greene turned to me and waited.

"I'm afraid I've never met her," I said.

"You've never met her? Well," she said. "Well." She shook her head and turned and nodded toward a tiny woman sitting by the window reading what looked like a child's picture book. She wore a white knit shawl over a pale green dress. Even from across the room, I could see the resemblances between her and Grandma Olivia. They were both small featured, however, as I drew closer, I thought Grandma Belinda's features were more dainty, more doll like. Her eyes were bluer and brighter and when something she read brought a smile to her face, her smile was warmer, happier.

With Mrs. Greene not far behind, I started across the room, my entrance drawing as much interest from these residents as it had with the residents in the lobby. Only Belinda didn't break her concentration. She turned the pages of the picture book and widened her smile.

"Hello," I said. She looked up slowly and I could see she had very young looking crystal blue eyes that highlighted her gentle, soft smile. Her skin didn't look as translucent as Grandma Olivia's. In fact, Grandma Belinda appeared healthier and more robust, with a richer complexion, despite being locked away in a rest home.

"Where have you been?" she asked quickly.

"Where have I been?" I looked at Mrs. Greene.

"This is a visitor, Belinda. She doesn't work here and she's not a volunteer."

She squinted at me.

"Oh," she said with great disappointment. "I thought you came here to read to me."

"I could do that," I replied and sat in the chair just across from her. Mrs. Greene turned to speak to

84

another resident, but she didn't move too far away from us. "My name is Melody," I told Grandma Belinda and waited to see if there would be any note of recognition. She simply widened her smile a bit.

"That's a very nice name." She paused and tilted her head a bit. "I think I once knew someone named Melody."

Had she heard of me?

"My mother's name was Haille," I said. I glanced again at Mrs. Greene, who was obviously leaning closer to hear our conversation.

"Oh." Grandma Belinda's lips remained in the shape of an O, as if she had just realized something significant.

"You know who I am then?" I pursued. She shook her head, more like someone who wanted to deny what she knew than someone saying she didn't know.

"Haille lived with your sister Olivia," I said, "and her husband Samuel."

"I haven't seen my sister today," she said. She turned and looked toward the door. "She's probably in her room, sulking as usual, just because, just because Nelson asked me to go for a walk with him and didn't ask her."

She gave a slight laugh that sounded like the tinkle of wind chimes. Her eyes brightened mischievously.

"I showed her the bracelet he bought me and she just sucked in her cheeks and turned her face into a big old sour puss. She said I asked him to buy it for me. Can you imagine? I wouldn't ask a man to buy me anything, especially Nelson Childs. I've never had to ask." She leaned forward to whisper. "But she does," she said and laughed again. "She asked Paul Enfield to take her to the Fleet dance Saturday night because no one had asked her. But he said he wasn't going. I knew he was going," she assured me with a knowing nod. "So . . ." She leaned back. "She had to go with Samuel Logan. Rather, he had to go with her. He didn't want to go. He wanted to ask me, but someone else had already.

"I don't ask men for things," she emphasized with another small nod. "I don't have to." She paused to drink me in and then nodded. "I bet you don't have to ask them, either."

I laughed. Mrs. Greene left the side of the other resident and moved directly behind us.

"What are you going to read me? Are you going to read me Sleeping Beauty? I like Sleeping Beauty," Grandma Belinda said emphatically.

"If you'd like," I said. "Where is it?"

"Don't you have it? Didn't you bring it?" she asked a little frantically.

"No. I'm sorry."

She pouted. I gazed at the pile of children's books on the small table between us and chose one.

"Would you like me to read this?"

She glanced at the cover and then nodded slightly. I looked about the room. The other residents were back to doing their own things for the most part. Only one or two continued to gaze our way. I started to read, putting as much drama into it as I would if I were reading to a five- or six-year-old child. She relaxed and turned back to me to listen. I noticed Mrs. Greene move around the room, in front of us, to the side, and then behind us again, circling, spending some time with others, but always keeping within earshot. It didn't take long to read the children's story, and when I finished Grandma Belinda clapped.

"Isn't that a nice story?" she said. "I love stories with happy endings. Olivia says there are no happy endings, only endings."

"Has she been to see you?"

"She's too busy to see me. She's in high society now. She has rich people to entertain. Her nose is up here," she said tilting her head back like someone who had a nosebleed and pointing to her forehead. "I'm an embarrassment to her. That's what she says. She sounds like the big bad wolf when she says it," Grandma Belinda said, lowering her voice to make it gruff. "You're an embarrassment. Stay in your room."

She stared at me a long moment and then she smiled impishly again.

"But even if I'm in my room, they come to see me. They knock on the window. And . . . sometimes, I open the window and let him in."

"Who?"

"Wouldn't you like to know," she sang and laughed. I had to laugh, too. She was obviously confusing time, mixing in events that had occurred years and years ago with events that had occurred more recently.

"Don't you know anything about me?" I asked hopefully. "I'm Haille's daughter, Melody. You know who Haille is, don't you?"

She stopped smiling.

"Can't talk about her or she'll have them heave me out on the street," she muttered.

"Is that what Olivia said?" I asked.

"Can't talk about her," she said and pretended she was zipping her lips shut.

"You can talk to me," I said. "I'm Haille's daughter. I'm your granddaughter."

She stared, her eyes blinking rapidly. Then she turned away and gazed out the window.

"Look how blue the sky is," she said. "I wish I could reach up and touch it. I bet it's soft."

Mrs. Greene was practically on top of us.

"Would you like to go for a walk? It's beautiful today," I said. Mrs. Greene's eyes widened. I looked up at her. "Can I take her for a walk?"

"Well, does she want to go out?"

"Would you like to go out, Grandma?"

"Yes," she said firmly, not even noticing I had

called her Grandma. I got up to help her, but she didn't really need any assistance. She rose quickly, turned her head as if everyone were watching her every move, and started out.

"Just stay in the garden and walk on the pathway," Mrs. Greene said. "There are attendants if you need any help."

"She seems fine," I said. "You were right. She's being well taken care of," I added, but Mrs. Greene didn't smile at the compliment. She watched us with the eyes of a hawk as we left the room.

I took Grandma Belinda's arm into mine and started down the corridor to the door that led out to the gardens. She was spry, energetic. She wore a flowery scent that smelled refreshing.

"I like your perfume," I said.

"Do you? Nelson gave it to me."

"Nelson? He was here recently?"

"Just the day before yesterday or the day before that. He brings me a bottle of perfume whenever he comes and we sit and talk about old times. Nelson is still quite a handsome man, don't you think?"

"You mean Judge Childs?" I asked.

"Yes," she said, laughing. "Imagine, Nelson's a judge."

When we stepped out, she paused to squint at the sunlight.

"Oh, it's warmer than I thought," she said. "It should be my birthday," she added and laughed. "I always say that on nice days. Olivia thinks it's very silly. What a silly thing to say, I wish it was my birthday. Like you could pick your birthday, she says. Your head is full of cranberries, she says."

I had to laugh at Grandma Belinda's imitation of her sister.

"Shall we go into the garden?" I asked.

"Oh yes. I love to smell the flowers."

We walked silently for a while and then she paused

and looked back to see if anyone were near us. One of the attendants had come out and was watching us.

"You know why she says all those things and calls me all those names, don't you?" Grandma Belinda asked in a deep whisper, snapping her head around to face me again. I shook my head. "Because she knows Daddy loves me more. Daddy buys me nice clothes. Daddy takes me places. Daddy is proud to introduce me to his friends. Daddy wants her to stay in her room." She smiled coyly. "Daddy told her to get married or else."

She leaned toward me again.

"I put my ear to the door and I heard him yelling at her. She was crying and he was yelling. But I felt more sorry for Samuel Logan than I did for her. He has to wake up every morning and see that grouchy face. I told him to sleep with his back to her so when he opened his eyes, he could see the sunshine and not Olivia with her puffed up eyes and her puffed up lips and her sour breath."

She started to walk again.

"You know he was here," she said softly.

"He was here? You mean, Samuel?"

She nodded. And then she stopped suddenly.

"But don't you tell. Promise?"

"I promise. When was here?"

"Last night. He came to my window and knocked and I opened it and I said, Samuel Logan, what are you doing here at my window the night before your wedding?"

"Wedding?" I shook my head. "I don't—"

"'If you don't let me in,' he said, 'I'll kill myself.'"

"Last night?"

"Shh," she said looking around. She continued to walk, moving a little faster. The attendant followed. "People here tell Olivia things. She has her spies everywhere. Let's sit on this bench," she said.

It was under a spreading maple tree with a row of

multicolored impatiens behind it. I sat next to her. She leaned back and waited as the attendant walked slowly by us, pausing only a half-dozen feet away.

Whispering again, Grandma Belinda continued. "I said, 'you won't kill yourself' and he said, 'I will. I will. I swear.' So I let him in."

"Let him in?"

"He crawled through the window and fell to the floor. It was quite a sight. 'Shh,' I told him. 'Someone will hear and how will that look? You here the night before you marry my sister?' He lay there on the floor so I sat on the floor and he told me how sad he was and how terrible it was to be sad on the night before your wedding. He wanted me to make him feel better. So I did. If Olivia knew, she would have them put poison in my food."

"She wouldn't do that, Grandma."

"Oh yes, she would. She poisoned my song bird. I know she did, even though she says she didn't. Daddy bought it for me on my sixteenth birthday and she was jealous. Nelson bought me something nice too," she added, "and that made her more jealous. He bought me a gold locket with a red ruby at the center. It had his picture inside." She smiled and then she grimaced. "Do you know where the locket is?"

"No. Where is it?"

"Ask Olivia. She took it and buried it somewhere. I'm sure. One day, it wasn't in my jewelry cabinet and that was that. You can kill my birds, you can steal my jewelry, but you can't keep them from liking me more, I told her. She said she didn't care, they were all ugly philanderers. But that's like the story about the fox and the grapes, right?"

"The fox and the grapes?"

"The fox couldn't reach the grapes so he said they were sour. Yep, sour grapes. That's Olivia all right."

She laughed and then took a deep breath.

"Look at the bluebird," she said pointing.

"It's beautiful."

"Yes. I wouldn't mind being turned into a bird. When people get old, they should be turned into birds," she concluded. "I read a story like that once." She turned back to me. "Are you going to read another story?" she asked.

"If you want me to, I will when we go back inside."

"Of course I want you to. I want to hear happy endings, only happy endings, more happy endings," she chanted.

She wanted to walk some more and then she decided it was time to go back. When we stepped back into the building, she said she was tired, already forgetting that she had asked me to read another story.

"I'm not as young as I was. I get so tired so fast now. Thank you," she told me. I knew she thought I was just someone else who worked there.

"Grandma," I said pressing my hand into hers, "I'm your daughter Haille's daughter, Melody. I'm your granddaughter and I'm going to come back and visit you often. Would you like that?"

"Haille?" she said. She shook her head slightly. "I know someone named Haille. Nelson told me about her. She's very pretty, isn't she?"

"Yes," I said. There was no point in telling her all that had happened. She had taken in too much already, I thought. She was physically strong for her age, but mentally, she was very fragile, as fragile as a little girl, and I knew, from personal experience, how easy it was to shatter a little girl's heart.

"She should go for her nap before lunch," Mrs. Greene said, suddenly appearing in the corridor.

"Yes, I was taking her to her room."

"I'll see to it she gets there," she said and nodded to the attendant who had been outside, hovering around us. He moved quickly to Grandma Belinda's side.

"I'll see you soon, Grandma. Have a good nap and then a good lunch," I said. I kissed her cheek and she touched it as if I had planted something very precious on her face. Then she turned and looked at me, blinking rapidly for a moment.

"You look like someone I know," she said. Then she smiled. "I remember. You look like me when I was your age." She leaned closer to whisper. "Don't give your heart away too quickly. They like to break hearts. That's what they like to do the most. Just ask Olivia," she said and laughed. "Ask her and tell her I told you to ask. What?" She looked at the attendant as if she had heard him say something. There was some mild chastisement in his expression and she straightened up. "Oh."

I stood watching them as the attendant led her down the hall.

"I'll show you the way out," Mrs. Greene said.

"I remember the way," I told her. "Thank you." I hurried down the corridor, through the lobby, and out the door, my heart thumping. Raymond sat up quickly the moment I appeared and then got out to open the door for me.

"Everything go all right?" he asked.

"Yes," I said. "Just fine."

I sat back, locked within my own thoughts, feeling rather sad and vulnerable. I wasn't looking out the window, so I didn't realize he wasn't taking me directly home until I noticed the driveway of Grandma Olivia's house.

"Why are you taking me here?" I demanded.

"It's what Mrs. Logan told me to do," he said and drove up the driveway.

"What am I supposed to do now?" I asked. He shrugged.

"I guess Mrs. Logan expects you."

"Be nice if she told me her plans for me," I snapped and got out.

She came to the door herself when I rang.

"Raymond said you told him to bring me directly here after my visit," I said.

"Yes. Come into the living room." She led the way and took her high-backed seat, which, as usual, made her look like some sort of dowager queen. "Sit," she ordered as if I were Ulysses the dog.

"Why did you tell him to bring me here?"

"I'm not accustomed to people standing over me when we talk," she replied and sat back, waiting for me to obey her and sit on the settee. I did so quickly.

"Well?" I demanded.

"I thought it best you speak to me about your visit before you spoke to anyone else. Tell me how it went and don't leave out any details."

"I'm surprised you don't know everything already," I said.

"What's that supposed to mean?"

"The way they were hovering around us, listening."

"Ridiculous."

Maybe it was, I thought, but it was easy to become paranoid where this family was concerned. I took a deep breath and wondered what I should tell her. I didn't want Grandma Belinda to appear foolish just because she loved children's books and confused time and places now, and I remembered Grandpa Samuel telling me to come to him with any stories first.

"She's very sweet and I thought she looked very healthy. She's only a year or so younger than you?" I asked deliberately. Grandma Olivia stiffened.

"Never mind that. What nonsense did she tell you? I'm sure she rambled on and on about something silly."

I shrugged.

"She told me about her youth, how many boy-friends she had, one of them being the judge."

Grandma Olivia's eyes narrowed into hateful slits.

"He wasn't her boyfriend when she was younger.

93

That is just one of her fantasies. This is exactly the sort of nonsense I'm talking about," she said, her words biting and sharp. I suddenly saw how vulnerable and helpless Grandma Belinda must have been, growing up with Olivia.

"She said you were often jealous of her and you poisoned her song bird and stole a locket the judge gave her," I said in an accusatory tone.

"Oh." She shook her head and smiled as though I had uttered the most ridiculous things. "She tells that story to everyone. That bird died of natural causes and I don't know why she carries on and on about it. When it was alive, I was the one who had to take care of it. She never fed it or cleaned its cage, and as for a locket, it was a present I received from someone and she fantasized it was for her. Men never bought her things. They didn't have to," she added dryly. "All they had to do was turn a flirtatious face in her direction and she was theirs. What else did she say?"

"She said your marriage was forced on you," I blurted, unable to hide my anger at the way she diminished and criticized my real grandmother at every turn. Is this why she brought me here? Did she get some sadistic pleasure from it?

"It wasn't forced on me, but parents had a great deal more to say about whom their children married then. It was better that wiser minds prevail. Far fewer of those marriages ended in divorce, and if she had listened to my father, she wouldn't be in this predicament today."

"She said you forbade her to mention my mother. Is that true?"

"That," Grandma Olivia said, "is the first true thing she told you. Yes, of course I forbade her to mention Haille. What sort of a situation would we have had with her babbling about this embarrassing event? You think I wanted the gossip mongers clicking their tongues? It was bad enough that some servants knew and the doctor knew, but somehow, I managed to keep everyone from suffering. You sit here now with your eyes full of condemnation and accusation, but do you pause to think what I provided for your mother? No, you don't," she said, answering herself quickly. "Well, I'll tell you.

"Your mother was a child born out of wedlock, normally a disgrace, but I gave her a home and my name and the best of everything. She could have had a fine education, met the most distinguished men, had a real future, but she was contaminated by Belinda's bad blood."

"And now you think I am too, is that it?"

"That remains to be seen," she snapped.

"Not by you. I'm not auditioning for your approval," I fired back at her, the tears burning under my eyelids, tears I would die before releasing in her presence.

"Nevertheless," she said, her smile sharp and her eyes bright and fiery, "you'll do nothing to risk my disapproval or—"

"Or you'll see to it I never get my inheritance. I know," I said.

"That's right," she replied and sat back.

There was a moment of silence, a truce between us.

"I wouldn't recommend that you return to the home to see Belinda," she said slowly. "She'll only fill you with more ridiculous fantasies and it might cause problems for everyone."

"She needs visitors, family. You can't leave her there like that, alone, lost."

Grandma Olivia laughed.

"She's far from alone and far from lost. She has the best care money can buy. If anything, she's spoiled, but she was spoiled all her life. That's why she ended up as she did," she concluded. "Don't go back there," she said standing.

"I will. She's my real grandmother," I said.

95

Grandma Olivia's eyes looked as if they could burn through my skull and sear my brain.

"She's a mental invalid, totally dependent upon my charity. I could have her put in a county poorhouse in minutes," she threatened. "What do you expect she can give you?"

"Love," I said not backing down or looking away.

Grandma Olivia sucked in her breath as if I had punched her in the stomach. She started to speak, but stopped, her eyes strangely softening, her look turning from anger and condemnation to an unexplainable look of pleasure, respect.

"Don't push me too far, Melody. I would like to see you have a good life, despite what you think of me, but you have to rise above yourself, your own contaminated blood."

"Am I dismissed?" I asked. I was trembling inside, but I wouldn't show it.

"Dismissed? Yes, but keep my advice hanging up front in your closet," she said. "Raymond will see to it you get home."

"Thank you," I said. I turned and marched out of the house, never welcoming the fresh sea air as much.

5
❦

Someone's Watching Over Me

Cary and May were already gone by the time Raymond brought me home. Aunt Sara said they had just left.

"Cary waited as long as he could, dear, but he felt sorry for May. He told me to tell you he was taking her to the Sea and Shell on Commerce Street and, if you came home early enough, to join them. How was your visit with Belinda?" she asked, but looked away quickly as if she didn't want to hear my answer.

"It was nice. She's very sweet," I said, "even if she is confused about events and time."

"Jacob asked me to make my meat loaf for dinner tonight," Aunt Sara continued, as if I hadn't said a word. "It's one of his favorites." She laughed, her laugh sounding as fragile as thin china. "He says I proved the old adage that the shortest distance to a man's heart is through his stomach. He says he fell in love with my cooking first and then looked up and saw there was an angel in the kitchen."

"Uncle Jacob said that?" I asked skeptically. Aunt Sara heard the note of doubt in my voice.

"Oh yes," she declared. "When he wants to, Jacob can say very sweet things."

"I guess he hasn't wanted to for a while," I muttered. "Aunt Sara, did you know my grandmother before she was sent to the rest home?"

Aunt Sara's smile faded quickly and she turned away.

"Not really, no," she said. "I mean, Belinda was always different. Jacob thought it best we didn't have much to do with her."

"Why? Because Grandma Olivia wanted it that way?" I asked pointedly.

"It's better not to say anything if you can't say anything nice about someone," Aunt Sara lectured. "Oh, I forgot. Could you pick up some garlic for me on the way home? Here, let me give you some money," she said, hurrying to her cookie jar. It looked more as if she were fleeing from my questions.

I went upstairs to change into a pair of jeans and a faded gray sweatshirt with our high school letters on the front. I put on a pair of sneakers, too, and then went running down the stairs, hurrying to catch up with Cary and May. Aunt Sara was waiting at the front door to hand me the money for the garlic.

"Thank you," she said, but she didn't move out of the way. After a moment she lifted her eyes and said, "Laura liked Belinda." It was as if guilt had been buzzing around in her head like a bee in a jar, threatening to sting her if she didn't open the lid.

"She did?"

"She even went to visit her at the home once." She lowered her voice to a whisper even though there was no one else around. "Olivia never knew, but Jacob found out and he was very upset with her for doing it. It was one of the few times he got angry at Laura. She promised never to go again and that was that."

"Why was everyone so mean to my grandmother?"

"It wasn't that we were mean to her, dear. She was . . ."

"What?"

"Telling horrible lies, and lies are . . . lies are what Jacob says they are, like termites. They get into your moral foundation and tear you down. Only sinners have reason to lie."

"Then Grandma Olivia might be the biggest sinner of all," I blurted and Aunt Sara's face nearly collapsed with shock. She turned white.

"If Jacob ever heard you say such a terrible thing—"

"Don't worry, Aunt Sara. I won't say it again. If you can't say something nice about someone, don't say anything," I reminded her.

"Yes." She nodded. "Oh dear, oh dear," she chanted as she returned to the kitchen.

I felt bad about shocking her with my outburst, but I was so frustrated and angry about the way this family treated Grandma Belinda that I felt like lashing out at all of them, all of them with their holier-than-thou attitudes, gazing down their noses at the rest of us as if they stood on Mount Olympus. Even if something was wrong with Grandma Belinda and she babbled silly things, confusing time and place, that wasn't a reason to ostracize her and forbid everyone from seeing her. Maybe there was another reason why destiny brought me here, I thought. Maybe it was for Grandma Belinda, who otherwise had no one to come to her defense but the shadowy figures of her flustered memory.

When I got to town, I found the streets jammed with people and traffic. There were many families, mothers and fathers walking with their children, everyone holding hands, their faces full of smiles, their eyes bright with excitement as they gazed at the pretty things in store windows or at other people rushing by on the way to restaurants, the dock, and the shops. I couldn't help standing wistfully and watch them walk by. Why couldn't that teenage girl be me and that man and woman be my real father and mother? Why couldn't I lead a normal life and be on vacation with my parents? What had turned fate in my direction and chosen me to be the one who had to flounder about searching for her identity?

A chorus of horns and then loud laughter shook me out of my self-pity. When I looked around, a smile returned to my face. Provincetown on weekends was filled with excitement. Yes, these people were tourists and some of them littered and some of them drove badly or complained vehemently about prices, but most enjoyed themselves and were appreciative of the ocean, and respected and admired the fishermen and boatmen. Shop owners, restaurant owners, hotel and bed-and-breakfast owners needed the business. To me, those who were securely planted in their wealth and property here and who looked down on all this were selfish and arrogant. They lived in their own world and Grandma Olivia was queen of it, I thought.

Well, as long as I lived here, I would never be like that. I wouldn't become one of them no matter how much money I inherited, I vowed.

I hurried on toward the Sea and Shell, a small, inexpensive eatery near the dock. When I turned a corner, looking back when I should have been looking forward, I rammed into someone who shouted, "Whoa, there!" I gazed up and into the eyes of the very handsome and distinguished looking man I knew to be Adam Jackson's father, T. J. Jackson, one of the most prominent attorneys in Provincetown. Before this, I had seen him only from a distance at school functions or on the street. Whenever he saw me, he looked at me with a very pensive look on his face. I thought that was because of something Adam might have told him about me, something nasty of course.

Adam, his sister Michelle, and his mother, Ann, a very attractive brunette who was just as tall as her husband, stood directly behind Mr. Jackson. Adam gave me his usual smirk of self-confidence, but Michelle grimaced with disgust. Her shiny braces glittered on her teeth, making her mouth as mechanical and cold looking as her dull brown eyes. She was thirteen, going into the eighth grade, and from what I had heard, just as snobby as a skunk.

"Well, hello," Mr. Jackson said, widening his smile when he recognized me.

"I'm sorry," I said.

"That's all right. No harm done. Where are you heading in such a hurry?"

"I'm late. I have to meet my cousins for lunch," I said, avoiding Adam's gaze. Ever since the time on the beach and the subsequent fight Cary had with Adam in the cafeteria, we had had little to say to each other. He had graduated and was going off to college in late August. He had told me he would become a lawyer like his father, although he didn't seem to have any great passion to be an attorney. He was doing just what was expected of him.

I had never really been this close to his mother before. She was a very pretty woman with big green eyes and a nose and mouth so perfectly shaped she could have been a model. She reminded me a lot of Mommy, because she had the same high cheekbones and elegant neck. I wondered if she had ever wanted to be a model, too. She didn't smile, so much as keep a soft and friendly look in her eyes and mouth.

"Well, if you're too late, you're welcome to join us for lunch," Adam's father offered. Michelle shifted her weight to her other foot and swung her eyes toward the sky with a grunt of annoyance.

"Thank you, but I'm sure they're waiting for me."

"We're going right in here," he continued, pointing to one of the more expensive Provincetown restaurants. "Come right back and join us if you've missed them," he insisted.

"Thank you."

"I never had the opportunity to tell you how much I enjoyed your fiddle playing at the variety show," he said. "Wasn't she something, Ann?"

"Yes, she was," Adam's mother said with a small smile. "A very nice surprise."

"How's your grandmother these days? I haven't seen her in quite a while," Adam's father continued as if we had all the time in the world to waste away. In truth, only Michelle seemed impatient and bothered. Adam continued his self-satisfied smirk, enjoying my discomfort. His mother looked patient and very friendly.

"She's very well, thank you," I said.

"Well, perhaps we can treat you to lunch another time," Adam's father said. I gazed at his soft blue eyes and gentle smile. I didn't know whether lawyers could turn the charm on and off at will because of the work they did in court before juries, but he seemed so sincere and warm, I almost wished I could have lunch with him. "It's the least we can do to show our appreciation for the fine performance you gave," he added. "Don't stop playing that fiddle."

"I won't. Thank you," I said and hurried away confused as to why he seemed so interested in me. It was hard to believe that someone as nasty as Adam came from such nice parents.

Cary and May were just finishing their sandwiches when I arrived at the Sea and Shell.

"Sorry I was late," I said sliding across from them in the booth. "I didn't know Grandma Olivia was having Raymond bring me to her after the visit for an interrogation."

"Interrogation?"

"An inquisition is more like it."

"Oh? I just thought you had decided to stay and have lunch with Belinda."

"I didn't eat lunch anywhere. Grandma Olivia didn't even offer me a glass of water."

Cary shrugged.

"That's Grandma. Go on and order. We'll wait and watch you eat," Cary said with a smile.

"Don't let me forget to bring home garlic for your mother," I said as I chose a sandwich from the menu. Then I told him about my literally bumping into Adam Jackson's father and family and how Mr. Jackson practically insisted I join them for lunch. Cary's eyes grew dark with anger just at the mention of Adam's name.

"Figures he'd want to show off. He was always like that," Cary said. "Like father like son."

"How do you know what Mr. Jackson was like when he was younger, Cary?" I asked, wondering at the venom behind his words.

"He went to school with my father and your step-father. Dad's told me about him. He was always spoiled, arrogant. That's just the way the Jacksons are and always will be."

"He didn't seem to be just now."

"Well, he is," Cary insisted. "They ought to be known as the Snobsons and not the Jacksons," he added. Whenever he got very angry, his ears would turn red at the edges. They were that way now, so I dropped the subject and began talking about Grandma Belinda instead. I had to remember to sign as I talked so May wouldn't feel left out. I didn't sign everything, of course. Cary shook his head with disbelief when I described what Grandma Belinda had said happened between her and Grandpa Samuel.

"I never knew any details, but I knew she was saying outrageous things."

"Now I understand why Grandpa Samuel wanted me to come to him with any questions," I said. "Grandma Olivia has little love for her sister and I think some of what Grandma Belinda told me may be true."

"I don't know," Cary said, shaking his head uncertainly. "I could probably count on my fingers how often her name's been mentioned in our house or at Grandma's."

"That's just it, Cary. There's got to be more of a reason why she is persona non grata in this family."

"What? Persona?"

"Not wanted," I explained impatiently. "You don't disown someone because she's mentally ill, do you?" He started to shrug. "Your mother told me Laura went to see her once."

His smile froze.

"She told you that?"

"Yes."

"My father was very upset with her."

"She told me that, too. Don't you think that was wrong, to treat a sick old lady like the plague? Well, don't you?" I pursued when he didn't respond. May was signing question after question, but I didn't turn from Cary.

"All I know is my father said Belinda was very immoral when she was younger and he didn't want Laura around that sort of woman," Cary said, a bit sheepishly. "I'm sorry."

"Your father . . . infuriates me," I wailed. Cary laughed. "He does! What makes him so high and mighty? Isn't there something in the Bible about judging others?"

"Judge not that ye be not judged," Cary said softly, nodding.

"Well?"

He shrugged.

"Tell him that," he said.

"I will," I declared, amazed at my newfound conviction to stand up for my poor, defenseless grandmother.

Cary smiled, doubting that I had the courage. It added fuel to the fire of wrath building in my chest. He glanced at May and then he leaned toward me.

"When you're angry, you're about twice as pretty as you are normally and that's a lot," he said.

His words brought a different shade of crimson to my cheeks. My thoughts became jumbled and confused, and when I realized that those words could have such an effect over me, I looked away quickly, not knowing whether I should cry or laugh at the turmoil that raged in my heart and in my head.

After we had gone to the supermarket and bought Aunt Sara her garlic, we headed home. There wasn't a cloud in the afternoon sky and the breeze had warmed up. The ocean looked soft and inviting with the sunlight glittering on the waves. The anger inside me was forgotten once I glimpsed the beauty of the sea, and our conversation returned to more pleasant subjects than family. Cary talked again about his desire to build real boats. He was full of ideas for customizing them and improving on their mobility. When Cary talked about his dreams he became a different person, more confident and intense, and I worried that Uncle Jacob's tyranny would slowly crush the hope and life from him.

"If your father really cared, he would want to see you turn your dreams into reality," I said, but he continued to make excuses for Uncle Jacob on the basis of family and tradition.

As we drew closer to the house, May said she wanted to go hunting sea shells, but Cary was determined to return to the model boat on which he was currently working. I sensed that this one was very important to him, so I offered to take May to the beach and keep her out of his hair.

"Come on up when you get back," Cary whispered. "I have something special to show you," he added. I felt a flutter in my breast and nodded.

May didn't seem unhappy that Cary wasn't accompanying us. She looked as if she wanted to be alone with me, and as soon as we reached the seashore, I saw why. She began to ask me questions about my life in West Virginia and boyfriends I had had. When I asked her why she wanted to know, she blushingly told me she had a boyfriend.

"What?"

I laughed, and we sat on a mound of sand as she explained how she had been partnered with this boy at school for different tasks and how they had grown to like each other. On Friday, when no one was looking, he had leaned over and kissed her on the cheek. She was so excited by it, she confessed, that she hadn't washed her face since.

I started to laugh, but saw how serious and intense she was about the experience and instead turned my thoughts to the first time a boy had kissed me. First times for some things were so special they stayed with you all your life, I thought, especially a girl's first kiss.

"Did Cary ever kiss you?" she asked. Apparently May, although deaf, was not blind to the attraction between Cary and me, how we looked at each other, how we spoke and touched each other, in ways that she knew were significant. Now it was my turn to blush. And worry that others in the family had noticed as well.

"We're just good friends," I said quickly, without really answering her questions. "What's your boyfriend's name?" I asked, desperate to change the subject.

"Laaaa . . . ry," she pronounced proudly. "Were you ever in love?" she signed quickly.

"I've had crushes on boys," I told her, "but I don't think I was really in love."

"How do you know when you're in love?" she asked.

"It's not an easy question to answer," I told her. "When you have a crush on a boy, you can't think of anything else. You write his name on everything and you walk about in a daydream and act so silly, people say you're lovesick."

"Sick?" She lost her smile. "Do you have to take medicine?" she asked.

"No," I said laughing. Then I realized she had been brought up with doctors and nurses and medicine most of her life. The word sick had only one meaning to her. "You're not actually sick. You're just . . . doing silly things all the time."

That made her thoughtful for a while. Then, she looked around to be sure no one was near before telling me that something was happening to her and that was why she was so worried when I mentioned sick.

"What do you mean?" I asked, concerned. She was still for a minute and then unbuttoned her blouse to show me the rise around her nipple. "Oh, you're just developing breasts," I said and told her as much as I could about a woman's body. When I mentioned the monthly period, she was astounded.

"Bleeding?" she made me repeat, grimacing as she signed.

"Hasn't your mother ever told you any of this?" I asked. She shook her head. "What about Laura?"

She reminded me that none of this was happening to her when Laura was alive and Laura probably thought she wasn't ready.

I told her more. Of course she knew that babies come from mothers, but the details of the process were still a mystery. She was shocked to learn that women carry eggs and men carry the sperm. When she asked me how the sperm got to the egg, I hesitated, wondering if I should be the one to tell her. Why hadn't Aunt Sara had a mother-daughter talk yet? How long did she think May would remain a child? Did she and Uncle Jacob assume that May's deafness made her immune to a young girl's thoughts and desires?

Had Mommy and Daddy thought I was immune to these desires? Mama Arlene took pity on me and all my questions and I told May about the birds and the bees the way I remembered Mama Arlene telling it to me. I described sex as Nature's trick to bring two people who loved each other together so they could create the greatest expression of their love: a baby. I didn't go into vivid detail, but I let her understand that a man and a woman had to join to make it all happen.

She was still, almost stunned, and then she signed a question that nearly brought me to tears: Would her baby be born deaf because she was deaf?

Of course, I didn't know for sure, but I told her I didn't think so. I told her her baby would be a separate person. She liked that and smiled again. I told her to come to me with any questions any time she wanted.

She looked up at me seriously and made the signs to indicate I had become her older sister. That did bring tears to my eyes and I hugged her. Then we got up and resumed our search for precious sea shells.

As May walked ahead of me along the beach, I now saw her as more than just a little girl. Sooner than Aunt Sara expected, May would become a young woman, a very pretty and sensitive young woman whose deafness made her even softer and more gentle than most. She would search for someone to trust, someone who loved her deeply. He would have to be someone special, I thought, because she was so special.

When we returned to the house, May went to her room to put away her new sea shells and I climbed the ladder to Cary's attic. As soon as I stepped through the trapdoor, I saw him hovering over his new model boat. He was working with such intensity, he hadn't heard me come up. Feeling like a spy, I stood there very quietly watching him concentrate. His mouth was slightly open, his eyes fixed on the tiny paint brush. He seemed to be holding his breath. After a few more minutes, he sat back and sighed with pleasure at his accomplishment. Then he realized I was there and turned quickly, blushing.

"How long have you been here?"

"Just a few seconds. I'm sorry. I didn't want to interrupt," I said.

"It's okay. Perfect timing. I just finished," he said, rising. "Come, take a look."

I stepped closer and gazed at the beautiful, sleek sailboat he'd been working on. He had just painted Melody on the hull. Surprised, I looked up at him.

"It's for you," he said.

"Really? Oh, it's beautiful, Cary."

"The engineering of its shape is my creation. If you look closely," he said, "you'll see two people inside the cabin. That's us."

I leaned over and peered through the cabin window. There were a tiny man and a woman standing beside each other, gazing into each other's eyes.

"It's so precious," I said softly, my breath catching in my throat.

"After it dries I'll bring it to your room," he said. "You can keep it on the shelf by your bed."

"Thank you, Cary. I'll always cherish it. Did you ever give anyone else a boat you made?" I asked.

Curiosity had gotten the best of me. I should have smothered the question, for I saw it brought back unpleasant memories.

"I gave one to Laura once, but she didn't think it was that special," he said turning away. "She was seeing Robert Royce then," he added, as if that explained everything.

"I didn't see it in the room," I said.

"That's because it's not there."

"Where is it?"

"Floating some place in the ocean," he said dryly. "Where's May?"

"Organizing her new sea shells," I said.

"Good."

"She told me she has a boyfriend," I told him.

"What?" He smiled. "A boyfriend? Our May?"

"Yes, really. There's a boy at school who likes her. She was full of questions about boys and love."

"Did you have the answers?"

"Some. She wanted to know how you know you're in love," I told him.

A small smile crossed his lips and a twinkle came into his eyes.

"What did you say?"

"I told her I didn't know for sure. It was different for everyone," I said, trying not to meet his eyes. "Then she wanted to know how babies are made. Apparently, your mother hasn't told her anything."

"What did you tell her?" he asked with some trepidation.

"The truth," I said. "Not in great detail, of course, but the basics at least. She's becoming a young woman, Cary. It's time she understood what was happening to her body and what *could* happen, don't you think?"

"I can't think of anyone I'd rather have tell her about it," he said after a moment's thought.

110

"Your mother, that's who," I countered, but he shook his head.

He continued to stare at me, and as his glimmering eyes met mine, my pulse quickened. He stepped closer, and as he leaned toward me, I lifted my mouth in anticipation of his kiss. We kissed and then we kissed again only harder and longer. He took my hand and gently brought me to the small sofa. When he sat, he pulled me onto his lap and brought his lips to mine once again. This kiss was more intense.

"Oh Melody," he said, moving his lips down my cheek to my neck. I lay back, enjoying the feelings rushing through my body. "I've gotten so I don't think of anything but you. Even on the boat, I'm dreaming of you, forgetting to do things. Yesterday, I wandered about for twenty minutes, forgetting why I had a wrench in my hand. Dad thought I was sick."

"Lovesick," I laughed and he pulled back as if I had shot him.

"Yes, lovesick," he said with a sneer. "I guess I'm not as sophisticated about it as, say, Adam Jackson." He stood up, pulling his hand out of mine as if he'd been burned.

"Cary, I was just kidding. I just told May all about that and—"

"What do you think, I'm acting like an eleven-year-old?" he asked astounded.

"No, I . . ."

He shook his head and turned away.

"Cary, I'm sorry. Really. I didn't mean to insult you. I don't want to drive you away from me," I added. He sat in his chair and sulked. I got up quickly and went to him. "I'm sorry," I said and kissed him on the cheek. He took a deep breath.

"I guess I'm just nervous," he admitted. "I don't have all that much experience with women."

"Neither do I with men," I said. "So we've got to be

kind to each other, gentle, loving, and most of all forgiving," I added.

He liked that and his smile was warm again.

"I forgive you. Now, where were we?" he asked and put his arms around my waist.

"I think right here," I said and leaned over to kiss him.

"Maybe I should have you tell me how babies are made, too," he kidded. "I'm not sure I've got it right."

"I doubt that, Cary Logan."

He laughed and then stood up, tightening his embrace around me. As we kissed, his hands slid under my sweatshirt. His fingers moved up my side and up my back until he found the clip on my bra.

I didn't move. He fumbled a while with the clip and then suddenly, it unfastened. The thrill that shot through my body made my legs weak. I moaned under his kiss and he brought me back to the sofa. When his fingers moved over my nipple, I thought my heart would shatter from pounding.

"Oh Melody, I am lovesick, but I don't care," he whispered. "I don't care if I die of it."

He started to pull my sweatshirt up but I stopped him. No one but Mommy and Mama Arlene had ever seen me undressed before, I thought. It was exciting, but it was scary, too.

"Don't you want to?" he asked.

"Yes, but slowly," I said. He kissed me again, and again he started to pull up my sweatshirt. He brought his lips to my breast and I slipped farther down under him. His right hand moved to my hip and over to the button that fastened my jeans. The suddenness with which he did it surprised me. For a moment, I couldn't catch my breath.

"No," I said. "Not yet."

He pulled his hand back, kissed my breasts, and pressed himself to me. I felt the small explosion building inside me and then I felt his hardness, even

112

through his pants, and I grew more frightened. It was happening, and if we let it go one second more, I thought, it would be like trying to hold back the tide.

"We'd better stop," I whispered. He held me tightly, his breathing coming hard and fast.

"Are you sure?"

"Yes, for now. Please, Cary."

"Okay," he said. After another long moment, he stood up and turned away, embarrassed by his obvious sexual excitement. I sat up quickly and reached back to fasten my bra. "I should be going down to help Aunt Sara with dinner."

"Right," he said. He returned to his desk and started shuffling model parts back and forth noisily.

"Are you okay?"

"Yes," he said, nodding but not looking at me. After a minute, he added, "I think it's easier for girls to stop once you start, especially when you've gone that far."

"I don't really know," I said, wondering if what he said was true.

"I do," he said harshly. "I don't need to practice too much to learn that lesson." He was trying not to be angry and frustrated, but I could see the battle within him had filled his eyes with fire and turned his skin cherry red.

I fumbled with my hair and realized my hair clip had fallen out. It wasn't on the sofa, so I looked beside it and then behind it.

"I lost my hair clip some place," I said. "It must have fallen behind the sofa."

"I'll find it for you," he said and started to get up.

"It's okay. I can do it."

I pulled the sofa back just a little and saw the clip. When I reached down for it, however, I saw something else, something that put a cold, shocking chill in my heart. It looked like the floor boards were parted. Light was coming up and through the floor. I leaned

113

closer and realized I was looking down into my room, looking right over the bed.

"What is this?" I asked. When I raised my head, Cary was staring at me, a look of terror on his face.

"It's . . . nothing."

"Nothing? It's an opening in the floor. Right over my bed."

"It was just there, just the way the boards settled or something. That's why I put the sofa over it," he said quickly.

When you're close enough to someone to see the love in his eyes, I thought, you can also see the deceit. Cary was lying.

"How long as it been there, Cary?"

"Since the house was built, I guess." He gave an exaggerated shrug of his shoulders. "I don't know."

I gazed at the hole in the floor again. I didn't know a lot about the structure of houses, but I knew that hole hadn't just formed there. He had obviously used one of his tools for constructing models to punch out the opening.

"Why did you do this, Cary?"

He shifted his eyes guiltily away and just sat there with his hands in his lap.

"I know you did this, Cary. Stop lying to me," I demanded, confusion again coming to take the place of my happiness.

He nodded.

"I did it when Laura started bringing him home and they spent time together in her room," he confessed angrily.

"Robert Royce?"

"Yes," he said, turning to me. He had his eyes squinted shut as he spoke. It was as if he were trying to block out some scene scorched on his brain. "I didn't trust him. I told her, but she wouldn't listen, so I thought I had to look in on her and be there if she needed me, if he . . . tried something."

"Don't you think she would have been able to stop him?"

He opened his eyes and shook his head.

"No. I don't know. What if she couldn't? I did it for her," he insisted. "I couldn't help it," he admitted. "But, I haven't looked down that hole at you, if that's what you think. I swear. I'm not a peeping Tom. Really," he pleaded, his face contrite with his effort to convince me and his need to have me forgive him.

"I believe you," I said, and he relaxed. "You should repair it though."

"I will. I just forgot about it," he said. "The sofa was over it, so I just forgot about it."

I nodded and put my hair clip back in. Then I started for the trapdoor. He reached out to take my hand.

"Melody, you don't think less of me because of that, do you?"

"No," I said. I smiled at him, but in my heart I was confused. I didn't know exactly what to think or feel at the moment. I needed time. "I better go down before everyone starts wondering where I am," I said.

"Maybe we'll take a walk after dinner or something."

"Maybe," I said. I nodded at the work table. "Thank you for the sailboat."

He smiled and watched me descend. When I entered my room, however, I gazed up at the ceiling. Now that I knew it was there, I could see the small hole. A second later, it was darkened. Cary had covered it.

But had he closed his heart on all that had made him drill the hole? Only time would tell, I thought.

What had he seen down here and what had it done to him? I wondered. How confusing and wonderful, exciting and yet frightening sex was, I thought. I didn't tell May, of course, but I could see it was the greatest mystery about ourselves. It inspired us, made us do creative things and yet strange things, weird things.

May had turned to me for answers on the beach, answers I had no idea myself where I would find. In a real sense both she and I were orphans. She had a mother who refused to acknowledge her needs and I had no mother to help me with mine. Whatever discoveries I made through my awkward stumbling, I would bring to May so she would benefit. Perhaps this was another reason why I was brought here, I thought.

But all these good plans and good intentions were soon to be shattered.

Uncle Jacob apparently had walked in on May and Aunt Sara just as May was signing a question that made Aunt Sara turn blue in the face. And what followed was about as furious as a hurricane. I had just gone down to see what I could do to help with dinner, but when I reached the bottom of the stairway, I heard Uncle Jacob call my name. He spit it out the way he spat out hateful Biblical names like Jezebel and Satan, Delilah and Cain.

I stepped into the living room. He was standing near the fireplace and when he turned, it looked as if embers from the fire had jumped into his eyes. There was no doubt that if he could have set me afire and turned me to ash, he would have done it in a heartbeat. I held my breath. No one had ever looked at me with such disdain. It chilled me to the bone.

"How dare you?" he said. "How dare you come into my home and pollute my child? I warned you about this. I told you it was in your blood."

I shook my head, tears of confusion clouding my vision.

"What have I done?"

"You have filled her mind with unclean thoughts, with pornography."

"I have not. All I did was tell her how babies are

made. What's wrong with that? She's old enough to know these things now and you and Aunt Sara should be telling her more."

His eyes widened.

"Your mother was a whore," he said through clenched teeth. "It's no surprise she bore a daughter like you." He nodded, satisfied with his thoughts. "The old sayings are full of truth. The apple doesn't fall far from the tree. I forbid you to talk to May on this subject, do you understand?"

I shook my head defiantly at him and recalled the Biblical quotation Cary had given me at lunch.

"Judge not that ye be not judged," I fired back at him.

He recoiled as if I had been big enough and strong enough to slap his face. His mouth moved, but nothing came out. He backed up a bit and then waved his finger at me, but not as firmly or with as much confidence as before.

"Just . . . mark my words," he said and turned his back on me.

I spun around just as Cary came down the stairs. I was crying now, the tears streaming down my cheeks.

"What's wrong?"

"The high and the mighty Logans have spoken again!" I spit through my teeth and charged up the stairs.

"Where are you going? It's dinner time."

"I'm not hungry. I'd rather starve than sit at the same table with him anyway," I cried and went into my room, slamming the door behind me. My body shuddered with my sobs. When I stopped to take a breath, I saw that Cary had put the beautiful sailboat on the shelf.

I went to it and wiped my cheeks as I stared at the tiny parts and the two people inside the cabin, looking happy and in love.

"No wonder Laura got into a sailboat with Robert," I muttered. "She just wanted to get away from here, get away from all this."

They did, but they died to do it, I thought. I looked at Laura's picture on the dresser.

Did you know what would happen to you that day, Laura? Did you deliberately sail into a storm? Maybe you were running away from a lot more than they all knew, or maybe you had seen something beyond the darkness, something more attractive and full of more hope. I wish I had known you; then maybe together we could have confronted the Logan misery.

I went to the window and gazed out at the ocean. The horizon seemed to mark the edge of the world. No wonder people believed you could fall off if you sailed too far. Tonight I wished I could do that. I'd rather take my chances in another world and escape the misery, the sadness, the deceit, and the loneliness I found in this one.

Almost two years before, Laura had stood at this window and looked out at that dark horizon. Did she see an answer? Did she see hope?

I wear your clothes and I sleep in your bed, and maybe, just maybe, I dream your dreams, Laura. Do I?

Answers, like the wispy clouds that drifted past the stars, lay beyond my reach. I gazed up, tantalized, tormented, feeling more and more lonely and afraid of what tomorrow would bring.

6

Revelations

The knock on my door was so gentle that at first I thought I had imagined it. I was lying on my bed, staring up at the ceiling, drifting with my own childhood memories, memories that floated by like an old-time silent movie, the characters and events passing in silence: silent laughter, silent tears, Mommy and my step-daddy being playful, Papa George gazing up from his paper, Mama Arlene standing nearby, a soft, loving look on her face, everyone waving, applauding, arms held out, my step-daddy lifting me into the air, Papa George standing over me as I practiced on my fiddle. The memories became more liquid, rushed by faster, scenes merged, faces were swept away, the silent music stopped and there was my step-daddy's gravestone before me, growing larger, taller until there was nothing else in my vision.

The knocking grew louder.

"Yes?"

The door opened and Cary entered sheepishly, carrying a tray with my dinner.

"Hi," he ventured.

119

"Hi."

"Ma wanted me to bring this up to you."

"I'm not eating anything in this house again," I said. "I'm just resting a while and then I'm leaving."

"Don't be silly, Melody," Cary replied and put the tray on the desk. "Where will you go?"

"I don't care. Anywhere but here. I'll find work as a waitress or a scrub woman some place."

Cary laughed.

"I mean it. You know I left before and I can leave again, Cary."

"Okay, but in the meantime, if you don't eat, you'll only get sick and spite yourself. Go on. I'll keep you company. It's good meat loaf. Ma does a great job on that."

"I know she does. She told me. It's your father's favorite," I said, spitting the words at him. Cary shrugged.

"Doesn't make it taste any better or any worse. I like it a lot too, and so does May. And so will you," he added. "Come on, eat so I can brag how successful I was."

I gazed at the food. I was hungry and it was stupid to permit Uncle Jacob to make me suffer. I rose from the bed and went to the desk. The aroma of the meat loaf was enticing and I had to admit, it tasted wonderful and succulent, all the flavors just perfectly mixed. Cary sat watching me.

"I think your mother became a wonderful cook just so she would have some place in the house where she could be away from your father much of the time," I said.

"They were different before Laura died," Cary revealed. "We were all different. We did more things as a family. Dad wasn't as uptight about everything. We went for rides, went to restaurants, took walks on Sunday. During the cranberry harvest, we were all out there working, and then there would be a big feast and celebration. Dad even danced with Ma."

"I don't believe it. Dancing is surely sinful," I said between mouthfuls.

"Everything became sinful after Laura's drowning. I told you. He blamed himself."

"Why was that, Cary? You've told me that, yes, but I don't understand. If your father lived such a moral life, read the Bible every night, made sure you were all so prim and proper, why would he feel responsible for an accident?"

Cary shook his head.

"That's between him and his own conscience, I suppose. I never asked him," he admitted.

"Maybe you should. If he's going to make everyone else suffer, he should at least explain why," I insisted.

"If we suffer, we suffer because of our own sins," Cary claimed. Then he looked away. I knew why.

"Maybe what you think is a sin isn't," I said softly. "It's not a sin to love someone too much."

"Yes, it is," he said quickly. "Remember Adam? Remember Original Sin?"

"Should I? Did I commit that, too?"

I started to smile. "All right, tell me."

"After Eve ate of the fruit and was doomed to be cast from Paradise, Adam ate so he would not be without her. That's loving too much," he explained.

"Just like a man to find another way to blame a woman for his own mistakes," I said. Cary's eyes widened.

"What?"

"That's just a Bible story, Cary. Do you really believe it?"

He turned away again.

"The Bible is full of lessons that prove true in our own lives," he recited mechanically.

I tried to see through his rehearsed words to the

true heartfelt feelings that lay behind them. There was something more he wasn't telling me. I could feel it in the silence and see it in the tight way he held his jaw.

"Everyone seems to want to bury his head in the sand in this family, Cary. It seems to be in the blood," I said dryly.

"What do you mean?"

"What do I mean? Right from the start, Grandma Olivia and Grandpa Samuel created a lie about who my mother was. My mother continued the lies and so did my step-daddy Chester. They put Grandma Belinda away so no one would learn the truth, whatever that is, and everyone went along with it, including your parents. Your mother told me lies are like termites eating at the moral foundation. If that were true, you'd all be living in rubble," I said.

Cary didn't argue. He nodded, looked horribly sad and tired. He stared at the floor for a while and when he finally lifted his head, his eyes were glassy, tearful.

"I lied too," he said. "I didn't make that hole in the floor just to watch over Laura when she was seeing Robert Royce. I made it before. I didn't know many girls and Laura was the softest, prettiest person in my life. Until she started seeing Robert, we did everything together. We never hid anything from each other.

"One day," he continued, "she started to lock her door. Everything in her life became so private and secret. She grew up faster, I suppose, even though we were twins. I felt left out, alone. I never had many friends at school. Laura was starting to make more friends, be invited to things without me. We were drifting apart. I don't know why I did it," he said. "She locked me out and I wanted to spy on her, I suppose, and see what it was that she would do by herself, why she wanted to be alone."

He raised his eyes to me again, this time tears emerging and trickling down his cheeks.

"I never told anyone this before."

"And you think that was your sin?" I asked softly.

"It was," he said. He took a deep breath. "I watched her without her knowing and at her most private times," he confessed.

My heart was pounding. The silence between the words was loud and revealing, as was the look in his eyes. I thought about the times I would have hated anyone spying on me. He was right: it was a serious violation.

"I'm sorry for it," he concluded. "The morning she left with Robert to go sailing, I was angry at her and she was angry at me and we never had a chance to make up. She had found out I had been watching her with Robert," he said. The pain in his voice made my heart ache.

"How?"

"I said something that only someone who had been spying on her would know. Maybe I wanted her to know; maybe I couldn't keep it inside anymore, the guilt. She never came back, so I could never tell her how sorry I was.

"That's why I went looking for her as long as I did. There were times during that search I stood up in my boat and shouted over the water, 'Laura, I'm sorry,' shouted until my throat ached. But she was gone. It was too late. She died hating me."

"I'm sure she didn't really hate you for it, Cary. She was angry, but you two were too close for hate to have a chance to set in any roots," I said trying to soothe his fears.

He shrugged, a small smile of gratitude on his lips.

"I was telling you the truth about the hole upstairs. I put the sofa over it and wiped it from my memory."

"I believe you, Cary."

123

"I didn't want you to think I was invading your privacy, too."

I smiled at him and he wiped the tears from his cheek.

"I believe you, Cary. I really do."

"Well, you ate. I guess I can brag," he said. He stood up, his eyes fixed on me, strong, loving, and very caring. "Don't run away, Melody. Ma's angry at Dad for what he said to you and he's feeling low. If you just pretend he never said anything—"

"More burying of the truth?"

"Sometimes, that's easier, I suppose."

"Easier, Cary, but there's always a price to pay when we hold a funeral for honesty, isn't there?"

"Maybe. All I know is I don't want you to leave."

"I won't leave," I said finally. "I still have some unfinished business, like finding out who my real father is," I added dryly.

Cary took the tray.

"I'll take it down myself," I said. "I don't need your father complaining about me being waited on, too."

"I don't mind waiting on you," Cary said.

Our eyes met again and the memory of our kisses and caresses upstairs in his attic workshop rushed back over me. I felt a flush come into my face, a tingling up and down my body. It was almost an ache, a craving, and it was so strong, it actually frightened me. Yet for all the warmth that flooded through me, I still felt an eerie chill as I thought of Cary's odd behavior and feelings for his sister. Thoughts and feelings that were definitely wrong, even sinful, Uncle Jacob would call them. I couldn't help wondering if the feelings Cary claimed to have for me were really leftover desires he'd had for Laura. Would I ever be loved or wanted for who I really was? But even as these thoughts flew through my mind I felt my body respond to Cary, felt the undeniable pull in my most

124

secret places. What was wrong with me that I could feel both repulsed and attracted at the same time?

Perhaps Uncle Jacob was right, perhaps I was truly a sinful wanton. Maybe there was something flowing through our veins, something lustful, sinful, evil. After all, I thought, I am Haille Logan's daughter. Maybe I would hurt Cary just the way Mommy had hurt young men, men like Kenneth Childs. Cary took a step toward me and I moved quickly to seize the tray and step around him.

"I'll take it down now," I said, avoiding his eyes. I knew if I looked, I would find two dark pools of disappointment.

When I reached the bottom of the stairway and turned, I saw Uncle Jacob in his chair listening to the news on the radio. May was sprawled on the rug by his feet, reading. Of course, she didn't hear me. Uncle Jacob's eyes fixed on me a moment and then shifted away, guiltily, I thought. I continued to the kitchen.

Aunt Sara wasn't there and the dishes were still piled in the sink. I rinsed mine off and put them in, too. I was going to clean up for her, but I was curious where she was. I saw that the back door was slightly open, so I went to it and peered out. There she was, sitting alone on the small bench, her arms folded across her chest, gazing into the darkness.

"Aunt Sara?"

"Oh," she said as if she had been caught doing something illegal or immoral. I stepped out quickly.

"I'm sorry," I said. "I didn't mean to ruin your dinner tonight."

She shook her head.

"Jacob doesn't mean half of what he says," she insisted. I tried to keep a look of disbelief from my face. It was something she had to believe to live in peace, I thought. "He always regrets his blustering," she continued. "I told him. I explained it. I was just

125

taken by surprise. May is just curious. I know it's natural. You didn't do anything terrible. I should have been the one to start to explain. It's just that it's all so overwhelming, isn't it? You're going along, growing alongside boys, even playing the same games, and suddenly you find you're very different." Her laughter trickled off into the darkness.

I smiled at the simple but true statement. Then I sat beside her.

"Did you have a lot of boyfriends before Uncle Jacob, Aunt Sara?"

"Me? No. I never—no," she said. "Well, there was someone I had a crush on," she confessed, "but every girl had a crush on him."

"Who was that?"

"Teddy Jackson. He was always so handsome, even when he was only twelve."

"Oh," I said. It didn't surprise me that any woman would see Adam's father as a handsome dreamboat, it was just that my dislike of Adam was so strong, I wasn't happy to hear about it. Aunt Sara was into her own memories, however, and didn't notice my reaction.

"Of course, he never gave me a second look. He had all the prettiest girls. I was never much to look at."

"That's not true, Aunt Sara. You're a very pretty woman."

"Oh, I guess when I fix my hair and put on something nice, I don't embarrass Jacob, but I'm no movie star," she said, laughing. "Laura, Laura was the prettiest one."

"Yes."

"And so are you. Your mother was always pretty. She had the kind of beauty that caused everyone to stop and take notice."

"You better not mention her name anywhere near Uncle Jacob," I warned her bitterly.

She was silent as she looked into the darkness again.

"He didn't always feel that way about her," she said, but the way she said it sounded almost as if she were jealous. "He used to think the sun rose and fell on her smile. Just like all the young men, I guess."

"You'd never know it," I said. This revelation was making my head spin. It was the first time Aunt Sara had really talked about the past.

"Oh, I know it," she replied quickly. She shook her head. "I know it."

"What are you saying, Aunt Sara?" I asked, holding my breath.

"What? Oh." She laughed. "I'm not saying anything. Not anything important at least. Don't you think anything of anything Jacob bellows," she emphasized, patting me on the hand. "He's just uncomfortable around women and women talk, is all. He shouldn't have taken it out on you and I told him so." She looked away again.

"Someday, Aunt Sara," I said taking her hand and forcing her to turn back to me, "everyone in this family is going to have to start telling the truth."

"What do you mean, Melody?"

"I don't know what I mean yet, Aunt Sara, but I have a feeling you do, and so does Uncle Jacob, and especially Grandma Olivia."

She stared, fear in her eyes.

"Maybe you shouldn't have gone to see Belinda," she said, her voice in a whisper, "maybe she put bad thoughts in your head."

"Or maybe she pointed me toward the truth," I replied.

Aunt Sara shook her head sadly.

"Don't go out too far, Melody," she said in a voice suddenly full of wisdom and firmness, a voice unlike any other she had used before. "It's what happened to Laura."

She turned away to stare into the darkness as if she half expected her lost daughter to come walking up the beach, in from the sea and the storm.

I left her alone and cleaned up the dinner dishes before going up to bed to ponder her warning.

"I guess you didn't have such a great weekend," Kenneth said after glancing at me when I got into his jeep Monday morning. He put it in gear and drove away before I could respond. He glanced at me again as we turned down the street and headed out of town. I sat stroking Ulysses and gazing out at the ocean. A number of times during the night I had wakened from sleep, nudged by a troubling image or the memory of harsh words. I would lie there staring into the darkness, listening to the creaks in the old house as the wind blew in from the sea. Even on the brightest of days, there were too many shadows in this home, I thought, and the wind sounded more like whispers on the stairs or just outside my door.

I wasn't the only one struggling with the past. There was a silent war being conducted here, a war with no guns, but fierce battles nevertheless, with the casualties being truth, happiness, and contentment.

"Don't want to talk about it?" Kenneth finally asked.

"I visited Grandma Belinda," I said.

"How did it go?"

"She said many things, some silly, I suppose, but some that infuriated Grandma Olivia."

"I bet," he said with a smile.

"She said Grandpa Samuel liked her more and she said your father was one of her boyfriends and that made Grandma Olivia jealous," I blurted.

His smile froze first and then metamorphosed into a hard, deep expression of pain.

"That's why she's in a rest home," he mumbled.

"She looks healthy and she's sweet, gentle, child-like," I continued. He drove, his face sullen.

"I'm sorry about what she said about your father."

"It doesn't surprise me," he replied. He turned to me with a smirk on his face. "I've heard such talk about him before. Dad was always what is euphemistically referred to as a ladies' man," he said, sarcastically.

"He can be very charming," I admitted.

Kenneth looked at me askance.

"You too?" He shook his head. "As long as it's in a skirt, he can't resist, no matter what the age."

"Is that why you don't get along?" I asked quickly, trying not to be offended by his callous remark.

"How he conducts himself is his business, not mine," Kenneth replied. "Let's not talk about him. It puts me into a bad mood," he said and then turned to me. "Just as you've been told, digging up the past is only going to revive unhappiness and we have enough to contend with in the present.

"Besides," he added, "you're my special model now. I don't want you coming around with a long, sad look on your face. I want you fresh, lovely, and curious about yourself, not others. Concentrate on our concept when you're with me," he added as we drew closer to his house and studio.

"You're the one who asked me about the weekend," I shot back.

He thought on that and then nodded.

"You're right." He held up his hand. "I'm guilty, which shows you, even I can be tempted into the wrong frame of mind. I'll make a pact with you," he said as he pulled into the driveway. "I won't ask you any questions about your private life and you won't ask me any about mine. We'll just be in the world of art, okay?"

"Art isn't a world separate from the real world," I

129

said, my eyes narrow, my gaze fixed and determined. "Ideas, images, colors all come from your experiences, don't they?"

He stared silently at me, a friendly, almost loving glint coming into his eyes before he smiled.

"You're quite a kid," he said. He said it with such admiration and pride, I had to blush. "Okay, you're right. But we'll do our best. Deal?" He extended his hand. I stared at it a moment. He wanted me to swear to be silent, to lock up my thoughts and questions, to put aside my quest for truth. I shook my head.

"I can't promise something I'm not sure I have the strength or even the willingness to do," I said.

He sighed with frustration and then smiled again.

"All right, but at least promise you'll try. It's important to my work." He waited.

"I'll try," I offered, weakly.

It was enough for now. He hopped out of the jeep and I followed, Ulysses at our heels.

"I've been working all weekend," he said as we went around the house to the studio. "Even without my star," he added, throwing a smile back at me.

When he opened the studio door, I saw what he meant. Near the marble block, there was a large papier-mâché mass shaped like a wave about to crash on shore.

"It's not exactly right yet, but that's something like the wave I've envisioned," he said. "Do you see the opening in the center?"

"Yes."

"I want you to go behind the wave, crawl under, and come up through that hole."

"Really?"

"That's the idea. I can picture you emerging from a wave, as part of the wave, this way. Understand?"

"Yes," I said, thinking it was a very clever idea.

"Just crawl in first and then I'll tell you how I want you to stand and so on." He went to his drawing table.

Then he nodded at me and I walked around the papier-mâché wave. I found where he had left room for me to go under and come up through the opening. At first, I felt a bit silly, but I did it.

"Okay," he said and stepped away from his table. "Okay." He nodded, stared, thought, walked about and then nodded again. "Okay, this is going to be a bit tricky, but don't worry. We'll get it right. Go back down and come up very, very slowly. I just want to see the top of your head at first."

I did as he asked.

"Stop," he said when my head was visible. "Very slowly now, keep coming up, yes, slower, stop. Perfect. Is that very uncomfortable for you?"

"Yes," I admitted.

He thought a moment and then moved quickly to the settee. He gathered up the big cushions and brought them behind the paper wave.

"Hold that position until I stuff these pillows under you," he said. "Okay, you can sit there."

He ran around to the front again.

"That'll work for a while," he said. "Come on out and I'll explain it to you in more detail," he said.

I wriggled out of the wave and took my place beside him. He had already drawn a sketch of the wave, but had left the middle undone, waiting for me.

"It's hard to think of a picture, a painting, a sculpture as having movement, but this is what I have to capture here because the movement is your development, your emergence from the sea into this beautiful young woman. Your body will first appear liquid, flowing, but it will start to emerge separate from the wave."

I nodded, although I wasn't sure I really understood.

"Now," he said, pausing and turning to me, "you wouldn't emerge dressed in a sweatshirt and a pair of jeans. Do you understand what I'm trying to say?"

My pulse began to throb, my heart racing at the thought of what he was alluding to. The idea of standing naked before Kenneth, whether he was my father or not, made me queasy.

"Yes," I said almost too softly to be heard.

"I have to have you comfortable, at ease. You've got to get past yourself and me and become part of this work, the essence of this work. Think of yourself as the sculpture and not as Melody Logan undressed in some barn, okay?"

I nodded, weakly.

"My shoulders are too bony and my collarbone sticks out too far," I complained. "I also have a patch of freckles all over here," I said, pointing to my chest just below my collarbone.

Kenneth smiled.

"I don't think that's going to be a problem for us, Melody, and you're far from bony. Look," he said more patiently, "I know it's unfair to ask you to achieve a professional attitude the first time you model for someone, and I won't expect perfection right away, but in time, you'll see," he said with a warm smile. "As hard as it is to believe, it will become very ordinary after a while."

He paused and looked at the door.

"You didn't tell anyone about this, did you?" he asked quickly.

I shook my head.

"Good."

The realization of what he feared made me laugh, especially when I considered how Uncle Jacob had reacted to the little I had told May about a woman's body. Suddenly, all the fear and nervousness left me, as I realized that modeling for Kenneth was just the thing to get Uncle Jacob's goat.

"What's so funny?" he asked, smiling.

I told him about May's revelation of her first kiss

and then her questions, and how I had described the changes a girl experiences as she matures. I explained that I had even given her some information about making a baby. And then I told him what had happened between me and Uncle Jacob when May, brought up something I had said in front of him and Aunt Sara.

"I can't wait to see Uncle Jacob's face when he sees Neptune's Daughter," I said, still unable to keep the laughter from my voice.

"Jacob's a horse's ass," Kenneth said. "He always was. He never had many friends and he was always the object of jokes and ridicule because of this high-and-mighty moral attitude of his, as if he were some sort of Old Testament prophet. Haille teased him a lot, too," he added with a small laugh.

"She did? Will you tell me about it?"

He sighed.

"All right. Here's the deal. I'll tell you about the old days when we break for lunch or rests, if you promise not to ask any questions, not to talk while I work. Deal?" he offered.

This time I seized his hand so fast, it brought a real laugh to his lips. Then he grew serious.

"We'll do this slowly," he said, "as slowly as I envision it in the work itself. Just take off that sweatshirt for now. I want to see you up to here this morning," he said indicating just above my breasts. "Your face, neck, and shoulders. Model, take your position," he ordered with a smile and wave of his hand.

I went behind the papier-mâché wave and pulled off my sweatshirt. Then I crawled through the opening and sat on the pillows, just my head emerging. He began to work, and as he did, I saw his face become so intense, his eyes so riveting, I couldn't keep mine off him.

After a while he said, "Another pillow."

I understood he meant for me to put another sofa pillow under myself so I would come up a bit more. When my head was as high as he had indicated he wanted he continued to work on and on.

"This is just the shape, the outline," he explained. "We're going to spend a lot of time discussing the expression on your face, how I want you to look, your eyes, your mouth. The best way to do that is to get you to think of something in your own past that will fit this, some event, some moment, some thoughts and experiences."

"Just as I told you: art isn't in a world by itself," I quipped smugly. He paused and smiled.

"All right. Don't be a smartass," he said and we both laughed.

Maybe I would be able to do this. Maybe I would be able to relax and help him create his greatest work, I thought.

"Break," he called after nearly another hour. He brought me a large bath towel to drape over my shoulders, and put on some water for tea. The towel covered my shoulders and bra. I used it to wipe the perspiration from my face and neck.

"It really is work just standing still," I said. He nodded.

"I'd rather be on this side of the brush," he admitted. "You take sugar, right?"

"Just one teaspoon, thank you."

"You know, what you were telling me about May and her questions is exactly the sort of thing I'm after here," he said. He sat at the small table and I sat on a stool beside him. "She's emerging out of childhood into the first stages of womanhood. Can you recall when this first happened to you?"

"Yes, I guess so."

"What was it like?"

134

"Scary and wonderful," I said. He nodded, obviously encouraging me to continue. I thought about it. "There were new feelings in old places." He smiled.

"Yes," he said. "Exactly."

"When May told me about her first kiss, I thought about mine and how I had run all the way home and gone into my room to be alone with my excitement. I wrote the boy's name about two million times and dreamed about more kisses, longer kisses."

"Did you tell your mother about it?"

"After a while."

"And?" he asked, very interested in what she had said.

"She laughed and told me not to believe in kisses or any promises made while kissing. She said to make them pay, that they're never too young to pay. I didn't understand at the time," I said, waiting to see what he would offer as an explanation for Mommy's bitter attitude about men.

"She ruined the moment with that kind of talk. You have to believe in the magic first. Haille didn't stop for magic. That was her problem," he said. "I don't think she enjoyed growing up, or gave herself enough time for innocence, understand?"

"Sort of. You mean she grew up too fast?"

"Worse. She gave herself away too young," he said. My breath caught.

"How do you know that?"

"She told me," he said, and I understood it hadn't been with him. "But let's get back to you. When you're coming up out of the wave, you're just feeling these new sensations and you're full of the same sort of questions May had about herself, questions you had, too. Understand? Think of that, concentrate on it." He paused and glanced at me. "Your body is developing. There are tingles, feelings, sensations in places there never were before. You're standing in

135

front of the mirror, naked, and you're seeing things that, as you said, surprise, frighten, and thrill you at the same time. Okay?"

I nodded. The air was so warm around me. I did feel as if I had slipped back in time. His words worked magic. My body remembered itself, the first tingles returned, the images—

The teakettle whistled, breaking my reverie. He poured us each a cup and offered me a cracker.

"How do you know so much about women?" I asked, and he laughed.

"Me? I'm far from the expert on women. You're confusing me with dear old Dad."

"Is that réally why you and he don't get along so well?"

"That's part of it," he said, taking a sip of tea. "Parents shouldn't try to force their children to follow in their footsteps, especially if their feet are made of clay," he said.

He talked a little about how his father had pressured him to go to law school and then how he had rebelled. I told him about Cary and his dream to leave fishing and become a ship builder of custom boats.

"I told him to tell his father."

"Did he do it?" he asked, his eyebrows raised in anticipation.

"Yes."

"And?"

"His father threw a fit, telling him it was family tradition to be a fisherman and a cranberry farmer and he had to continue."

"Horse's ass," Kenneth said.

"Cary will do it. Some day," I said firmly. Kenneth stared at me, a softness in his eyes.

"You like him a lot, don't you?"

"Yes," I admitted.

"Romantically?"

136

I nodded, sensing Kenneth wouldn't judge me for my relationship with Cary.

"Not your first boyfriend, is he?" he asked. He was sounding more like my father now, a father who hadn't seen his daughter growing up.

"No, but he's the most . . ."

"Serious?"

I nodded again and sipped my tea.

"Don't give your heart away too quickly, Melody. It's the most precious gift you can give any man," he advised.

"I won't be like my mother, if that's what you mean," I said sharply.

He smiled.

"Good," he said. "That's good."

We returned to work. Kenneth put more detail into his drawing. He explained that he intended to do at least a half dozen of these pictures, each taking the metamorphosis to another stage so that it would be like doing an animation. When he flipped the pictures quickly, he would get the illusion of movement and that illusion would be embedded in his mind as he hoped it would be in the marble block.

After lunch he showed me how to use some of the carving tools to do the preliminary work on the block. Even though it was hard work, I enjoyed it, enjoyed knowing I really was contributing to this artistic masterpiece. The day flew by and I didn't have much time to tend to my usual chores, but when Kenneth announced it was time to stop, I was actually disappointed.

"It's all right," he told me when I complained about not being able to clean and organize his house, especially after a weekend. Mondays were always the hardest because he seemed to get even sloppier on Saturdays and Sundays. "This is what an artist's life is like. Now you can understand and appreciate why I'm

137

not the neatest, most organized individual you've met.

"Anyway," he added, "you can do what you can here for twenty minutes or so. We're finished for the day. I'm just going down to the beach for a while to think. Then I'll come back and take you home," he said.

He left with Ulysses at his heels and I went to work cleaning and organizing the studio. I swept up the dust and chips from the marble block, cleaned and arranged the tools, and fixed the sofa again. As I was moving about, I paused at the drawing desk. I hadn't looked at the pictures yet. Kenneth hadn't offered and I was afraid to ask. Now, they were covered with a white sheet, and I wondered if Kenneth was the type who hated anyone looking at a work in progress. I hesitated.

I couldn't help feeling we had grown closer because of this project and I hated to do anything that might threaten our relationship. Little betrayals, indiscretions, and lies eventually tore down a foundation of love and friendship, I thought. I had enough evidence of that, and now, because of how things were going between us, I regretted permitting Cary to take off the lock on Kenneth's storage room so that we could invade his private and secret cache of paintings, even if they were paintings of my mother and stirred more mystery.

I continued to clean and organize the studio, but my attention kept returning to the drawing table. What harm would one peek do? I thought. Surely, if Kenneth really wanted me not to look, he would have said something. I listened for him, heard nothing, and returned to the drawing table. Slowly, I lifted the sheet and gazed at the first drawing.

There was far more detail in my face than I had anticipated. This was more than a sketch, but the face I saw on the paper looked more like my mother's face than it did mine. At least, I thought it did, and that caused me to drop the sheet quickly when I heard Kenneth's footsteps. He entered just as I moved away. His eyes shifted from the table to me and then back to the table.

"Well," he said, crossing the studio, "you've got this place looking proper again. Makes me feel guilty every time I mess it up," he said with a smile. He paused at the table and lifted the sheet. "What do you think?" he asked gazing at the picture.

"What?"

"I'm sure you snuck a peek, Melody. I would have."

"Oh. I . . . yes. I did. I was surprised at how much detail you got into it already," I said, trying to keep the disappointment out of my voice.

"Uh-huh. That sounds diplomatic."

"I'm not an art critic. Not yet, at least," I said. "But it looks like the beginning of something special." If only it was my face that would grace his masterpiece, I thought.

"Yes. It's only a figment of my imagination right now, but soon, it will grow. You know, this is going to take us all summer," he said.

"I'm not going anywhere," I replied. "I was going to run away yesterday, but then I thought, where would I run to?"

He stared at me and I held my breath, hoping he would offer his home as a sanctuary should I need it. But he remained silent. If the words were on his tongue, he swallowed them.

"I guess the bottom line is none of us can really run away. We can escape but we can't run away," he said.

"How can we escape if we don't run away?" I asked.

"You find another place to go inside yourself," he said, staring at the block of marble.

"As you found with your art?"

He nodded.

"What were you escaping from?" I asked and

waited as he hesitated, his eyes still on the block of marble.

"Myself," he said.

"Yourself?"

"Who I found out I was," he said. He shook his head. "Give me time, Melody. Give me time to find a way to tell you what you want to know."

My heart skipped a beat.

The rebirth Kenneth was creating out of this block of marble might truly be my own.

7

Sing for Your Supper

Cary was in the driveway washing Uncle Jacob's truck when Kenneth brought me home. He was in cut-off shorts, shirtless and barefoot. May was helping, soaping up the fenders, getting almost as much suds dripping down her arms and legs as she was putting on the truck. Unhindered by clouds, the late afternoon sun was still strong enough to make things gleam, especially Cary's bare shoulders and back, emphasizing his muscularity. He turned toward us as we slowed to a stop.

"Good-looking boy," Kenneth muttered. "He has the best of the Logan features, softened by his mother's side fortunately. I see why you're drawing hearts in the sand," he added with a wink. I blushed so crimson, I was sure I looked sunburnt.

Cary's face lit up with a smile as soon as he saw us, and May came rushing over to play with Ulysses.

"Hi, Mr. Childs," Cary said, approaching. "I'd shake your hand, but . . ." He held up his soapy fingers.

"It's all right. I'm not allergic to soap and water,

141

even though Melody might have told you otherwise," he said.

My jaw dropped.

"I wouldn't—"

"How's the catch these days?" Kenneth asked Cary after laughing at me.

"We had a very good day. Dad's quite pleased," he said, glancing at me. "It's put him in a good mood. For once."

"That's good. And the cranberries?"

"Looks as if it's going to be a heavy harvest," Cary replied. "Heavier than last year."

"Melody tells me you're into boat building."

Cary shot me a look of surprise.

"Well, yes, I am but—"

"I have a boat plan I'd like to show you one day. Maybe I'll have Melody bring it home and you can take a quick look at it and make some suggestions," Kenneth said. Cary's face changed from surprise to genuine awe.

"Really?"

"I've always had it on the back burner, but perhaps it's time to get the construction under way," Kenneth said. "See you bright and early, Melody."

"I'll be early, but I don't know how bright I'll be," I said.

He laughed, checked to be sure May was not standing too close to the jeep, then shifted the gears and pulled away. Cary, May, and I watched him and Ulysses disappear around the turn, Ulysses facing us all the way, looking like a small child who wished he could stay with his friends.

"Was he kidding about the boat?" Cary asked.

"It's the first time I've heard him mention it, Cary. But he's full of surprises and secrets, no different from anyone else around here."

Cary nodded, the soap suds dripping off his forearm.

142

"Need some help?" I asked.

"No, we're just about finished. May and I will just dry her off." He signed instructions and May returned to the pail and sponge.

"I have to shower," I said. "I'm full of marble dust." I started toward the house.

"How about a quick dip instead?" Cary suggested. "Just throw on your suit and we'll go down to the beach."

"Then I'll have to wash the salt out of my hair before I sit down at the dinner table," I complained.

"Women," he said, groaning.

"Why don't we go after dinner—a night swim," I suggested. His eyes brightened.

"Really? Great." He looked at May. "Ma doesn't like her swimming at night so—"

"We'll bring her tomorrow." I said, hoping that May wouldn't mind.

"Okay. I'll find something for her to do while we're gone, so she won't feel left out," he said and returned to the truck.

Cary was right about Uncle Jacob. He was in a rare happy mood, actually buoyant. He didn't apologize for the way he had yelled at me the night before, but his tone of voice was softer when he asked me to pass him things at the dinner table and when he thanked me. Also, whenever he spoke, he actually spoke to me, rather than around me. Apparently, today's catch was as good as they used to be. It was like striking gold.

The happiness in Aunt Sara's face made her eyes younger as well as brighter. It was nice to hear her laugh, and even to hear Uncle Jacob laugh. As I gazed at them, all full of smiles, everyone treating everyone politely, considerately, the food as wonderful as ever, the cranberry wine sparkling in the glasses, I was able to envision this family before Laura's tragedy and I was able to see what Cary had described. Even if it were destined to be short lived, the joviality warmed my heart and made me feel I was part of a real family again. There was no better music to drive away the shadows than the sound of laughter.

Suddenly, as the meal was coming to an end, Uncle Jacob leaned on his elbows toward me, his eyes dark and fixed, his smile gone.

"What say you earn your supper tonight, Missy?" he said. I glanced at Cary, who shrugged, and then at Aunt Sara, whose mouth hung open.

"How?" I asked.

"You know, like people did in olden times. Found a way to pay for their dinner."

"What do you want me to do?" I asked, my throat tightening, my voice hardening.

He slapped his hands together.

"We'll all adjourn to the living room and have a private concert. What do you say, Sara? Can you let these dishes wait?"

"You mean, you want me to play my fiddle?" I asked, astounded.

"It's somethin' you do real good," he replied. Cary was beaming like the cat that had gotten to the fish on the counter in the kitchen.

"I—" I gazed at Aunt Sara. She'd never looked happier. For a moment I felt as if I had sat at the dinner table in the wrong house.

"Well?" Uncle Jacob pursued.

"Okay," I said, still amazed at his request.

"Then it's settled," he said slapping his hands together and standing. "Mrs. Logan?" He held out his arm and Aunt Sara giggled and joined him. "We'll adjourn to the sitting room for a private concert," he said and held his other arm out for May. Cary had signed a quick summary of what was happening. She leaped to her feet and took her father's arm.

144

"What's going on?" I asked Cary as we watched them leave the room.

"I don't know. But as Dad often says, don't look a gift horse in the mouth. Shall we?" Cary held out his arm and I took it, still quite shocked and confused. When we got to the stairway, I went upstairs to get my fiddle.

They were all sitting in the living room waiting for me with great expectation on their faces when I appeared in the doorway. Uncle Jacob was settling back in his chair, puffing his pipe. Aunt Sara sat on the couch with Cary on one side and May on the other.

"May has a way of hearing this," I explained and gestured for her to come to me. She understood. When I put the fiddle up, she placed her hand on the case so she could feel the vibrations while I played. I did seven tunes, singing along with three of them. Aunt Sara looked very pleased and Uncle Jacob nodded and tapped his fingers along with the rhythms. Cary never took his eyes from me.

"Well, that's real nice," Uncle Jacob said. "You earned yourself a few dinners."

"I'll see to the dishes," Aunt Sara said, rising. "That was wonderful, Melody. Thank you."

"I'll put away my fiddle and come help you clean up, Aunt Sara."

"Oh no, you don't," she said. "You heard Jacob. You earned your keep. Just go enjoy yourself," she insisted.

I went back upstairs to put away my fiddle. While I was busy returning it to its case, Cary poked his head in the door.

"How about that dip in the ocean?" he asked.

"What about May?"

"I gave her something to do on one of my models. She's painting."

"You mean you bribed her?" I said, laughing.

"Whatever works," he said.

"Okay. I'll put on my bathing suit."

"Put it under your clothes," he said. "I'd rather it be our secret."

I nodded and did as he said. We met down by the front door and left quickly, letting Uncle Jacob and Aunt Sara think we were just taking a walk.

"I don't like doing things behind their backs like this, Cary," I complained.

"Why make Ma nervous, which is what would happen," he said. "It's not really a lie when you're doing it to help someone else, Melody. It's only a lie when you hurt someone or you can't live with it," he added.

Maybe he was right, I thought. Maybe I was holding up too high a standard because I had been lied to so much and for so long. He took my hand and we first went to the lobster boat where he said there were towels. After we got them, we crossed the sand toward one of his favorite places on the beach. It was a small cove, hidden by two small dunes.

I didn't really notice the stars until Cary spread out the biggest towel and we sat for a few moments, gazing out at the ocean and then up at the sky. Cary pointed out the Big Dipper, the North Star, and what he said was Venus.

"A sailor has to be able to read the stars," he explained. "They're his map."

"I've never been on a boat at night, but I can imagine how lost and alone you could feel if you didn't know how to steer your boat," I said.

"Without the stars, the darkness is so thick, you feel as if the ocean has risen all around you and you're sailing into it," Cary said. "Of course, we have our compasses. I think I was on the water before I could walk on land. Dad wanted me to have my sea legs first."

I laughed and he pulled off his shirt and stood up.

"It will be cold at first," he warned, "but after you're in it a few seconds, it will feel great."

It was a warm night, wonderful for a dip in the ocean. I stood up and unbuttoned my blouse. He stepped out of his pants and then kicked off his shoes. I took off my dungarees, placed my shoes and socks on the towel and then reached out to take his hand when he offered it. We walked down to the water slowly. When the white foam ran over my toes, I jumped.

"Easy," Cary said putting his arm around my waist.

"It's colder than I thought," I said and tried to retreat, but he tightened his grip on my waist.

"You'll love it."

"Cary, I don't think so," I said shaking my head. He laughed and tugged until I stepped farther down the beach. The water reached my ankles.

"You've just got to go for it," he advised. He let go of me and turned to dive right into the waves. When he popped up, he was laughing. "It's great," he claimed. "Makes you feel alive all over."

"Sure," I said, hesitating.

"Come on. Be brave."

My heart was pounding. Suddenly, the stars looked more like drops of ice above me. Cary splashed about to demonstrate how comfortable he was. He called again, urged and pleaded. I took a deep breath and ran forward, falling into the water. The shock made me scream. Cary was at my side, laughing. He embraced me and we stood with the sand washing out from under our feet as the tide rushed in around us. I grew a little afraid, even with his arms around me, and started for shore.

"I'm freezing!" I screamed, "and I'm going to be washed out to sea."

He laughed but followed. We splashed through the

water, and ran up the sand to the beach towel. Cary unfolded another towel quickly and put it around my shoulders, hugging me and rubbing me at the same time.

"Aren't you cold?" I asked, my teeth chattering.

"Not when I'm with you," he said and kept rubbing me dry. "How's that?"

"A little better," I said, still shivering. The chill on my skin tingled. I sat on the beach towel and Cary wrapped a towel around his own shoulders and then began to massage my feet, my ankles, and my calves.

"Weren't you really cold in the water, Cary Logan?"

"I guess I'm just used to it," he said.

"It looked so warm all day, I thought it would still be." My body shook with a spasm and he laughed.

"Nature can be deceiving," he warned and sprawled beside me.

"I don't know if I can stay out here much longer, Cary," I said. It was as if the chill had gone deep into me and turned my stomach to ice. "It's the wet bathing suit."

"Why don't you take it off then?" he said.

"What?"

"Slip out of it, dry yourself, and put on your pants and shirt," he suggested. "There's no one around," he added. I gazed back. The dunes were empty, not a soul in sight. All we heard was the sound of the surf. He moved closer to me and then he kissed me.

"Your lips are warm," I said, "even though your face feels cold."

He laughed, rubbed my shoulders, and then kissed my neck. The mixture of the chill and the warm tingle that shot down my spine made me shudder and then moan. Cary's fingers slid beneath the straps of my suit, lifting them off my shoulders. As he shifted me into a sitting position, holding me closer to him, the straps slid further down my arms. Then he ran my

148

towel under the suit, drying me as the suit fell away. He reached around the side of my breasts.

"Cary," I whispered, "don't."

"Shh. I'll warm you up again," he promised. My heart was pounding, the blood rushing through my body, making me feel lightheaded and dizzy. I felt as if I would spin into unconsciousness if I lifted my eyes toward the sky of blazing stars. Cary gently lifted my arms, one by one, until they were both free from the straps. Then he peeled the front of the suit away and my breasts were uncovered, my nipples tingling in the cool night air. They were so erect, they arched. Cary lowered me slowly to the blanket and continued to peel away my suit. I started to resist until he lowered his head and kissed my breasts, moving his tongue quickly over one nipple and then the other. I closed my eyes and lay back, lifting myself gently to help him take the wet suit from my body. When it fell beneath my hips and I realized I would soon be totally naked, I gasped.

"Cary."

"It's all right," he said. "It's only me. We're alone." I lifted my hand to touch his face and then he pulled the bathing suit down and over my knees. Immediately, he wrapped me in my towel and held me close, so close I could feel his heart thumping. Then he rubbed the towel all over me, wiping me dry, warming my body until I felt absolutely comfortable and content.

Cary then lay down beside me, kissing my cheeks, my nose, my eyes, nibbling softly on my chin and then kissing my neck and shoulders as his hands continued to rub my body in circles, finding my breasts, moving his palms in circles over them and then coming down the sides of my body until he held my hips. He leaned over me, gazing down at me. His face was in darkness, but just enough light came from the stars to allow me to see his gentle lips in a small smile.

"Melody, you were meant to be here. Ma's right. You were brought here to make us all well again, especially me," he said.

He kissed me long and hard on the lips and then he slipped beside me, moving about until I realized he was taking off his own bathing suit.

"Cary, wait—"

"Just touch," he said. "We'll just touch."

Then he was naked too, and I felt him throbbing, moving in between my legs as he threw his towel over us like a blanket.

"Cary, don't," I said. "We could make a baby like this."

"I know. I'll be careful," he said, but he didn't stop. The sensation that flew through my body when he touched me where no boy had ever touched me before made me tremble so, I thought I would be unable to stop him if things started to go too far. He nudged me again and again. I began to cry softly, but his lips drank my tears before they could go far down my cheeks. He kept reciting my name, chanting it like a prayer.

"I love you, Melody," he said. "I couldn't love anyone as much as I love you."

I didn't know if I could speak. My heart was racing. Cary was out of control. In a few more moments, I was sure I would be too.

This is what happened to your mother, I heard a voice inside me say. Remember what Kenneth said? Remember him telling you how she would jump on the back of a motorcycle and end up on a beach blanket? Well you're on a beach blanket now, Melody Logan, and you're naked and about to do what she did.

I shook my head at the words resounding inside me.

"No," I cried and pushed at Cary's chest.

"Melody, I love you."

"Please, stop Cary," I said.

150

"I can't," he said. "I can't."

But he pulled back, his sex exploding on the blanket, his head against my chest, his whole body shuddering and then coming to rest.

Neither of us moved. It was as though the world revolved around us as we stayed perfectly still. Caught in a moment of time. My heartbeat started to slow and my breathing came easier. Still, neither of us moved, neither said anything. We lay there, holding each other, both equally amazed at our discoveries about ourselves and each other.

"I'm sorry," he finally said. "I'm so clumsy and inexperienced. You were right. I shouldn't have started to do this without the proper protection. You probably think I'm an idiot." He sat up quickly.

"No, I don't, Cary. I'm not very experienced at this either, no matter what you might think." I sat up, too, holding the towel around me.

"You're not?" he said skeptically.

"No, I'm not. Why?" I asked, turning on him. "Do you think I'm like my mother when she was my age? Is that it?" I asked hotly.

"No," he said.

"Maybe I am. Maybe it is in my blood," I said bitterly. "I shouldn't have let you go as far as you did, but . . ."

"But what? It's not a sin if you love me as much as I love you," he said. "You wouldn't do this with any other boy, would you?"

I shook my head.

"So? Don't you see? That means we love each other." He leaned toward me again to kiss me, but I pulled back.

"No more, Cary. I just want to get dressed and go back to the house."

"You're not mad at me, are you?"

"No. I'm just a little confused about everything. Please try to be understanding," I insisted.

"Okay," he said. He stood up and we both dressed silently in the darkness.

"I probably look as if I've been rolling around on the beach," I moaned.

"We'll stop at the boat and you can straighten up," he said, but his voice was different, strained. I knew he was displeased with my reaction, but I really was confused. I had wanted this and yet, when it started to happen, I was too afraid to continue. Was I just like my mother or was I really as in love with Cary as I imagined? Was it the fact that so many people would frown on our relationship that worried me?

He gathered the towels and we started away, carrying our wet suits. Cary walked a little faster, remaining a foot or so in front of me.

"Don't be angry at me, Cary," I said. "I have too many confusing things going on inside me right now to think clearly about anything. Do you really, truly believe that it is right for there to be love between us, when there is also blood? I want to believe that it is right Cary, but aren't you afraid of what everyone will think?"

He plodded along, not answering me.

"Cary?"

"It will be all right," he said. "I'm not angry at you. The truth is I'm just as confused. Nothing is as simple as we think, I suppose, even love."

I went into the bathroom on the boat, where there was a small wall mirror, and repaired myself the best I could. When I came out, Cary was sitting and gazing out at the ocean. I came up beside him and put my hand gently on his shoulder. He put his hand over mine and continued to look out at the water.

"The water keeps moving," he said. "It looks the same, but it never is. Everything's in a constant state of change. Trees grow new leaves. They look the same as last year's leaves, but they're different. Even the sand on the beach moves. The wind shifts it. Maybe we're changing all the time, too," he said. "Maybe I was different yesterday, even though I look the same today."

"That's what they say in science class. We're always breaking down and rebuilding cells."

"So," he said, turning quickly, "what about our feelings? Do they break down and change, too? If I love you today, will that love be different tomorrow?"

"I don't know."

"I don't think love changes. I think that it stays the same even though everything around it becomes different. I'll love you the same way when you're old and gray and I'm old and gray. No matter what anyone thinks Melody, I know it is right between us. Our love is special."

I smiled.

"You believe me, don't you?" he asked with worried eyes.

"Yes, Cary."

"Then, don't be afraid to love me too," he said. "No matter what your mother was or did. You're not your mother."

"I know," I said. "I just need a little more time to figure everything out. I want to be ready, Cary. I need to be sure."

He nodded and then turned back to the ocean. I stood by him and we both watched the waves dance with the stars until we grew tired and walked home, holding hands, silent, full of wonder.

I noticed something different about Kenneth immediately the next morning. Even Ulysses appeared changed, more subdued, as if he had been chastised just before they arrived to pick me up. Kenneth mumbled a quick good morning and pulled away with an awkward jerk that sent me back against the seat. He drove fast, the wheels squealing as he made the turn and accelerated, pulling around a slower car and going even faster. He never took his eyes off the road. I was afraid to say anything. Artists were so moody. One minute they were ecstatic, the next, they were melancholy. We bounced hard on the dune road because he took that faster than usual also. I was relieved when we finally came to a stop in his driveway.

He got out, slammed the door behind him, and then, to my surprise, instead of heading for the studio, turned and walked toward the beach. Even Ulysses looked confused, turning from Kenneth to me and then back to Kenneth.

"Aren't we going right to the studio?" I asked, running to catch up with him.

"No. I have to calm down first," he said over his shoulder, not even bothering to turn around.

"Calm down? Why? What happened?"

Instead of replying, he sped up and walked on. I followed, slowly this time, until we reached the top of the rise on the beach and he stood there gazing out at the ocean, his hands on his hips.

"What's this all about, Kenneth?" I asked, my heart thumping now. "Did I do something wrong?"

"Did you?" he snapped, spinning on me. His eyes were just as full of pain as they were of anger.

"No," I said softly, feeling shame flush my cheeks. He smiled with disdain.

"Lying is just in the blood, is that it? It comes so quickly, so naturally to you people." He turned away again.

I couldn't keep the tears from climbing over my eyelids and sizzling down my cheeks.

"I'm not lying," I said.

"Really?" He reached down to take a handful of sand and watched it fall through his fingers. "Then you didn't go into my private storage room?" he said without looking at me.

I stopped breathing, the breath that was already

caught in my throat choking me. After a moment, I found the strength to reply.

"Yes, I did," I admitted. The shame that had made me hot with embarrassment turning to cold fear.

He turned slowly, nodding.

"I noticed the hasp had been removed. Whoever broke in did a fine job, but in haste one bottom screw was left a little too far out. I wouldn't have thought anything of it, however, if, when I opened the door myself last night and entered the room, I didn't notice that the cobwebs were all broken and the canvases had been moved and not put back as neatly as they were. Got a good look at everything, did you?"

"No," I said.

"Did you take the hasp off yourself?" When I didn't answer immediately, Kenneth made the right conclusion. "No, you didn't. Who went in there with you, Cary?"

I nodded and looked down.

"I took you into my home, trusted you with my privacy, my possessions, my work. Now you can understand why I don't have many people out here," he said. "People." He spit the word as if it burned his tongue to utter it. "They always let you down."

"I'm sorry, Kenneth," I said. "I—"

"Yes? Tell me. How do you justify breaking and entering my private place? Go on," he taunted and challenged. "Let me hear your excuse."

"I was looking for the truth," I cried through my tears.

"The truth?"

"About you and me and my mother," I said. "Everyone thinks you're my father, and you told me that you couldn't tell me what you knew, so I thought . . . I thought you were ashamed of it or just didn't want to have a daughter," I wailed back at him.

He shook his head, speechless for a moment. I couldn't stop my crying. My shoulders heaved and fell and my stomach felt so weak and twisted, I had to wrap my arms around myself.

"Everyone thinks I'm your father? Who's everyone?"

"Uncle Jacob, for one. He says that's why you offered me the job. It was your way of trying to amend for your sin of never acknowledging me."

"Jacob would say something like that." He laughed. "It's nice to know how his parents treat him," he said.

"I don't understand," I said, shaking my head in confusion.

"Never mind. Look, Melody, if you were my daughter, I would tell you immediately. I thought by now you would have realized that I admire you and certainly wouldn't be ashamed to acknowledge you were mine, but it's not true. I wish it were true. You have no idea how much I wish it or how long I've wished it.

"That," he continued, "is the real reason why your mother sent me the picture of you and her and wrote 'I'm sorry' on the back of it." He took a deep breath and sat on the sand. "She wasn't just apologizing for not living up to my hopes for her; she was apologizing for not being able to be the woman I loved. It wasn't all her fault either," he added, sighing as he closed his eyes and leaned forward, his knees up, his arms around them.

I stopped crying, sucked in my breath, and sat beside him.

"Then you loved my mother?" I asked softly.

"Yes, very much."

"And those pictures of her in the room?"

"She enjoyed posing for me. She was so beautiful I wanted to capture her forever and art was a way to do it. Eventually, it became the only way to do it, and that made it both wonderful and painful for me. I got so I couldn't look at those pictures and had to keep them under lock and key, almost as if I were locking them away from myself as much as anyone else.

"As you and your boyfriend saw when you went in there," he continued, bitterly, "there were cobwebs over the door. That's how infrequently I enter to gaze upon those pictures. After you arrived, I thought about Haille constantly and I couldn't resist going in there again. That's when I made the discovery."

"I'm sorry, Kenneth," I said. He was silent, so I reached out and touched his hand. He nodded.

"Well, I can understand what you're going through, I guess. Living with Jacob, hearing his moralistic trash. He never really knew or understood your mother. He was always jealous of her affection for me, too. And when Chester came to her defense—" He shook his head. "Did anyone tell you they actually had a fist fight on the beach?"

"Yes, Grandma Olivia mentioned it."

"Chester whipped him, of course, which helped widen the chasm between them and the whole family. Haille enjoyed having men fight over her. All that I told you about her was true," he said. "She was bedazzling, tormenting, a tease with a capital T, but all of us let her get away with it."

He smiled, remembering. Then he looked at me.

"I should have made it perfectly clear to you that I wasn't your father, that Haille and I never . . . that I never had the opportunity to be your father."

This revelation came as a shock to me, but I knew now was the time to press on for more information. "Then who is my father? Is he someone here in Provincetown?"

"I really can't say, not because I don't want to, but because I don't know." He shook his head. "It all happened so fast. She and I weren't seeing each other much at the time."

"Why not?"

"That's something very personal to me, Melody. All of us have to hold on to something. It doesn't have anything to do with what you want to know. Just like everyone else close to your family at the time, I heard that Haille was pregnant, and the next thing I heard was she had accused Samuel. I knew that was untrue. I had been at their house often enough to see that Samuel treated her the way he would treat a daughter and not a lover. He was always charming and kind and probably spoiled her. It's sort of an example of biting the hand that feeds you. When it came time to blame someone, for some reason, a reason she wouldn't reveal to me, she turned on him. He seemed the most logical, I guess."

"Why?"

"Olivia was harder on her. Anything she got, she got because of Samuel. He bought her the clothes, the jewelry. He doted on her. Olivia was the ice queen who treated her the way the evil step-mother treated Cinderella. If Olivia demanded she do a chore, Samuel would find a way to get her out of it or pay someone else to do it. If Olivia punished her for misbehavior, Samuel got her a reprieve. I suppose she played him the way she played all the men around her at the time, even me," he said.

"She wasn't very nice then, was she?"

"Well, she was like a beautiful but dangerous creature," he replied with a smile. "I think some men like being manipulated. Samuel certainly had to know she was beguiling him, using him, but he enjoyed it. He had no daughters and one of his two sons took after his wife and treated him as poorly as she did. His other son . . . his other son became jealous of him, I think."

"Jealous? My step-father? Why would he be jealous of his own father?"

"He was jealous of how Haille treated him and how

158

he lavished gifts on her. Chester was always in love with Haille. So was Jacob, but Jacob thinks his own feelings were sinful. In his case it might be true. Jacob hated her because he loved her, if you can understand that. Chester, as I told you before, worshiped her and eventually paid a dear price for that worship: his family.

"That's really all I know about it, Melody. She named Samuel as the father of her baby. Chester either believed her or wanted to believe her and they ran off. So as I've told you, your father could be someone here or could have been someone just passing through. I'm afraid the truth died with her."

He turned to me again.

"This is why I advised you to stop the search. Stop trying to look back on the painful past and look to the future now. Take advantage of the situation, take anything you are given from that mad family, and go on to be your own person. You're bright, talented, and beautiful. You have far more than most girls your age, even the ones with parents."

I turned away. The ache around my heart felt like a hand closing on it, squeezing the very life from me.

"It's not easy to do that," I said.

"Yes, I know, but essentially, it's what I've done, Melody."

I turned back to him.

"Because of how you think of and treat your father?" He didn't reply. "That's the one private thing you want to keep to yourself, isn't it?"

"Yes," he admitted.

We were both quiet. The surf roared and the terns cried to each other above the water. In the distance we could see an oil barge creeping along, looking as if it slid against the sky. The breeze made strands of my hair dance about my forehead and cheeks. The lines in Kenneth's face deepened with his grimace. Ulysses, lying quietly at our feet, lifted his head with curiosity at the sudden silence. Kenneth reached out to pat him. I wiped away my lingering tears.

"Well," I said. "I guess we have to get back to work. That is, if you still want me to be the model."

"What do you say, Ulysses? Should we keep her?" Kenneth asked. As if he understood the question, Ulysses wagged his tail vigorously and we both laughed. "That's it," Kenneth said standing. "The boss has spoken."

I stood alongside him and then we started back to the house. He wasn't my father, I thought, but there was still something strong binding us. Perhaps it was the fact that we had both loved my mother.

"Kenneth," I said as we turned toward the studio, "please don't be mad at Cary. He only did it because of me."

"I bet," he said. "He won't be the last young man who does something to please you."

"I won't be like my mother was," I insisted, my eyes narrow but firm. He gazed at me.

"No, I don't think you will. The fact is, I think you're twice the woman she was," he said. "Now let's get all that into the sculpture."

I followed, buoyed by his words and yet saddened by them as well.

Cary was right, I thought. We're in a constant state of change. Nothing was permanent except real love, deep love, love that transcended time and place. It was the rope we cast to each other to keep each other from drowning in the sea of turmoil otherwise known as life.

I wondered if I should take hold or swim on, searching until I discovered there were no more answers waiting for me, at least in this world.

8

Daydreams

In the days that followed, Kenneth and I did grow closer. I felt something magical being born between us because of the artistic work he was creating, with me as his muse. The way he included me in his creative thinking made me feel I was so important to the vision that I gradually began to believe it, to feel as if I really were an essential part of his work. And then one day after I had finished chipping away on the block where Kenneth had told me to chip, I stepped back. As I gazed at the partially carved marble, I began to see it take form. It was just as he said: the sculpture was emerging. Kenneth was using his talent, his vision to bring it out, and because I had grown closer to him, I could share somewhat in that vision. It was as if I had been staring and staring at the same scene and suddenly I saw the colors, the shapes, the movement I had been told were always there, but until now had never been able to see.

He had warned me that once we got into this, he would eat, sleep, and drink it. He reminded me of a deeply religious person who had taken a vow and dedicated his life to a single prayer. I was always the first to become hungry and ask if we could break for lunch. Usually, he never heard me the first time I spoke. He would be looking at me, but it was as if he had already transcended this world and was living and breathing on another plane. He was in the world of his creation, traveling over the highway of his own imagination, and I was afraid he would leave me somewhere far behind.

"Kenneth, my stomach is growling," I moaned.

"What?"

"I've been pleading for the last half hour. Aren't you hungry?" I cried.

I was still basically in the same position he had originally placed me. It seemed that whatever he was doing was never good enough to please him. He would rip off pages and crumble them with frustration and then start anew, pacing, studying, coming up to me and adjusting my shoulders or my head, changing a strand of hair, finding something to do with the most minute detail of my being before making a new attempt to satisfy his artistic appetite. Meanwhile, my lowly, earthly appetite whined and groaned.

"Oh. Yes. Right. Is it lunch time already? It seems like we just started."

"We've been at it for nearly three hours, Kenneth. Even to a fanatic like you, that's more than just starting, isn't it?" I asked.

He laughed and threw up his hands.

"Sorry. Okay, go fix us some lunch. I'll be right there," he promised.

"I'm not going to call you, Kenneth. This time, I'm going to start eating without you if you don't come," I warned.

"A model is not supposed to nag the artist," he decreed. "She has to remain subtle and discreet, very unobtrusive, or the artist will lose the vision and have to start all over again," he threatened.

"That's blackmail," I told him as I pulled on my sweatshirt.

"No, it's basic artistic survival," he replied.

I paused before leaving the studio and looked at him sharply. It caught his attention.

"What?" he asked.

"You're not above taking advantage of your art to escape from things," I accused. He started to grimace and then turned it into a smile.

"Looks like the model is beginning to develop some vision herself," he said nodding. "Go make lunch. I'll be right in. That's an artistic promise."

I laughed and hurried out. Whenever he smiled at me and spoke warmly to me, it changed the face of the world. Every day had become more interesting and a little more exciting for me since Kenneth and I had had our heart-to-heart discussion, confessing more to each other, finally being honest with each other. It was as if another barrier had crumbled between us. Realizing that Kenneth could not be my father changed everything. Something different, some new feeling was emerging from the deepest places in my secret, put-away heart. Even when I was away from him, home from work, helping Aunt Sara in the kitchen, playing with May, I couldn't stop thinking of Kenneth. I would go over the things he said to me that day, the way he'd looked at me; it all took on new meaning. I even imagined that the long, slow looks he'd given me while we were working were looks not of an artist in love with his art, but of a man in love with his model.

Cary lost patience with me a number of times because I wasn't listening or paying attention to him. I resembled someone going in and out of a coma, drifting, walking about with a soft grin on my face,

163

nodding at sounds, but never really hearing anything but the whispering voices emerging from my own tingling heart. Through the fog of it all I knew that I was disappointing Cary, letting him down, but I just couldn't help wanting something more from Kenneth, something I was afraid Cary could never give me.

No matter how I tried, I couldn't stop fantasizing that Kenneth was falling in love with me.

In the library, I read stories about famous artists who had developed passionate affairs with their models, affairs of love that drove them mad with desire. Age didn't matter when it came to such strong emotion. It would be the same between Kenneth and me, I thought. After all, we had so much in common, and that came from his own lips. He had said we were both like orphans, rejecting and rejected by family. Most important, he had been in love with Mommy, and now, he surely saw something of her in me, enough of her to stir his suffering heart. It went deeper, I told myself, and he not only saw Mommy in me, but something more. He had said that, too. He had told me I was twice the woman. Could that mean he cared for me twice as much as he'd cared for Mommy?

Perhaps because of these new feelings, as well as my growing understanding of the artistic process, I was even more anxious to go to Kenneth's studio each day. I even offered to work overtime at no pay and come Sunday as well as Saturday if he wanted.

"We'll see," he said. "An artist can't rush things, can't overdo them either. I'm not complaining, you understand. I would never complain about it, but the work is very intense, exhausting. When you leave here, I usually crash."

"And don't even eat the supper I prepared for you, right?"

He shrugged.

"I know you don't because when I return the next day, I can see how much food is still there. I should stay longer, eat dinner with you," I suggested hopefully.

"Don't they expect you home to help?"

"If I don't eat there, I don't have to earn my keep," I told him.

"We'll see," he said, always the cautious one.

Twice during the week, however, I got him to permit me to serve him dinner and eat with him. I pretended that this was our house and Kenneth and I had long discussions over the meal I'd so lovingly prepared. One night our discussion turned to family, and, as always, our words became heated.

"I'm not looking for any confrontations with Jacob Logan," he said. "Not now."

"He wouldn't dare cause any trouble. I would just—leave. That's all." When Kenneth didn't say anything, I added. "I could just move in here, sleep in your other bedroom."

"Are you kidding? Jacob would set the authorities on me, get me arrested for corrupting the morals of a minor," he said.

"I'm not a minor," I snapped. He started to smile but stopped when he saw how lobster red with indignation my face had become.

"In the eyes of the law, you most certainly are a minor. You're miles above the average girl your age, I admit," he added to soften the tension between us. "But we have to be careful, Melody. Many people would not fully understand or appreciate what we're doing here."

"I haven't told anyone anything," I said.

"Not even Cary?" he asked, his eyes narrow with suspicion.

"Not even Cary. I realize he's not mature enough yet to understand what we are doing," I replied,

165

throwing my hair back and gazing at him with a defiant air that brought a small, but intriguing smile to his face. I was a little sad, though, that what I'd said was true; Cary wouldn't understand. He was too much like Uncle Jacob.

Kenneth shook his head and laughed lightly, the specks in his brown eyes brightening.

"You've got spirit, Melody. I am really lucky to have found you," he said.

I thought my heart would explode with joy. Every night afterward, I went to sleep with his words on my lips: "I am really lucky to have found you."

"And I you, dearest Kenneth." I hugged my pillow and dreamed of the day he would come to me and say, "Forget society. Forget what those busybodies would say. You and I will make great art together and should be together forever. I can't sleep without saying your name over and over until it becomes a song in my heart. Melody . . . Melody."

Was I the lovesick schoolgirl I had warned May she had become? Or was I really mature enough in heart and spirit to attract the romantic interest of an older man, a handsome and interesting older man?

Cary misunderstood my daydreaming and deep thoughts and grew impatient with me often during our walks after dinner. It wasn't that I'd lost all feelings for him as he accused, just that being with Kenneth made me realize the limitations of my relationship with Cary. For as much as Cary was my confidant, my only true friend here on the Cape, he just would never understand the thoughts and yearnings I discovered growing within myself as I helped Kenneth create his most prized work of art. Nor would he understand the role I played in its creation. I feared that Uncle Jacob had been too much of an influence on Cary, that no matter how he fought it, Cary would always be his father's son.

"You're just being polite spending time with me, is

that it?" he accused one night as we walked along the surf.

"Pardon me?" I asked, startled by his tone and sudden outburst.

"I talk and talk and you nod but you hardly say anything to me unless I pull it out of you like pulling on a fish line that's gotten tangled on a sunken barge. And when you kiss me it's quick, with your eyes slammed closed, and then you rush off to bed just like—just like—You're just different," he finally stammered, unable to complete the thought. But I knew. I knew all right. Cary was accusing me of being just like Laura!

"I am not," I said defensively, though I knew in my heart he was partially right. I wasn't like Laura. Oh, no. I wasn't as saintly as his beloved sister. But I was different, changing before his very eyes.

"Yes you are. It's because of what happened that night on the beach, isn't it? You think I went too far too fast and you're punishing me."

"Cary, that's ridiculous," I insisted.

"No, it isn't. I know girls can be like that. They'll sulk or pretend you don't exist until you come pleading and begging for a kind word or some attention. I don't know why they call you the weaker sex," he said bitterly. "We're the ones who act like clowns or lose our self-respect just for a favor or a kiss. Men are the powerless ones," he concluded.

"That is so untrue, Cary Logan," I said, spinning on him, my hands on my hips. "Men break the hearts of women much more than women break the hearts of men. Men are usually the unfaithful ones. They make all sorts of promises that are supposed to last forever and ever, and they buy expensive presents to convince us of their love, and then, after a while, they go looking for love with someone else.

Cary's eyes widened.

"I wouldn't," he said. "And that's not just an empty

promise. I thought you knew me," he said sadly. "I thought I knew you, too. I guess we're both fooling ourselves." He marched off, leaving me standing alone on the beach.

"Cary!"

"I'm tired," he called back without turning. "I've got to get up early tomorrow."

I watched him march back to the house, his fists balled with rage. I shook my head in pity.

He's been through a lot, I told myself, but he's still a boy compared to Kenneth. In time he'll be a much stronger person, but it's not my destiny to wait. "Is it?" I asked the stars. They blinked but had no answers, yet I felt sure that even if Cary were right and I had changed, it wasn't wrong for me to change. It simply meant I was growing up.

Later that evening, Aunt Sara called me to the telephone. It was Alice Morgan, my best friend in Sewell. She was very excited because her mother had finally given in and said she could make the trip to Provincetown to visit me.

"I can leave the day after tomorrow!" she exclaimed. "Is that all right?"

"Oh Alice," I said and thought a moment. What would I do with her now? How could I bring her along with me to Kenneth's studio? What was happening there had to be kept private for a number of reasons, not least of which was the growing feelings we were developing for each other.

Alice was always the immature one, even though she was one of the brightest students in school. Her family was one of the richest in Sewell, but she had never had a boyfriend. She was much too interested in books and studying to be bothered with clothes and makeup, which seemed to be the only thing that boys our age noticed. Despite our differences, she was a faithful friend. I hated hurting her.

"What's wrong, Melody? I thought you would be

happy about it. We're finally going to see each other after all this time apart," she cried.

"I know. It's just that . . ."

"Just that what?"

"Just that I've taken a job and I won't have time to properly entertain you. You'd have to spend hours and hours alone, and I couldn't leave you alone at this house. My uncle Jacob would make you miserable and Aunt Sara would drive you crazy. It wouldn't be much of a holiday for you."

"What about Cary?" she asked timidly. Was that her real motive for wanting to come?

"Oh, he works long hours too, Alice. He's never around."

"I see," she said, her little voice drifting away. It brought tears to my eyes as I imagined her in her room, her bubble of excitement bursting. "What kind of a job do you have?"

"I work with a local artist," I said. "Sometimes, he uses me to model for his pictures."

"Really? A model?"

"Just simple things," I said quickly, "like a girl walking on the beach or walking with his dog on the dunes. But I have to do a lot more. I'm there from early morning to dinner and sometimes later, so you see why it wouldn't be a very fun vacation."

"Oh."

"Maybe before the summer's over, I'll have a break and you can come. I'll stay in touch and call you as soon as I know when I can get some time off, okay?"

"Okay," she said, but her disappointment was more than obvious.

After I cradled the receiver, I felt just awful. There wasn't anything Alice wouldn't have done for me if I had asked her, and when I was desperate, she was ready to give me money, have me move into her house, anything. Cary was right, I thought. I was becoming a different person, but perhaps when you became mature, you also left part of yourself behind with the little girl in you. Becoming an adult seemed to mean becoming a little more selfish in different ways.

I promised myself I would put aside a few days for Alice before the summer ended. Once the sculpture was almost finished Kenneth was sure to need me less and then I could call Alice and have her come for a visit, I thought. It eased my troubled conscience and helped me to put her voice and probable tears out of my mind for the time being. I couldn't dwell on it anyway. I was too busy.

Kenneth had me work a half a day on the following Saturday. When Cary heard, he was full of questions. He came to my door, knocked, and started asking.

"Why does Kenneth need you on Saturday? What does he want you to do?"

"Same things I do all week, Cary," I said. I still hadn't mentioned my modeling and now I probably never would.

"Doesn't he take time off?"

"It's only for half of the day and he takes off Sundays. When he gets into a project, he becomes totally involved, absorbed by it."

"Sounds like he has nothing else to do with his life," he muttered. "Did he mention that boat again?"

"No, not yet."

Cary smirked.

"Thought so. Everyone is so full of . . . seaweed," he remarked.

"Kenneth doesn't say something if he doesn't mean it, Cary Logan. He'll bring it up soon. I'm sure."

Cary raised his eyebrows.

"How come you're so sure of whatever he says all of a sudden?"

"I just am," I said. He nodded, smirked again, and went up to his workshop.

After breakfast on Saturday morning, Uncle Jacob had the nerve to ask me if my working on the weekend meant Kenneth was paying me time and a half.

"Yes, he is," I said.

"Good. Don't forget to put half of the overtime as well in the pot," he ordered.

"I'm sure if I did forget, you'd be the first to remind me," I said brazenly, knowing I was sure to get a lecture.

"You're old enough to know responsibility and obligations," he replied. "Your mother never had an inkling of what those words meant and that was because everyone spoiled her. Spare the rod and you spoil the child," he recited.

"I am not a child," I fired back, but he didn't retreat an inch.

"Kids today don't grow up as fast as we had to grow up. They're given too much and don't have to give back much in return. It's gettin' harder and harder for me to find anyone under forty who wants to do a day's work. They all think it's just going to come to them," he declared.

"Yes," I said dryly. "I'm the living proof of a spoiled person."

He blinked, twisted his lips, and then shoved his pipe into his mouth, grumbling to himself.

I recalled how Kenneth had called him a moral horse's ass. It brought a smile to my lips.

"What's so funny?" he demanded.

"What? Oh, nothing," I said as I hurried out, praying harder for the day Kenneth would suddenly turn to me and say, "Come live with me and be my love."

He was already waiting for me. I hadn't heard him drive up, but it cheered my heart to see him there early. He was just as anxious to be with me as I was with him, I thought, and got into the jeep. We sped off and I saw there was something different on Kenneth's mind, some new excitement painting itself on his beautiful face.

"What are we going to do today?"

"We're moving ahead," he said. "I've completed the first stage and now I want to get into the meat of it." He glanced at me. "Neptune's daughter is coming up higher and revealing more of herself as she emerges out of the sea. She's filling out the female form."

I knew what he meant and it filled me with so much excitement I could barely breathe. I sat back, my heart thumping, the wind blowing my hair. Was I ready? Yes, I thought, I was ready. Almost overnight, I had grown up. I was ready to shed my innocence and share myself with Kenneth.

Ulysses barked because I had been ignoring him. I laughed and gave him a quick hug as we drove onto the dune road and Kenneth's studio.

The studio looked different to me this morning, perhaps because of what I knew was about to occur. It seemed darker, the shades drawn lower on the windows. As soon as we stepped through the door, Kenneth did something he had never done before: he locked the door behind us. His eyes shifted guiltily away when he saw my surprise.

"I'm too far into this to bear even the smallest interruptions," he explained. Since we had never been interrupted before, I didn't think much of his reason, but I smiled and nodded anyway.

He went to the model of the wave and studied it intently, his hands on his hips and his right hand stroking his beard as he continued to think and envision.

"Okay," he finally declared. "Here's what I want. Undress to your waist, take your usual position, and then come up until you're exposed up to here," he said drawing an imaginary line just above his stomach. Got it?"

I nodded. He returned to his easel and waited as I went around the wave and pulled off my sweat shirt. I hesitated a moment, my fingers actually trembling so badly I couldn't get them to undo the fastener on my bra. Finally, it was unfastened and I slipped the bra down my arms.

I had studied myself often in the mirror in my room, anticipating this moment. Mommy used to say I was a late bloomer, but that when I bloomed, I would bloom fast. I imagined it had been that way with her and that was why she knew. When I was fourteen, I barely had the bumps on my chest May now had. I thought I would never develop the curves and figure Mommy had.

And then, suddenly, between the ages of fifteen and sixteen, I began to develop quickly, finding a change in my body each succeeding day. I once went to Mommy and cried, pleading with her to get me to a doctor, afraid that my breasts would never stop growing. She just laughed and told me not to worry; they would stop growing eventually, and in the meantime I should learn to enjoy all the attention they brought me. I tried to do as Mommy suggested, but it was hard to enjoy yourself when you felt as if an alien had taken over your body.

Soon though, I did gain self-confidence. The boys no longer teased me about being flat as a board and instead took long looks at me and began spending more time trying to win my attention.

But now, I couldn't help thinking of all the beautiful, mature women Kenneth had seen naked. I was terrified that he would gaze at me and think of me as just a teenager and not a young woman. Cary had been in awe of my body, but was I shapely enough for a man like Kenneth? Would he gaze at me naked before him and think he had made a big mistake in asking me to model for him? What if I was not the budding beauty he envisioned?

All the while I was trying to gather up my courage, to calm my trembling limbs, Kenneth was preoccupied with his preparations and never noticed my shyness and fears.

"Ready," he called.

I took a deep breath, crawled through the opening, and started up and out of the wave. As I rose, my heart began to pound, my legs picked up the trembling that had begun in my fingers, and I held my breath.

"Keep your eyes open," he ordered.

I swallowed and moved another inch or two, still not revealing my breasts. He waited, his drawing pencil in his hand.

"Come up," he instructed. "That's it. Good, good."

And there I was before him. He stared a moment. I felt the crimson color in my neck and face. It was as if Kenneth had walked over and run his brush over my skin. After what seemed like an hour, Kenneth nodded. If he noticed, he didn't mention my blushing.

"Just turn a bit to your right and then, if you can, pull your shoulders back a little. Lift your chin and concentrate on the ceiling. Don't be too stiff. Relax."

"I'm trying," I said.

"I know. Easy. That's it. Good. All right. Let's start with this pose first," he said and began.

Whenever I shifted my eyes to glance at him and see what sort of expression he had on his face, I saw only the same intense scrutiny I had seen before. There was no look of appreciation and none of disapproval. The total neutrality of his eyes, his lips, his entire being surprised and then annoyed me. I jerked my shoulders back.

"Getting tired?" he asked without taking his eyes from his paper.

"A little."

"Just a few more minutes and we'll take a short break. I think I have the curve I want and the lift in your head. Yes, this will work. This is it," he said.

"What about the rest of me?" I asked sharply.

He just nodded and kept working. It amazed me that I had been right when I told Cary an artist was like a doctor when he looked at a woman. I had expected more than this—this impersonal artistic eye.

"You're perfect," he finally declared as he stepped back and looked at me. "You're just what I wanted, what I needed."

"Really?"

"There's this innocence about you, this freshness in your body that makes the statement," he said.

"Statement?"

"My statement. Beauty emerging, the birth."

"Oh."

"Okay, let's do some more." I groaned, but he didn't pay attention. After another twenty minutes or so, he put down his pencil.

"You can take a rest. I want to map out some of this on the marble. I'm getting this faster than I thought I might," he declared proudly.

"Then I'm doing well as your model?" I fished.

"Outstanding."

I stood there, still undressed, facing him, waiting for him to look at me differently, to smile differently, to step up to me and take me in his arms, to kiss me long and deeply, my naked breasts turned into him, waiting.

Instead he went straight to his cold marble block and left me dangling in my own imagination. I didn't bother putting my bra back on. I slipped into my sweatshirt without it. Then I came up beside him, hoping he might still turn and look at me as a woman instead of a model, an object of love instead of an object of art.

"If you'd like to get some fresh air, take Ulysses for a walk on the beach," he suggested. "I might be a while."

"Fine," I said sharply, sharper than I had intended, but he didn't appear to notice. I don't think he even heard me. I started for the door and Ulysses got up as quickly as he could to follow.

"Come along, Ulysses. I can always count on your wanting to be with me at least," I said loud enough for Kenneth to hear.

"What's that?" he said after a moment.

"Nothing. I'll be right back."

"Take your time," he said and returned his attention to his precious block of marble.

I slammed the door hard behind me and marched toward the beach, Ulysses at my side, trotting, his ears flapping.

"Men," I fumed and planted myself with a hard thump on a hill of sand. Ulysses looked disappointed that I wasn't walking any farther, but I wasn't in the mood.

"Now when he looks at me," I told Ulysses," he looks right through me. He's not seeing me, he's seeing that—that vision of his."

Ulysses panted, his tongue hanging over his mouth, his eyes wide as if he understood my indignation.

"I bet when you see a female you like, you see a female," I told him. He sniffed as if in response and plopped down beside me, convinced I wasn't going to move.

I stared at the ocean. Maybe I'm being too sensitive, I thought. Maybe I'm being too selfish. After all, Kenneth has made art his life and he has decided to include me in it. That's significant. He probably could have chosen any of a number of pretty girls in town, or maybe imported one. He was very successful; he could afford a very expensive model if he wanted. Yet he had chosen me. I was his special vision.

As I looked out over the ocean a lone cloud in the distance seemed to take the shape of a heart. A good omen, I thought. I lay back and Ulysses suddenly put his head on my stomach. It made me laugh. I closed my eyes and felt the sun on my face and the warm sand beneath me. It was all so soothing. In minutes I was asleep. I don't know how long I slept, but I woke to the sound of Ulysses barking. He was up and facing the road that lead to and from Kenneth's house. I sat up and turned to see a small purple car with what looked like astrological signs painted all over it in white come bouncing down the sandy ruts. The driver tapped out long, loud beeps on the horn as the car came to a stop in front of Kenneth's studio.

"Who's that?" I asked Ulysses. He gazed at me and then ran down the sand hill toward the driver as she emerged from the car. She was wearing a long, one-piece green and white dress, the hem actually touching the ground. Even from this distance, I could see long, silver earrings dangling from her lobes. Her dark brown hair was down to her shoulder blades.

"Ulysses!" she cried, kneeling to open her arms to hug him. Ulysses was all over her, licking her face, her neck, her hair. Her laughter was carried back to me in the wind. The woman stood up, shaded her eyes with her hand, and gazed toward me. Without knowing who I was, she waved and then turned as Kenneth came strolling around the house. I watched as she ran to him with the same enthusiasm Ulysses had run to her. He opened his arms in welcome and she was in his embrace an instant later. They kissed on the lips. I felt my heart do flip flops.

When she pulled back, her musical laughter trailed up to me. She was looking my way and he was obviously explaining who I was. She waved again and I got up and started toward them, my heart thumping with anticipation, a small fist of fear growing tighter and tighter in my stomach until I felt as if it would burn right through my skin.

"Melody," Kenneth said as I approached, "I'd like you to meet Holly Brooks."

"Hi, Melody," she exclaimed, her eyes wide with excitement. She wore a purple tinted lipstick that matched the color of the car. When she extended her hand to shake mine, the half dozen silver and copper bracelets on her arm all bunched up at her wrist. On each of her fingers she wore a ring, some simply silver embossed with a shape, two looking like some sort of polished stone.

She was a small woman made to look smaller in her oversized broomstick dress. She looked as if she were swimming in it, yet when the material shifted, I could see that she was braless, her breasts pressing up against the thin cotton. She wore a thin leather collar around her neck with tiny multicolored stones embedded in the material.

There was something very bright and airy about her smile, and her eyes were filled with a happy light, making them look more hazel than dark brown. She had a small nose and soft cheeks that dipped just slightly to diminish the roundness in her face and make her mouth small enough too, so that her iridescent lipstick looked pretty, not garish. There were the tiniest freckles on her forehead and down the sides of her temples.

"Hi," I said offering my hand. She seized it and shook firmly.

"When's your birthday?" she asked quickly.

"June twelfth," I said, looking at Kenneth. He wore a deep smile and nodded slightly.

"A Gemini," she declared. "I knew it."

"Holly is an astrologer," Kenneth explained. "As well as an artist."

"Oh. Aunt Sara believes in that."

"Really? Well, your aunt's a smart lady."

"Please," Kenneth said. "Spare us the hoo-doo voo-doo for a while."

"Oh Kenny," she said. "You know I come to see you only when it's the right astrological time and you know we're always good together, right?"

He shot a quick glance at me, his eyes full of embarrassment.

"Right. Melody," he continued, anxious to change the subject, "is my model for the new project."

"Oh yes. I can see why," she said, turning back to me. "She's so pretty. She must make a wonderful model, Kenneth."

"She's doing a terrific job," he said looking at me. I smiled, enjoying my moment in his sunshine.

"Good," Holly said. "It's so beautiful here, so conducive to art, to inner expression. There's a positive energy here. I feel it," she said, closing her eyes and embracing herself. She took deep breaths.

I looked at Kenneth and he smiled as we both waited. She popped her eyes open and gazed into my face with such intensity, I nearly laughed.

"The first time I drove up here, I knew Kenneth had felt the energy and that had brought him here. Remember, Kenneth? Remember how we just sat for hours and hours holding hands, soaking up the twilight and feeling the vibrations?"

"Yes, Holly," he said in a tired voice. "Why don't I help you with your things?"

"Oh, yes. It's *so* wonderful to be here again. You don't know how something like this can recharge your batteries, Melody, until you're away in the world of chaos, drowning in tension."

"I think she has some idea," Kenneth said with that inscrutable smile of his.

Holly turned back to me.

"Oh? I can't wait to get to know you, Melody. Kenneth hasn't told me very much. You're like his little secret," she said.

I glanced at him, wondering what that meant, delighted that he'd mentioned me to Holly. That meant I was important to him. But then, why had he invited her here? Who was she?

"He hasn't told me anything about you," I said. "You must be his other little secret."

Holly laughed and for the first time, I saw Kenneth Childs blush deeply.

"Your things?" Kenneth reminded her firmly.

"Oh, yes, my things." She uttered another little musical laugh and went to the trunk of her car. It was stuffed with small, battered suitcases. "Let's just take in these for now," she said pulling out the two largest. Kenneth took them from her and started toward the house. She opened the rear door of the car and something rolled out. It looked like a large, clear stone. The back seat was filled with clothes, books, and art supplies, and a lamp lay on the floor.

"Can you take this for me, Melody," she said, lifting the stone object. "I'll get the other things."

"What is it?"

"My crystal," she said. "The energy is drawn into it and then I draw it into myself. I never go anywhere without putting it alongside my bed. Kenneth doesn't mind," she said.

"Excuse me?"

"Oh, you'll see. We have so much to tell each other," she declared.

"How long are you staying here?" I asked.

She paused, gazed around a moment, took a deep breath, and then nodded, before closing and opening her eyes.

"Until I stop hearing it," she said.

"Hearing it? Hearing what?"

"The voice that called me here." She smiled.

180

"You'll understand. I promise," she said and reached down to pick up a packet of incense off the floor in the back of the car.

She closed the door and we started toward the house.

"I only know a little about Kenneth's new work, but from the way he talks, I can see it's the most exciting thing he's done in years. I'm glad he found it. He was beginning to worry me," she said with a serious face, her eyes darker, her lips tighter. "I was beginning to think the shadows of the past were overtaking his bright light and dimming his spirit. I'm so happy for him, and if you had anything to do with it, I'm grateful to you," she added.

I just looked at her, failing to find the words to respond to all this. I turned to carry her crystal to the guest room and she stopped me.

"Not that way, dear. I told you," she said, "that has to be beside the bed." She nodded toward Kenneth's bedroom and smiled.

I hesitated, my chest feeling hollow, no heartbeat, no blood, no lungs, just an echo chamber full of surprise and disappointment.

Kenneth appeared at the bedroom door.

"I put your suitcases by the closet. Anything else you want brought in right now?"

"No, Ken. Thanks."

"Okay. I'm going back to the studio." He turned to me. "Are you sure you don't mind staying the whole day?"

"I think I'm getting a little stomachache. But I'll be fine. I can stay," I said.

"Oh?"

"Stomach ache? Don't you worry, Ken. I'll help her. I have just the herbal medicine for stomach aches. Come along, Melody," she sang.

Reluctantly, my legs feeling like twin sticks of lead, I followed her into Kenneth's bedroom. She took the crystal and placed it beside the bed on a night stand and then she turned to me and smiled.

"Time of the month?" she asked.

"What? Oh. No," I said.

"Did you eat something nasty this morning?"

"No."

"Just stress then," she concluded. "I have just what you need."

"I doubt it," I said harshly. She stared at me curiously.

"You have a lot of negative energy coming out of you, Melody. If you let me, I'll help you."

"No thank you," I said. "I'll just walk it off. That usually works." I turned and fled the bedroom.

Outside, I hesitated, not sure if I wanted to walk home or walk on the beach.

Why hadn't he told me she was coming? Why hadn't he told me anything about her?

"Is every man a liar?" I shouted at the sea and the sea roared back what sounded like a resounding yes to me.

Just when I had gotten to the point where I thought I knew Kenneth, I discovered he was more of a stranger than ever. Perhaps we never get to know anyone, I thought, not even people we love and people who claim to love us.

I took a deep breath and walked toward the sea, hoping that the roar of the waves I heard would grow louder and louder and drown the angry voices chattering away inside me.

9
∞

It's in the Stars

I took a long walk down the beach toward where I could see the Point's end and the vast North Atlantic. As I let the sea spray wash over me, I wished I could just drift away with the tide, away from Kenneth, away from the Logans, away. How could I have been stupid enough to think that Kenneth could love me? Holly and all her eccentric, exotic ways were what an artistic man like Kenneth wanted. I was just a silly teenager who bored him. But I hadn't bored Cary, Cary who truly loved me, Cary whom I rejected to follow my childish dreams of Kenneth and his love for me.

I felt awash in self-pity as I continued down the beach, noticing that the seaweed was thicker on this part of the Point. It looked like the ocean had been in a rage here, tearing up the underwater vegetation like a madwoman might rip out her hair. There was driftwood everywhere, made shiny from the constant scrubbing of the salt water. I spotted something that had washed ashore. As I drew closer, I realized that it was a doll, her hair matted, her face bleached by the sun so that even the black button eyes were a dull gray. The lower half of her body was embedded in the sand where the tide had deposited her and would no doubt return to carry her back out to sea.

I plucked the doll from her temporary grave and brushed her off, imagining how this had once been a little girl's prize possession. In my mind's eye, I envisioned the little girl as sweet and as innocent as May perhaps, preparing a fantasy tea party with the doll seated at a toy table, the teacups and teapot set out. Surely the little girl had told her doll all her wishes and secrets. In the beginning, when she first had been given this doll, she probably slept with it beside her and carried it everywhere. It had become her precious little companion in which she had trusted her love and her dreams.

For whatever reason—maybe the girl had just grown up and left it at the bottom of a toy chest—the doll drifted from her private world and was forgotten, discarded, to take her place among all the other forgotten toys. Later, there might have been a house cleaning and toys were thrown away to make room for other things. Her mother might have held it up and asked, "Do you want this anymore?"

The little girl thought for a moment and remembered her childhood best friend fondly, but she was older now and her eyes had turned to boys; dolls were as embarrassing as an annoying little sister giving away intimate family secrets. Who wanted her new boyfriend to know she used to whisper I love yous to a doll instead of to him.

"No," she said, and sentenced her precious friend to the dump. How it came to be in the ocean was another story, but it had, and it had found its way to this beach. Even with her eyes bleak, her face lackluster, I thought I could hear the tiny doll's plea. She looked up at me, begging not to be left alone, condemned to this horrible fate.

I brushed her off and carried her back with me, really not sure what I would do with her. I wished someone would find me on the beach like this and brush off my grains of sadness and salty tears before carrying me off to a new and better home. Like this doll, I felt discarded and perhaps with even less fanfare. But hadn't I done the same to Cary? Was Holly's arrival my punishment for treating Cary so selfishly?

As I rounded a bend and approached the beach in front of Kenneth's house, I saw Holly seated on a blanket, her legs curled in a lotus position, her arms folded under her breasts, her head back so her face was awash in the afternoon sunshine. She was barefoot and wore a light green and white tie-dyed tank dress that came barely to her knees. She also wore different earrings. These looked like jade and glittered along with whatever she was wearing around her neck.

Ulysses hadn't come out with her. I imagined him pouting in the studio with Kenneth because I had rushed away without so much as glancing at him and beckoning for him to join me.

I was going to ignore Holly and go into the house, when I heard the exotic, Far Eastern–sounding music, and drew closer. Somehow, she sensed me and turned.

"Hi," she called.

I stepped closer and saw the small stream of smoke rising from a tiny bronze pot.

"What are you doing?" I asked.

"Greeting the zodiac. I've got to get in tune with the vibrations, the energy here, as soon as possible. Come," she said, shifting on her blanket to make room for me, "join me."

"To do what?" I asked with a smirk.

"Plug into the universe," she replied as if it were the

185

most obvious thing. "All the answers to your questions and your problems are in here," she said, pointing to her heart, "but you have to find the way to reach them, unlock the doors, and to do that, you have to strip away the worldly confusions, the tensions and the turmoil. You've got to lift your spirit from this bondage and free your inner self. I'll show you how if you want," she said.

I started to shake my head and laugh at her. Did she really expect me to believe these things?

"It won't cost you anything but a little of your time and energy," she said quickly. "And it might be just what you need, Melody."

"How do you know what I need?" I snapped back at her.

She smiled softly.

"I know you need some peace, some strength, some light. I know you have to rid yourself of your burdensome anger, and I know you're looking for meaning and love," she added.

I couldn't deny it. My face must be a window through which anyone could see my troubled heart, I thought, if someone who had just met me already knew all this.

"How can sitting on a blanket and staring at the sky and the ocean help?" I asked disdainfully.

"I'll show you if you give me a chance," she promised with friendly eyes.

"Why should you care about me?" I challenged.

"Why shouldn't I?" she responded quickly. "Come on. I don't bite." She patted the blanket beside her. I drew closer.

"What's burning?"

"Incense," she said.

"It smells funny. What is it?" I asked, grimacing.

"My own recipe of frankincense, styrax, and cascarilla bark. You've never smelled incense before?"

"No."

"It's really very pleasant. What do you have in your hand there?" she asked, leaning to see what I was carrying at my side.

"Someone's old doll. I found it on the beach," I said unashamedly and more possessively than I had expected.

"All my dolls were handmade for me when I was a little girl," she said. "My mother was a tailor and very talented. She made all my clothes and all my brother's and my father's clothes, too. She learned it from her mother. I don't know how far back the skill went, but it was something they brought over from Europe. Of course, all my friends made fun of my clothes because they knew practically everything I owned was home-made."

"Where did you live?" I asked, unable to prevent myself from being interested in her, especially when she talked about her mother. She seemed so open and free, revealing intimacies about herself without any fear. After living on the Cape for a while, I thought she was a breath of fresh air.

"Yonkers. It's just outside of New York City. My mother worked for a manufacturer in the Bronx. Ever been there?"

"No," I said.

"I haven't been back in ages, even though I live only a train ride away in Greenwich Village," she explained.

"I don't know where that is exactly," I said. "I know it's in New York City."

"Yes. It's where a lot of artists and writers, folk singers and musicians live. I have a shop there on Christopher Street. I do readings, sell candles and crystals."

"Readings?"

"Astrology," she said. "Personal horoscopes."

"Oh. My uncle Jacob thinks it's mumbo jumbo, even heathen. He's always bawling out my aunt Sara for reading her horoscope in the paper, but she does it anyway."

"It's not mumbo jumbo," she said softly. "Astrology was studied among the ancient Egyptians, Hindus, Chinese, Etruscans, and the Chaldeans of Babylonia. It all started with the Chaldeans about three thousand BC. It was very logical to them. When they noticed how the sun and the heavenly bodies affected seasons, crops, they just assumed it all affected human life as well."

"I don't really know all that much about it," I said. "Just that it's like fortune telling."

"Yes, in a way. Your destiny is dependent upon the sign of the zodiac under which you were born and the relationship of the planets at the time and throughout your life, but more depends upon the position and power of the sun and the moon at birth than upon all the planets of our solar system combined. The sun and the moon are the transmitters of the stellar forces. I make charts on a horoscope, working out the location of the sun, the moon, and the planets within the twelve segments of the zodiac known as houses," she continued. "Each house is named for a constellation and each takes up thirty degrees of space, the whole making the three hundred sixty degrees of a circle. That's why the number three hundred sixty is the symbol of completion," she lectured.

"It all sounds silly," I said. Why would Kenneth like someone who believed in these things? I wondered.

"Oh, but it's not. It's all logical. Listen," she insisted. "We all have five positive points of projection and four positive centers of energy. Four plus five makes up the mystical nine, the symbol of deity. The head, hands, and feet are the five points of projection

188

from which streams and streams of vital force are constantly radiating. We symbolize that with the five-pointed star," she added and showed me her wrist where she had a five-pointed star tattooed.

"The positive centers of energy are the brain, the spleen, the heart, and the generative organs, while the great center of reception is the solar plexus." She held her hand against her stomach. "Just think about it. When trouble or anxiety crosses our path, the first place we feel it is here, right? Usually we have no appetite. We have butterflies."

I nodded. That did make sense.

"Mental and psychic goodness depend upon the perfect freedom of the body. Anything that cramps, binds, or twists us out of natural proportion is fatal to real spiritual progress. That's why people in India, Chaldea, and Egypt wore loose-flowing robes and why the high priests did the same. It's why I dress like this, too," she explained. "Does that help you understand it a little better?"

I nodded.

"I can do a chart for you while I'm here, if you want."

I didn't reply. In a real sense I was afraid of knowing what was in store for me. The future seemed far more terrifying than the present, and I was also afraid that if she told me good things, it would only give me false hopes. I had had enough of that.

"Aunt Sara is impressed with the fact that my twin cousins were born under the sign of Gemini," I revealed.

"Yes. Castor and Pollux represent the twin souls. See?"

"No," I said sharply.

"I can explain it," she said.

"I'm not interested."

She just smiled.

"Well, if you change your mind, I'll be here."

"Who's watching your store while you're here?" I asked.

"A friend of mine, Billy Maxwell. He's paralyzed from the waist down, the result of a bullet wound he got when he was fleeing from a mugger. The mugger shot him in the back," she said without sadness or tragic overtones. "Billy's a poet so it didn't stop him from doing what he loves to do."

"Isn't he still bitter and unhappy?" I asked.

"He was in the beginning, but I helped him find a new wavelength, a new highway to travel spiritually, and he's become a happier, more beautiful person."

"Was he your boyfriend?"

"We loved each other, but it wasn't boyfriend-girlfriend in the way you mean."

I nodded and looked away.

"You're Kenneth's girlfriend though, aren't you?" I asked, my voice shaking.

She laughed.

"As much as anyone could be Kenneth's girlfriend. Kenneth is like a comet. He can't be chained to anything or anyone, except his art, of course."

"But you're here, living with him, aren't you?" I practically spit back at her.

"We touch like two meteors passing in the universe when the stars are lined up correctly, but he knows and I know it's not permanent in the sense you mean. It's permanent in our universe though. He and I will be this way for eternity, our two spirits touching," she said.

She saw the look of confusion on my face.

"You'll understand if you let me open a door for you."

"What door?"

"The door to yourself," she said. "First, you have to free your mind of turmoil, rid yourself of negative energy."

"How do you do that?"

"I'll show you how. First, close your eyes and concentrate on your own breathing. Don't breathe fast or slow. Just tune into yourself. Go on, try it," she urged. She patted the blanket again. "Come on."

I lowered myself slowly to the blanket, still looking at her skeptically.

"Concentrate on my breathing?"

"Every time a thought tries to enter your mind, drive it away, and the easiest way to do that is to concentrate only on your breathing. Go on."

"This seems very silly," I said.

"Everything new seems silly at first. It can't hurt you to try, can it? Just stare at the water and concentrate on your breathing. Go on," she urged.

I sighed and did what she said.

"It's not working," I declared after just a few minutes. All the sounds of the ocean invaded, the terns, the surf, even the wind whistling around my ears.

"You're not concentrating. Push the noise away, chase out the thoughts. Your breathing is all you want to know at the moment. Keep trying."

I did, and soon I didn't hear those other things. I felt and heard only my own breathing and a wave of relaxation and contentment washed over me. After a few more minutes, I felt her hand on mine.

"Did you do it?" she asked.

"I think so," I said, a bit impressed with myself.

"It takes practice. It's called meditation and it will allow you to travel to your inner self," she said. Then she lifted off her necklace and handed it to me. There was a deep cloudy green crystal in gold suspended from it. "Here, wear this."

"What is it?"

"Moldavite. It's from a meteorite that fell to the earth about fifteen million years ago."

"Really?"

191

"Yes, really," she laughed, amused by my amazement.

"What's it supposed to do?" I asked turning it in my fingers.

"It aids alignment with your higher self, channeling extraterrestrial and interdimensional sources. It's good for balancing and healing the body and the mind," she explained.

It was my turn to laugh. "No thanks," I said, trying to hand the necklace back to her.

"Why don't you give it a chance?" she said and pushed my hand away.

I thought for a moment and then shrugged and put it on. She smiled.

"There, you see. You've taken the first step: a little faith, a little hope."

"Every time I have a little faith or a little hope, I get disappointed," I said.

"Maybe you've been putting your energy into the wrong things, the wrong places."

"How do you know which is right and which is wrong?"

"That's why you have to develop a clearer vision," she said. She looked out at the sea and held that gentle, angelic smile on her lips. "You're very fond of Kenneth, aren't you?" she asked, not turning back to me.

"Yes," I said.

"It's not unusual to imagine things—wonderful things—with such a person. When I was your age, I did a lot of that, too." She looked at me, her eyes still warm, but smaller, more intense. "You're angry with me, aren't you? Angry that I showed up?"

I shifted my own eyes away quickly.

"Well," I said, "Kenneth and I are doing something very special. It takes a lot of concentration and—we can't be interrupted," I declared firmly.

"I'm sure you won't be, especially not by me. I've

known Kenneth a long time. I know when to be in his face and when to be out of it," she said, laughing. Then she looked at me very intently, her eyes soft but determined. "I know I'm good for him, Melody. I know I give him something he needs, something that helps him be the artist and the man he wants to be."

Tears came to my eyes. I was hoping that was what I would give him and who I would be.

"You'll do that for someone special someday, I'm sure. It's not something that happens overnight. It takes time."

I twirled the coarse, faded doll's hair in my fingers and stared at it.

"Do you have a boyfriend?" she asked.

"Sort of," I said thinking of Cary. The boy who loved me and who I had put aside to chase a silly dream.

"You'll have to tell me all about him," she said, "and I'll make up a chart for him too and tell you if you're destined to spend a long time together."

I had to laugh at that, thinking of Cary hearing Holly's ideas.

"He's like his father. He wouldn't listen or believe in anything you said."

"Oh. Well, let's wait and see," she said as if she knew something about Cary that I didn't. "What I like about coming here," she said, gazing out at the vast ocean again, "is the great privacy. I really feel as if I'm on the edge of the world and I can do whatever I want. Don't you feel that too? That sense of freedom?"

"Yes," I admitted.

"Well then, while you and Kenneth work, I think I'll just get some sun."

She started to unbutton her dress. I watched with surprise as she peeled it off to her waist. She wasn't wearing a bra. Topless, she turned on the blanket to expose her back.

"It feels like a warm bath," she said and moaned with pleasure. Then her eyes popped open. "Don't you ever sunbathe nude out here?"

I shook my head.

"I love the sense of abandon, the freedom. It's like getting back to basics. You oughta try it."

She closed her eyes again. Her Far Eastern music continued playing on her tape recorder and her incense continued to send tiny spirals of smoke into the wind. I sat with her a few minutes more and then I got up.

"I'm going back to work," I said.

"I hope I don't fall asleep out here," she muttered. "One year I got a bad burn. Kenneth got involved in what he was doing, of course, and completely forgot about me. Scream if I'm still out here when you finish."

"Okay," I said.

She lifted herself to continue talking to me before I walked away.

"Why don't you come back tomorrow and we'll have a picnic on the beach?"

"I have to go to my grandma Olivia's for a Sunday brunch," I said with a grimace.

"You don't look too anxious to go."

"I'm not. I hate going to her house. We have to tiptoe around and remember not to speak unless we're spoken to. My aunt is constantly on pins and needles, afraid one of us will do something to irritate my grandma Olivia."

"Oh. Sounds dreadful," she said, "but I guess we have to put up with family sometimes."

"She's not really my grandma. My real grandma is in a rest home," I said.

"Really? You'll have to tell me about it all," she said. "Maybe at our picnic. Couldn't you skip the brunch?"

"They'll have heart attacks," I said. "Especially my uncle Jacob." She laughed. Then she shrugged.

"So, wake up under the weather."

"What?"

"You know, use the old reliable," she suggested.

"What's that?"

"Female problems," she said. "Your uncle Jacob's not going to challenge that, is he?" I shook my head, laughing at the thought of it and amazed that she would join me in a conspiracy so quickly.

"Hardly," I said.

"So there. I'll come pick you up around eleven."

"But what will I say when they come home and find me gone?"

She shrugged.

"You felt better, thought you should get some air, and went to town or something and met me. What would you rather do, be out here with Kenneth and me or go to your stuffy brunch?"

"Be out here, definitely," I replied without hesitation.

"So? Do what makes you feel good. You have to be honest with yourself and then and only then, can you be honest with others," she said, smiling as she gave me another drop of her wisdom. "If you come, I'll do your chart," she threatened with a laugh.

I had to smile. Despite the conflicts raging within me, I couldn't help liking her. I started away, still undecided about her suggestion.

"Eleven o'clock?" she called. I walked a little farther and then I turned impulsively and yelled back into the wind.

"Okay. Come get me."

I ran down the small hill to the studio, clutching the discarded doll in my arms, feeling more confused and more excited than ever, but, strangely, more hopeful, too. It was as if I had finally found an adult who could

195

be completely honest with me. An adult I could truly trust as my friend.

"I see Holly's begun to convert you," Kenneth said when I entered the studio. I had gone through the house, leaving the battered doll in the kitchen until I was ready to leave for home.

"What? What do you mean?"

"She gave you one of her crystals," he said, nodding at the necklace. Even Ulysses looked up with new interest.

"Oh. Yes. It's fifteen million years old and from a meteorite."

"Is that so? Did she show you the warranty?"

"What?"

He laughed.

"Nothing," he said with a wave of his hand.

"She wants to have a picnic tomorrow. She's coming to pick me up at eleven," I said quickly to see if he would disapprove. He just looked surprised.

"Really? What are you going to tell Jacob?"

"I'll take care of it," I said firmly. He widened his smile and lifted his eyebrows.

"I see. Holly wouldn't have given you any ideas on what to say to Jacob now, would she?"

"Maybe."

He shook his head.

"I thought so. It doesn't take Holly long to get right into the heat of battle when she sees an emotional conflict," he said.

"She's interesting," I offered cautiously. He laughed.

"Interesting? She's like a rain storm in Technicolor, psychedelic clouds, neon lightning with the wind playing tunes from the Zen Buddhists. Wait until she reads you some of her poetry," he continued.

"Don't you like her?" I asked, confused. It sounded as if he were making fun of her.

"Of course. She's fresh air. There's not a phony bone in her solar and lunar body. Come on, let's finish this," he said and nodded at the papier-mâché wave. I pulled off my sweatshirt and then took my position quickly. Maybe it was because I had done it before and the shock and excitement were over, or maybe it was because of some of the things Holly Brooks had said, but whatever the reason, my nervousness and inhibition were gone. I felt as if I had done this often.

"How long have you known her?" I asked after I'd gotten myself comfortable.

"A long time."

"Did you meet her here in Provincetown or in Greenwich Village?"

He paused.

"Melody, you know I can't talk and work at the same time," he said.

"Sorry."

"Just lift your chin a little and turn slightly to the right. Good."

"Could you just answer one question?" I begged.

"Okay. I can see if I don't, I won't have any peace anyway. What is it?"

"Do you believe in all this—the power of the crystals, the energies in the universe?"

He stared at me a moment.

"I don't believe in anything but my art," he said, but he didn't sound proud of that. He said it with an underlying tone of sadness and defeat. "Let's work."

I could tell by his tone that he was in no mood to continue the conversation, so I resigned myself to silence so Kenneth could begin.

When we were finished, I hurried out to see if Holly had fallen asleep on the beach. She was in the house, however, and greeted me as I passed through to pick up the doll and wait for Kenneth at the jeep.

"I have something else for you," she said, holding a large paper bag. She dipped into it and brought out some sticks of incense. "Burn these in your room while you're meditating. It will help relax you," she said. Then she reached in again and pulled out a roll of yellow material. "You can wear it tomorrow when I come for you."

"Wear it? I don't understand. How do you wear it? What is it?"

"It's called a sari. It's traditionally worn by Hindu women. Here, let me show you how to put it on," she said. She wrapped it around me and even draped it over my head. Then she stepped back and bowed with her hands together.

"How do I look?" I asked, turning.

"Wonderful. It fills your face with a spiritual light," she said.

I took it off and practiced wrapping it around myself.

"Perfect," Holly said.

"Thank you," I said. She looked back to be sure Kenneth wasn't in earshot. "Don't wear anything else underneath. Remember what I said about confining the natural form."

I nodded, blushing, and put the sari back into my bag as Kenneth appeared.

"What are you two plotting?" he asked.

"Nothing more than a trip on a star," Holly replied.

"That's what I thought," he said. "Hop in, Melody, for an ordinary trip in a jeep." Ulysses got in with us.

"Bye," I said.

"See you in the morning."

"Be right back, Holly," Kenneth told her. "Are you going to make us one of those spiritual dinners tonight, all grain, vegetarian, organic?" he asked. She nodded.

"I'll be losing a few pounds before she leaves," he told me. Holly laughed and we drove away. "Where did you get the doll?" he said gazing at it in my hand.

"I found it on the beach."

"A bit beat up, isn't it?"

"I just didn't want to leave it there," I said. He looked at me askance for a moment and then smiled. "And what's in the bag?"

"A sari," I said. "And some incense."

He laughed.

"What's so funny?"

"I wish I could see Jacob's face when he sees you burning incense, walking around in sandals and one of Holly's dresses with crystals around your neck," he said, his brown eyes sparkling with mischief.

"It's not any of his business what I wear," I said firmly. He turned and stared at me. I tilted my head, questioning those intense eyes.

"What?"

"Just for a minute there you sounded so much like Haille it threw me back in time," he said in a wistful tone, his eyes darker.

He drove on, pensive, while my heart pounded as I wondered what it all meant.

Aunt Sara didn't pop her head out of the kitchen to greet me when I came through the front door. The house was deadly quiet, so quiet it made me uncomfortable. I glanced into the living room, saw there was no one in there, and then hurried down to the kitchen. It too was empty. Where was everyone? I started up the stairs.

Cary heard me and stepped out of May's room with May beside him.

"I thought you were only working a half-day today," he said, his eyes cold and accusing.

"Kenneth asked me to stay longer. He had a friend arrive today. Holly Brooks," I said. "Do you know her?"

"No. What's that around your neck?" he asked, like an attorney cross-examining a witness.

"It's a crystal with special healing qualities," I said and he smirked.

"That's pagan."

"It's not pagan if it makes you feel good. It happens to have a lot to do with spirituality, too, Cary Logan. You don't know anything about this."

May was signing and pointing to the doll in my hand. I signed back, describing how I had found it on the beach. She wanted to look at it. Even though it was so faded and ragged, May looked at me with that ecstatic rapture only the very young could express. She understood my rescue mission immediately and turned to Cary, signing. He shook his head.

"What is she asking?" I inquired, because she had her back to me.

"She wants me to fix that mess of a doll. What are you doing with it?"

"I found it on the beach and it's not a mess," I insisted and marched into my room. Cary came to the doorway with May.

"Well, what are you going to do with it?"

"I don't know, but I know it's not a mess. It was once a very pretty little doll." I spun on him, my eyes burning with swallowed back tears. "People cast each other aside just as easily as they cast aside their possessions these days," I complained.

A deep silence fell between us.

"Maybe I could do something with it," he finally said. "Can I look at it?" he asked in a softer tone. I handed it to him and he turned it over in his hands. "Body's still okay. Needs some paint and a new head of hair, as well as a new little dress. It's not so much, I suppose."

He saw the warm appreciation in my eyes.

"Could you do that?"

"I have all that paint upstairs and the tools. I'll just get something for the hair and May will make the new dress." He signed that to her and she nodded emphatically. "What color do you want her hair?"

"My own," I said quickly. He nodded and explained all to May, who looked almost as happy as I was about it.

"What else do you have?" he asked, nodding at the bag in my hand.

"A dress Holly gave me and some incense."

"Incense?"

"Yes. You light it and it helps when you meditate."

"Huh? Meditate? You mean like a Buddhist monk or something?" he asked with a smirk.

"Where's Aunt Sara?" I asked instead of replying. He was getting me angry. "I thought I'd find her in the kitchen and help her with dinner," I said.

"She's not here. She and Dad went to dinner at the Wilson's," he said. I stepped back, surprised.

"Your father and mother went out to dinner?"

"Well, you know Ma. She prepared our dinner first," he said. "All we have to do is serve ourselves and clean up afterward. Dad and Jimmy Wilson are talking about buying a cranberry bog together. Ma put up quite a fuss when she heard she had to leave us, but I promised her we'd take care of everything."

"Oh. Well then, I'll clean up and go down and get our dinner set out," I said.

"I'll just put this up in my work room," Cary said, indicating the doll.

I signed to May, describing what we would do, and she told me she would set the table while I showered. After I finished towel-drying my hair I took out the dress Holly had given me and wrapped it around myself. When I stood before the mirror, I laughed at how I looked and then thought I would wear it to dinner to see Cary's reaction. He was downstairs in the kitchen and when he saw me, he stopped what he was doing and dropped his jaw.

"What is that?"

"It's called a sari."

"I'll say it's sorry," he remarked and laughed.

"Cary Logan, all you're doing is showing your ignorance," I accused. His smiled faded.

"Well, what's it supposed to be?"

I explained that it was the natural dress for Hindu women and a very special gift given to me. Cary started to smile after I finished, but when he saw the serious expression on my face, he tightened his own, swallowed back his ridicule, and sat at the dinning room table, tonight taking his father's seat.

It was as if the chair had powers, for Cary's face took on Uncle Jacob's serious demeanor. May and I took our usual seats. There was that same moment of quiet that preceded all of our dinners. May looked expectantly at Cary and he reached for the Bible.

"Dad left a marker where he thought I should read tonight," he explained and began. "'Love not the world, neither the things that are in the world.'" He paused as if the words were choking him.

"Why don't you choose your own selection tonight, Cary?" I suggested. I could see the indecision in his eyes as he thought about my suggestion. It was like challenging the king, doing something deliciously forbidden. His eyes brightened with mischief.

"Okay," he said. "I will." He turned the pages, paused, and gazed at me as he read. "From the Song of Solomon. 'How fair is Thy love, my sister, my spouse! How much better is thy love than wine, and the smell of thine ointments than all spices! Thy lips, O my spouse, drop as the honeycomb: honey and milk are under thy tongue.'" He paused and gazed at May and then at me with his face bronzed in pride and defiance.

"Not one your father would have chosen," I said, impressed with the intensity of his reading. He had never sounded more grown-up to me. For a second, he had actually taken my breath away.

"You wanted me to make my own choice and I did," he said with firm defiance.

He and I gazed at each other.

"I'm glad you did," I said.

He smiled.

"Actually, you look pretty in that dress," he said. "Sort of special."

I smiled.

"Thank you."

May began to sign, wondering why it was taking us so long to begin eating. Daddy never made us wait this long, she emphasized.

We laughed, grateful for the light moment, and started to pass the dishes to each other.

Afterward, Cary helped May and me clean up and put everything away. We left the kitchen as spotless as Aunt Sara did.

"What's this meditating all about?" Cary asked, and I told him some of the things Holly had told me. Of course, he was skeptical, raising his right eyebrow higher than his left as I spoke. I described what I had felt when I did what she instructed and concentrated on my breathing.

"You got like that just by listening to yourself breathe?" he asked with doubting eyes.

"By tuning into myself," I corrected. "Would you like to try?" I asked. "Or are you afraid of what you'll find?"

His eyes sharpened and then narrowed at my challenge.

"Okay. Show me."

"Wait in the living room," I said and ran upstairs to get the incense. I brought it down quickly and set it in a sugar bowl. Then I lit it and placed it in front of us on the floor. May sat by, watching with fascination as

203

I got Cary to assume the lotus position—or as close as he could get to folding his legs over one another without toppling over.

"I wish I had her music, but we'll try without it for now," I said.

"I can hum something. How about 'The Battle Hymn of the Republic.'"

"Cary Logan, if you're not going to be serious . . ."

"All right. I'm sorry," he said, holding up his hands and laughing. "That stuff sure smells."

"It's supposed to. Okay, concentrate, drive away all thoughts and just listen to yourself take breaths, but don't hurry or slow your breathing, understand?"

"Gotcha," he said and we began.

"Melody?" he said after only a few seconds.

"Shh. Concentrate," I said.

We were both quiet. I felt him gaze at me and then he stared ahead. I think he was really beginning to get into it, too, when suddenly, the front door opened and Uncle Jacob and Aunt Sara appeared.

"What burned?" Aunt Sara cried, worrying about the dinner she had prepared.

"What in the name of God is going on in here?" Uncle Jacob demanded from the living room doorway before we could get up. He looked from me to Cary and then back at me. Then he rushed past us and pulled the incense sticks from the bowl. He thrust them at Aunt Sara. "Get rid of this. Run water on it first."

"What are they doing?" she asked.

"Something pagan," Uncle Jacob said. He turned his fiery eyes on Cary. "I warned you, boy. I told you to watch for the devil and now you've gone and let him into our home."

"Dad, listen—"

"I don't understand," Aunt Sara said meekly. "Where did you get that dress, Melody?"

"From the devil himself, I'll wager," Uncle Jacob

204

said. "Satisfied now, Sara? Satisfied she ain't your dead and gone Laura? She's about as different from Laura as night is from day," he said.

"Stop it, Dad!" Cary cried.

Jacob moved forward quickly and slapped Cary across the cheek so hard it turned his head. Aunt Sara cried out, and Cary looked at me, his eyes burning with hot tears.

"Cary," I began, but before I could say another word, he shot from the room and out the door.

"Cary!" Aunt Sara cried after him.

Uncle Jacob turned to me.

"Now you've done what you came to do, what Haille brought you here to do. It's her revenge," he said.

"You're ignorant! You're ignorant and narrow-minded and cruel!" I fired back. I charged out of the house and after Cary, while poor May struggled with her hands to express the pain and confusion that had burst upon her like a hurricane.

10
&

Shelter from the Storm

I ran from the house out into the darkness. Heavy, ominous clouds had come sweeping down from the northwest, rolling and rumbling over the night sky, burying the stars and the quarter moon, shutting out any brightness and light. I had hoped to find Cary either right in front of the house or on the road, but he was nowhere in sight. When I walked around the house and toward the beach and the dunes, I couldn't see very far. He could have gone in any direction, I realized and groaned my disappointment. I walked over the sand and put my hands to my mouth to cup them in the shape of a megaphone.

"Cary!" I cried, but the wind tossed my desperate call back in my face. Perhaps he had walked toward the ocean, I thought, and continued on. My eyes grew used to the darkness, but the wind was so strong, I actually had to struggle to walk forward, my feet slipping and sliding in the soft sand that easily gave way beneath them. I took off my shoes because it felt easier to walk in bare feet. Every once in a while, I screamed Cary's name, but with the ocean roaring

louder, the surf riled up by the approaching storm, waves slamming onto the beach, and the wind now howling around me, I realized he would have to be only a few feet away to hear.

My sari flapped against my legs. Sand flew into my face so often I had to keep my eyes closed, my hands up for protection. My hair whipped around my forehead and temples, and then I felt the first drops of rain, cold, sharp, heavy. Nevertheless, I charged forward over the dune and looked toward the dock. Then, just as I was going to turn back, I saw a small light on the lobster boat. Lowering my head to keep my face protected, I ran as hard and as fast as I could toward the dock. The rain grew heavier, stronger, each drops feeling like a glassful. My hair was soaked to the scalp in seconds and my dress was drenched, the material now clinging to my wet skin.

I reached the dock and hurried onto the boat. It rocked hard in the water, but I managed to get to the cabin door and open it. A gust of wind blew behind me so fiercely, I was practically driven into the room. I struggled to close the door and then I turned and saw Cary sitting on the bench, his head down. There was a small lantern lit. I leaned against the closed door and caught my breath.

"Cary, are you all right?" I asked. How could he be so lost in his thoughts and not hear the commotion I made arriving? He lifted his head slowly, his eyes catching the glow of the lantern.

"Why did you follow me?" he replied.

"It was all my fault," I said. "I'm sorry. I didn't mean to get you into trouble."

"It's not your fault," he said bitterly. "I don't do anything I don't want to do. You're right about him. He's narrow-minded and stupid and cruel."

"You're just very angry right now, Cary. You don't mean those things. He's still your father," I said, although I was pretty sure I meant those things.

"How can you ask me to forgive him? He practically called you the devil's own daughter!"

"It doesn't matter what he calls me or what he thinks about me," I said. "He's not my father. He's yours."

Cary shook his head in confusion. He looked like a little boy, overwhelmed by the events that raged around him.

"I'm not going to live in his home forever, Cary. I don't need his blessing or approval. Don't worry about me," I said.

"Well, he's got no right. He can't call someone else evil. He's not special just because he reads the Bible at dinner and talks about sin and redemption all the time. I'm not going to forgive him and I'm not going to work with him. I don't care. I'll leave and get a job on my own working for some other fisherman, if I want. Or maybe, I'll just find a boat-building company and take a job there," he vowed.

"You're just upset, Cary. You can't leave your family. They need you more than ever now, especially your mother and May."

He shook his head and looked down. I went to him and sat beside him on the bench. When I put my hand on his shoulder, he raised his head slowly and turned to me, his eyes full of pain and sadness.

"What about you? You don't need me any longer, now that you have your work with Kenneth and your new friend, is that it?"

"Of course not," I said. "I need you very much."

"Really?"

"Yes. I'm just helping Kenneth with his most important art project. It's not anything more," I said. "And as for friends, you're the best friend I have right now."

His eyes warmed and his lips softened.

"You mean that?"

"Yes, I do. I mean it," I said firmly. His smile

widened. He stared at me a moment and then he looked very concerned.

"You're soaked to the skin. Look at you."

As soon as he mentioned it, I felt the cold and shuddered. Then I laughed at how I looked: the strands of my hair pasted together, the sari full of sand.

"I guess I'm not really dressed for the weather," I said. The rain was pounding the roof of the cabin now and the boat continued to rock. "Is it supposed to be a bad storm?"

"No, but it will be like this for a while," he said and hurried to light the kerosene heater. Then he opened the closet and pulled out some towels. "It might even be an all-nighter. There's not much here in the way of clothing," he said. "But I do have this raincoat."

"I remember putting it on right after you rescued me from Adam Jackson's clutches," I said smiling.

"Yes."

"And here you are, rescuing me again," I said.

"You should have turned back when it started to pour."

"I was worried about you," I said. We stared at each other for a moment.

"Your sari is pretty sorry right now," he said smiling. I laughed and rose to unwind it, pausing when I realized I had taken Holly's advice and worn nothing underneath. Cary gazed at me. His eyes were so full of love and desire, he made my heart pound. I kept my gaze fixed on his and continued to unwrap the garment until I was naked, the lantern flickering the shadows over me. Cary lost his breath for a minute and then he thrust a towel at me.

"Dry yourself off before you get pneumonia," he advised.

I took the towel and scrubbed my stomach and legs and then the rest of me while Cary turned up the heater. He gathered up the sari.

"This isn't going to dry so fast," he said. "It's really soaked through and covered with streaks of grime." He draped it beside the heater and turned back to me.

I had the towel wrapped around myself, but I still shivered. Cary hurried to get the raincoat over me and then he pulled out a rolled up thin mattress and untied it, spreading it out on the floor near the heater. The rain continued to beat a drum roll over the sides of the cabin and the roof, drops zigzagging down the windows. Just the sound made me shiver. Cary stripped off his shirt.

"Here," he said. "Put this on too."

"But aren't you going to get cold?" I asked.

"Don't you remember? I don't get cold," he said smiling. I took the shirt from him and slipped it on. Then I lowered myself to the mattress and rubbed my hands together in front of the heater. Now that I was dry, I began to feel a bit cozy and my shivering stopped. Cary stood, staring down at me, the light from the lantern glittering on his chest and shoulders.

"I was just getting into that meditating, too," he said, going to his knees beside me. His polished smile shone again.

I laughed and he reached past me to take some empty sacks out of a cabinet near the bench. He crunched them together to form something of a pillow for both of us. He patted it and lay back, his hands behind his head, gazing up at the ceiling. The rain thumped, but the wind seemed to die down a bit so that the boat rocked less.

"Maybe you and I can just get a boat like this and live in it," he said.

"Oh sure. I'll break into my piggy bank tomorrow," I said and sprawled out beside him.

"No, really," he said turning. "Why can't we do something like that? I could find a job and make enough to do payments on an old boat. It doesn't have to be seaworthy, just liveable."

"Cary, I'm not exactly legally on my own yet," I pointed out. "Do you think Grandma Olivia would permit us to live like that within her precious world? Or your father?"

"I don't care. We'll defy them all. We'll just run off and get married."

"What?" I started to laugh, but saw he was serious. "I'm not going to start life the way my mother did," I said. "I'm not going to be impulsive and then regret it every day and make everyone else's life miserable."

"Is that what she did?"

"Yes. She made my step-father hate himself, hate what he was doing, hate his family. The more unhappy she was, the more unhappy he became. And then we all suffered."

"I'd work myself to the bone to make you happy, Melody," he said. His green eyes were soft and luminous in the dim light of the small lantern.

"Sometimes, you can't help what happens around you, and then you only feel guilty and hate yourself, Cary. Let's not be foolish. Let's be smarter than our parents, okay?"

He nodded.

"As long as you promise not to run off and marry the first rich man who proposes to you," he said.

"I would never do that," I said. "I want much more than a hefty bank account."

He laughed, and then looked serious again, his eyes burning with such love that the stretch of silence between us began to palpitate with sensuality. He kissed my right cheek and then my left before he cupped my head so he could tip it at an angle that made his next kiss a kiss on my lips, intense enough to take my breath away.

He leaned over me and then pressed his lips to my wet hair.

"Melody," he whispered as if my name were a prayer. His lips were at my ear. "Melody."

He was doing exactly what I dreamed Kenneth would do. But this wasn't Kenneth. It was Cary who loved me, Cary who made my body respond quickly.

The tingling in my body became long, overwhelming waves of deep passion that filled my thighs and made me moan through my slightly opened mouth. He caught my breath between his own lips and kissed me again, his hands finding my breasts, the thumbs rolling over my nipples.

Above us the thunder crashed, and through the window I could see lightning crackle. The towel I had wrapped around my waist came apart. I closed my eyes and lay back as he moved his mouth down over my lips, over my chin, to my neck and then my breasts. I heard him fumbling with his pants.

"Cary—"

"I'm ready this time," he whispered. "You don't have to worry about getting pregnant."

My eyes snapped open.

"Cary, no."

"I love you, Melody, completely, fully."

Was this going to happen? Would I let it happen? The dark voice of my heavy conscience began to warn me, but all I could see was Uncle Jacob's face of displeasure smeared into one giant blob with huge, hostile eyes. It was as if he were the voice of my conscience now and that was a voice I wanted to defy, to despise.

I am not evil. I am not the devil's own daughter. There is nothing bad in my blood and my mother's sins are not my sins, I fired back in my thoughts.

Cary and I were doing exactly what Uncle Jacob had forbidden, but who was he to forbid anything? What Cary and I felt for each other at this moment was pure and good, I cried. I will not feel guilty for loving him.

I felt him against me, throbbing, lifting me gently, kissing me with lips so hot they drove away even the thought of a chill. And then he was there, pressing forward. The sharp, short pain I felt frightened me for an instant and then that passed and was replaced with a sensation so thrilling it vibrated throughout my body. Soon we were both clinging to each other with a passionate desperation that pressed me back to the border between consciousness and unconsciousness. I rose and fell with the waves that lifted the boat beneath us. The storm that raged died away and was replaced by a blazing sun inside me. We quivered against each other, both of us exploding, our sex sweetening our lips.

"I want to be one with you forever and ever," he pledged as we reached the end and eased our bodies, folding softly into each other's arms, our breaths still heavy, our hearts still pounding. We lay there, waiting for it to all to subside. I kept my eyes closed and after another few minutes, I heard him move away and start to dress himself.

When I opened my eyes, I felt as if I had just wakened from a dream. Cary had his back to me. I watched him a while before wrapping the towel around myself again and curling up on the mattress. He took the raincoat and put it over me for a blanket, kissing me softly on the cheek. Then he went to the door and looked out.

"It's still coming down pretty hard out there," he said.

"We should go back. They'll wonder where we are."

"I don't care. Let them. Let him," he corrected. He closed the door and returned to my side, brushing my hair back and gazing down at me. "I love you, Melody. I feel I am truly free when I am with you. I am not afraid of saying anything, telling you anything, revealing anything to you."

"I'm glad, Cary. Trust is the most important part of loving someone."

"Then you do love me, too?" he fished.

"I do," I said, convinced it was so. "Yes."

He smiled.

"Then nothing that happens matters. Nothing he can say, nothing anyone can say matters. I can say good-bye to nightmares, to dreary days and dreary, lonely nights. We'll be together forever now, won't we?" he asked.

I started to nod, but stopped. After all I had been through, I was afraid to let too much sunshine come into the shadows of my heart.

"Let's take it a day at a time, Cary. When promises get too big, they have a way of turning into great disappointments."

"I'm not afraid to make a big promise," he said, smiling. He lay beside me and put his arm under my head so I could lie in the softness. He stroked my hair and we were both silent for a long while. The movement of the boat became softer, undulating, hypnotizing. I felt as if I were in a big cradle being rocked.

"Love me half as much as I love you and we'll be all right," I heard Cary say.

It was the last thing I heard before I fell asleep.

We were lucky it was Sunday, for neither Cary nor I woke with the light of morning until the sunshine blazed through the window and wiped over our faces to wash away dreams and sleep. If it had been a weekday, Uncle Jacob would have come through the door before our eyelids had opened and he would have discovered us wrapped in each other's arms, asleep, me still half naked, with only a towel and Cary's shirt to cover me.

I stirred first and then Cary blinked, closed his eyes, ground the sleep from them, and sat up, a look of confusion on his face. We gazed at each other.

"It's morning," he said as if he had made a most wondrous discovery. The look of fear on my face wiped the stunned expression from his. He shot up, gazed around a moment, and then scooped up my dress. "It's not completely dry."

"It's all right. I have to put something on," I said.

He handed it to me and I began to wrap it around my body quickly while he put on his shirt and straightened up the cabin. I put on my shoes and he put his on, too. When he opened the door, the glitter of the morning light on the sand made us both squint.

"What are we going to tell them, Cary?" I asked.

"The truth. We got trapped by the storm and slept in the boat," he replied. "And if he says one nasty thing about it, I swear I will leave for good," he vowed.

My heart thumped like the slow drumbeat of a military funeral march as we made our way over the dunes to the house. I just hoped Uncle Jacob wasn't waiting by the door. When we arrived, we paused, looked at each other, and then Cary turned the knob. To our surprise, it was locked.

"Why did he do that?" I asked.

"He just wanted us to ring the bell so he would know exactly when we came back," Cary said. "That way Ma would wake up too." He shook his head and then smiled. "Follow me," he said and we walked around the house, where there was a ladder lying beside the wall. Cary lifted it carefully and gently laid it against the house just under my bedroom window.

"What if he locked the windows, too, Cary?"

"The window in Laura's room doesn't lock," he said. "It broke a long time ago and we never fixed it. I'll go up first and get it open," he added and started up the ladder. When he reached the window, he opened it gently, smiled down at me, and then came back down the ladder.

"Why didn't you go in?"

"You go first. I want to be sure you climb up all right," he said, stepping back.

I gazed around. It was very early, so there were no

215

other people or cars about. Surely, they might suspect burglars if they saw us, I thought. I looked up the ladder at the open window and shook my head in amazement.

"I can't believe we have to do this," I said, but I started up the ladder slowly. I trembled a few times, but I made it up to the window sill and climbed in, Cary right behind me. He closed the window softly, indicating we should be quiet. Then he went to the door and peered out.

"They're still asleep," he whispered. Then he leaned forward to kiss me and slipped out of my room.

After I got out of the damp sari and into a nightgown, I crawled into bed and fell asleep again, not waking until I heard Uncle Jacob shouting in the hall, complaining about our getting into the house through a window. Obviously he had gone out and seen the ladder still leaning against the house.

"Like common thieves, Sara. They used the ladder and broke into the house. Like thieves in the night!"

"Shh, Jacob. Let them sleep," I heard her say.

"Let them sleep? Where were they? How dare they climb up a ladder to get into the house?"

"You locked them out, Jacob," she reminded him. "Now hush up," she said sharply.

I heard him mumble loudly and then stomp noisily down the stairs. Not ten minutes later, there was a gentle knock on my door and Aunt Sara entered.

"Melody?" she said. "Are you asleep?"

I turned to face her.

"No, Aunt Sara. I'm sorry about climbing up a ladder and through a window, but we couldn't get into the house without waking everyone otherwise," I said.

She nodded, but looked dreadfully sad.

"Where were you?"

"We got caught in the storm and spent the night in

the lobster boat," I said. It was the truth, albeit not all of it.

"What were you doing last night when we came back from the Wilson's?" she asked.

I explained meditation the best I could and apologized if I had caused any trouble. I emphasized that it wasn't Cary's fault.

"Laura never did anything like that," she said, shaking her head woefully.

"She might have if she had lived to learn more about it," I said and Aunt Sara nodded, pleased with that thought.

"Yes, that's true. She might have," she said. "She might even have worn that dress, just for fun once. Yes," she said. Her face brightened. "Well, do you think you'll be up and about soon? We do have the brunch at Olivia's today."

"I don't feel up to it this morning, Aunt Sara. Please give Grandma Olivia my apologies," I said.

"Oh dear. I just hate when we have to do that. Olivia gets so upset. What will I tell Jacob? He'll just get even more riled," she moaned.

"If he has to know, tell him I'm having cramps," I said.

"Cramps?"

"Time of the month," I said but shifted my eyes quickly so she couldn't see I was lying.

"Oh." She brought her hand to her mouth. "I see. Well, will you be all right by yourself?"

"I'll be fine as long as I can rest a while, Aunt Sara."

"Yes, yes. It can be debilitating," she said. "I'll tell him. I'll look in on you before we go," she added and left.

I just hated lying, especially to Aunt Sara, but I could see that this time it was the better thing to do. It got her off the hook as well.

I was still in bed when Cary came by, knocked softly, and peeked through the opened door.

217

"Hi," he said smiling.

"Hi. What's happening?"

"Nothing. I told Dad we got caught in the storm. I guess you had already told Ma. He didn't say anything about it, but he was fit to be tied. I've never seen his face so red or his eyes bulge with so much frustration. Glad you missed it," he added. "You're not going to the brunch?"

I shook my head.

"I heard Ma tell Dad it was woman trouble. First time I ever wished I was a girl too," he said and I laughed. "I'll see you later. If I'm still alive," he added and pretended he was in a noose and being hanged.

"Stop it!" I said laughing. He threw me a kiss and backed out.

Aunt Sara stopped by as she had promised and I pretended to be asleep. She stood by the bed a long moment. I felt her hand on my forehead and then I heard her sigh before she turned to leave.

When the house was deadly quiet, I rose, showered and dressed, and went down to make myself some hot chocolate. A little before eleven, I heard the muffled beep of Holly Brooks's car horn. The beep that funny little car made sounded more like a groan.

Holly was wearing a pink, blue, green, and white tie-dyed one piece with a matching headband, and she was driving barefoot. She wore a rope of crystals around her neck. I was wearing the Moldavite, but I couldn't put on the sari because it was still a little damp and needed a good washing. I was dressed in jeans and a sweatshirt with a pair of light pink sneakers and no socks.

"How did it go this morning?" she asked as I got in.

"It worked," I said and she laughed.

"It always does," she said, driving away. "You should have worn the sari this morning."

I explained how I had gotten caught in a storm and it was still wet and full of sand and grime. I didn't want to tell her why I was out in the storm, but she asked and I had to describe the events that led up to Cary's flight and my searching for him.

"Pagan? Devil? Is that what your uncle thinks? I thought I was in Provincetown, not Salem," she added. "You have a rough road to travel here. How did you come to live with these relatives?" she asked. Apparently, Kenneth hadn't told her much about my past, which I found curious.

I described it as quickly as I could and when I finished, she shook her head.

"I'm almost afraid to do your horoscope," she said and then laughed. "I'm sure it's all going to change for you now. You'll see."

When we arrived at Kenneth's, I saw his car was gone. Ulysses came running at the sound of the engine. I couldn't imagine Kenneth leaving him. He never did unless I was there, I thought.

"Where is he?"

"He had to go to Boston," she said, "so it's just the two of us. Do you mind?"

"No," I said, even though I was a little disappointed. I hadn't spent much time just relaxing with Kenneth and I wondered how different he would be away from his studio and his work.

"Besides, it's good to just be around feminine energy from time to time. Masculine energy throws us off. Too much of the other sort of static. Let me lend you something more comfortable to wear on the beach."

I followed her into the house and the bedroom where she had her things unpacked and hanging in Kenneth's closet. She pulled out a frilly, one-piece tie-dyed dress similar to her own.

"Why don't you just throw this on for now? I've almost got our picnic all packed, just need to throw in a few last-minute things," she said. She went out to finishing packing while I changed.

I noticed that the bed was still unmade, the blanket twisted, the pillows practically on top of each other. Holly's bowl for incense was on the nightstand, full of ashes. Like Kenneth, Holly was obviously not much of a housekeeper, I thought.

"Now that's much better," she said when I came out wearing her dress. I was barefoot, too. "Wait," she said and ran into the bedroom. When she returned, she had a pink, blue, and white headband. "Here, wear this."

I put it on and she clapped.

"Now you're a true guru."

She gave me one of the baskets to carry and we headed out to the beach.

"I have a favorite spot," she said and pointed to a place not far from where I had found the discarded doll. Once there, we spread out a blanket. Holly turned on her tape recorder to play her music and then she assumed the lotus position, instructing me to do the same.

"It takes practice to get good at meditation," she explained. "Someday, you'll be at the point where turmoil can be raging around you, and you'll just close your eyes and tune it all out. Everyone will be amazed and then jealous of your power," she promised. "People who bother you and get under your skin will become meaningless."

After what had occurred the night before, what she was promising sounded wonderful. I listened to her instructions and did what she said. The two of us sitting in the lotus position on the beach and facing the ocean must have made quite a sight. We were so far away from the tourists however, there was little chance of anyone discovering us. I understood why she cherished coming here.

"There are places in the world that have more spiritual energy than others," she said, "and Kenneth's beach is one of them."

After we practiced our meditation, Holly took out her charts and books and asked me questions, beginning with all I knew about my date of birth. It happened that I had been told the actual time of day I was born, which meant she could give me an even more detailed reading. She plotted out the location, the sun and the moon at the time, and began to work on my horoscope.

"Gemini is in the constellation of the planet Mercury which absorbs an energy that appears to be a compound of all other planets. It's why he is known as the messenger of the Gods," she said. She reached into her basket. "Now that I've gotten to know you better, I want you to have this."

She handed me a ring with an emerald set in silver.

"What is it?"

"Emerald, the mystical gem of Gemini, which is the talisman stone."

"Oh, I can't take another thing from you."

"Of course you can. It's good karma for me to give something spiritual to you. The emerald," she continued, "is a variety of beryl. It strengthens the heart, liver, kidneys, immune system, and nervous system. It's a tonic for the body, mind, and spirit. It enhances dreams and deeper spiritual insight as well as meditative powers."

"It does all that?" I asked staring at the ring on my finger.

"It does," she said firmly. She returned to her charts and then looked up at me and began my horoscope.

"You have a sensitive, active mind. Emotionally you are quite affectionate, generous, and impulsive. You have great powers of observation and are able to grasp facts quicker than the average individual.

"You are somewhat of a dreamer and when those dreams are shattered you are deeply disillusioned and hurt. You can be too romantic. You are sensitive and affectionate as a lover. Your imagination plays an important role in your love life." She paused and looked up. "Does that sound accurate?"

I shrugged.

"I suppose," I said. I guess I was something of a dreamer. She looked at her chart again.

"You have a mind of your own and want independence, so be careful whom you choose as a lover and especially whom you choose to marry."

"What if I choose another Gemini?" I asked. She smiled and nodded.

"I thought you would ask that." She studied her charts, made some notes, and looked up. I held my breath. "You'd be compatible because you would understand each other. The sexual demands and needs would be mutual. I have to know his date of birth, time, and so on, because the one exception to all this would occur if one or the other has Scorpio rising at the time of birth. You didn't."

"What would happen?" I asked, breathless.

"The demands of Scorpio would prove to be too much for the mercurial Gemini nature. Your approach to sex is more spiritual. The Scorpio influence is more physical. Just wouldn't work," she concluded.

"I don't think that's true for us then," I said quickly, too quickly. Her eyes widened.

"Oh?"

I blushed and turned away.

"Somehow, I have the feeling you already know you could be compatible, is that it?"

I nodded.

"The first time you made love?" she asked and I nodded again.

"I remember my first time, although it seems like one of my previous lives by now," she added with a laugh. I looked up with interest. "It's all so new and surprising, you expect it will be that way all the time, but often it's not," she warned. "Even with the same man."

"How many men have you—"

She laughed.

"Let's not talk about me. You think you're head over heels in love, is that it?"

"Yes."

"Maybe you are; maybe you're just discovering love itself," she said. "Compassion for each other is so important," she continued. "That's why I made the point about Scorpio. When one lover is more self-centered than the other, when all he or she wants is to satisfy himself or herself, it becomes something different and soon leads to unhappiness. Find a man who cares for you more than he cares for himself and you've found love.

"But, alas," she said, gazing at the ocean again, "that can be as hard to find as a drop of water after it's been spilled in the ocean."

"You never did?" I asked.

"Once, but unfortunately he died young. That was how Kenneth and I met. He and Brad, my lover, were roommates in college."

"Oh. Kenneth never told me. Actually, he hasn't told me all that much about his past."

She smiled.

"Don't be put off by that. Kenneth lives in the moment, in his art. I've done his horoscope. He'll never change, Melody. Events in his past mirrored the movement of the sun and the moon and produced the dramatic disappointments. They're sewn forever into his being and into his future.

"That's why he and I get along so well. He knows I won't make any demands, won't stay long. I come and go like . . . a cloud," she said, looking at the sky.

"Can't he live like a normal person ever?" I asked, still unable to let go of the dream that Kenneth just might have feelings for me. Though in my heart of hearts, I knew whatever feelings he had would never be able to compare to Cary's love for me.

"Kenneth? Kenneth Childs is one man who is terrified of becoming normal in the sense you mean. Responsibilities, obligations, and the guilt that follows on their heels is very frightening to a true, pure artist. God forbid he had to do something for the house or family just when he was about to begin his work. In the end he would only hate his own wife and children. He doesn't want to be involved in anything or with anyone that will lead to something permanent, something demanding his time and energy. His only commitment is to his art, because it's safe. If he fails, he only fails himself," she concluded.

Then maybe Kenneth is my father after all, I thought, and what Holly was telling me about him was the reason why he would lie or avoid the truth. Would I ever really know the truth?

"What did you mean by Kenneth's dramatic disappointments?" I asked.

"I really don't have a right to talk about it, Melody," Holly said. "Kenneth's memories of happiness and sadness are his possessions. He has to be the one to share them with others."

"It has to do with my mother," I said. "I know it does."

She just held her soft smile.

"Sometimes, I gaze into the stars and I see things I know I must not touch, must not disturb, must not reveal. Sometimes, Melody, it takes more strength to leave a discovery where you found it."

"Is that what Kenneth did?" I shot back at her.

Her smile faded a bit.

"It's something we all do, Melody, sometime, at some place in our lives. Hungry?" she asked, changing the topic.

"Yes," I said. After all, I had skipped breakfast.

As we ate, Holly told me more about her own past, about Kenneth's college roommate, Brad, and how much they had been in love. She read me some of her favorite poetry and she talked more about the power of her crystals. We took a walk on the beach, searching for sea shells, and then sunbathed in the afternoon sun. For one day, at least, I felt as if I had an older sister who would listen to my deeper thoughts and fears and who wasn't afraid to tell me about some of her own.

The sun began to show its descent toward the horizon and I thought I should probably head home soon. The family had surely returned from Grandma Olivia's by now. I changed back into my own clothes and Holly drove me home. I didn't see the car and the truck was still in front. The house looked dark, too.

"It doesn't look as if they've come back yet," Holly said.

"They would have had to by now."

"Maybe they went some place else. Your uncle might have taken his family for a Sunday drive," Holly suggested.

"Not likely," I said. "Not in the mood he was in." I got out. "Thanks for a wonderful day. I guess I'll see you tomorrow when Kenneth brings me to work."

"Okay. Watch that sunset. You'll feel a lot of good energy," she said and drove off. When I entered the house, I found it empty, dark. In the kitchen, my empty mug was right where I had left it.

Upstairs I found everything quiet and just as deserted. Why weren't they back yet? I went into my room, showered, put lotion on my browned face and shoulders, and then dressed again. Still, I heard no one in the house. I descended the stairs, thought for a moment, and then stepped outside and decided I would sit and wait facing the road. Nearly another hour passed.

Finally, I saw the Logans' car come around the turn

225

and head toward the house. I stood up in anticipation, but was surprised to see Cary driving, Aunt Sara in the front seat, and May in the rear. Where was Uncle Jacob?

They drove in and parked. I walked toward the car as Cary got out, his face drenched in worry and sadness. Aunt Sara had apparently been crying.

"What's going on? Where's your father?" I asked.

"He . . . had chest pains at Grandma Olivia's," Cary said, "so we had to rush him to the hospital. The doctors said he had a heart attack."

"Oh no! Is he—"

"He's still alive, but he's critical," Cary said. "We were there most of the day."

I bit down on my lower lip and then rushed to help Aunt Sara go to the house.

"I'm all right," she said. "We've got to stay strong. No one's really eaten all day. See to May," she said. "I'll fix us some dinner."

"Oh no, Aunt Sara. Let me do it."

"No, no. I have to do it. I always do it. See to May," she said.

May looked like a small flower, wilted, her little face pale, her eyes wide and full of fear. I embraced her and we all went into the house. At the stairway, Cary turned to me, his eyes wet with tears.

"He's going to die," he said. "I know he is."

"No, Cary. Don't say that."

"I did it to him, you know."

I shook my head.

"Yes, it was my fault. I drove him away just the way I drove Laura and they both left angry at me."

"No," I insisted, but he turned and started up the stairs to his attic hideaway, his shoulders slumped, his head down, drowning in his own guilt.

May clung to me harder. Her little hands moved like small sparrows seeking answers and all I could do was keep telling her it would be all right. Everything would be all right.

My hands trembled like lips caught in lies as I signed.

If there was any place on earth where everything wouldn't be all right, it was in this house, I thought, and took her back with me to the kitchen to help Aunt Sara face another night of agony and loneliness.

11
&

Last Confession

Aunt Sara had prepared a meat loaf for us before she left for the brunch at Grandma Olivia's. She moved about the kitchen like a robot, not really looking at things. Her eyes resembled two glass orbs, lifeless on the outside with no light of their own, merely reflecting what was in front of her. I imagined that inside, her thoughts were lightning bugs zigzagging from one end of her head to the other, tracing her fears, anxieties, and sorrow across the black wall of her despair.

May set the table and I worked on the mashed potatoes while Aunt Sara checked her meat loaf and prepared some steamed vegetables. We all kept busy, avoiding each other, and taking solace in our labors.

"We were just sitting around talking," she suddenly began as if she had heard me ask what had happened. "Everyone was having a good time. The food was as delicious as ever and Samuel was very jolly, I thought. Olivia had invited Congressman Dunlap and his wife Joan. We were all having such a good time."

She paused to look at me.

"Olivia was very concerned about you. She asked me dozens of questions, wanting to know how you were, what you had been doing, how well you were getting along at your job. She was very disappointed about your not coming. I think Samuel was even more disappointed. The judge kept asking about you, too. Finally, Congressman Dunlap burst out with, 'Who is this young lady everyone is so interested in? I have to meet her.'

"Everyone laughed. Even Jacob."

"What about Cary?" I asked.

"Oh, he had taken May down to the beach. They weren't far off."

She sighed deeply and continued to prepare dinner, talking as she went to the stove.

"They got into a political discussion and the judge had an argument with Congressman Dunlap about taxes. They were getting pretty riled up. No one noticed Jacob rubbing his chest and taking deep breaths until suddenly—" She paused and looked at the wall as if the scene were being projected onto it. "Suddenly, he struggled to his feet, made a strange guttural sound, and fell forward on the grass. The congressman was the first at his side. He had been in the army and had some training in CPR. Jacob complained about pressure on his chest and pain up his arm to his shoulder. The congressman said it looked like a heart attack and we should get an ambulance quickly.

"I was no good to anyone. I couldn't move. My legs turned right to butter. All I could do was hold onto the chair and cry.

"But Olivia. You should have seen her, Melody," she said with a wide smile of appreciation and admiration on her lips. "She stood up and like a general, coolly dictated commands," Aunt Sara said and then demonstrated, pointing this way and that.

"Samuel, go make the phone call. Nelson, go get a

pillow and a few blankets from the maid. She even told the congressman's wife to pour some water for Jacob. In minutes, everyone was moving about, doing something. Then she turned to me," Aunt Sara said, imitating Grandma Olivia's expression.

"'Sara, get a grip on yourself. Go get the children immediately,' she ordered, and I tell you when she turned her eyes on me, I felt my buttery legs harden into stone and my spinal cord turn to steel. I nodded and went down to the beach.

"Cary was devastated. He couldn't believe his father was—had collapsed. Jacob's been such a tower of strength. He's never been sick, never missed a day's work, and he never complains about muscle aches and pains, no matter how hard he works and how miserable the weather. I've seen him come home with his face blue from cold, but he never so much as moaned.

"When the ambulance arrived, Olivia hovered over the paramedics making sure they did everything as quickly and efficiently as possible. Then she organized us into two cars and we followed the ambulance to the hospital. Cary drove our car. When we arrived, she went to the emergency room doctor immediately and got him to go see to Jacob. He reported to her before he reported to anyone else. It seemed like only minutes before they had a heart specialist beside Jacob and Jacob in the CCU. I never saw Olivia any stronger. She inspired me and I kept myself together.

"After a few hours, she came to us and said we should go home and get some rest. There was nothing more to do but wait to see how his condition developed. All the while I kept thinking, if Olivia, who is Jacob's mother, can be so strong, I have to be strong, too. So I kept my tears back and did what she said.

"Cary worries me now," she continued. "He didn't say a word until he spoke to you."

"He'll be fine, Aunt Sara," I promised, even though

I didn't know if I had any right to make such assurances. I certainly had no track record of success when it came to predictions about people.

She sighed again and returned to the meat loaf.

"Everything's ready," she declared. "Can you get Cary, Melody?"

"Of course, Aunt Sara."

I went to the stairway and called him, but he didn't respond, so I went upstairs to get him. I called him again from the bottom of the attic ladder and still he didn't answer me. When I looked in the attic room, I found him sitting and staring at a model of a lobster boat.

"Cary, dinner's ready," I said. "Your mother wants you to come down. She needs you, Cary."

"I made this when I was only seven years old," he said, staring down at the model. "Dad was really surprised at how well it came out. For a while we kept it downstairs on the mantle so Dad could show it to his friends. He wasn't always the way he is now. When I first started to go out on the boat with him, we were more like brothers than father and son. He taught me everything about the boat and the business and said I was his good luck charm. We had much better catches in those days.

"After Laura's death everything changed. Sometimes I think we all died with her," he said, "in different ways, I guess. Dad kept too much of it inside him, eating away. Then . . . I became a disappointment to him."

"You're not a disappointment to anyone, Cary. Anyone who says that just doesn't know. You've been a better son than any boy I ever met, but you are your own person and it's not a sin for you to want things that are different from your father's desires. Deep inside himself, your father knows that. You had nothing to do with this. I'm sure," I said.

He raised his shoulders slowly and turned.

"But after last night . . . He hasn't struck me for years," he said.

"And he shouldn't have last night. I'm sorry, Cary. I don't mean to say anything bad about him, now, of all times, but he was wrong and I think he realized that right away and that's what bothered him the most. You have to be strong for your mother, Cary, and for May. She's so dependent upon us and especially you. She's like someone who's fallen overboard and is barely floating on a tiny raft of hope. You know how much harder it is for her."

He nodded.

"Yes. You're right, of course."

"You've got to be as strong as your father has been for this family," I said and he straightened up even more. "Now come on down and eat something," I ordered.

He smiled.

"Aye, aye, Captain," he said, saluting. He rose and followed me down the ladder and into the dining room. When Aunt Sara saw him, she brightened a bit. Serving the meal helped her keep herself together.

"We'll need a special reading tonight," she told him when we all sat at the table. He nodded and opened the Bible.

" 'The Lord is my shepherd,' " he began, and read the psalm so beautifully, it brought tears to my eyes.

None of us had much of an appetite, but even May saw how important it was to eat as much as she could to please Aunt Sara. After dinner, we all helped with the cleanup and then Cary announced he would drive us all to the hospital.

"Oh dear," Aunt Sara said. "Maybe I should change into something fresh, and maybe May should put on—"

"None of that matters, Ma," Cary said with authority. "We're only there to be at Dad's bedside and give him comfort."

She nodded. Cary had already taken the reins. He was at the helm and in control of our actions and direction. We got into the car and he drove us to the hospital, no one saying much until we arrived.

The cardiac-care unit permitted only immediate family visits, for five minutes every hour on the hour. Cary decided May should wait in the lounge with me while he and Aunt Sara went in to see how Uncle Jacob was doing.

Grandma Olivia and Grandpa Samuel had gone home for the night and left orders for the doctor to call them if there were any dramatic changes. I kept May amused and answered her questions about the hospital, people we saw working, and as much as I knew about heart attacks. One of Papa George's friends had died of a heart attack two years before and I recalled some of the details about blocked arteries, destroyed muscle, water in his lungs.

I didn't tell May any gruesome details, but her eyes were dark with worry and fear when I explained how the heart worked. She was closed up so tightly in her silent world, and now all this tightened the doors and windows, bringing her more darkness. A touch, a smile, constant signing and embraces helped bring back some light to her face, but in the pauses, the silence grew more deafening and drove her down deeper and deeper into her own loneliness.

We feel like strangers to each other so often in our lives, I thought. It's hard enough as it is for most people to explain, express, and communicate their feelings, fears, and dreams to each other. May was born with a disadvantage and given another obstacle to overcome. It was at times like these when that handicap would announce itself most loudly and make the rest of us feel even more frustrated trying to help her and, therefore, help ourselves.

When Cary and Aunt Sara came out, they both looked glum. Aunt Sara was dabbing her eyes with a

233

handkerchief. Cary looked pale. Even his lips had lost most of their color. He guided his mother to the settee and then he turned to me.

"It's hard seeing him hooked up to oxygen and all those heart monitors clicking away. He looks so small in that bed—he looks like a corpse," he blurted and his tears broke free to burn down his cheeks. May started to cry and move her hands about desperately for news.

Cary signed to her that Uncle Jacob was still sick but getting better and told her to go sit with their mother. She did so and Aunt Sara embraced her. The two rocked gently on the settee. Cary turned back to me.

"He can talk," he said. "Just barely whisper, but he can talk. Just before we left, he asked me about you and I told him you were out here."

"He asked about me?"

"Yes. Then he said—" Cary paused, looked back at his mother and then back at me. "Then he said he wanted you to go in to see him alone."

"What?"

"That's what he said, Melody. I told the head nurse and she said to wait fifteen minutes and then send you in to see him. She said it would be all right. I told her you were my sister," he said.

"Why does he want to see me?" It felt like a hand of ice was stroking the back of my neck and then moving down my spine.

"He thinks he's going to die tonight," he said, "and he wants to tell you something before he does," Cary replied, taking a deep breath before going to sit with his mother and sister.

I felt as if I had swallowed a dozen goldfish and they were all flopping about in my stomach. Cary checked his watch and looked at me across the small lobby. It seemed he was looking at me across a chasm so wide and deep we could never reach each other again.

I sat back. Of all people for Uncle Jacob to want to see. Me! Maybe he wanted to lay some curse on me or blame me for his condition. Maybe he wanted me to promise to leave his house for good. Or maybe, maybe one of those deeply buried secrets was about to rear its ugly head.

I took deep breaths. May gazed at me with her eyes big, the expression on her face mixed fear and hope. Aunt Sara bit down on her lower lip and nodded to unheard voices. Cary stared ahead. I vaguely heard the voices of other people around us and heard the footsteps of nurses and technicians. My heart pounded harder with every passing minute.

And then Cary gazed at his watch again and looked up at me.

"It's time," he said. "Go on. They'll show you where he is," he added.

I didn't think I could stand, but I did. I gazed at Aunt Sara, who looked up at me with curiosity and confusion, and yet with a prayer on her lips and in her eyes. I smiled at her and at May and then I started toward the door to the cardiac-care unit, my legs and feet floating over the hard tiled floor. I opened the door and entered the large room with the circular nurses' station in the center, a bank of monitors reporting the heartbeats of the patients around them. Everyone looked efficient and serious, emphasizing the critical care and the possibility of life-and-death choices that were made there each and every day.

I sucked in my breath and started across the room, passing elderly patients, until the head nurse greeted me.

"Melody Logan?" she asked with a brief smile.

"Yes, ma'am."

"Right this way," she said and nodded toward the last bed on the right where Uncle Jacob, hooked to his life-saving machinery and his monitors lay waiting, inches from death's grasp. Cary was right about him, he did resemble a corpse, pallid, small, withered.

I looked at the nurse.

"You can stay here a few minutes and see if he wakes. Otherwise, come back later, on the hour," she suggested. She checked the drip in his I.V. bag and then walked back to the nurse's station. Timidly, I drew closer to Uncle Jacob's bed and gazed down at him. The beep, beep, beep of the monitors seemed to mirror my own drumming heart.

Half of me wanted him to remain asleep, while the other half couldn't contain my curiosity. I was tempted to flee and also tempted to touch his hand to see if he would waken. His eyelids trembled and I saw his lips writhe and then stiffen.

"Uncle Jacob," I said, or at least, I thought I did. Maybe I had just thought it. He didn't acknowledge me. "Uncle Jacob?" I said a little louder.

His eyelids fluttered and then opened. He turned slowly and looked at me. There were oxygen tubes in his nostrils and tiny beads of sweat had broken out on his brow. I took a cloth from the table beside the bed and wiped his forehead. As I did so, he mouthed my name.

I leaned in because he was barely whispering.

"Melody . . . come closer," he said. I looked back at the nurses' station and then brought my face as close to his as I could.

"What is it, Uncle Jacob? You should just rest, get better."

He shook his head.

"Won't get better," he said. He swallowed, the effort causing him to close his eyes. His Adam's apple strained against his skin and bobbed. Then he opened his eyes again. "My fault," he said. "It was my fault."

"What was your fault, Uncle Jacob?"

"Haille."

"My mother? I don't understand, Uncle Jacob. What are you saying?"

"Haille . . . When I was a young boy . . . she was barely thirteen but I . . . did a terrible thing . . . made her do it. She never told, but it was my fault . . . my fault she became what she became and we had all the family trouble."

I stared at him. His eyes were watery, dark, the pupils smaller.

Suddenly, he found my hand and squeezed my fingers as hard as he could, which wasn't very hard.

"I didn't mean to be so hard on you, but I feel more responsible," he said after a big breath. He closed his eyes and then opened them quickly. "A sin can last forever, be passed on from mother to daughter, from father to son . . . forever. Be a good woman and end the devil's hold on us all." He swallowed hard and closed his eyes. Then he whispered, "My poor Laura. Poor, poor Laura . . ."

His head fell to the right and the monitor began a long, shrill humming sound. I released his hand and stepped back.

"Stat!" I heard behind me. Two nurses rushed past me and the doctor on duty came across the CCU. I backed away slowly as they all gathered around Uncle Jacob's bed. Electric pads were being placed on his chest.

Someone shouted, *"Clear!"*

I saw Uncle Jacob's body jump and heard the doctor say, "Again, clear!"

I fled the CCU. Cary was waiting in the hallway and I ran into his arms.

"What?" he cried.

"Something's happening to him. I—"

"Dad!" he groaned and charged through the doorway into CCU. I waited a moment and then turned to see Aunt Sara and May standing in the lounge, Aunt

Sara's hand on May's shoulder, both of them gazing at me with the same horrified look in their eyes.

I started to cry. My stomach felt hollow, just the way it had felt when I learned Daddy had been killed in the mining accident. Aunt Sara started to shudder with her own sobs. May's face wrinkled with pain, her moans distorted by her great fear and sadness. I went to both of them and the three of us embraced, held each other, and waited, all of one heart, small and trembling, alone and helpless against the dark cloud encroaching, moving with the wind raging around us.

"He's back!" Cary cried from the doorway. He was laughing through his tears. "It's a resurrection."

We turned and gazed at him. He wiped his cheeks with the back of his hand and took a deep breath.

"Back?" Aunt Sara said.

"What does that mean, Cary?" I asked.

"His heart stopped but they got it started again," he said, "and he's doing okay for now."

"Oh, praise God," Aunt Sara cried. "Praise God." She held on to May and rocked with her on the settee.

I took a deep breath, closed my eyes, and said my own prayer of thanks. When I fled the CCU, I believed I had caused him to have the heart failure for sure. It was the great effort he had made to speak to me.

Cary regained his calm demeanor and strength.

"How about a cup of hot tea, Ma? I can get it from the machine downstairs," he said.

"Yes, thank you, Cary."

"I'll get May a soda. Melody, you want something?"

"I'll come with you," I said and got up. We walked to the elevator. When the door opened, he took my hand and we stepped in and he pressed the button.

"I really thought he was a goner," Cary muttered. "I watched them struggling, but that doctor hung in there and suddenly, the monitor began clicking away again. Everyone cheered. They waited and his pulse built up. It's a miracle," he added. "Don't you think?"

"Yes, Cary."

He nodded, so filled with joy he was beside himself. Then, he remembered I had been in there. As the door of the elevator opened, he turned to me.

"What did he want?"

"I think it was something he wanted only me to know right now, Cary. I don't feel right talking about it. I hope you understand."

"Oh. Sure," he said, although his eyes betrayed his hurt. It wasn't a time for a father to keep secrets from his son. "I understand. It must have been pretty important to him, though. He was willing to chance dying to do it, huh?"

I nodded and we went to the vending machine. We brought Aunt Sara her tea and May her soda and then Cary went to check on Uncle Jacob one final time. He returned to say Aunt Sara could go in with him now and Aunt Sara decided they should take May so she would see Uncle Jacob was still alive.

I waited for them in the lounge, thinking about the things Uncle Jacob had said. He sensed death at his door and felt he had to confess to me. I realized how much blame he had carried in his heart all these years, but I doubted if he was the main cause of any sins Mommy had committed afterward.

"He's stabilized," Cary told me after they emerged from CCU. "Let's go home and get some sleep. We're all exhausted."

I couldn't argue with that. May actually fell asleep in my arms on the way home and Aunt Sara looked as if she would topple herself any moment. Cary helped her out of the car and into the house. She wanted to go to the kitchen to do some final cleanup, but he insisted she go right upstairs and get to bed.

"Dad's going to need you stronger than ever, Ma. You can't run yourself down now," he said with authority. She nodded.

"Yes, yes, you're right, Cary. Thank God we have you. You're my strength now," she said and squeezed his arm. He kissed her and watched her go upstairs, taking May along with her. Then he turned to me.

"What a day, huh?"

I smiled.

"I can think of better ways to spend our time, if that's what you mean," I said. He laughed. It was good to see his face brighten. "But I confess I am tired, too."

"I'll make sure everything's off and put away," he said. "Then I'll stop by to say good night." He leaned over to kiss me on the cheek and walked off.

I hurried upstairs, washed, and dressed for bed, putting on a light blue cotton nightgown. If there was ever a time to practice Holly's meditation, it was now, I thought, and sat in the lotus position on the bed and concentrated. I was so deeply involved, I didn't even hear Cary come up to my door. I felt his hand on my shoulder and opened my eyes.

"Did it work?" he asked. "Your meditating?"

"Yes. I felt the tension drain from my body, just as Holly said."

"I guess I'll have to learn how to do it then," he said.

I unfolded my legs and sat back against the pillows.

"Mind if I stay here with you for a while?" he asked.

"Of course not."

He took off his shoes and sprawled out beside me on the bed, putting his head on my lap. I stroked his hair and he closed his eyes.

"When Laura and I were very little and one of us got scared, we would lie together like this for a while. I

240

think we did it until we were about fourteen or fifteen," he admitted. "It's nice having a safe haven in a storm, whether the storm's in your heart or out there."

"You were lucky to have each other," I said.

He opened his eyes and looked up at me, thinking.

"It must have been difficult for you, growing up alone, away from family."

I smiled.

"I had Papa George and Mama Arlene, as well as Daddy. Sometimes, Mommy was there for me, too."

He nodded, still thoughtful. Then he smiled.

"Sing me one of those fiddle songs, a soft one," he asked. I laughed and then I began, singing one Papa George had taught me. It was really the prayer of a miner's wife, praying her husband would always be safe in the bowels of the earth, and it ended on a happy note because he always came up, smiling through the coal dust.

Singing it reminded me of Daddy and I couldn't help the tears that burned under my eyelids. But Cary didn't notice the crack in my voice. When I looked down at him, I saw he was fast asleep, his chest rising and falling gently. I didn't have the heart to wake him, so I crawled under the blanket and fixed the pillow under his head, too. Then I reached over and turned off the light.

Darkness fell like a heavy blanket. The moon peeked out from between two passing clouds and sent a ray of white light through the window, washing over us both. Then the clouds closed and shut out the illumination. I closed my eyes and in minutes, I was as deeply asleep as Cary.

Hours later, I awoke with a start. For a moment I forgot what had happened. It all came rushing back and I sat up, realizing Cary was no longer beside me. He was at the window, gazing out.

"Cary?"

"Oh," he said turning. "I should have just gone to my room. I didn't mean to wake you."

"You didn't. Are you all right?"

"Yeah. I just woke up and felt a little nervous. I like looking out at the ocean whenever I'm nervous or afraid. I guess that's where I find my meditation. Laura's room always had a better view of the coast than mine. I would either come here or go up to the attic. I'll leave and let you sleep," he said, turning from the window and starting toward the door.

"No, don't leave," I said. He paused.

"I can't stay here all night. Ma wouldn't understand," he said.

"Just stay a little while longer."

"I'll fall asleep again," he threatened.

"I won't let you do that," I said. Something in my voice brought a smile to his face that was so bright, I could see it even in the darkness. He returned to my bed and sprawled out beside me. Then he leaned forward and kissed me gently on the lips. We embraced and kissed again. His hands moved over my shoulders and down my arms. He brought my fingers to his lips and then he put his head against my bosom and moaned. I closed my eyes and drank in the warm feeling that comforted me as much as it must have comforted him.

"I feel guilty thinking about you, wanting you at a time like this," he whispered.

"You mustn't feel that way. If we care for each other, we can't be ashamed of needing each other," I told him, though I was worried that Aunt Sara or May might hear us.

"Oh Melody," he said. "I do care for you, love you, need you more than I will ever need and love anyone."

"Then throw your guilt overboard," I said and he

laughed. He rose, pulled off his shirt, unbuttoned his trousers, and crawled under the cover beside me. We kissed, held each other tightly, and then his hands went under my nightgown until they found my breasts. Our lovemaking was different, more like a dream. We weren't driven by sexual appetite as much as we were by the need to reassure each other. We moved gently, slowly, and when it was over, he slipped away so quietly and smoothly, I wondered if it had actually happened. But his place beside me in my bed was still warm from his body. I ran my hand over it and moaned softly to my pillow.

Then I closed my eyes and didn't open them again until the first light of morning kissed my face.

I was almost afraid to rise, yet I couldn't escape the vivid memory of Uncle Jacob's heart stopping right before my eyes. As I showered and dressed I tried to think of something else, anything else, but still the memory returned. With trembling legs, I started down the stairs. Apparently, everyone else had risen before me. Aunt Sara was already in the kitchen making pancakes and Cary and May were at the table.

"Why didn't anyone wake me?" I asked.

"Oh you wouldn't be sleeping if you didn't need it," Aunt Sara said. I looked at Cary. His face had the shine of polished stone, his eyes luminous with joy.

"I called the hospital. Dad spent a good night and the doctor was already there."

"That's wonderful, Cary."

"He told the nurse to tell me not to bother coming to the hospital and waste my time standing around. He'd rather I take the boat out and check our traps," he said laughing. "I'll do both. Grandma Olivia and Grandpa Samuel are coming by to take Mama over to the hospital. May's going to go to school."

I nodded. Cary apparently had things organized.

"You can go to work as well," he said.

243

"Oh, I should stay and help Aunt Sara."

"Nonsense, dear. I'm fine," she said. "Cary's right."

"Cary is becoming a bit bossy, isn't he?" I asked, fixing my eyes on him.

"He's the man of the house until Jacob's back on his feet," Aunt Sara said. Cary beamed.

"As long as he doesn't get too big for his britches," I remarked and then signed the idea to May, who thought it was very funny.

"Now just a minute," Cary protested. "Let's have a little more respect for the captain of this ship."

"We'll give the captain the respect he deserves, but if he's an ogre, there's always the chance of a mutiny," I countered, and Cary laughed.

It was good to wake up to sunshine and hope and happiness again. I prayed it wouldn't be short lived.

Kenneth had already heard about Uncle Jacob, as had most of the local residents in Provincetown. Like any small town, news traveled fast, but bad news traveled even faster. When Kenneth came to pick me up, I brought him up to date.

"It doesn't surprise me, this heart attack," Kenneth said. "The man was always brooding, grinding away at his insides, even as a teenager. You all right?" he inquired.

"Yes."

"Sara must be a mess."

"She's doing okay," I said. "Cary's been a source of strength."

"Really? Good for him. Are you going to be able to work?" he asked cautiously.

"Yes. It's the best thing, the best way to deal with worry, work it under the sand."

Kenneth laughed.

"That sounds like some beachcomber's wisdom," he remarked and drove on.

We did work hard that week and Kenneth made a great deal of progress, deciding by week's end that he was ready to begin the actual sculpture. Holly did some painting of her own while we worked. By her own description, her work was ethereal, spiritual, abstract, full of bright colors and ghostly shapes. In one painting, the woman she'd painted had stars looking down instead of eyes. Kenneth said she usually sold all of her works in New York at her shop.

Holly was always upbeat and pleasant and fun to be with, which proved refreshing during these troubled times. During my breaks, or if Kenneth finished with me early, Holly and I usually walked along the beach, practiced meditating, talked about crystals and astrology, sunbathed, and dressed in her headbands and saris. One day she decided to repaint her car and I helped her create new images over a pea-greenish yellow exterior. Kenneth thought our work was so far out, Holly might be pulled over on the highway for violating sanity. Everyone laughed. I felt very comfortable being with the two of them, especially with Holly.

During this week Cary had taken over his father's role and actually had some very good days at sea, which he said buoyed Uncle Jacob and helped his recovery. I didn't go back into the CCU with them, but two days after they moved Uncle Jacob to what they called Step Down care, I accompanied the family on a visit. I noticed that Uncle Jacob avoided looking at me the whole time and then, just before we were about to go home, he whispered something to Cary. As we were all leaving the room, Cary asked me to remain.

"My father wants to talk to you privately again," he said. "We'll wait for you in the lobby."

I looked at Uncle Jacob, but he kept his eyes closed and lay back on his pillow. It wasn't until the others left that he opened his eyes. Actually, they snapped open, and he gazed at me with that all-too-familiar look of accusation.

"Cary said you wanted me to stay for a few minutes?" I said, approaching his bed.

"Yes." He looked away, sipped some water, and then turned back to me. "He tells me I asked to see you while I was in the CCU."

"Yes," I said, surprised that he had to be told. "It was only for a few minutes, but—"

"I have no memory of this, but my doctors tell me I could easily have hallucinated and said ridiculous things. You are to disregard anything I might have said under the condition I was in," he ordered. "I hope you haven't gone blabbering any of it to anyone."

"No. I wouldn't do that," I said.

"Not even to Kenneth Childs?" he asked, his eyes shifting to me.

"No."

"Good. Then forget it all. It was gibberish, the babbling of a confused, sick man. Do you understand?" he asked. "Do you?" he insisted.

"Yes, Uncle Jacob."

"Good," he said again. "I hope you're helping Sara during this hardship."

"Of course I am."

"And you're not taking advantage of my incapacity," he added.

"I never took advantage, even when you were well, Uncle Jacob."

He widened his eyes and I looked away. I didn't want to get into any arguments with him now. If something should happen, I would surely be to blame. Maybe that was what he hoped.

"Just remember this discussion."

"Okay," I said. "I hope you feel better," I added and turned to leave.

"Oh, I will," he said. It sounded like a threat. I didn't look back. I couldn't wait to get away from him, and I marched out quickly.

Cary looked up expectantly when I stepped out of the elevator. Aunt Sara had been talking to a hospital aide, but stopped and looked my way, too.

"Everything all right?" Cary asked quickly.

"All right?" I thought a moment. "Everything's . . . back to normal," I said dryly. Cary raised his eyebrows.

Aunt Sara heard my words and misunderstood.

"Yes," she said. "Isn't it wonderful? The doctors think Jacob will be home sooner than we thought. Of course, it will be hard for us to make sure he doesn't try to do anything he shouldn't. He'll have to rest and avoid stress of any kind," she added.

"Sounds as if I should move out then," I muttered under my breath. I thought Cary might have heard anyway because he looked very troubled.

I took May's hand and we left the hospital. As we walked to the car, my mind went to how important family could be at times like this. I thought about Grandma Belinda and how long it had been since I had visited. I decided I would return this weekend. Even though she wandered about in a state of semiconfusion, I felt there was a possibility of love between us. Or at least I hoped there was.

I knew I would need it. The days that lay ahead were full of bleak promises and even more obstacles to my happiness. But I had no idea just how much more, no idea at all. Not even Holly's horoscopes could reveal that.

12

Showdown

After work on Saturday, I told Kenneth and Holly of my plans to visit Grandma Belinda again.

"How will you get there?" Kenneth asked.

"I guess I'll take a taxi. Olivia practically forbade me to visit, so I won't get Raymond to take me, and Cary has his hands full with Uncle Jacob in the hospital as well as having to do all the work. He's very worried about this year's cranberry harvest, too."

"I can take you," Holly offered. When I started to shake my head, she insisted. "Really, I don't mind."

I thought about it and started to laugh, thinking what it would be like for us to drive up in Holly's psychedelic car. It would certainly catch everyone's attention. Kenneth saw the wide grin on my face.

"Melody is imagining what sort of an entrance you two will make dressed in your saris, headbands, crystal earrings, and sandals, Holly," he said, staring at me with laughter in his eyes.

"Why?" Holly asked.

"Why? This is a rest home for New England bluebloods. They haven't seen anything like you, even in their senile hallucinations," he replied.

Holly thought a moment and then smiled.

"Well, then we'll be a special treat for them, won't we?"

"I don't think I can dress that way," I said softly, not wanting to hurt Holly's feelings. "I've only just met my grandmother. She might not even recall the meeting, so I had better not do anything to confuse her. I was thinking I would wear what I wore the first time."

"Oh, dress any way you want, Melody. So will I. This might be fun," she squealed. "I like talking to elderly people. Often they have a better understanding of the cosmic center."

"That's because they're closer to becoming pure energy," Kenneth quipped and then winked at me.

Once Kenneth had determined he was ready to begin sculpting the marble block, he became more relaxed and more confident about focusing his creative energy. He declared that the work was already completed.

"Completed?" I looked at the block and then shook my head in confusion.

"In here," he said pointing to his head. "It's done. All I have to do is bring it out, follow the blueprint. I become a mere tool of my artistic consciousness. Do you understand?"

"Oh. Yes, I think I do," I told him. A month ago I might have thought him weird, even mad, but after having him lecture to me daily about the creative eye, and after hearing Holly talk about the power of focused energy, I really did appreciate what he was saying. He was pleased I understood.

At the end of our work days now, Kenneth would pour the three of us a glass of cranberry wine, my glass being only a third or so full. It was really Holly's idea.

"People who work as hard as you two do have to

step back and permit their spirits and their bodies to join hands again," she said.

We usually sat on the small patio between the house and the studio and watched Shell, the turtle, navigate around the rocks and the fish in the small pond. The sun was still high enough in the sky to provide warm rays, but it wasn't unbearably hot and there usually was a late-afternoon breeze coming off the sea. The conversation was mostly between Holly and Kenneth, the two of them talking about people they had known and things Holly did in New York City. I never felt like a mere observer, however, because one or the other would often turn to me to explain something or someone. It was from these conversations that I gleaned an idea of what Kenneth had been like when he was only a few years older than I. There appeared to have been a bright period to his life, a period when he was as bohemian as Holly, carefree and far more sociable.

And then, from what they said, I understood that he had lost contact with all their mutual friends and had done little or nothing with anyone, even here in Provincetown. Holly constantly complained about his failure to visit her and her shop in New York. Kenneth merely smiled and promised he would some day.

"When the stars are correctly aligned for it," he added, shifting his eyes impishly to me.

"The stars have been aligned for it many times, Ken. You've got to be aligned," Holly replied and we all laughed.

Holly was right about our quiet time. Although I was tired, our half hour or so of relaxation always put me in a good mood and I was able to bring some of that joviality home to help cheer up Aunt Sara during this troubled time.

When I arrived at the house after work this particular Saturday however, I found Aunt Sara was more upset than usual. Cary was still out on the lobster boat and she was worried about visiting Uncle Jacob.

"He's called three times asking for Cary," she moaned. "I can't imagine what's keeping him. He knows how his father worries up there and he knows we can't let him worry," she said, her face full of a thousand anxieties.

"Uncle Jacob surely understands that things can keep Cary busy and working late. It's happened many times before, hasn't it, Aunt Sara?" I asked.

I knew that since Uncle Jacob had been given phone privileges, he called a number of times during the day, giving Aunt Sara orders, making demands, and questioning her to death. I assumed many of those questions had to do with me.

"It's hard for him," she said. "He feels like a prisoner chained to his bed by doctors and nurses, fed medicines, and prohibited from doing the simplest things. They had to give him bathroom privileges faster than they wanted because Jacob refused to sit on a bed pan," she added. "He's been hounding the doctor to let him go home."

I wanted to say it was very hard for Cary, too, and especially hard for her and May, but I put a zipper on my lips and helped her get dinner ready instead. However, when Cary wasn't home an hour later, even I became worried. Uncle Jacob called to speak to him, complaining that Cary had neglected to report the day's catch. Aunt Sara had to tell him Cary wasn't there.

"I don't know," I heard her say. "I'm getting very worried. Should I send Melody down to the dock?" she asked him. I saw her eyes shift from me as she listened to him speak. She nodded and promised to call him as soon as she had news. Then she cradled the phone and wrung her hands.

251

"What did Uncle Jacob say? Should I go to the dock?" I asked her. May sat staring at us, her eyes full of worry, too.

"He said you wouldn't know what to look for or what to ask anyone," she replied, shaking her head as she did so.

"I can see if the boat's there, can't I?"

"Yes," she said. I saw that it took great courage for her to disagree with anything Jacob uttered.

"Then I'll go," I declared and started out of the kitchen. May called to me and then signed her desire to go too.

I nodded and she leaped to her feet and took my hand. The two of us marched out of the house and over the dunes, both straining to see the activity at the dock. We had only to go a few thousand yards down the beach to discover there wasn't anyone there. The lobster boat was nowhere in sight either.

"Where is he?" I asked myself aloud. May tugged on my hand and signed the same question. I shook my head and continued toward the dock. When we got there, we stood looking out at the sea, searching in every direction for a sign of the boat. I saw an oil barge going south and larger cargo ship, but no sign of the lobster boat. I just hated returning to the house with no news, but I knew the longer we remained here, the more Aunt Sara would worry, and Uncle Jacob was sure to call again.

Maybe there was a reason to worry, I thought. This wasn't like Cary. Even though the weather was picture perfect, accidents do happen at sea. It would be just horrible if something bad had happened now, with Uncle Jacob still in the hospital, I thought. Since I had been practicing tuning into the cosmic energies with Holly, I paid more attention to my feelings and instincts, and I didn't like the heavy little ball of worry that was growing in my chest. There was nothing to do but go home and wait with Aunt Sara.

I started to turn away when May tugged hard on my hand and then pointed north. I looked, but saw nothing.

"What?"

She pointed more emphatically. Her eyes were more seaworthy than mine, for she had grown up here and she knew how to read the twilight glitter on the surface of the ocean. I strained to see as two almost indistinguishable dots grew into shapes that were slowly moving closer to the shore.

"What is it?"

We walked to the edge of the dock and waited as the shapes became two boats, one looking like a tugboat. Finally, I could make out the lobster boat clearly. It was being towed toward the dock.

"Oh, thank goodness," I declared. May smiled and started to sign an explanation. She recalled something like this happening before. The boat had broken down at sea and Uncle Jacob had to radio for help.

When Cary drew close enough to see us, he waved from the starboard bow. The sun had almost completely dipped behind the horizon as the lobster boat was delivered to the dock. Cary and Roy Patterson got it tied up and Cary hurried off to tell us the story.

"The catch was good, but suddenly our engine died and we weren't able to fix it. How's Ma?" he asked quickly, knowing she would be concerned.

"She's very worried, Cary. Uncle Jacob keeps calling from the hospital."

"Let's get up to the house," he said.

Roy said he would take care of everything and we hurried back. Cary looked exhausted. His hands were full of grease, and there were streaks of it across his face, which was darker, even red at the crests of his cheeks.

"I'll wash up and go right to the hospital," he said, taking such long, deep strides over the sand May and I had trouble keeping up with him.

253

"You have to have some supper first, Cary. Just call him."

He nodded, but he looked more concerned about his father than he was about the problems with the boat.

"He's going to blame it on me," he muttered, "but I didn't do anything different. We had oil pressure problems."

"I'm sure he'll understand. May said something like this happened before anyway, right?"

"Right," he said, but he didn't sound confident.

Aunt Sara was at sixes and sevens by the time we arrived. She had practically worn the skin off her fingers wringing her hands with worry. Cary quickly explained what had happened, and she told him to call Uncle Jacob.

"You guys just eat," he said after he had the conversation with his father and hung up. "I've got to wash up and run up to the hospital."

"But Cary—"

"It's okay," he said. "He wants to know the details. I'll eat something later. Go on. Don't wait."

"But—"

He charged up the stairs before I could protest any more. I looked at Aunt Sara. She shook her head and went about serving our dinner.

"Be back as soon as I can," Cary called from the front door less than ten minutes later.

"I don't know why you can't get something to eat first," I called back, but he was already out the door. I looked at Aunt Sara. She was troubled, but silent. "Uncle Jacob's being pretty selfish, Aunt Sara. Cary's had a miserable day. He's tired and hungry. You should have made him eat."

"I can't worry Jacob now," she cried in defense. "He's still recuperating."

I choked back my angry words and drank them down with water. If Uncle Jacob had been an ogre before, I thought, he would be a bigger monster now, for he was sure to take advantage of his own illness at every opportunity.

It was nearly three hours later before Cary returned. Aunt Sara had been trying to do needlepoint, but her eyes lifted every time she heard a creak in the house or the sound of an automobile outside.

"I should have gone too," she muttered.

When Cary entered, she threw down her needlepoint and jumped up to greet him at the living room door.

"He's fine," Cary said quickly. He looked more exhausted than I had ever seen him, and I saw that the fatigue didn't come from his day's labor so much as from the emotional tension he had just experienced. "I think he might even be released in a day or so."

"Really? Oh, that would be wonderful," Aunt Sara cried, clapping her hands together. She quickly signed the news to May, whose face lit up with a smile.

It occurred to me that no matter how I saw Uncle Jacob or what I thought of him, he was still Aunt Sara's husband and May's father. They loved him, and in his own way, he surely loved them. I had no right to be critical of him, I thought, especially now when he was recuperating from one of the worst illness anyone could have.

"But one of his doctors stopped me in the hallway," Cary continued, "and made it perfectly clear that Dad can't go back to the way he was, not for some time. If he doesn't rest, eat right, and exercise, he could have a relapse."

"Oh dear. Did they make that clear to Jacob?" Aunt Sara asked, her hands flitting about, nervously tugging on her dress and brushing at her hair.

"Too clear," Cary said, shifting his gaze to me. I understood this was a major reason why his visit was so long and difficult. "He's furious about it. Says they don't know what they're talking about, that it's work

255

that makes a man strong, emotionally, physically, and spiritually. He vowed he won't be anyone's cripple and the doctors threatened to keep him in the hospital. You'll have to tell him, Ma. You'll have to put your foot down too," Cary said.

Aunt Sara nodded, her eyes wide with fear and worry.

"Of course, I will, Cary," she said. "Yes. All of us will do what we can to help him understand, won't we?" she asked, turning to me. I smiled.

"Yes, Aunt Sara. Did you eat anything, Cary?"

"I had a candy bar. Got it from the machine in the hospital."

"Oh. Well I kept everything warm for you, Cary," Aunt Sara said. "Just sit and I'll get you a plate."

"I'm not hungry, Ma."

"Of course you are, especially after the day you've had," she insisted. "Now," she added when he opened his mouth, "if you expect me to tell your father what to do, at least listen when I speak to you," she said.

Cary laughed.

"Okay. Let me just call Roy and see about the repairs on the boat. I have to give Dad a report before he goes to sleep, too," he said and went to the phone.

Afterward, May and I joined him at the dining room table and watched him eat. When Aunt Sara went back into the kitchen, he leaned over to whisper to me.

"He's bad, Melody, cranky and meaner than ever. He swears he's going to sneak back on the boat first chance he gets. I told him I wouldn't go out then and he fumed at me for a good half hour until I calmed him down. When I first got there, he accused me of not checking the oil before I took out the boat. I always check the engine, Melody," he assured me. "I know what can happen out there," he said.

"I believe you and I don't know why he wouldn't."

"It's just his condition, I guess. It makes him ornery."

"Well, he should be just the opposite. He should be pleased and proud he has a son who can step in during this emergency and keep the business going. I'll tell him, too," I threatened.

"No, please. That's all I need, him thinking we were conspiring against him while he was ill."

"He thinks it of me anyway, Cary."

"No, he doesn't," Cary said, but I saw the way he dropped his eyes quickly.

"What did he ask you about me? Come on," I urged. He started to look up and reply but Aunt Sara returned. When she left again, I repeated my question. Reluctantly, he answered.

"His brain is all jumbled from the heart attack, I'm sure."

"Come on, Cary."

"He wanted to know if you were spreading stories about him and your mother. I told him he had to be hallucinating to think of something like that and he got so mad at me, I had to leave the room for a while. That's when I met his doctor and heard what was going to happen. Can you think of any reason why he would ask me that question?" Cary asked, his gazed fixed on my face.

"No," I said quickly. What Uncle Jacob had said to me in the CCU was never meant to be repeated. It was as sacred as a dying person's confession to a priest. I had no intention of uttering a word of it, ever.

Cary shrugged and returned to his dinner.

"That's why I said he was hallucinating," he muttered. He eyed me scrupulously as he chewed his food and I turned to May and asked her if she wanted to play Chinese checkers.

Before we rose to go into the living room, I told everyone I was going to visit my grandmother tomorrow. Aunt Sara stopped clearing the dishes.

"Oh dear, is that wise, Melody?" she asked.

"Very wise," I said. "I like her and she likes me. We have to get to know each other before it's too late."

"Yes, I suppose you do," Aunt Sara said, "but I'm sure Olivia—"

"Has nothing to say about it," I chimed in quickly.

"Oh dear," Aunt Sara said. "All this commotion at once. Oh, dear." She hurried back to the sanctuary of her kitchen.

Cary gazed up at me with eyes of appreciation and glee.

"Grandma Olivia has met her match in you, Melody Logan," he said, struggling to contain his amusement.

"Yes, she has. Whether she likes it or not," I fired back, and Cary gave in to a fit of laughter.

Confused at all the commotion, May tugged on my hand for explanations. Instead, I took her into the living room for our game of Chinese checkers. Cary came in to watch us play and fell asleep in his father's chair. No one had the heart to wake him.

"Jacob does that often now," Aunt Sara said gazing at Cary with her eyes twin pools of sadness. She sighed. "Let him sleep."

May and I went up to bed. Aunt Sara tinkered around the house until she had gotten herself tired enough and came up, too. Hours later, I heard Cary's footsteps on the stairway. He paused at my door and then went on to his own room. The boy in him was being shoved further and further back into his memory as he was forced to become a man of responsibility and duty. How lucky were those who could have a full and happy youth.

Holly was there in the morning as she had promised. It was the first time Cary had seen her car, or her, for that matter. She wore one of her long, flowing dresses, a matching headband, opal earrings in a silver setting, a jade necklace, and her pink and green sandals. She had even painted a small pink and green dot on each of her cheeks.

At first Cary was amazed and then he thought it was all very amusing. Aunt Sara merely dropped her jaw and retreated into the house with May. I introduced Cary to Holly and she immediately asked him his date of birth.

"Why?" he asked.

"I know you're a Gemini," she said, "but I need more details about your birthday."

"Huh?" Cary turned to me.

"We have to go," I said quickly. "I want to make visiting hours."

"Oh yes," Holly said. "Perhaps I'll see you soon and we can talk again," Holly told Cary.

He nodded and I got into Holly's car.

"I made something for your grandmother," she told me as we drove away. "It's right on the back seat."

I turned and found a crystal embedded in a blob of silvery-gray stone that looked like petrified scrambled eggs.

"What is it?" I had to ask.

"It's a paperweight," Holly explained, "but that's lepidolite in the center. It aids muscles, strengthens the heart, and is very beneficial to the blood. What is most important, it aids sleep, which I know is a problem for the elderly. Try to get her to keep it close to her bed," she advised.

"Thank you, Holly," I said, wondering not only what Grandma Belinda would think, but what Mrs. Greene and her assistants would do.

Holly thought the rest home was in a truly beautiful and tranquil place.

"Whoever chose the location was sensitive to positive energy," she declared. "I can feel it. It's ideal for meditation."

There were a half dozen or so other vehicles in the

visitors' parking lot when we pulled up. I saw a man and a woman helping an elderly lady walk along a garden pathway. The two elderly gentlemen I had met when I came the first time were on the porch again, sitting in the same seats. Only today, both were wearing suits and ties and had their hair neatly combed.

"Well now," the one who had first spoken to me last time said, "you come to entertain us, have you?" He was looking at Holly.

"No sir," she said. "We're just visiting someone."

"That them?" the other man shouted.

"No, they're just visiting someone."

"Who'd you say they were?"

"Just visiting," he repeated. Holly laughed and followed me through the front entrance.

Mrs. Greene was in the lobby, talking with some of the residents, who were apparently waiting to be entertained. One of the attendants, a tall, dark haired man with a pock-marked face and thin, very red lips, stepped out from behind the desk on our right, where he had been talking to a young girl. Mrs. Greene straightened up quickly and hurried toward us, the attendant moving to join her.

"Yes?" she said.

"I'm Melody Logan. Remember? I visited my grandmother, Belinda Gordon, recently."

"Yes, I recall." She pulled her shoulders back and stiffened her jaw. "I remember I specifically asked you not to give her any candy," she said sharply.

"What?"

"I explained how important it was that she not be given any candy. They share what they are given and they don't know who is diabetic and who isn't. I thought you understood that. It's a simple enough request," she added, drawing her lips thin.

"I didn't give her any candy," I said.

"No? Well she had it in her room right after you left," Mrs. Greene said with a twisted smirk.

"I don't think Melody would lie, ma'am," Holly said softly. She had a way of disagreeing with someone that made it sound pleasant, but Mrs. Greene stepped back and drank her in with a look of disgust.

"And who might you be?"

"Just a friend," Holly said.

"Yes, well, I'm afraid I can't permit anyone but immediate family to visit," Mrs. Greene said, "and we do ask that our visitors dress decently. We value our reputation here. Our clients are highly respectable people and there are a number of them visiting their loved ones at the moment."

"Decency comes from the heart, not from our outer garb," Holly said, still speaking softly.

Mrs. Greene ignored her and turned back to me.

"I have spoken with Mrs. Logan," she said, "and she has left instructions that for the time being, no one is to visit her sister. I assumed she would have told you."

"What do you mean, no one? I'm her granddaughter!" I raised my voice. "I'm not just anyone!"

The attendant moved closer. Some of the residents stopped talking and turned our way.

"Please, lower your voice," Mrs. Greene said shooting a glance at some people who were visiting a relative.

"Why can't I see my grandmother?" I demanded.

"Her condition is very delicate. We're just trying to do what's best for her," Mrs. Greene replied with a smile so phony it dripped.

"Surely, having a loved one visit can't be anything but good," Holly said. Mrs. Greene shot her a look that, if it had been a dart, would have pierced Holly's pleasant smile and gone right through her head.

"I'm not leaving here without seeing my grandmother," I fired at her and planted my feet so firmly, it was as if they were nailed to the floor.

Mrs. Greene studied us a moment. I saw a look of retreat in her eyes, which quickly fell to the gift in my hand.

"And what is that you're bringing her?"

"It's a crystal paperweight and it has healing powers," I said.

Mrs. Greene smiled coldly.

"I can't permit it. We have to have control over what is brought into the rooms."

"What harm can this do her?"

"I can't permit it," she repeated. "It's against my better judgment, but I will permit you, and you alone, to visit with your grandmother for half an hour."

"Why am I limited in time? No one else is," I protested.

"That's my final decision. I have a major responsibility here. The welfare of my guests, all my guests, must be taken into consideration. And I repeat, only immediate family," she said, sending another look of disgust Holly's way.

Holly put her hand on mine and smiled.

"I'll just wait for you out on the porch," she said with a wink. I knew she would enjoy speaking with the two elderly gentlemen. She took the paperweight from my hands and turned to Mrs. Greene. "Perhaps I can make this a present to you," she said. "One of the qualities of lepidolite is that it enhances one's expression of inner light and joy."

"Ridiculous," Mrs. Greene said and pivoted. "Gerson, show Miss Logan to Miss Gordon's room."

"She's in her room?" I asked. It was such a beautiful day, and most of the residents had been brought to the lobby for their entertainment. Why was Grandma Belinda shut up in her room?

"Yes," she said, lifting the corner of her mouth until it cut into her cheek. "She's not feeling well today.

That's why I want to limit your visit. Your cooperation will be appreciated," she added and returned to the people with whom she had been talking when we arrived.

"This way," the attendant said. He wore a sharp, sarcastic smile on his lips. Holly pressed my hand and nodded.

"Go on. I'll be fine," she said.

I followed the attendant through the lobby and down the corridor toward the residents' rooms, my heart thumping with every furious thought that bounced from one side of my brain to the other.

I was even angrier when I saw Grandma Belinda. Her door was shut and she was sitting in her rocking chair near the window, gazing out like a child who had been punished and sentenced to stand in a corner. The lights were off, so the room was full of shadows. She was wrapped in a shawl and appeared smaller than I remembered her. Her eyes were red, her face pale, and it looked as if she had been crying. I waited for a moment, but she didn't even notice I had entered her room.

"You got a half hour," the attendant reminded me firmly and stepped out, closing the door behind me. I went to Grandma Belinda and touched her hand. She turned slowly and looked up at me, expressionless, indifferent, a lost lamb.

"Hi Grandma. It's Melody. I came to see you again. How are you?" I asked quickly. "Why are you sitting in the shadows?"

She stared at me blankly, her eyelids blinking rapidly.

"I told her I was pregnant," she began, "and I told her it was Nelson's baby. She got very angry and swore at me and called me a liar. She called me terrible names and said she wouldn't help me if I told my lie to anyone else, ever, but I wasn't lying. I wouldn't lie."

"Nelson? You mean Judge Childs?" I asked and sat on the bed, facing her. She rocked and nodded.

"Yes. There were other young men. I've always been very popular," she said with a flirtatious smile. Then, in a heartbeat her face changed expression until she looked older, serious. "But I should know who is the father of my child, don't you think?" Her face turned angry. "How can you doubt me, Olivia? You want to doubt me; you don't want it to be true because you've always loved Nelson. Well, don't blame me because he loves me more than he loves you."

"Grandma," I said softly. She seemed to be looking through me and not at me, her gaze distant.

"Stop that laughing. I'm not lying. I'm not!" she said, straining her throat until the veins in her neck were well outlined.

"It's all right, Grandma. It's all right. I believe you," I said and took her hand.

She stopped rocking and looked at me. She began to blink rapidly again. And then, like magic, her face brightened with a childlike smile.

"It's a nice day," she said, glancing through the window. "It should be my birthday."

She laughed and rocked. Then she stopped again and her face grew darker, her eyes small, her lips taut. She shook her head.

"I was screaming upstairs, screaming at the top of my voice. It's time. It's time! The door was locked. She wanted me to lose the baby, you know. Oh, don't look at me that way," she said, turning to me. "You're always taking her side."

"Grandma," I said softly. "It's Melody."

She shook her head. Was she telling me the truth or was everything so jumbled in her mind that her words were like one crossword puzzle confused with another, the answers all to the wrong questions?

"She left me, no doctor, no midwife, no one. I guess you never knew that part, huh?" A crazed twist

264

shaped her lips and she smiled so coldly it put ice in my veins. "I delivered my own baby and when she came up and found the baby was all right, she nearly died herself with disappointment. You never knew. I can see it on your face, Nelson. You never knew."

She turned and rocked. I held my breath until I saw her chin begin to quiver and the first tear emerge.

"Grandma," I said. "Please, try to look at me and see me. Please."

What had they done to her? Why was she so much more confused, lost. How long had she been kept in this room? Her rocking stopped again. She took a deep breath and lowered her face until her chin rested on her chest. Then she closed her eyes and in moments was asleep.

I sat, waiting to see if she would wake and go into another exclamation, drawing thoughts, memories, words from some secret place in her mind. The minutes ticked and she slept.

If Nelson Childs was the father of her baby . . . then he was my real grandfather, after all, and that made Kenneth my uncle. Did he know? What if none of this were true? What if it were?

Oh please wake up, Grandma, I thought. I want to know more; I want to be sure.

There was a gentle knock on the door. When I turned, a short, plump nurse entered carrying a cup and some water.

"She's dozed off again, has she?" she remarked.

"What's wrong with her? She's so different from the way she was the last time I was here, and it wasn't that long ago," I questioned.

"When they reach this age and they've been sick or lived a hard life, changes can occur from hour to hour," she said. "She's falling into Alzheimer's," she added. "In some cases that's merciful."

"Well not in hers. She has a lot of years left and she can get better," I cried.

The nurse raised her eyebrows and looked at me as if I were the one who was suffering mental aberrations. She shook Grandma Belinda's shoulder.

"Come on, Belinda. Time for your medicine," she said.

Grandma's eyes fluttered open and she turned slowly.

"Come on, dear. Take your pills. Remember?"

"Pills? Again? Why so many pills, Olivia? Did the doctor really say I should take these, too?"

"Yes, he did."

The nurse looked at me.

"Who's Olivia?" she whispered.

"Her sister."

"Oh. Yes, Belinda, he did. Come on, honey. That's it," she said. "Now wash them down. Good girl."

"What are those pills?" I asked.

"They're just a form of a tranquillizer to keep her calm," she said.

"Maybe they're doing her more damage."

"Are you a doctor?" the plump nurse asked with a face full of ridicule.

"No, but—"

"Well, her doctor has prescribed them. If you have a problem with that, speak to Mrs. Greene," she added and left the room.

"I'd rather speak to the wall," I mumbled.

Grandma Belinda was staring out the window again. I touched her hand and she turned slowly, very slowly, toward me, her eyes so sad, they put tears in my heart.

"Grandma, it's me, Melody. Remember?"

She smiled.

"Yes. He told me about you. He said you look just like your mother." Her smile evaporated. "Only, I can't remember what she looked like."

"She looked like you," I said.

"Did she?" She smiled again and then gazed out the

window while she spoke. "It's my birthday you know. We're having guests and a cake."

"Happy birthday, Grandma," I said, tears now building under my eyelids.

"Everyone's going to sing Happy Birthday to me." She turned. "Even Olivia, because I'll look right at her and she'll have to sing. Right?"

"Yes," I said and smiled.

"Happy birthday to me, happy birthday to me, happy birthday, dear Belinda, happy birthday to me."

She closed her eyes.

There was a harder knock on the door and the attendant appeared.

"It's time," he said.

"It can't be a half hour."

"It is," he insisted. "Don't make it hard for me, will ya," he muttered with threatening eyes.

"No," I said standing. "I'll leave that to Mrs. Greene."

I leaned over and kissed my grandmother on her cheek. She didn't open her eyes. Then I turned and marched past him and down the corridor.

The residents were being entertained by a singer in the lobby. She played the accordion as well. Mrs. Greene was standing in the rear with some attendants, a receptionist, and some visitors. She glared my way and I glared back as I left the lobby and stepped out of the building, my heart thumping so hard I thought it would drown out the singing.

There was no one on the porch, but I saw Holly on a bench talking softly to some song birds who stared up at her as if they really understood. Even though I was still shaking, the sight brought laughter to my lips. She saw me and hurried up the walkway.

"How was your visit?" she asked.

"Very bad," I said. "They're medicating her into oblivion and I have the feeling it's Grandma Olivia's fault. I've got to pay her a visit."

"Oh, that's so sad. If we just taught them how to meditate, there would be no need for chemical therapy."

"There's no need for it now," I said. "Unless keeping the truth buried is a good reason."

Holly's eyebrows lifted into question marks, but I didn't want to say anything until I was certain what I had heard was really the truth. At least now I understood why Grandma Olivia had been so interested in learning what her sister had told me the first time. I felt as if I were opening the door to a vault, a vault covered in dust and cobwebs, its hinges rusted. This was no time to walk away.

"Could you do me a favor," I asked, "and take me to my Grandmother Olivia's house? It's just a little out of the way."

"No problem," Holly said. "If that's what you want."

"Oh, it's what I want," I said nodding. "I never wanted it more."

13
&

Accusations

When we turned into Grandma Olivia's driveway and came to a stop, I sat quietly while I tried to catch my breath. Confronting Grandma Olivia was always difficult, but this was going to be twice as hard and the anticipation made my heart race.

"Are you all right?" Holly asked.

"Yes. You don't have to wait for me," I said. "I might be here a while."

"But how will you get home?"

"Grandma Olivia's driver will take me, I'm sure."

I gazed at the house. Despite the bright sunshine glittering on the windows, the beautiful rainbow colored flowers and perfectly trimmed hedges, the house looked dark and full of foreboding to me. Holly sensed my tension.

"Maybe she's not home. Maybe nobody's home," Holly said.

"I'll wait for her," I said in a tone of voice that indicated I would wait forever, if need be.

Holly gazed at me and then at the house. She

squinted, closed her eyes, and then opened them and nodded as if she had reached a conclusion.

"There's a lot of static here, a bed of negative energy. Remember what I told you about my friend who went to India and walked on a bed of hot coals?"

"Yes." I smiled, recalling the story and how animated Holly had been when she told it.

"You've got to build a wall between yourself and that which can hurt you, Melody. You have the power in your own mind. Rely on your concentration, focus."

"I'm doing just that," I said. "Thank you." I got out. She remained in the driveway, watching me walk up to the front door. I pushed the buzzer and waited and then pushed it again. Holly was still in the driveway, unwilling to leave me here. Finally, Loretta, the maid, came to the door. I looked back and waved to Holly to indicate it was all right. Reluctantly, she backed out. I didn't want to send her away, but I knew that if she came into the house with me, Grandma Olivia might use her as an excuse to refuse to talk to me. I was determined she wasn't going to find any avenue of escape from the truth this time.

"Hello, Loretta," I said. "I want to see my grandmother. Is she here?"

"Mrs. Logan is upstairs in her bedroom. She wasn't feeling well today. I just brought her a little lunch, but she didn't eat much."

"I have to speak to her," I insisted.

"She's in her bedroom," Loretta said, intending that I take that as a reason why I couldn't. She was a tall, thin woman with a face that looked as if it were made from porcelain and would crack and shatter if she smiled or laughed.

"People talk in their bedrooms," I said and marched past her.

"Oh, but Mrs. Logan doesn't want to be disturbed," she cried.

"No one wants to be disturbed, Loretta," I replied and started up the stairway.

I had been upstairs only once before, when Cary had given me my first quick tour of the house, but I had seen Grandma Logan's bedroom. I remembered she had a bed next to a wide, dark cherry wood, three-drawer nightstand on which sat a large Tiffany lamp. Behind the bed were two big windows over which hung sheer wine-colored drapes. The bed was on a matching oval area rug. On the right was a cherry wood desk and on the left, adjacent to the door, were the closets, dressers, a very uncomfortable looking spindle chair, and a side table. The walls were covered with a light brown wallpaper that had what looked like tiny flowers stenciled around the borders. I saw no paintings on the walls and thought the room was rather cold for a bedroom.

At the moment the door was closed. I knocked and waited and then knocked again.

"What is it?" I heard Grandma Olivia cry with sharp annoyance. Rather than answer and announce myself, I just opened the door.

My appearance was almost as shocking to her as hers was to me. She was sitting up, her face covered with some sort of milk-white facial cream. Her watery red eyes peered out of the mask of lotion and her bland lips looked like a line drawn with a broken crayon. Her blanket was folded back at her waist. Surrounded by her oversized pillows, her thin hair down, her egg-shell white silk nightgown loosely clinging to her bony shoulders, she appeared smaller than she did when dressed and moving about the large rooms. The portion of her chest that usually remained covered now revealed age spots and tiny moles. Minus her jewelry and her hair combs, and wearing this skin lotion, she looked naked, vulnerable, caught unpro-tected by her wealth and power, a queen without her crown. My seeing her like this filled her face with immediate rage. She stuttered and gasped before she could get out her angry reprimands.

"How—how dare you come up here without being announced? Who do you think you are barging into my bedroom? Where do you get the audacity— Haven't you learned anything about manners?"

She reached over the bed to fetch a towel and wipe the cream from her face, whipping her eyes back at me as she did so. There was so much fire coming from them that if I had been made of ice, I'd have been a pool of water in seconds.

"I just came from visiting with Grandma Belinda," I said in response.

She threw the towel to the floor and pulled her blanket up until it covered her to the neck.

"Where's Loretta? Did she permit you to enter the house?"

"Don't blame Loretta. She told me you were up here and I insisted on coming up to see you."

"Well, you just turn yourself around and march back down those stairs and out of the house. I am not entertaining guests today. I have a splitting headache, a sinus problem and—"

"I'm not here to be entertained, Grandma Olivia. I'm here to confirm the truth, once and for all," I fired back. Her eyes widened as her anger peaked.

"How dare you speak to me like that? And with all the family trouble now, too. Poor Jacob and Sara having to contend with Jacob's heart attack and now your insolence. I warned you about your behavior. I told you—"

"I said I have just come from seeing Grandma Belinda," I interrupted, raising my voice just enough to grab her attention. She stared a moment, her lips pursed.

"What of it?" she demanded.

"First, I was told you left orders for no one to see her," I began in a smaller, quieter voice.

"That's correct."

"Why?" I asked, my eyes narrowed as I took a step toward her.

"I don't think I have to explain myself to you and I will not be cross-examined in my own home. Get out," she said, pointing to the door.

"I'm not leaving until I hear the truth from your lips. It may burn your tongue, but I want to hear it," I said.

My calmness fanned the flames of her rage even more. Her mouth opened and closed without a sound emerging as she choked on her own fury.

"Grandma Belinda was not in good health," I said. "She was under some medication that's turning her into a zombie."

"Oh, so you've become a doctor, too, is that it? You want to go up there and tell them how to treat their patients. Is that why you've come bursting into my home?" she added with a cold smile spreading from her twisted lips to her steely eyes. "This is exactly why I left orders for no visitors. She's not well. She's not up to visitors anymore, and I'm disappointed that you were permitted to see her. I will have a stern talk with Mrs. Greene."

"Mrs. Greene knew if she didn't permit me to see my grandmother, she would have a bigger fight on her hands with me than she would have with you," I said.

"Oh, so you pushed your way in there just as you've done now, is that it? You think I'm going to tolerate this sort of behavior? You think just because my son is in the hospital that I won't call Sara and tell her to throw you out on the street? Don't you know that it's only because of my generosity that I permit you to live here? By all rights you should be in some foster home until they find a family strong enough to stomach you," she spit back at me.

"I'm not going to be intimidated by your threats this time, Grandma Olivia. If you threw me out on

273

the streets, I would just go down to the Provincetown newspapers and tell them about this family and its dark secrets."

She laughed.

"Do you think anyone in Provincetown would do anything to upset me?" she challenged. "You don't know how ridiculous you sound. Now do as I say and—"

"Grandma Belinda told me the truth about my mother's birth," I blurted. I didn't add that she had babbled it in what sounded like insane rambling. "She told me she was kept shut up in the house, not even provided with proper medical care, in the hope that she would lose the baby. She told me how you made her deliver her own baby."

"What? That is such a preposterous story, I don't think it requires a response."

"And then she told me who the father was, my mother's father, my grandfather," I added.

Grandma Olivia seemed to sink a little in her bed. She leaned back against the pillows, her ashen face almost transparent now. Then she brought the corners of her mouth up and into her cheeks, thinning her lips so they looked like strings of pale pink wool strained to the point of tearing.

"Which one of her many, many lovers did she call the father of her baby? This time," she added.

"She said it was Judge Childs."

Grandma Olivia's lips trembled and then broke into another, very forced, hard smile.

"Oh she's gone back to that story, has she? Last year it was Samuel, you know. And before that, it was Martin Donnally, a policeman who died two years ago. Once it was Sanford Jackson, Teddy Jackson's father. I told you not to go up to see her anymore. I knew she was going to tell you with one ludicrous story after another. She was always a liar, always fantasizing about this or that man. Belinda never had

274

more than one foot in reality and most of the time, not even a toe. She was always doing terrible things and then making up stories. In her deranged mind, she thought the wealthiest, most handsome men in Provincetown were going to rush off and marry her. Nothing was further from the truth.

"She was crazy even before she began drinking and sleeping around. All that just put her over the top, and after she gave birth, she went completely mad. Why, if I hadn't had the judge's help at the time—"

"The judge's help?"

"Yes. That's why she's making up this story now. It was Judge Childs who came to my aid and helped me place her in the home where she was treated well and where she has lived comfortably in her madness up until now. I needed his political influence. You can imagine the waiting list for that place. That's why she accuses him of such a thing."

She wagged her head and then nodded.

"Belinda's getting worse. I didn't know how bad things were until very recently and that's why I left orders for her not to have visitors. Satisfied? Now that you know all the nitty gritty dirt I've been trying to keep swept out of sight?"

She leaned forward, strengthened by the venom of her lies. For I could tell, she *was* lying.

"We are one of the most respected and well known of the original families here," she continued. "Reputation is as important as money in the bank. Despite the unfortunate circumstances surrounding Belinda and your mother, I was able to protect my family. Now, after we've been overly generous and permitted you to live amongst us, given you opportunities, you continue to threaten our peace and well being. How dare you come here with your accusations? I shut my sister up pregnant? I didn't give her medical assistance? What do you think I'm doing now?"

"But, that's what she told me," I said, weakening.

She laughed again and shook her head.

"So you will go around and tell people what a deranged, mentally ill woman who has been institutionalized for years and years said? This is why you come running here? This is how you threaten me?

"Please," she said, wagging her head and waving her hand as if she were chasing away flies, "go home and try to be of some assistance to my son's wife during this trying time. If you can't, well, we'll see about making some other arrangements for you," she said, but not as a threat, more like a logical conclusion.

I stepped back. Was I wrong? Was Grandma Belinda just fantasizing? Oh, why couldn't the truth be as plain as day? Why was everything to do with this family so cloudy and confused? Was it like that in all families?

Grandma Olivia leaned back and moaned.

"You've made my head pound again. Please, send Loretta up immediately. I need her to get me more of my medicine," she said in a thin, breathless voice.

"Where is it? I'll get it," I offered.

"I'd rather do without it and suffer," she retorted. "Just send Loretta up on your way out." She thought a moment and sat forward again. "How did you get here?"

"A friend brought me."

"A friend? Is your friend downstairs, too? Is my house full of strangers?"

"No, I sent her away."

"And how do you intend to get home then? Go walking on the highways so I hear about it?"

"I thought maybe if Raymond were here—"

"He's not. He's running errands. And of course Samuel is down at the docks wasting time with fishermen. Damn your insolence," she muttered. "Hand me my pocketbook and I'll give you taxi fare," she said.

276

"I don't need your money. I've been working and have my own," I said.

"Suit yourself. Actually, that's good. I'm glad you have some independence. I have a feeling you're going to need it. Go downstairs and call your taxi and take yourself and Belinda's idiocy home," she ordered.

She fell back against her pillow and put her hand over her forehead.

"Loretta!" she cried.

I turned and went out the door. Loretta must have been waiting at the bottom of the steps, for she heard Grandma Olivia's cry and was already coming up quickly.

"I told you not to go up," she said. "I told you. Now she'll be furious at me." She glared angrily at me as we passed each other on the stairs.

I hurried down and went to the phone in the kitchen where the telephone numbers for various services were posted on the wall. I found the number for the taxicab company and called for a car. Then I went out front and sat on a stone bench and waited. As I sat there, I thought about Grandma Belinda. She didn't seem mean enough to make up a story about Judge Childs just to get back at him. How I wished there was someone else to talk to, someone who had been around at the time. Grandpa Samuel was there, but he wouldn't contradict Grandma Olivia. That was certain. There was no point in asking him anything.

I longed to be with people like Papa George and Mama Arlene again, people who had no affectations, who didn't connive and plot against people they supposedly loved. I longed for people who meant what they said, people who didn't hide behind innuendo and double meanings, whose pasts weren't cloaked in shadows, simpler people who wore their hearts on their sleeves and whose smiles had nothing behind them but love and affection. They weren't rich and they didn't live in big, luxurious homes. They had

277

no political power and influence. No one feared them, but they were more content and they could sleep with crystal-clear consciences.

Everyone had some regrets, some choices they wished they hadn't made. Everyone's life was stained with mistakes and blotched with sadness, but simple, honest people had more smiles and more laughter in their hearts. Their wealth wasn't as easily counted, but it was there, and I longed to be with them again. Maybe I really should leave, I thought. Maybe I should welcome being thrown out on the street. Grandma Olivia's threats could be rewards in my way of thinking.

The taxi arrived and I got in quickly. The driver was an older man with curly, gray hair and a round, red face.

"Where to, Miss?" he asked as we moved down the driveway.

I thought a moment.

"Do you know Judge Childs?" I asked.

"Nelson Childs? Sure do. Everyone who's lived here most of his life knows the judge, Miss."

"Good. You know where he lives then?"

"Sure. Post Hill Road, about a mile from here. You can't miss his house. It's one of the biggest on the Cape. Is that where you want me to take you?" he asked.

I hesitated.

"Yes," I said firmly. "That's where I want to go."

"Then we'll pull up anchor and set sail," he said and turned left instead of right, which was the way back home.

The jovial taxi driver was full of questions, but if he had hoped to make a meal of my answers, he was going to starve. I answered everything with a yes or a no or a maybe. When it came to being closed-mouthed, I had many models to learn from in this New England community.

Post Hill Road was a paved street that turned for a quarter of a mile or so up a rise and then toward the beach. There were only two other homes on the street, both small Cape Cod houses. But the judge's home was a true New England mansion, even more impressive than Grandma Olivia and Grandpa Samuel's home.

"You know this is a historical house, don't you?" the taxi driver asked.

"No."

"The judge bought it for a song and then he and his wife restored it. It's even been featured in a few magazines. My wife knows all about that stuff," he added. "It's a three-story colonial," he said as we drew closer. The house had been restored in a weathered grey cladding and had a semicircular entry porch. What made it even more unusual was its large octagonal cupola.

The driveway was circular. Like Grandma Olivia and Grandpa Samuel's grounds, the lawn was pampered and designed with fountains, walkways, and small rock gardens, but there was almost twice as much acreage here. When we entered the circular drive, I looked off to the right and saw the dock, the moored sailboat and motor boat, and some small dinghies. Just behind the house was a large gazebo and another area for flowers, where I saw a swing seat under a large maple tree.

The judge's car was in front of the garage so I felt confident he was home.

"How much would it cost to have you wait for me?" I asked the taxi driver.

"How long?"

"About twenty minutes," I said. He shrugged.

"I have to charge you another fifteen dollars for half hour or part of," he replied.

"That's fine," I said and got out. I think he would have waited for nothing just to satisfy his curiosity. He didn't take his eyes off me as I stepped up to the front door and rang the bell. I heard a deep ding-dong sound on the inside and waited. Moments later, a short, balding man who looked to be in his early sixties opened the door. He wasn't dressed like a butler or a servant. He wore a white shirt opened at the collar and a pair of dark slacks. The small ridges of gray hair resembled steel wool over the sides of his head and down the back where it was a great deal thicker. He had a caramel complexion with dark brown eyes and his nose was thick at the bridge and his lower lip was fuller than his upper.

He took a pair of wire-rimmed glasses from his top pocket and placed them slowly over his eyes to gaze out at me. They magnified his eyes and made them look even rounder. Without speaking, he looked over at the taxicab and then he turned back to me.

"Didn't hear you drive up," he said. "How can I help you?"

"My name is Melody Logan. I'd like to see Judge Childs," I said.

"Judge expecting you?" he asked. He seemed astounded by my visit. Didn't the judge ever have people calling on him?

"No, but he asked me to drop by when I had an opportunity," I replied.

"That so?" he said and stood there chewing on the idea for a moment. Then he shook his head. "He don't usually see people unless they have an appointment with him," he added.

"Can you please tell him I'm here?" I asked, not hiding my impatience.

He didn't move.

"He might be nappin' in the den. That's where he usually is if he don't go someplace on Sunday. He falls asleep after he reads the papers."

"I have a taxicab waiting for me," I pointed out so he would appreciate the time he was wasting. He nodded.

"Yeah. Okay. I'll go check." He started to close the door on me. "I suppose you could wait inside," he decided and stepped back to let me enter. He closed the door. "Be right back," he promised and started down the short corridor.

The only illumination in the entry way and the living room on my right came from the sunlight that penetrated the windows with their curtains drawn back, but I could see some decorative wood ornaments applied to the walls in the corridor. There were paintings on these walls as well, but I didn't think any of them were Kenneth's. They weren't his style. They were original oils depicting colonial scenes, realistic with subdued colors, all set in thick, ornate frames.

All the furniture I saw looked antique. It was as if it had come with the house and it, too, had been restored. I felt as if I had stepped into a museum or one of those reconstructed homes open to tours. It didn't feel lived in, warm. Yet from somewhere deep in the house came music I recognized. I listened hard until I recalled it from music class. It was Debussy's *La Mer*.

Moments later, the balding man appeared, followed by Judge Childs dressed in a maroon satin robe with matching slippers. His hair was a little disheveled, and as he drew closer, I saw he hadn't shaved. His eyes were somewhat bloodshot and he looked flushed, as if he had been jolted out of a deep sleep.

"Melody, my dear. What a wonderful surprise," he said, holding out his hands. "When Morton told me I had a beautiful young lady visiting, I thought he was joking. You did right to wake me, Morton," the judge told his butler.

"I didn't mean to disturb you," I said.

"Oh nonsense. Old men like myself need to be

disturbed. Otherwise, they would just waste away musing about their glorious lost youth. How about something to drink? A lemonade perhaps?"

"That would be fine," I said.

"Morton, we'll be in the sitting room," the judge said. "Two lemonades if you please."

"Very good, Judge."

"My maid, Toby, is off today," he explained. "This way, my dear," he said, moving toward the room to our right. When we entered, he rushed over to turn on the lamps. "Please have a seat," he said, indicating the strange looking bench to his right. I hesitated. "Oh, you can sit on it," he said with a smile. "It's actually comfortable."

"I've never seen anything like it," I said.

"Neither had I until my wife bought it at an auction in Boston. It's called an empire hall bench and it was made around 1810. Most everything in this house is an antique of one sort or another. Our furnishings are quite eclectic, as is the artwork. My wife made the house her life. She would rush off for hours, go miles and miles if she heard there was an auction or a sale of antiques, and New England has an antique shop or an auction every ten feet," the judge remarked. "I swear—"

He sat in a high-backed, ornate gold chair with a red cushion backing and red seat. He looked uncomfortable because the chair was small, but he didn't complain.

"But I'll say this for her, she never bought something and didn't put it to use. No showcase furnishing for her. We had to use it all. Wait until I show you the dining room. The table is from the early eighteenth century, Baroque style, I think. I can't remember it all. Anyway," he rattled on, "you can see where Kenneth got his first education in art, architecture, and the like. I blamed his mother for that," he said.

"He's a wonderful artist though, isn't he?"

"Yes, I guess he is. People do pay large sums of money for his work. Ah, here's our lemonade," he said as Morton returned with two tumblers on a silver tray. "The glasses are contemporary, but that tray—what about that tray, Morton?"

"French, 1857," Morton recited.

"There, you see. Morton knows it all. He drove my wife everywhere in those days, didn't you, Morton?"

"Yes sir."

"Morton's been with me, what, forty years now, Morton?"

"Forty-two years and four months, Judge."

Judge Childs laughed.

"What a memory. I depend on Morton for all my dates and responsibilities now, don't I, Morton?"

"I do my best, Judge."

"That he does, that he does. Well, drink up. Thank you, Morton."

"Yes sir," Morton said and left.

"Don't know where I'd be without him. When I lost my wife, I was lost myself. I didn't know where my own medicine was kept. So," he said, his eyes shifting to me, "you came to visit, did you? How did you get here, by the way?"

"Taxicab," I said. "I have him waiting."

"Oh, that's terrible. Unheard of. Let me take care of that," he said. He started to get up.

"It's all right, Judge Childs."

"No, no. Morton will drive you home. I don't want any taxicab driver hanging about. It will only be a moment," he insisted and left. I heard him whispering to Morton in the hallway and then I heard Morton go out.

"I have to pay him," I said as soon as the judge appeared again.

"That's taken care of, my dear. I'm honored you've come to visit. The least I can do is take care of the cab driver. Now then—oh, how's Jacob? I should have

283

asked you that first thing," he said returning to his seat.

"He's doing well and might come home very soon. Maybe even tomorrow."

"That's wonderful." He sipped his lemonade. "Yes, I have antiques that would make a museum curator's mouth water," he continued. He seemed driven to talk, nervous. It suddenly occurred to me that Grandma Olivia might have called him and told him the gist of my conversation with her.

"You know I've been visiting my grandmother Belinda," I began.

"Oh?" He said, nodding. "I do think Olivia mentioned that. Yes. How is Belinda doing?"

"Haven't you visited her yourself, Judge Childs?" I asked.

"Me? Oh, not for some time," he said. "Why, did she say I was there?"

"Yes."

He laughed.

"Poor Belinda. Even before she was, well, disturbed, she had a problem with reality," he said. It sounded like a line he and Grandma Olivia had rehearsed.

"But you have visited her?"

"Oh sure. You see that painting there," he said nodding to a large portrait on the wall behind me. "My wife found that in a sale just outside of Hyannis Port. Bought it for two hundred and fifty dollars. Turns out it's an original and probably worth ten thousand if it's worth a penny. She was good at making finds like that.

"So," he said without taking a breath, "how's your fiddle playing?"

I put the lemonade down slowly on the small marble table beside me. Morton had left a wooden coaster that looked as if it, too, was some sort of antique. Then I turned to the judge. My silence made him swallow hard. He stared a moment and then he nodded softly.

"This isn't just a casual visit, is it? You came here to ask me something specific, didn't you?"

"Yes sir," I said. "I think you know what it is, too," I said. He nodded again, put his own glass down, and took a deep breath, closing his eyes and then opening them.

"You sure you want to ask me these questions?" he said.

"Yes. I know everyone tells me there's no point in stirring up the past, that it just brings a lot of pain to a lot of people. But I grew up believing I was one person and then I found out, in a hard and shocking way, that I was someone else, that the people I had loved and trusted all my life were lying to me about the most basic thing of all, me, my identity," I said.

The judge nodded.

"When you get to be as old as I am, you look back on your life and it seems as if you've led at least two different lives. I wasn't a wild young man. I never did much that would make my parents ashamed, and I did do a lot that made them proud. Funny thing is, if you've had good parents and you've loved them and known they loved you, even after they're dead, you worry about doing things that would make them ashamed. I guess that's what people mean when they say you can live on in your children."

"I don't know both my parents," I said. "I may never know who my real father is, but I know my mother and now I know my grandmother. Are you my grandfather?" I asked bluntly. He stared at me. "Grandma Olivia doesn't want me to know the truth, but I think she has her own private reasons for that."

He smiled.

"You're a bright young woman. Any man would be proud to call you his granddaughter."

"Are you that man?" I pursued.

He brought his head back and gazed up at the ceiling. When he lowered his head, his eyes were glassy with tears. I held my breath.

"My Louise knew, but she was too much the lady to ever bring it up," he said. "And you should have seen her around Haille. She never made that girl feel unwanted. Hers was a heart so full of charity and love, it could forgive Judas.

"Oh, I could say I drank too much in those days. I could blame it on bourbon, or I could say Belinda was beautiful and enticing, which she was, but in the end, I have to bear the burden of my own sins."

"Then you are my mother's father and, therefore, my grandfather?"

"Yes," he said. He shook his head and smiled. "Look how simple it is to say it now. Maybe because I'm looking at you and I see the pain. I can't lie in the face of that. At least, I can't now," he said. "I never had to lie to Louise. She never came right out and asked me," he said. "Isn't that wonderful? I didn't deserve her."

"Did my mother ever know?"

"Yes, but not until she was much older. Actually, not long before she got herself into trouble and she and Chester left Provincetown."

"You mean pregnant with me?"

He nodded.

"I think I suddenly need something stronger than this," he said, holding up the lemonade. "If you'll excuse me a moment." He rose and went to a cabinet to take out a bottle of Tennessee whiskey. He poured himself a half a glass and drank most of it in a gulp. "Fortifies the courage," he explained, poured himself another, and stood by the window.

"How did she find out?" I asked.

"I had to tell her eventually. When I discovered she and Kenneth were getting too serious about each other. It broke my heart to do it, but under the

286

circumstances, I had no choice." He turned, looking as if he had aged years in minutes. "They both resented me for it."

"Especially Kenneth?"

"Yes," he said, bowing his head in sorrow. "It's terrible enough when a son learns his father was unfaithful to his mother, but when that infidelity steals away the woman he loves, the pain is far more and the chasm it creates between father and son . . . well, it would be easier to step across the Grand Canyon than bridge the gap that's grown between my son and me. I'm afraid, I'll take that to my grave."

"Why was my grandmother locked away in that place?" I asked, my eyes narrow with suspicion. Judge Childs shifted his eyes away guiltily and gazed out the window as he spoke.

"I never approved of how Belinda was treated during her pregnancy. Olivia was embarrassed about it, of course, and kept her out of sight, literally a prisoner in her home. I wasn't the one to complain, for obvious reasons, although I did express as much disapproval as I could.

"In short, the pregnancy, the imprisonment, her history of promiscuity, drinking, they all took their toll and she became a rather disturbed woman after Haille's birth. We consulted with a doctor, a psychiatrist friend of mine, who recommended an institutionalized setting. In the beginning we—I hoped it would be temporary, but it went on and on."

"Because that was what Grandma Olivia wanted—her embarrassment shut away."

He looked at me and then lowered his eyes with shame.

"You have to understand my predicament at the time. I was married. I had children. Kenneth had recently been born. I was in politics."

"She threatened you. If you didn't cooperate, she threatened you," I concluded. He didn't deny it.

"Ironically, it might have been the best thing for Belinda anyway. I did visit her whenever it was possible."

"To ease your conscience," I accused, my eyes fixed unflinchingly on him. He returned my gaze and shook his head.

"When you look at me like that, you resemble Olivia more than Belinda. I could never hide my weaknesses from her, nor my shame. I know Olivia holds you in higher regard than you think," he added.

"It's like being complimented by the devil."

"Oh, she's not all that bad. She's had a difficult life and she's done well. She's actually been Samuel's strength. He owes his success to her."

"I know. She lets everyone know how indebted they are to her, especially me," I muttered. I looked up at him again sharply. "Since I first visited Grandma Belinda, Grandma Olivia has had them give Belinda medicine that keeps her in a daze, and she tried to keep me from visiting."

"Oh? I didn't know that."

"Well now you do."

He nodded.

"I'll see that it stops," he promised.

"Somehow, someone should make it possible for her to come home," I said, tears in the corners of my eyes.

"Yes," he said in a tired, defeated voice, "only where is her home now? Where she is, I'm afraid," he replied to his own question.

"Maybe someday I'll be able to make a home for her."

"Maybe you will," he agreed.

"First, I have to find my own home," I said. "I want to know who my real father is."

"If I knew, I would tell you, but Haille never confided anything intimate to me. I just know it's not Kenneth, thank God. What a mess that would have

288

been. Sins of the father," he muttered and shook his head.

"For what it's worth to you," he added, as I started to turn away, "my home is always open to you."

I thought about this and then just nodded without reply.

"I wish there was some way I could earn your forgiveness, Melody," he said.

"It's not my forgiveness you need."

Unable to look at me, he finished the whiskey in his glass.

"I've got to go home," I said.

"Of course. I'll fetch Morton."

We walked out into the hallway.

"Do you think," he began, "there will ever be a time when you can look at me as your grandfather?"

"For as long as I've known you, you've pretended it wasn't true."

"I know, and I regret it," he said.

"So do I," I replied. "I suppose it comes down to who regrets it more."

He smiled.

"When it comes to regrets, I have the edge."

I softened my eyes. He did look like a broken, remorseful old man and for the moment, I felt pity more than I felt anger. Anger was a sword, sharp and hot, but it also burned and cut the person who held it in their vengeful grasp.

"What's Grandma Olivia going to do when she learns you've told me the truth?" I asked.

He thought on this and then smiled.

"Pretend I didn't," he said, which brought a smile to my face, too.

Then he leaned forward and kissed me on the cheek.

"I'm glad you came here today, Melody," he said. "Morton will be right with you."

I stepped out and took a deep breath. My lungs felt

289

full of hot air, enough to make me explode. From practically every point around this house, there was a good view of the ocean. The front steps were no different.

I saw a sailboat bucking the waves, the ocean spray shooting up around it, its sails full of wind. It was too beautiful here to plant a garden of lies. Eventually, the ocean, like time itself, would wash them away and leave us with the naked truth on the beach.

I wasn't as afraid of tomorrow as I had been yesterday. In fact, I looked forward to it.

14
&

Jealousy

*F*rom the way Morton spoke about Judge Childs
when Morton drove me home, it was apparent to me
that he loved him as he would love his own father.
Apparently, my grandfather had helped Morton when
he had gotten himself into trouble with the law. He
was about twenty at the time. My grandfather offered
him a job driving for him, helping around the house,
being his all-around assistant, and Morton had remained with Judge Childs ever since. I wondered just
how much Morton really knew about the family
secrets. However, I could see he wasn't one to tell
tales out of school, especially if it involved my grandfather. He'd rather cut out his own tongue than speak
a word against him.

I wondered about my grandfather, a man who could
earn so much respect and such devoted loyalty from a
complete stranger. I wanted to believe that meant he
had some very fine qualities, but what the judge had
done to Grandma Belinda was wrong, very wrong. He
compounded the sin by cooperating with Grandma
Olivia, who wanted her sister kept out of sight. He

succumbed to Olivia's jealous rage and paid a high price to protect his own name and reputation. It cost him his peace of mind at a time in his life when he most needed it, and most important, it cost him his son's love. Despite his wealth, his big house full of valuable antiques, his beautiful property, his position in the community, he really was someone to be pitied. That much Morton did reveal.

"You made the judge happy," he said with admiration. "I could see it in his face. He hasn't worn a smile like that for years. At least, not since his wife died."

"Did you like her as much as you like Judge Childs?" I asked.

"Oh surely yes. Mrs. Childs was a real lady. She never let down her hair in public, and she always treated everyone with the utmost respect, no matter what color he or she was, or what their family did for a living. She was a pretty woman, too, and she wrote poems. She published some in those small magazines, and once in a big magazine from New York City. I don't recall exactly which one, but I know it was an important magazine. Mr. Kenneth was right proud of her at the time."

"I work for Kenneth, you know," I told him as we drove into town.

"Oh, that's right. You're Mrs. Logan's granddaughter. The judge told me you were helping Kenneth around his house and such." He shook his head. "The next time you see him, you tell him he should come visit more."

"Do you know why he doesn't?" I asked softly.

"That isn't my business. I just know a son should visit his father when his father is along in age. That's where you're living, right there?" he said, nodding at Uncle Jacob and Aunt Sara's house.

"Yes."

I saw the car in the driveway beside the truck and

knew Cary was home. Why wasn't he visiting Uncle Jacob at the hospital? I wondered.

"Here we are," Morton said, pulling into the driveway. "You come visit again. I know the judge would like that," he said.

"Thank you."

I got out and hurried to the front door. As I entered, Aunt Sara was climbing the stairs with a tray in her hands. There was a bowl of clam chowder, crackers, and a piece of filleted bass with some vegetables on a plate. She swung her head around to see me come in and flashed a smile at me, her eyes full of sparkling light.

"He's home!" she announced. "Jacob's home. He insisted they release him today instead of waiting until tomorrow. I'm just bringing him some home cooking. He said he didn't miss anything as much as my cooking. You can come up to see him in a little while," she added and continued up the stairs.

"Where are Cary and May?" I called.

"In the kitchen having a late lunch," she shouted back. "Go on in there if you're hungry."

I walked down the hallway and paused in the kitchen doorway. Cary was signing to May as she ate her sandwich, explaining more to her about their father's illness. Her eyes widened and he turned to see me standing there.

"Hi. How was your visit?"

"There's a lot to tell," I said. "You brought your father home already, I see."

"He threatened to get up and walk out anyway. The doctors had no choice. They weren't happy about it. We've got to keep him quiet, resting, taking his medicine. I hope he doesn't wear out my mother. She's been up and down those stairs a half dozen times for one thing or another already and she insists on doing everything herself."

"I'll help her anyway," I said.

"You'll be away working with Kenneth," he reminded me.

"Well, I'll help her every chance I get, and so will May." I smiled and signed the same to her. She nodded eagerly and told me Aunt Sara had already agreed to let her stay home tomorrow to do just that. "See? It will be all right," I said.

"Sure," Cary said without enthusiasm. "You hungry?"

"Actually, now that I see you eating, I realize I am. I've been going ever since I left this morning."

"Going where?" he asked.

"From Grandma Belinda to Grandma Olivia and then to Judge Childs's home," I replied. His face brightened with curiosity.

"Oh, so that's what you mean by having a lot to tell?"

"I'll make myself a sandwich and tell you everything from start to finish," I promised and I did just that.

Cary shook his head, amazed at the revelations when I completed a summary of my travels and experiences.

"If Dad knew, he never let on to me," he said. "I guess this family does have its closets full of skeletons. Didn't the judge have an idea who your father might be?" Cary asked.

"No," I said. "He just told me that it wasn't long after Kenneth and Haille found out about him that she got herself into trouble and she and my stepdaddy left Provincetown."

I gazed at May, who had been watching us with curiosity as I told Cary everything. Somehow she sensed she shouldn't interrupt, but my intensity and Cary's firm attention piqued her curiosity. I quickly told her I was describing my visit with Grandma Belinda and then, to get away from going into it any further, I suggested that we take a walk on the beach after I said hello to Uncle Jacob.

"We'll all go for a walk," Cary decided.

The three of us went upstairs. The bedroom door was open. Uncle Jacob was sitting up, his back against two large, fluffy pillows. He wore a nightshirt, and although he didn't look as small as he had in the hospital bed, he still looked pale and quite a bit thinner to me. Aunt Sara was sitting at his bedside trimming his fingernails. It looked as if she had just brushed his hair, too. If Uncle Jacob was happy about being home, you couldn't tell by looking at him. He didn't smile when we appeared.

"You're sure that engine's working fine now, eh Cary?" he asked.

"Yes, Dad. She's purring better than she was."

"Doubt that," he muttered. "I always took good care of my boat."

Cary glanced at me to see if I read a reprimand in Uncle Jacob's remark.

"Hello, Uncle Jacob," I said, refusing to be ignored. "I'm happy you're home."

He grunted what sounded like a thank you, but avoided looking at me.

"You send Roy around after work tomorrow," he told Cary. "I want a word with him."

"Sure. You need anything? We're just going to take a walk on the beach."

"I have a list of groceries, Cary," Aunt Sara said.

"Oh."

"Let's do that first, Cary," I suggested.

"Sure. Where's the list, Ma?"

"Right beside the tea kettle. Add a five-pound bag of sugar, please," she said. Cary nodded and we started out.

"You have money?" Uncle Jacob called.

"Yes," Cary said.

"Stay close to home afterward. Your mother can't do everything herself," Uncle Jacob warned.

"I'll help as much as I can," I said. He finally focused his gaze on me, his eyes searching my face to see if I were looking at him any differently since our conversations in the hospital. I forced a smile and he turned back to Aunt Sara to tell her to open the window a little more.

At the supermarket, we split up the list, giving May a half dozen items to fetch herself. As Cary and I walked down the aisle pushing our cart, he grinned at me, his eyes glittering impishly.

"What's with that look you have on your face, Cary Logan?" I asked him.

"I was just pretending you and I were married and shopping together, pretending May was our little girl."

"We're kind of young to have a daughter as old as May, aren't we?"

"I just pretended she was much younger," he said with a shrug. If everything was as easy as pretending, we would all be forever happy, I thought.

"Suppose she was that young? Do you think I would let her go off by herself like this, Cary Logan? What sort of a mother do you think I would be?"

"A perfect one," he responded. "Don't you think I'll be a good father?"

"Maybe," I teased.

"Maybe? Why—" He stopped when the man in front of us turned around. It was Adam Jackson's father.

"Well, we meet again," he said, fixing his soft blue eyes on me. He wore a pair of jeans, a heather grey sweater, and sneakers and looked rather young and athletic. There was a warmth in his smile that went beyond mere cordiality, I thought. Despite Cary's discomfort, I didn't mind Adam's father.

"It's nice to run into you again," I said.

"At least you're not knocking me over this time," he kidded. I couldn't help blushing. "Hello, Cary."

"Hello," Cary answered, rather sulkily I thought.

"How's your father doing? I was sorry to hear about his illness," Mr. Jackson said.

"He's home," Cary replied and leaned over to get some cans of soup.

"That's good. Give him my regards." Mr. Jackson looked at me again. "Cary's father and I used to go fishing together once in a while. He ever tell you about that marlin we caught, Cary?"

"No sir, he didn't," Cary said. "We have to move along. My mother needs these things," Cary added gruffly.

"Oh sure. Well, don't forget to give him my best, and if he needs help with anything . . ."

"Okay," Cary said.

Mr. Jackson winked at me.

"I bet if you play the fiddle for him, he'll feel a lot better a lot faster," he said.

"Thank you."

I smiled and we walked past him. When I turned back, he was still looking our way.

"Don't look back at him. He's just flirting with you," Cary muttered.

"What?"

"Everyone knows T. J. Jackson's reputation here. Like father like son," he said. "And he doesn't care about age either. That's why he can't hold onto a secretary long."

"Really? But he has such a beautiful wife," I said, gazing back at him again despite Cary's admonition.

"Some men are never satisfied. It's an ego thing."

"Oh. Since when did you get so wise about these matters?" I asked, perhaps a bit too sharply.

He shot me a pained look.

"I'm just looking out for you, Melody," he said. He walked on in a sulk until I put my hand on his and he turned back to me.

"I'm glad you are, Cary," I said. It brought the lightness and gaiety back to his face.

May met us at the dairy counter and we finished our shopping. As we left the store, I saw Mr. Jackson putting his groceries into his car. He saw me, too, and paused to wave. I started to wave back when I saw Cary was watching out of the corner of his eye.

"Damn flirt," he said under his breath.

Was he right? I wondered. I didn't know whether to be flattered or frightened by the attention of an older man. After all, look where daydreaming about Kenneth got me. Nowhere but sad. It made sense, however. Even Mama Arlene used to use that expression as if it were gospel: Like father like son. Except, what about Kenneth? I thought. He wasn't like his father, and Cary wasn't like his.

I wondered. Was I anything like mine? Unfortunately, I doubted that I would ever know.

When we arrived home, we found Aunt Sara halfway up the stairs again, this time carrying a tray with a mug of hot tea and some biscuits.

"He wanted a cup," she explained. "I'll be right there to help put it all away," she added, nodding at the bags of groceries we carried.

"We'll take care of it, Ma," Cary said, his jaw taut with anger. "He's going to wear her out completely," he told me as we watched Aunt Sara continue up the stairs.

It wasn't a wild prediction. Uncle Jacob had a bell next to his bed that he would ring about every five minutes it seemed. He interrupted supper twice that night demanding things from Aunt Sara. She never uttered a word of complaint, she was so happy to have him home, but it was apparent to both Cary and me that she couldn't run up and down the stairs all day and night. She wasn't even able to relax enough to eat!

"Maybe you could get them to hire a special duty nurse for a while, Cary," I suggested. "If your family needed the money, maybe Grandpa Samuel and Grandma Olivia would help."

"It's not the money. You know how my father is when it comes to strangers in his house," he replied.

"Then maybe we can get him to sleep in the living room until he's a lot better," I said. "At least your mother wouldn't have to go up and down the stairs so much."

Cary thought it was a good suggestion, but when he brought that idea to Uncle Jacob, he roared with anger.

"Turn my house into a hospital, would you? I'll be up and about soon. I don't need people walking in here and seeing me laid out on some sofa like a sick child," he declared. "Who came up with that idea?" I heard him shout.

"It was my idea," Cary said. "Sorry."

"Just keep your mind on your work. That's enough for now," Uncle Jacob told him.

Aunt Sara became flustered because Uncle Jacob lost his temper. I felt so bad because Cary was upset with himself. I told him it was my fault.

"It's not your fault," he snapped at me. "I thought it was a good idea and it is."

He climbed upstairs to his work room because he was just as embarrassed by his father's reprimands as he was angry. I entertained May, playing Chinese checkers until she couldn't keep her eyes open. I kept looking for Cary to come down to the living room, but he didn't leave his attic retreat until after I had gone to bed myself.

So much for Uncle Jacob's first night home from the hospital, I thought. In any other house, it would be a night of joy, but in this one, it was a night of tension.

During the night I heard Aunt Sara leave the bedroom and go downstairs to fetch something for him, and before morning, I heard her do it again. At breakfast, the fatigue was still planted well in her eyes. She got herself up early enough to give Cary his breakfast before he went down to the dock, and then she began bringing things up to Uncle Jacob. I tried to help, but she said it would be better for now if she did it herself.

"He's a little grouchy about being so confined," she explained.

I hated to leave for the day, but at least May was going to remain at home to be of some assistance. If Uncle Jacob would let her help, that is.

I wondered when Grandma Olivia and Grandpa Samuel would be by to visit. I asked Aunt Sara.

"Later today," she told me. "Olivia's mad at Jacob for forcing the doctors to release him from the hospital. She wasn't going to come at all, but I begged her and told her Jacob would only become more upset and it wasn't good for him."

"She wasn't going to come?" I asked, astounded.

"Oh, she was just blustering about," Aunt Sara explained. "I swear. This is the most stubborn family." She bit down on her lower lip as if she had uttered the worst profanity or heresy. "It will be all right. Please, God, everything will be all right," she said.

I heard the sound of a muffled car horn and hurried out, but instead of Kenneth, Holly was there to pick me up.

"He can't drag himself away from his block of marble," she explained. "I think I saw him for ten minutes yesterday. So, how was your visit with your other grandmother?"

"Interesting," I said in a neutral voice. She raised her eyebrows.

"Oh? Aren't you the cool one? Trying to teach the teacher a thing or two?" she added and I had to laugh.

"There are some things I have to work out yet. Myself," I added.

"Okay. Remember though, I'm here for you if you need me," she said.

"Thanks."

"I hope someone needs me soon," she declared. "I'm beginning to feel like a piece of furniture around Kenneth's house."

I laughed, but we arrived at Kenneth's I saw what she meant. He was so involved in his work, he barely acknowledged my arrival. I wanted to tell him about my visit with his father and all I had learned, but I was afraid of breaking his concentration. I didn't need someone else mad at me, especially Kenneth.

"I need to check something," he said. "Would you pose for me for just a few minutes?" I did so while he studied me, thought, studied and then nodded.

"Okay, I'm fine," he said and returned to the block. "You can return to work on the base," he said when I didn't move. I gathered my tools and began. We worked quietly for a while, only the sound of the chipping and the tapping of the hammer echoing in the studio.

Finally after what seemed like hours, he stepped back, wiped his face with a towel, nodded at the block and then turned to me. I was on my knees, staring up at him. He blinked and refocused his eyes as if he were returning to this world.

"So," he said, "Holly told me you had an unpleasant visit when you went to see Belinda yesterday. What was she, sick or something?"

"No, not exactly," I said. He stared at me. I'd never make a good Logan, I thought. I couldn't keep the truth from pressing its face right up against the window pane.

"You have something to tell me?"

"Yes."

He nodded and looked away. Then he wiped his hands and walked to the window that faced the ocean. He stood there for a while staring out. I wiped my hands and brushed down my clothes. He took a deep breath and then turned back to me.

"Grandma Belinda told me things," I said. "They were keeping her shut up and giving her some medicine that made her dopey, but she told me things."

"What sort of things?" he asked.

"Things about my mother, about how she was born."

"Uh-huh," he said staring at me so oddly, his face so still, it looked chiseled from marble itself.

"As Holly told you, I then went to see Grandma Olivia. She denied everything," I said with disgust. "She continued the lies, but I knew they were lies. I just knew it," I said.

"And so?"

"I went to see your father."

"I see." He looked out the window again. "Might get some rain later today," he said. "Looks like some boomers coming out of the northeast." He looked down and then crossed to the sink to get himself a glass of water. "Want some?"

"No thanks." I didn't move. He went to the sofa and sat down. After a moment he turned back to me.

"I didn't lie to you, Melody," he said. "I just didn't tell you everything I knew. It was more painful for me, believe me," he said.

"I think I understand," I said. His raised his eyebrows.

"Really? I don't," he muttered bitterly and sipped some more water.

"It was terrible for them to keep the secret so long and permit you to grow up thinking my mother was someone else, someone you could love," I said.

He nodded, a small, tight smile on his lips.

"Yes," he said. "Terrible is a good word, but I'm afraid I can think of many others not suitable for a young girl's ears."

"Your father's a very sad man, Kenneth. I think he's very sorry," I said. Kenneth widened his smile.

"You? You want to forgive him? He let you grow up without ever knowing he was your grandfather. He never sent you a dollar or inquired about your well-being. He let Haille and Chester run off without a penny to their names to live in the hills of West Virginia, and when you arrived here, he made no attempt to tell you who you were and who he was to you. If Belinda hadn't babbled to you in the rest home, you still wouldn't know the truth," Kenneth pointed out. "Forgive him?"

He shook his head.

"I don't want to hate him," I admitted.

"Just like him to win you over even after all that. The master charmer strikes again," he said bitterly.

"I just want everyone to tell me the truth. I just want to know who my father is," I said, my throat tightening as my tears built a reservoir beneath my eyelids.

"He didn't say?"

"He told me he didn't know. He said my mother wouldn't confide in him and that all he knows is that she got into trouble after she found out the truth."

"That's right. It was his fault," Kenneth spit out. "Especially the way he told her. What did he expect would happen?"

"How did he tell her?" I asked, breathless.

Kenneth turned away. I saw by the way he was working the muscles in his jaw that it was not just difficult but painful for him to resurrect these memories. This was just why everyone was warning me about raking up the painful past, but unspoken suffering just festers like sores in your heart and eventually bursts and eats you alive inside.

303

"One afternoon while I was away, my father invited your mother to go sailing with him. Haille and I had gone with him before, and on one other occasion, she and my mother joined him on the sailboat. I thought there was nothing unusual about this particular time, and she certainly didn't.

"Imagine her," he said, turning to me, his eyes bloodshot with tears, "young and beautiful and still very innocent, dressed in one of her newest sailing outfits, her face fresh and tender with the morning dew. She liked my father, actually loved him for his charm and sense of humor. None of us ever put any special importance on the attention he rained on Haille. He flirted and beguiled every female who was in reach of his smile."

Kenneth smiled to himself for a moment, lost in some memory.

"She used to say being with my father was second best to being with me."

His smile faded.

"We were all so happy-go-lucky, the rich kids enjoying our sailboats and our cars, our clothes and jewelry, able to go almost anywhere we wanted to go, almost any time we wanted. We could have parties on the beach and pay for everything without the slightest concern. Everyone else envied us. College was nothing more than an expected promise. If we worked, we worked only to fill time and amuse ourselves. We didn't work out of necessity.

"What could go wrong for us?" he asked, shaking his head. He wasn't looking at me so much as he was at his memories now. "If we got sick, we received the best medical attention; if we broke something, it was replaced, no matter the cost. Our entire futures seemed to be laid out on a primrose path. All of us knew how lucky we were and we had only a vague interest in those who weren't. Maybe that was because, deep inside, the smartest of us knew life can be a bubble that bursts at any moment and everything you thought was so important can vanish in an instant."

He sighed deeply, his shoulders rising and then falling as he lowered his head.

"She arrived early that afternoon. Surprise! My mother wasn't going along this time. It was to be just her and dad."

He raised his head.

"She described every little detail about that day to me afterward, alternating between crying and laughing, her laughter thin and on the verge of insanity.

"Dad looked dapper, handsome, younger than ever. She noticed he was more talkative than usual when she arrived, but his talk was about new things my mother had bought at auctions, plans he had to redo this and redo that around the house, small talk. Until they got out to sea, that is.

"He sailed into a cove and started to talk about his own youth. Pretty soon he was talking about Belinda. Haille began to feel a little uncomfortable as he described his own romantic interest in Olivia's sister. And then, he just lowered the boom on her and told her he was her father. He said it the way you might say: I have to confess, I broke that piece of china yesterday.

"Haille was stunned of course. This man sitting across from her in the sailboat, this man she had known all her life as my father, this charming friend of Olivia and Samuel Logan, one afternoon chose to tell her he was her father. He took her out to sea so she was more or less trapped on the boat and had to hear his side of the story, of course. She said she was tempted to jump into the water and swim to shore, but she was trembling so badly she couldn't trust her body to be strong enough to make it.

"The impact of hearing he was her father was great, but what was even greater was the realization that she and I—that we were half-brother and sister and the budding love between us was incestuous and forbidden. Imagine the feeling of betrayal she felt at that moment.

"My father defended himself by saying that if she and I had never shown any indications of becoming serious lovers, he would never have told her the truth. Isn't that incredible? He would have kept it secret forever, for as you know now, who would believe poor deranged Belinda, right? Oh, they made sure of that, my father and Olivia Logan.

"Of course, he insisted Belinda was really in need of psychiatric help and they were giving her the best, most expensive treatment possible. All men who have affairs and impregnate their lovers should have his opportunity and logic."

Kenneth laughed.

"Some force their lovers to have abortions, some pay them off and send them away, some deny having ever known them, if they can. The fortunate rich and powerful stuff their lovers into rest homes where they can be kept institutionalized, medicated, and humored. Everything Belinda said after that was just fantasy or lunacy.

"And you want me to forgive him," he said. He lay his head back again.

"That's because I see him now, Kenneth," I replied in a small, trembling voice. "I wasn't there from the beginning and I didn't know the details as you do. What did my mother do when he finally brought her back to shore?"

"She got away from him as quickly as she could. At first she called him a liar, thinking Olivia had put him up to it to keep her and me from being together."

"Why?"

"That's something only Olivia can answer. She and Haille never got along, and I think—" He hesitated and gazed up at me, deciding whether or not I was old enough to understand or whether he had a right to say it. He decided to continue. "I think Olivia always loved my father and was jealous of her own sister. That jealousy manifested itself in her relationship with Haille. Olivia treated her like Cinderella, the beautiful but inferior step-daughter.

"Anyway, Haille came home and shut herself in her room. No one knew why yet, I suppose. When I got home that night, Dad called me into the den and, fortified with a half dozen bourbon and waters, told me what he had told Haille.

"Now it was my turn to call him a liar. Who wanted it to be true? I, too, was hoping it was just a connivance to keep Haille and me from becoming boyfriend and girlfriend and eventually marrying, but he broke down and cried and confessed and blabbered like I had never seen.

"I was stunned. I rushed out of the house and over to see Haille. That was when she described the sailing and the way Dad broke the news. She was already different," Kenneth said, nodding to himself.

"How?"

"I sensed this abandon, this feeling that whatever had been keeping her in check was gone. She was like a kite whose string had broken and she was being tossed about, but not minding it. She was laughing a lot, acting like the daughter of a mentally disturbed woman. I got frightened, especially when she embraced me on the beach and said, 'Let's not care. Let's do what we want and let's do it right now, right here.'

"I panicked. It was as if a vampire had asked me to become a vampire with her. I broke her hold on me and ran from her, hearing her laughter trail after me. I still hear it sometimes.

"Anyway," he said, "the rest you know. Haille became the woman Olivia accused her of always being: promiscuous, uncaring, indifferent, reckless, and wild. The rest is as I told you. Oh, I tried to be friends anyway, tried to give her good advice, come to her aid whenever she needed me, but it was like holding back the tide, the inevitable disaster. Dad was right. It wasn't very long afterward that she became pregnant with you and then Chester came to her defense. Blindly in love with her, he stood by while she accused Samuel of unthinkable things. Maybe that was her way of getting back at my father, attacking his close friend. To her, they were all the same: Olivia, Samuel, my father, all part of the conspiracy. Anyway, shortly after that, they ran off to West Virginia.

"I don't know who your father is," he added before I could ask again. "I'm not holding back anything anymore, especially since you have spoken with my father. Haille never told me. When I asked her, she laughed and said, 'You are Kenneth. In my heart, you always will be.'

"That was why I was so taken aback when you told me you suspected I might be your father. It was eerie, as if Haille were speaking again through you. I know how much you want to know. I wish I could give you the information, give you that gift, but I can't. The truth is buried with your mother, Melody. I'm sorry."

I didn't realize I was crying until I felt the tears drip off my chin. Kenneth rose and handed me a handkerchief. I blew my nose, wiped my eyes, and took a deep breath. He smiled and nodded at me.

"You know this makes me your uncle, don't you?"

"Yes."

"Do you mind?"

"No," I said but I meant yes. I minded because for a while I had dreamed of him as a lover, too. Now, that looked even more ridiculous. I felt so ashamed, so lost. Will-o-wisp dreams never came true for me and never would. There were too many clouds in the skies over my family's past.

"Well, we'll have to give all this some serious thought now," he added and turned back to the sculpture.

"Serious thought? What can we do about any of it?" I wondered aloud.

"Depends," he said, picking up his chisel.

"On what?" I said, following him.

"On whether Dad is really ready to reveal the sins of the past, and on how Olivia and Samuel react. You're related to Olivia through Belinda, of course, but you're not a Logan." He smiled. "So," he said, bringing the hammer and the chisel to the block, "you might move in here with me, if you want." He turned. "Being as I'm a close relative now."

My jaw dropped and I gaped at him.

"Move in with you?"

"And not have to put up with that horse's ass," he added.

"You would want me to live with you?"

"Look at it from my point of view. I get a great cook and housekeeper for free," he joked. He started to tap the chisel and then stopped. "Of course, that means I would have to do something legal like file to be your guardian or something. I suppose that means I would have to attend a parent-teacher's conference, too, doesn't it? And sign your excuses for absence, parental permission slips, all that stuff?"

He looked at me but I just stared. Live with Kenneth?

"Do I have to go shopping with you and see to your dental appointments?"

"Are you serious?"

His eyes darkened a little as his face lost its touch of lightness and humor.

"One way or another I knew Haille would come back into my life," he said.

He turned and tapped the hammer harder. Chips began to fall. The echo resounded.

One way or another?

I hadn't found my father, but perhaps I had found the next best thing.

15

&

The Damage Is Done

Kenneth and I spent the rest of the day so involved in our work, we lost track of time. Now I appreciated why Kenneth devoted his life to his art. It was truly an escape from the heavy burdens and the turmoil that often rained down around us. Working together, he and I developed a rhythm that overtook and absorbed us. We were aware of each other, but never spoke and rarely even looked at each other. It was almost a religious experience as Kenneth's hands began to mold shapes and bring his vision out of the block of marble.

So lost in the artistic effort, we were both surprised to hear Holly's knock on the door, followed by her plaintive cries beseeching us to come up for air.

"I ate lunch myself. I meditated, did two personal charts, walked Ulysses until he begged for mercy. Don't you people get tired?" she exclaimed.

Kenneth and I looked at each other.

"What time is it?" he asked.

"Five-twenty," she replied.

"Oh no," I said. "I promised I'd be home early to help take care of Uncle Jacob."

"Five-twenty?" Kenneth repeated. He looked at me, astounded. "Did we eat lunch?"

I shook my head, amazed my stomach hadn't reminded me or complained.

"Fanatics," Holly accused.

I looked at myself, full of dust, my hair almost gray, my face streaked. Kenneth, too, resembled a ghost, the chips and dust turning his beard practically white.

"Someone has to take me home right away," I wailed.

"I will, if only to have some human company for a while," Holly said, glaring at Kenneth, who shrugged off her look of reprimand with that boyish smile that could charm the heart of the most wicked witch.

I brushed myself off as quickly and as best I could and then hurried out to Holly's car.

"The man's dangerous, a bad influence," she said when we started away. "Hang around him long enough, and you'll start to look like him. You might even grow a beard!" she growled. "Do you realize how long you two were shut up in there?"

"Funny," I said. "I don't feel tired. I should, doing that so long, but it's . . ."

"Invigorating?" she suggested.

"Yes."

"Well, I suppose for Kenneth, and maybe now for you, it's so deep an involvement it's like meditating, moving to a higher plane of consciousness, leaving this burdensome world of woe," she said and smiled. "You do look a lot happier than you did this morning."

She gazed at me again, her eyes narrowing suspiciously.

"You're wearing a very coy smile, Melody Logan. Something is afoot."

"Maybe," I said and laughed. "Maybe."

"Whatever it is, I'm happy for you." We rode a little longer in silence and then she turned back to me with a face of concern. "When am I going to know, or is it something so secret I may never know?"

"You'll know soon," I said.

She nodded.

"I saw it in your chart, but I didn't say anything."

"What?"

"A big change, something very dramatic involving family."

I raised my eyebrows.

"Am I warm?" she wondered.

"Overheated," I said and we both laughed. I hadn't felt this cheerful for a long time. A ray of sunshine had sliced its way through the dark, brooding clouds. But my light and happy mood vanished as soon as we arrived at the house. There was something about the way it looked that put a hard and heavy feeling in my chest. Maybe it was all in me, in my trepidation and anticipation, or maybe some of Holly's powers had rubbed off and I could sense negative energy even before it reared its ugly head.

"You all right?" she asked when we pulled into the driveway. I hadn't realized I had sighed so deeply and loudly.

"Yes, I'll be fine. Thanks for the ride."

"It's okay." She thought a moment and then said, "If Kenny goes back into the studio again tonight after dinner and stays there all night, I think I'll start planning my return to New York."

"Oh, really?" I was genuinely disappointed.

"This is just not the right time for me to visit, but I'll be back," she promised with a smile.

"When will you go?"

"I'll see. Not tomorrow anyway," she added. "There is still some battery recharging I want to do for myself here. Bye."

"Bye and thanks," I said and got out.

313

I found the house ominously quiet when I entered. I closed the door softly and practically tiptoed. There were no lights on in the living room and no sounds coming from the kitchen. No one appeared to greet me. As I walked from room to room I wondered if there was anyone home.

Oh no, I thought. I hope Cary didn't break down in his boat again. Maybe Uncle Jacob had had a relapse.

Just as I turned to go upstairs, I heard someone sobbing. I went down the hallway to the dining room and peered through the door. There sat Aunt Sara, her head down on her folded arms, her shoulders shaking.

"Aunt Sara," I cried and rushed to her side. "What's wrong? Did something happen to Cary? Uncle Jacob?"

She lifted her head slowly and then smiled through her tears.

"Oh Melody, dear. You're home. Good."

"Why are you crying?"

"Oh, it's nothing," she said quickly and dabbed the tears away with the hem of her apron. "I'm just a little tired, I guess."

"I'm sorry I didn't get home earlier, but I just didn't realize the time."

"That's all right, dear." She smiled weakly and took a deep breath. It was as if she carried a lead weight on a chain around her neck.

"Where is everyone? Where are Cary and May?"

"May's upstairs in her room. Cary just left for the supermarket. I made a meat loaf, but I forgot to tell you kids to pick up the beer he likes. He likes it with my meat loaf."

"He had to have it tonight?"

She stared at me.

"That's why you're crying, isn't it? He was upset so you got upset? And Cary had to run out as soon as he got back from work, right?" I asked, the whole scenario flashing before my eyes.

314

"It's nothing. I should have remembered." She sighed. "I usually do."

"I bet he's not even supposed to be drinking it," I exclaimed. "And after all you've been doing for him, for him to make a scene and—"

"It's all right, dear. Cary will be back soon. I have the meat loaf on low and—"

"That's not the point, Aunt Sara. If he drives you until you get sick, too, where will everyone be?"

"I'll be fine," she insisted. "I wanted to have an earlier dinner tonight, though. Olivia and Samuel were here today. We had a nice lunch and their visit cheered Jacob, but before they left, Olivia told me to tell you she would be sending Raymond for you about seven."

"What?"

"She said she wanted to see you and—"

"Well, maybe I don't want to see her," I snapped.

Aunt Sara's face filled with shock. She shook her head as if to deny the words.

"Not want to see her?"

"Who is she, the queen? Demanding this and that? I'm tired and I was looking forward to relaxing tonight. I have a lot to think about," I added, but Aunt Sara heard nothing. Her huge scared eyes stared woefully back at me. "Oh, just forget it, Aunt Sara. Forget I said anything. I'm going up to wash off this marble dust and then I'll come down and help you with supper or anything else you need."

I turned and left her, a sailboat drifting in a windless sea. She was kind and loving, willing always to sacrifice her own happiness and comfort for someone else, especially for Uncle Jacob. Yet she was the saddest and most tragic person I knew right now. I wished I'd had Holly there. I'd ask her what went wrong with Aunt Sara's stars? Where were the sun and the moon when Aunt Sara was born?

May was waiting for me in my room. She was

315

sitting on the floor, her knees up, drawing on her pad, her back against the frame of the bed. She saw my feet and looked up quickly.

I asked her why she was waiting in my room and she quickly signed back that she was upset for Cary. He had come home exhausted, his head drooping, his shirt off and over his shoulder, looking forward to a shower and a good meal, but Aunt Sara greeted him at the door and told him what Uncle Jacob demanded. May said Cary didn't even set foot in the house. He turned and hopped into his truck. May claimed she had gone out after him, trying to get him to wait. She wanted to go along, but he shot off angrily and drove so fast, he nearly turned over making the turn! she exclaimed through her hands and eyes. May told me she had come into my room afterward because she was actually frightened by all this. She had been hoping I would soon come home and comfort her.

It filled me with rage, but rage that wasn't aimed at Uncle Jacob as much as it was at the whole situation. How could I go down there later and tell Aunt Sara that I was going to move in with Kenneth Childs? How could I desert her and May and Cary at this point? Aunt Sara still thought I had been sent to fill the gap made in her heart by Laura's death. Cary and May needed me more than ever. I felt frustrated, turned and twisted. Aunt Sara wasn't the sailboat in a windless sea, I was. I was the one who had little or no control of her destiny. Capricious fate blew at my sails or left me in a state of dreary calm whenever it had a whim to do so.

I assured May that everything would be all right. I promised her I would help Aunt Sara and we would make Uncle Jacob comfortable and happy again. Then I went into the bathroom and took a quick shower, feeling as if I had swallowed a lump of bread dough and it was stuck in my chest. As I was toweling my hair dry, I heard shouting in the hallway and hurried to my door.

What was going on now?

Cary was standing outside his father's bedroom, his head lowered until his chin rested on his chest, listening to Uncle Jacob rant and rave.

"We never had a catch that bad! What the hell was Roy doing? I bet he's been slacking off without me looking over his shoulder, is that it? The man works for you. You can't treat him like a friend. You treat him like an employee or else he'll take advantage."

"It wasn't his fault, Dad, or mine. We did everything we always do."

"Two lobsters! Two lobsters! And each barely a pound and a quarter?"

"I told you we have to get out of the lobster business, Dad," Cary said softly.

"Never mind that nonsense. I see I've got to get myself up and out of this bed faster. Tell your mother I'm ready to eat," he snapped.

Cary nodded and turned. He saw me wrapped in a bath towel standing in the doorway. His eyes brightened for a moment and then became dull again when he realized I had been there while Uncle Jacob verbally whipped him.

"Hi," I said.

"Hi. I thought you'd be home before me," he added as he walked with me down the hallway.

"We got so lost in the work, we didn't realize the time until Holly came knocking on the studio door."

Cary smirked at my excuse.

"I have to go down and tell Ma to bring up his food."

"He's becoming a real monster," I declared, glaring furiously at Uncle Jacob's doorway.

"He's just frustrated," Cary muttered and started for the stairs.

"Your mother was crying when I got home, Cary."
He paused and looked at me.

"She's near the breaking point herself," I warned strongly.

"I'm doing the best I can!" he cried, tears filling his eyes.

"I didn't mean—I'm not blaming you, Cary."

He spun around and stomped so hard down the stairs, I thought he would crack a step. The last thing I had intended was to upset him. The look on his face turned my heart to glass which was quickly shattered by my boiling blood.

It's Uncle Jacob's fault, I fumed. Damn him. Without hesitation, I marched across the hallway to his bedroom door. He was sitting back against his pillow, anticipating his tray of food, looking like some spoiled member of royalty who thought everyone else existed merely to please him.

"Uncle Jacob," I said, addressing him as sternly as a schoolteacher.

He opened his eyes slowly, but when he saw me, they widened quickly and drank me in from head to foot. For an instant I thought he looked pleased, but it was as if the realization of that heightened his anger.

"How dare you come here dressed like that?"

"Forget about how I am dressed. I don't care. You're being unreasonable, throwing tantrums like a baby when everyone is doing their best to make you comfortable and help you get well. But if you don't stop shouting and demanding, you'll make Aunt Sara sick, too!"

His mouth opened and closed without a word. Then he waved his fist at me.

"Get out! Get out of my sight you daughter of temptation."

The veins in his neck strained and he fell back against his pillow, his face red.

"I'm just telling you this for your own good as well as everyone else's," I concluded.

He slammed his eyelids shut as if he had to wipe out the sight of me. It's futile, I thought. The man's too selfish. I returned to my room and got dressed. Just as I finished, I heard Cary coming up the stairs. He was carrying the tray of food and Aunt Sara was trailing behind, her every footstep a monumental effort now. Cary and I exchanged glances as he continued down the hallway, but Aunt Sara paused.

"Everything's ready downstairs, dear. May's at the table. Just serve the dinner. I have to stay with Jacob and help him eat his meal."

"When will you eat, Aunt Sara?"

"I've already had more than I need. Please, just be sure May eats."

"Okay, Aunt Sara. Don't worry. I'll take care of her."

"Don't forget," she said. "Raymond's coming for you at seven."

Cary looked back, his eyebrows raised with curiosity.

"I'm sure Grandma Olivia wouldn't permit me to forget," I muttered and went downstairs.

"What does Grandma Olivia want?" Cary asked when he joined May and me at the dinner table.

"I don't know. All I know is I'm being summoned to the palace. But she might be in for a surprise," I added and went to the kitchen to get the meat loaf. May had already set the table and brought out the bread and the jug of ice water.

"What sort of surprise?" Cary asked when I sat at the table. He was in his father's seat again, the Bible opened and ready for his reading.

Instead of answering, I stared down at my plate and kept my head lowered.

"What surprise, Melody?" he asked.

"The meat loaf's getting cold, Cary."

Reluctantly, he picked up the Bible. I lifted my eyes toward May and saw her looking small and frightened. It amazed me how although she was deaf, she could still pick up on the tone of conversations. Years of silence had made her perceptive when it came to a turn of the head, a movement in the eyes, a twist of the lips. She could read people's moods better than most people who had no trouble hearing.

"Luke, Chapter 6," Cary began. There was a bookmark stuck at the pages his father wanted read. Cary opened to them and then, in his father's voice, he read, "'For a good tree bringeth not forth corrupt fruit; neither does a corrupt tree bring forth good fruit.

"'For every tree is known by his own fruit . . .'"

He read to the end of the chapter and then put the Bible down without another word. I began to serve the meat loaf, thinking that Uncle Jacob was always with us at this table as long as he chose the Bible selections to be read.

"You have some new secret?" Cary asked after he took his first forkful. When I didn't reply, he added, "I kind of thought we weren't keeping secrets from each other."

"It's not a secret, Cary." I glanced at May. She watched me with question marks in her eyes, too. I turned to Cary. "I already told you what Judge Childs told me."

"So?"

"So since Judge Childs is really my grandfather, Kenneth is my true uncle."

"What does that mean?"

"It means he could be my guardian," I blurted.

Cary stared at me, his fork frozen in the air. Then his eyes darkened with the realization.

"You mean, you're thinking about going to live with him?"

"Maybe," I said. "At the moment he's my closest true relative," I added.

He continued to stare at me instead of eating.

"Your food's getting cold, Cary."

"I'm not hungry."

"Look, this might even be better for now, considering the way your father is," I said.

"How could it be better?"

"He doesn't want me here. It's only irritating him and he has to recuperate."

"Do what you want," Cary snapped and pushed his plate away. "Everybody should just go and do what they want!" he cried and rose from the table.

"Cary!"

He marched out of the dining room and out of the house. I heard the front door slam.

May's hands were going like birds chasing each other.

"He's just upset about your father," I signed, "and your mother. He'll be all right. Could you clear the table when you're finished? I'll go after him."

She nodded and I hurried down the hall and out of the house. He hadn't gone far. He was leaning against the truck, his arms folded across his chest, his head down. The sky had changed to a dark plum color streaked with crimson that looked like freshly spilled blood and the ocean had an inky-gray sheen. I saw no boats, and with no traffic on our street and no other people about, I felt smaller, alone, like the two of us were the last people on earth.

I put my hand on his shoulder. He didn't look up.

"First Laura and then you," he said.

"If I move in with my uncle, I won't be leaving you for good, Cary. I'll still be in Provincetown. We'll still see each other whenever we want to see each other."

"Will we?"

He raised his head. His green eyes were darker and strangely haunted.

321

"Yes," I said emphatically. He smiled as if I had said the silliest thing. "I promise," I added.

"Promises," he muttered and gazed toward the ocean. "You of all people know they're like balloons. When you first get them, they're fresh and bright and full and then time passes and they lose air or simply explode. Laura and I used to make all sorts of promises to each other."

"I'm not Laura, Cary. I never intended to be. I'm not your sister. I'm—"

He looked at me, his eyes full of expectation.

"Yes?" he said.

"I'm your girlfriend, or at least, I hope I am."

"Do you?"

"I wouldn't say it if I didn't mean it, Cary. You know how I feel about lies."

He smiled.

"Yes, that I know," he said, nodding. He took a deep breath and looked up at the windows on the second floor of the house. "I'm never going to please him, you know."

"That's his fault, Cary, not yours," I said.

"It doesn't matter whose fault it is. I've been at his side all my life. Ever since I was old enough to walk out to the dock with him. He's a good sailor—the best. I never felt anything but safe being out there with him."

"That's good," I said. "That's the way a son should feel about his father."

He shook his head. And then he shut his eyes as if a vision so terrible it cut through his brain like a knife had appeared.

"What is it, Cary?"

"I didn't tell Ma everything," he said after a short pause and another deep sigh.

"What do you mean?"

"The doctor doesn't think he will ever be what he was. He wants him to go on disability and stop working altogether," he said. "Too much damage to his heart."

"Oh." I slumped back against the truck beside him, suddenly feeling guilty about yelling at Uncle Jacob. "He doesn't know?"

"He knows; he just won't accept it," Cary said. "When I brought him home, he said, 'I don't want to die on land. I'll die on my boat.'"

I thought about Aunt Sara and how she would fall apart like a figure of ice surprised by the spring sunshine.

"You've just got to make him understand, Cary."

"Understand? I might as well shout at the wind or stand on the beach and try to scare away the tide. The sea is in his blood. Almost every day of his life, he got up and went to sea." He smiled. "He always says he wobbles when he walks on dry land. He says he gets land sick the way most people get seasick.

"And, he'll worry about the family, making a living. He was planning on expanding the cranberry business, you know."

"You can do all that, Cary."

"It won't be the same for him. Dad's not a man who can spend the rest of his life sitting in a rocker, waiting for me to come home with a report."

"Well what's his solution?" I cried.

"There is no solution," he said. "We'll just do what we have to do when we have to do it, I guess." He took a deep breath and looked at the house. "Let's go back before Ma comes down and finds we ran away from her dinner."

I took his arm and he turned his troubled, dark green eyes to me.

"I'll be at your side to help you whenever I can, Cary."

His eyes brightened and he looked young again, young and strong and hopeful. Then he leaned closer and we kissed. It was just a soft kiss, a moment, but it

323

was like a promise, and not a promise that would burst like a balloon.

At least, that's what I believed in my heart.

Raymond was there promptly at seven. Aunt Sara came down from Uncle Jacob's room to be sure I was ready and that I would go. Why pleasing Grandma Olivia reigned so importantly in her mind, I would never understand. But it did. It was as if Grandma Olivia left her shadow on the walls here and Aunt Sara always felt that shadow hovering above or behind her, waiting to pounce and approve or disapprove of anything she said or did.

I hurried out and into the car. The moon was out now, big and bright, full and smiling, with long dark clouds streaking its face and making it seem sinister one minute and gay the next. It was as if a voice whispered in my ear, telling me to beware everything, for nothing was what it appeared to be.

"Probably get some showers tonight," Raymond said as we drove off.

The weather again, I thought. And then I thought, maybe it was a secret language; maybe it was another way of revealing what was in your heart.

"As long as it's not a storm," I replied.

"No, nothing like that. Just a refreshing downpour to drop us out of this unusually humid and warm air," he said.

"And tomorrow the sun will shine?"

"Expect so," he said.

I smiled to myself and we drove on.

The great house was surprisingly dark when we arrived. Raymond got out quickly and opened my door. I hurried up to the front and rang the bell. Loretta opened the door and glared out at me. She still hadn't forgiven me for bursting in the day before, I realized.

"Grandma Olivia wants to see me," I said sharply. She grimaced as if she had a bellyache.

"In the living room," she said, stepping back.

There was only a small light on in the hallway, and there wasn't much light coming from the living room either. When I entered, I saw a single lamp lit on the table beside the chair in which Grandma Olivia sat, perched like a buzzard, her eyes in half shadow, her face wearing the darkness like a veil. She was dressed in a very plain, dark blue dress, and less jewelry than usual. Her hands grasped the knobby ends of the arms of the chair as if she were afraid she might be shaken out of it.

"You sent for me?" I asked. Her deathly silence actually frightened me and I lost much of the confidence and anger that had helped me feel firm and secure. There was a long, ungodly pause that started my heart thumping.

"Sit down!" she said sharply.

I backed myself to the sofa, not taking my eyes from her. Anyone watching me would have thought I was afraid to turn my back on her. I folded my hands in my lap and waited. She moved forward just enough to bring her face fully out of the shadows and into the light. Even so, she looked ghostly, her face so pale that her dark eyes seemed to leap out at me. I actually gasped.

"So you went from here to Nelson's house and you heard his pathetic tale," she recited, as if telling the last line of a ghost story.

"I knew my grandmother was telling the truth," I said. "I didn't believe you."

"Men," she said so disdainfully it sounded as if she thought they were the lowest form of life. "They are so weak, so at the mercy of their lust. Every man I've known, my own father, his father, my child of a husband, even my sons, even Jacob, marrying that

325

dishrag who wallows in her own tears. I told him she wasn't strong enough to be a Logan's wife, but he didn't listen to me, not even Jacob," she moaned. The tone surprised me, and I actually thought she might start crying.

"Aunt Sara is a sweet woman who's had more than her share of terrible tragedy and—"

"Oh stop it," she snapped. "You don't have any more respect for her than I do. You're too much like me," she declared. "You're more a Gordon than a Childs, believe me," she added and with some sense of pride. It sounded like a compliment, and hearing her give me one so unexpectedly took the wind from my sails.

"I respect her," I said, but without as much firmness as I thought I would have.

"You don't respect her. You pity her. Would you like to be like her?" she asked with a wry smile on small, tight lips. "Is she the sort of woman you see yourself becoming after you marry?"

"Everyone's different," I said.

She laughed.

"You don't like to say unpleasant things, even if you believe them in your heart."

"How do you know what's in my heart?" I replied, regaining my self-assurance.

"I know," she said, nodding. "In many ways you remind me of me when I was your age, even younger."

That surprised me. She, admitting she was like me?

"You will find it a disadvantage, this need to always be pleasant and do what Sara idiotically preaches: 'don't say anything about anyone if you can't say something nice,'" she recited, wagging her head in mimicry. "Isn't that what she always parrots?"

"She's a very kindhearted, considerate person who thinks the sun rises and falls on your wishes," I said. "And if she knew how you felt about her, she would feel just terrible."

"She's merely afraid of me," Grandma Olivia said with a wave of her hand. "She has about as much love for me as you do, but I don't mind. If you spend your time worrying about who loves you and who doesn't, you'll end up—end up like Belinda," she concluded.

"Why didn't you tell me the truth?" I demanded.

"It wasn't my truth to tell," she said with a pained sigh. "And it's not something I care to remember." The sadness dropped from her face and was quickly replaced with that habitual take-charge look. "Besides, what good does that do now? Belinda is in a rest home. Your mother is dead. Your real father remains a mystery. You have only what I can give you. Nelson may have confessed to his youthful sins, but believe me, he has nothing more to give you than agony. He's wasting away in that house, living alone, his other children content to be far away, his son Kenneth unforgiving."

"Kenneth told me everything he knows. He's my uncle. I have that now," I retorted.

She snickered.

"Relatives. If you ask me, they're just additional burdens. You inherit their weaknesses and problems on top of your own. If you have a relative who committed a crime, people treat you as if you committed the crime. You're tainted. Overcoming the burden of my sister has been a lifelong endeavor for me," she said. "I've done well and I'm not about to countenance any setbacks," she added, leaning forward to focus her steely eyes on me.

"What's that supposed to mean?"

"It means that I called you here tonight after speaking with Nelson and hearing him slobber like a baby over the phone, because I wanted to be certain, absolutely certain that what he told you goes nowhere else. I'm too old to do battle with a new scandal. He was a fool to break down and tell you."

"I had a right to know. It's my life, too," I protested. "Now, I know that Kenneth Childs is my uncle," I continued. "He's asked me to move in with him and permit him to become my guardian."

She recoiled as if stung by a bee.

"What? Absolutely not. Why, that would be as good as standing on the street corner and announcing it all. Is he mad?"

"He was in love with my mother," I said. "You know when he learned about his father and my grandmother, that ended their hope of becoming man and wife. He wants to do this for me."

"I will not permit it," she insisted. She reached for a small bell on the side table and rang it. Loretta appeared as if she had been dangling above the doorway. "Call Kenneth Childs for me," she ordered.

"He doesn't have a telephone," I reminded her.

"Send Raymond to his house immediately and tell him I want to see him tonight."

"Stop!" I shouted. Her eyes widened into two small balls of fire as her shoulders lifted. "He's in the middle of something very important. He can't be disturbed."

The fierce anger that sprang to Grandma Olivia's face shocked me, and Loretta just stood in the doorway, afraid to move a muscle.

"That will be all for now, Loretta."

"Should I send Mr. Raymond for Mr. Kenneth?"

"No, not at the moment," Grandma Olivia said. She sat back after Loretta left, and we contemplated each other warily. She nodded slightly, as if reaching a conclusion.

"You don't like living with my son. I imagine he's going to be especially difficult now that he'll be home so much," she added as an afterthought.

"That's not the only reason I want to move out and live with my uncle," I said.

"Nevertheless." She stiffened in her chair like a

monarch. Then she leaned toward me again, stabbing me with her hard, penetrating glare.

"You will move in here," she declared, "and live with Samuel and me for your remaining year of public school. Then you will attend one of the finer colleges and pursue whatever interests you."

"What?" My jaw hung open.

"Naturally, I will expect the most exemplary sort of behavior. I will, in return, provide you with all of your needs, a fine wardrobe, one that reflects what a granddaughter of mine should wear, and Raymond and the car will be available to take you wherever you have to go. We will tell the world that you didn't want to be an added burden to Jacob and Sarah at this time, with Jacob so sick and all. Actually, that's not far from the truth. I imagine you and Jacob don't see eye to eye and your continued presence won't help his recovery."

"You expect me to move in here with you?" I asked, still astounded at the suggestion.

"It's a much better solution. Kenneth will approve of it as well, I assure you," she said with sickening confidence.

I stared, amazed. Once, I was almost homeless, without anyone, and now, three homes were available to me.

"You and I don't have to fall in love with each other," she continued, "but we can have respect for each other."

"You, respect me?" I almost laughed.

"You have shown some resourcefulness that, as I said, reminds me of myself at your age. I'm a good judge of character, and I think you are even more like me than you want to admit. It's not a sin to be strong, Melody. And Lord knows it's up to the women in this family to be strong, since the men are all weak."

"Cary's not weak," I blurted.

"What Cary is or isn't remains to be seen. He was too attached to his twin sister to show any independence from her. Even since her death I still haven't seen Cary show any sign of backbone. There is a large fortune here and much responsibility to be assumed."

"And you're saying that I will be the one to assume it?" I asked, even more amazed at her proposals.

"We'll see. Let me just say that I am running out of good candidates." She sat back. The grandfather clock bonged the hour.

"Aunt Sara will be heartbroken," I muttered, thinking aloud.

"What would she be if you moved in with Kenneth Childs? Ecstatic? Can you imagine the gossip, Jacob's ranting? Oh, I know what my son is like. I don't need you to tell me."

"I always thought he was trying to be like you," I said. She laughed.

"Do I behave like a woman enveloped in religion? I have no false modesty nor do I pretend to be the most moral person, looking condescendingly on all those who don't pray as much. I attend church on occasion, contribute heavily to its coffers. My son Jacob is a moral snob. Don't look so shocked. I've often told him as much to his face.

"So you see, my dear Melody, you and I might have more in common than you care to admit. You'll move in immediately," she concluded and started to rise.

"I'll have to talk about it with Kenneth first," I said.

"I will not permit Nelson Childs's maudlin confessions to paint profanities across this family's good name," she declared with regal authority. "No one should doubt the firmness of my determination, nor the intensity and impact of my wrath should I be crossed."

Her words resounded like church bells, vibrating through my bones.

"Make your arrangements as soon as possible," she ordered and left the room.

As soon as she was gone I was left to contemplate her words, which still echoed in the room. I gazed about this large house. Once, my mother had lived here, and now, Grandma Olivia was proposing I do the same, ordering, I should say.

I would much rather be with Kenneth, I thought. Despite Grandma Olivia's threats and dire predictions, I was determined to make that my first choice, but I trembled, wondering just what her threats could do. Right now, the last person I wanted to hurt was Kenneth.

Confused, frightened, feeling like a leaf prematurely torn from the branch, driven this way and that by capricious winds, I left the house. Raymond looked up from where he stood by the car as I started toward him. He barely moved. Everything seemed so still. It was as if the world had frozen and I was the only one left moving through the air on a crystal breeze.

And I had no idea where it would take me.

16

&

A Glimmer of Hope

May saw that Cary had looked up sharply from their Monopoly game when I entered the house and paused by the living room door. She turned too, her eyes as wide and as filled with curiosity and worry as her brother's.

"You were gone a long time," Cary said.

"Where's Aunt Sara?" I asked.

"Upstairs with Dad," he replied. His eyes searched my face. "You all right?"

I started to nod and then stopped and said, "No."

Cary glanced at May and then back at me.

"Want to go for a walk?" he asked. "We can get some ice cream in town or—"

"I'd rather just walk on the beach, Cary, and then go to bed early tonight," I replied.

He nodded and signed to May to ask her to run up and tell Aunt Sara we were all going for a walk. She jumped to her feet and hurried upstairs. Cary took my hand and we went outside to wait for May. The sky had become overcast, not a star in sight. There was a strong breeze coming from the northeast. I laughed to myself, thinking that the people I knew back in West Virginia would be so impressed with my knowledge of weather systems, they would start calling me The Weather Girl of Sewell.

"Why are you smiling?" Cary asked.

"I was just thinking about people back home and how different I would seem to them now," I said.

"I wish you thought of this as your home," Cary said softly. "It's the only place you have any real family, the only place where someone who really cares about you lives."

I didn't reply, even though I felt his eyes on me and my heart had warmed with his soft words. Instead, I looked out over the dark blue-black ocean that seemed to flow into the sky. Terns, barely visible, looking more like ghost birds, called to each other. To me there was a note of desperation, fear in their cries. It was as if they were afraid they would lose each other forever in the darkness.

Off in the distance, I saw the lights of a tanker just emerging on the horizon. It looked so small and far away. The sea is a place for people who don't mind being alone, I thought, for people who actually crave being away from the din and clatter of society. Out there, the sky must be overwhelming at night and make one feel either tiny and insignificant or part of something much bigger than anything one could experience on the shore.

"I'd like to go for a real sea trip one day, Cary."

"You mean like overnight, days?"

"Yes."

"Okay," he said. "When?"

"Someday," I said with a smile.

"Something very, very serious is happening, isn't it, Melody?" he asked in shaky voice.

I nodded just as May came out to join us. I took her hand and the three of us began our familiar walk over the sand. Although it was harder to see it because of the thickening darkness, the ocean was just as loud, if not louder, than ever.

"Looks like a storm, but it's not," Cary said. "These clouds will all be gone before morning."

"Nevertheless, it's a bad night for astrologers," I said.

"What?"

"People who read the stars to tell your future." I explained.

"Oh, you mean like your new friend Holly?"

"Yes."

"She read your future lately?" he asked in a timid voice.

"Yes."

"And?"

"She predicted a big change involving family and she was right."

As we continued along the beach, I told him about my discussion with Grandma Olivia and what she had suggested, or rather, what she had demanded, backing it all up with threats. Cary was astounded.

"She wants you to live with them?"

"I think she can make a lot of trouble for everyone if she doesn't get her way."

"I'll go talk to her tomorrow," he said firmly. "She can't run everyone's lives."

"No, Cary. I don't want to be the cause of any more family turmoil."

We plodded on in silence for a while and then Cary turned back to me.

"What's Kenneth going to say about it?"

"I don't know. I'll tell him in the morning."

"Then you've made up your mind?" Cary asked, stopping. I felt May's grip tighten. We had told her nothing, but she surely sensed the tension in my fingers.

"Maybe I can do more good this way, good for Grandma Belinda, too. I think Grandma Olivia and I have reached an understanding. We're like two pit bulls who've faced each other, claimed our own territory, and backed away. Besides, she's not all wrong about men," I said with some bitterness. "Judge Childs, my grandfather, wasn't exactly thinking about how his actions would affect people he supposedly loved. I feel sorry for him now, but I don't approve of what he did. Every time I think of Kenneth's face when he described what happened with my mother, I get a little sick about it all. Kenneth blames him for my mother's bad behavior, for everything. It's terrible for a son and a father to be so estranged. I don't want anything like that to happen between you and Uncle Jacob, Cary."

"It won't. It doesn't have to happen if you stay here, either," he said.

"It might. And then in the end, you would only hate me for it."

"I would never—"

"Besides," I offered, "you and I will probably have an easier time seeing each other this way. We would actually go on dates."

He thought about it and I saw that pleased him. We walked on until we came to a small hill, spotted with scrub bushes. We all sat there a while, the wind making my and May's hair dance over our foreheads and faces. She laughed about it as we brushed the strands away from each other's eyes.

"May's not going to understand your moving out," Cary said.

"I'll explain it to her somehow so she doesn't feel terrible about it."

"She'll miss you almost as much as I will," he warned.

"You'll bring her to see me and she'll spend lots of time there."

"It won't be the same for her. She's never been

335

comfortable at Grandma Olivia's. She's always afraid of breaking something valuable or tracking in dirt."

"I'll see to it that she's more comfortable there," I assured him.

"You're not thinking you will change Grandma Olivia, are you, Melody?" Cary asked with a smile.

"You never know," I said and he laughed.

"I swear you have more blind faith than Laura had and that's saying a lot, too."

May stood up and went to fetch something in the sand. While she was away, Cary leaned over and kissed me softly on the lips.

"It's going to be hard for me not having you right across the hall, Melody," he whispered.

"I won't be far away," I promised and he kissed me again.

May returned with what looked like a girl's light brown shoe. The discovery excited her and she handed it to Cary and signed questions quickly. He shook his head.

"Someone could have lost it running on the beach," he explained. Turning to me, he added, "She thinks it comes from a boat that sank, but the ocean doesn't give up its treasures that easily," he remarked. May wanted to keep it. However, Cary didn't want her to have it, calling it garbage. "In the back of her mind," he muttered, "she thinks it's a gift from Laura. She's always expecting some sign to prove her sister hasn't forgotten her."

"It's not a bad thing to hope for, Cary," I told him, but he shook his head.

"It's useless and painful. It's better we don't give her any encouragement," he insisted.

Reluctantly, May left the shoe and we walked on, making a circle before returning to the house. Aunt Sara was downstairs preparing tea and some biscuits for Uncle Jacob. I told Cary I wanted to hold off telling her about my discussion with Grandma Olivia.

"Grandma Olivia will probably tell her herself," Cary said, and sure enough, Aunt Sara revealed that Grandma Olivia had called to say she was coming to visit again tomorrow.

"Two days in a row. Isn't that nice?" she added.

Neither Cary nor I said anything, suspecting the real reasons for the visit. May was tired, so we went upstairs and I helped her get ready for bed. I watched her sign and mouth her prayers and then kissed her cheek and fixed her blanket. As I started away, she seized my hand and told me she had a secret. I watched as she described how she was going back tomorrow to get that shoe and put it with the other things she had found on the beach. They were all in a box in her closet and she had shown them to no one but me. I promised I wouldn't tell Cary. All of us, especially little girls, needed someone to trust, someone with whom we could share our deepest secrets. She looked relieved, happy, and wished me a good night.

I lay awake for a long time, listening to the sounds in the house. The wind died down just as Cary had predicted it would. I could hear Aunt Sara's and Uncle Jacob's muffled voices. They sounded like ghosts in the walls. After a while, they were silent and there was nothing but the creaks in the floors and ceilings. One of those creaks grew louder and then I heard my door open and close. Cary's silhouette moved quickly to the side of my bed where he knelt. My heart was pounding.

"Cary, if your father knows you've come in here——."

"Shh," he said, putting his fingers on my lips. "I can't sleep. I keep thinking I'm going to lose you."

"You won't," I said. His fingers moved over my chin and down my neck. I could feel the thump, thump, thump of my heart chasing my blood through my veins. My body began to tingle in all my secret

337

places. Cary lifted the blanket away and brought his face closer, laying his cheek on my stomach and then bringing his lips up to kiss the small valley between my breasts.

"Cary," I whispered weakly. His left hand moved down over my shoulders and across my breasts to my stomach. He rose gently and slipped in under my blanket. The bed springs groaned and we both froze because it sounded so loud. "Cary, you better—"

"Let me just lie beside you for a while," he pleaded. I tried to back away, but it was as if there were two voices inside me: the voice of my body that wanted his touch and the voice of my conscience that clamored for me to be good. Soon, my body's voice grew louder, drowning out the warnings and the pleading. I felt my resistance crumble. His lips found mine. We kissed and held each other tightly. His hand was on my thigh, inching toward the hem of my nightgown.

Weakly, I urged him to stop, but it was as if I wanted to stifle my own voice; there was barely any force behind my words. It wasn't until I felt him between my legs that an electric chill of panic shot down my spine.

"Just let me get close to you, please," he begged. My resistance collapsed like a sand castle at high tide and he was pressing forward. The bed groaned again and then we heard a door open and close in the hallway.

Cary and I became paralyzed, both of us hardly breathing. There was a gentle knock. Cary slid quickly off the bed and to the floor. The door opened and Aunt Sara appeared.

"Melody, dear, are you still awake?" she called in a loud whisper.

I didn't speak, but she stood there, silhouetted in the hall light.

"I just—felt bad about not getting to speak to you after you returned from Olivia's," she muttered, more to herself than to me. I remained silent, actually holding my breath. My heart drummed so loudly, I thought she would feel the vibrations if she didn't hear the beat.

But after another minute, she backed out and closed the door softly.

Neither Cary nor I moved for a long moment. Then he got back into bed with me and started to caress me again. I put my hand over his and stopped him.

"You better go back to your room, Cary."

He moaned.

"Please. I'm too frightened."

"All right," he said.

"Be careful she doesn't see you leave, or your father hear you in the hallway."

"I will," he said, his voice dripping with disappointment. He leaned over to kiss me goodnight. "I love you, Melody," he said. "I really do."

"I know," I said. It sounded almost sad. I hadn't meant it to sound that way, but it made him hesitate.

"You love me, too, don't you, Melody?"

"Yes," I said, truly believing I did. It felt more like love than anything I had ever felt for any other boy, and no one had become a part of me as quickly as Cary had.

"I don't trust my grandmother," he said before leaving. "She probably knows how we feel about each other and she wants to do something to stop it."

"She can't," I said. "Not even she is that powerful."

Through the darkness I could see him smile, his face was that bright with happiness at my response.

"Good night," he said again and quietly slipped out of my room.

I waited, holding my breath, hoping and praying neither Uncle Jacob nor Aunt Sara caught him leaving. The silence continued and I let out my trapped breath.

Maybe moving into Grandma Olivia's wasn't such a bad idea after all, I thought.

Something had to put the brakes on this roller coaster Cary and I were riding. I had just proved to myself that I certainly couldn't.

To calm my raging blood, I practiced the meditation techniques Holly had taught me and soon I found the doorway to sleep.

Once again it was Holly instead of Kenneth who came for me in the morning. Cary was already off to work and May to school. Aunt Sara was on her way upstairs to bring Uncle Jacob a second cup of coffee and the morning paper.

"I've got a lot to do today," she told me. "Olivia always looks at the house through a microscope and she'll be here before lunch."

"You have your hands full with Uncle Jacob, and besides, few people take as good care of their home as you do. She has no right to pass judgment anyway. She has a housekeeper and probably never lifted a broom in her life."

"Oh no. When she was younger, she had to do all the housework because her father wouldn't employ a maid, and Belinda—"

She stopped and bit down on her lower lip, realizing she was about to violate her own rule: if you can't say something nice about someone, don't say anything.

Holly beeped her horn and I knew it was she who had come for me because her horn sounded like a goose with laryngitis. This time I was more definite about my promise to be home early enough to help with dinner and then I left the house. Holly was wearing half moon silver earrings that dangled nearly to her shoulders and a shimmery tank top and a dark blue full-length skirt with sandals. Her toenails were neon pink.

"He slept in the studio if he slept at all," she muttered as I got into the car. "I didn't realize he

340

hadn't come to bed until I woke this morning. Either he's hypnotized himself or the sculpture has possessed him. Artists," she said raising her eyes. "When they get hooked on their own work, they're worse than those monks who take vows of silence. But," she added, turning to me, "I must admit I've never seen him so taken with anything else he's done."

She blinked and took another look at me.

"What's with you this morning? You look as serious as a truck driver with hemorrhoids."

"I've got to make some very important decisions," I said.

"Oh? Well, I told you that your day of birth indicates you possess an imaginative mind coupled with excellent powers of observation. Don't trust too much to luck. Depend more on your own intuitive vision."

"Luck," I said with a laugh. "Whatever I bet on is sure to lose."

"Don't be down on yourself. Remember what I said about negative energy," Holly warned. "Your personal planets are Saturn and Uranus," she continued. "Under favorable influences, it's good for seeking favors from elderly people, but use tact and diplomacy instead of force."

"And under unfavorable influences?" I asked.

She nodded.

"Postpone change and long journeys."

"Is it a favorable or unfavorable time?" I asked.

"I'll study my charts and let you know later," she promised.

Holly was so serious about her beliefs, I couldn't laugh. Who knew? Maybe there was some truth to it.

Kenneth was in the studio when we arrived, but I wasn't prepared for what he looked like when I entered. He was pale and drained, his beard scraggly and his cheeks and neck unshaven. His clothes were wrinkled and looked slept in. His eyes were distant, bloodshot, the eyes of someone who was looking beyond everything that stood before him. He barely muttered a good morning when I greeted him.

I saw he had made considerable progress on the sculpture, especially with the face. It was becoming the face in the drawings, the face of my mother, more than it was my face. There was that slight turn in the upper lip that Mommy had, especially when she was being coy.

Kenneth's hands did have miraculous artistic power, I thought. As I gazed at the work in progress, I felt the movement. It was almost as if the stone girl would become flesh and blood at any moment and pull herself up and out of the base. Under his surgical fingers, the marble looked malleable, easier to form than clay. The figure's shoulders and face already showed skin-like texture, down to the way it rippled over the embossed cheekbones and breastbone. Perhaps, I thought, an artist was a person born with more life in him than other people and he puts some of that life into the work itself, diminishing himself every time he creates something as great as this, until one day, he is just an ordinary man surrounded by his creations, but comforted by the thought that he could never die as long as his work lived.

How was I to compete with this for his attention and love? I wondered.

"Did you have any breakfast yet, Kenneth?" I asked. For a while I thought he either hadn't heard me or didn't care to reply. Then he paused and looked at me.

"I had some coffee and a piece of something," he said.

"Piece of something?"

"A doughnut, I think." He thought another moment. "Or was that yesterday?" He shrugged and looked at his sculpture.

"Grandma Olivia sent for me last night, Kenneth, because your father told her what he had told me."

"Oh?" He brushed off the left earlobe on the sculpture and stepped back to study the face of Neptune's Daughter. "Just a minute," he said. "I want to check something."

I thought he was going to look at me to compare, but instead, he went to his drawings. He nodded to himself and wiped his hands on a rag.

"What were you saying about Olivia?"

"She sent for me because Judge Childs told her about our conversation."

"What did she want?"

"She wanted to be sure I told no one. She's afraid of a new scandal and she is so concerned about it that she wants—she practically ordered, I should say— me to come live with her and Grandpa Samuel. She forbade me to live with you."

Kenneth stared at me and, just when I thought he was going to say something, turned back to his drawing.

"The way you just raised your right eyebrow," he said, "I never saw you do that. It's interesting. It sort of indicates some mature insight. I like it, but Haille never did that," he muttered more to himself than to me.

"Did you hear what I said, Kenneth? Grandma Olivia wants me to live with her. She says it would be better for Uncle Jacob's recovery if I was living there right now, too, and it would only fan the flames of scandal if I came to live with you."

"She's right about that," Kenneth said. "Olivia's always been the sensible one, the one with solutions in that family."

"You think my moving in with her and Grandpa Samuel is the right solution?" I asked and held my breath.

343

"Might be," he said and turned again to his sculpture.

I stood there, fighting down a throat lump and swallowing back my tears. I had hoped he would tell me not to go to live at Grandma Olivia's. I had hoped he would insist I move in with him, that there was no other real solution, no other place I belonged but at his side. Why should he care about scandals?

"One thing's for sure," he said as he approached the marble, "you'll get the best of everything living there."

"Except love," I muttered sharply. At first I thought he hadn't heard. He just stared at his work. Then he turned and looked at me with his eyes finally focusing on me.

"Don't put too much stock in that, Melody. Love is fragile at best and often a burden or something that blinds us. It's fodder for poets and song writers and they build it into something beyond human capacity. Falling in love means enrolling yourself in the school of disappointment. Being human means failing each other often, and no two people fail each other more than two people who pledge to do things for each other that they'll never do because they're just incapable of it."

He gestured toward his sculpture.

"That's why art is enduring. The look of love or hope, or the look of compassion, bravery, whatever, is captured forever. We spend our lives trying to get someone to be as enduring as a painting or a sculpture and we can't because feelings crumble as quickly as the flesh."

"That's not true, Kenneth," I insisted.

He turned back to me and sighed. Then he shook his head and smiled.

"You know what I miss the most about my youth? My gullibility. It's nice believing in everything and everyone. It makes you feel secure, but be strong and depend more on yourself and you'll be ready for disappointments. That's the best advice I can offer you.

"Go live with Olivia. She's the real guru, not Holly with her stars and moon. Olivia can read the future better than anyone. She's the true captain of her soul and the master of her fate. She's endured and she's stronger than anyone. Disappointment withers in front of her. She can stare down disaster. My father cries in his beer, mourns his lost youth and his mistakes, while Olivia will rage on until the day she dies. And even death gets little satisfaction when it takes someone like her. For death, Olivia is a reminder that it, too, is a slave to something bigger. It's just an errand boy for Nature.

"So live with her and learn from her," Kenneth concluded. Then he took up his tools and returned to his marble creation, not seeing the tears brim in my eyes.

I sucked in my breath and left the studio. He didn't need me there, I thought. The vision is all in his head now anyway, just as he always claimed.

Holly was sitting in front of the house on a stone bench, Ulysses at her feet as she worked on a chart and thumbed through her books. When I appeared, she looked up with surprise.

"Why aren't you working?"

"There's nothing for me to do in there. You were right about him," I said.

She raised her eyebrows.

"Oh? Ignored you, too, huh?"

"Something like that."

"Were you crying?" she asked after she gazed at me closer.

"No." I turned away quickly and took a deep breath.

"Oh honey, don't let him get to you. Artists are so moody and—"

"It's okay," I said and smiled at her. "Could you take me home? I'd do more good helping Aunt Sara today."

"Sure. Oh," she said, "about your chart, the planets . . ."

"Yes?"

"It's a favorable time, a time for change," she said. She didn't have to tell me. I already knew.

Grandma Olivia's Rolls Royce was just leaving the house as Holly and I made the turn. The sight of the luxury limousine made my heart do flip-flops for I was afraid of how Aunt Sara would react to what Grandma Olivia was proposing. I was sure Uncle Jacob was ecstatic.

"I've made up my mind," Holly said as we pulled into the driveway. "I'll be leaving the day after tomorrow."

"Oh, no! I'll miss you," I said. She smiled and leaned forward to squeeze my hand and give me a kiss on the cheek.

"And I'll miss you too, sweetheart. You're a very nice girl, Melody, full of good energy, compassion, and love. Someday, you'll make a lucky man a wonderful companion."

I hurried into the house, worrying more about Aunt Sara than myself at the moment. May was in the kitchen washing out the pot in which Aunt Sara had made some hot oatmeal for Uncle Jacob. She was surprised to see me and obviously did not yet know what Grandma Olivia had wanted. She told me Aunt Sara was upstairs with Uncle Jacob. I waited for her to come down, but when nearly a half hour passed and she still hadn't, I went upstairs. The door to Uncle Jacob and Aunt Sara's room was closed. I hesitated and then knocked softly. They must have thought it was May and wondered why she was knocking.

Aunt Sara opened the door and looked out at me with bloodshot eyes. Uncle Jacob was dressed in a cotton flannel shirt and pants. Aunt Sara was helping him dress.

"Melody. You're home already?"

"Yes, I thought—" I looked past her at Uncle Jacob, who struggled to pull on one of his socks. He did look stronger, with more color in his face. I was sure the news Grandma Olivia had brought had cheered him. "I thought you might need me here more."

"She doesn't need you," Uncle Jacob snapped. "Everything's fine here."

"He insists on getting up and going downstairs," she said mournfully.

"Did you ask the doctor, Uncle Jacob?"

"I don't need the doctor to tell me what I can do and what I can't," he said and pulled on the other sock. Aunt Sara hurried to kneel at his feet and help him put on his shoes. He turned to me as she did so.

"Good you came home early though. You can start packing," he said. "Your grandmother can send the car over for you earlier than she thought," he added, and Aunt Sara uttered a cry and then pressed her hand against her mouth as he glared down at her. "Now Sara, you heard it all and you know that it's best for everyone all around. We're just lucky to have my mother and father alive and strong enough to handle the problem."

"Is that how everyone sees me now?" I asked. "The problem?"

"She's never been a problem for me," Aunt Sara said. "And the children—"

"Everyone will be better off," Uncle Jacob insisted. "Especially the children."

"I'm not full of contamination, Uncle Jacob."

"You're Haille's daughter," he said as if that ex-

347

plained everything. "We can't help what's been passed through the blood. It takes someone as strong as my mother to keep things right," he said.

"Yes, she's got a wonderful track record," I snapped.

"Now don't you be insolent and disrespectful. You ought to be grateful someone wants to take you into her home. You're the result of lust and sin and—"

"Jacob!" Aunt Sara exclaimed. She stood up and he turned his head away.

"I've got to get some exercise," he muttered, "so I can build myself up and get back to work."

He started to stand, wobbled, and sat down hard on the bed.

"Jacob!"

"I'm fine. Just a little bed weary," he said. When he started to stand again, Aunt Sara put her arm around his waist and he reluctantly leaned on her shoulder. "There," he said, standing. "That's a start."

Aunt Sara looked at me with eyes so full of sadness, I had to turn away.

"I'll go pack," I said.

"Good," Uncle Jacob muttered.

My throat tightened and my tongue felt glued to the bottom of my mouth, so all my words were swallowed back. There was nothing more to say to him anyway, I thought. After his confession in the hospital, I was a constant embarrassment to him. He couldn't look at me and not feel guilty. It brought him much needed relief to see me go. Grandma Olivia didn't know how right she was when she suggested my moving out would improve Uncle Jacob's chances for recuperation.

May was waiting for me in the hallway, her eyes full of questions and confusion. She wanted to know if we could go for a walk to town. I smiled at her and took her hand. I brought her into my room and sat her on the chair by the desk.

I began by reminding her why I had come, why I had been left there, and why I had been forced to stay.

She was sad about my mother, but she quickly told me she was happy I was there. I thanked her and then told her about Grandma Olivia's offer and why it would be good for everyone. I didn't tell her about my grandfather or his sinful history. I tried to make it seem as if I would be gone only for a short while. I would always be nearby, I told her, and she would come to visit me as much as she wanted, that Cary had promised to bring her often, but she was still confused.

How could it be good for everyone? Didn't I help her mother?

How could I explain it all to her? I wondered and then I did the one thing I had tried never to do: I told a lie to make things easier. I told her Grandma Olivia needed me.

The idea of Grandma Olivia needing anyone surprised but interested her. May was so forgiving and compassionate she couldn't deny anyone anything, even someone like Grandma Olivia, who seemed to have everything she could want.

In the end she accepted it. It brought tears to her eyes, but she didn't cry. She offered to help me pack. I explained I had very little to bring with me. Grandma Olivia was going to buy me many new things. When I heard Uncle Jacob and Aunt Sara in the hallway, I told her she had better see what she could do to help her mother and she left.

Uncle Jacob and Aunt Sara made a lot of commotion going down the stairs. Uncle Jacob got dizzy once, but when I came out to help, he made a miraculous recovery and completed the journey. Aunt Sara brought him outside to sit on the porch.

As I sifted through the things I would take with me, I recalled when I had first come to stay in this room. I looked at Laura's picture and thought about her again. Cary insisted Laura and I were alike in so many ways. Holly would call it a kindred spirit. There were nights when I had lain here and felt another presence, felt encouragement and comfort, as if someone warm and loving had touched my cheek or stroked my hair or taken my hand during the night. It turned my nightmares into sweet dreams.

I had no idea what sort of a room Grandma Olivia would provide for me. Chances were it would be bigger, of course. I hadn't done very much to change this room. So much of what was in it still had significance and great importance for Aunt Sara. Laura's love letters were where they had always been. Her clothes remained in the closet and bureau. Her dolls and music box were undisturbed.

Aunt Sara was sure to return the room to its shrine status after I moved away, I thought. Now, she would mourn her daughter's death a second time. I had tried to be a daughter to her, but the truth was no one could replace Laura, and the hole in her heart Aunt Sara had hoped I would fill would always be there. Maybe it was more painful, even deceitful, for me to wear Laura's clothes and sleep in Laura's bed. Maybe as Kenneth had said, Grandma Olivia was the real guru for this family. She knew best.

I was tired of fighting anyway, tired of pursuing the elusive truth, tired of uncovering lies, tired of expecting love to simply blossom like a flower and beam under the sunlight of my smiles. People like Grandma Olivia always get what they want in the end, I thought, and those of us who think we can fight them find we are just living in a fantasy world.

I wished there was a way I could say goodbye to Laura's memory, a way that made sense or made me feel better about what I had done and what I would now do. But everything I looked at had seemed unmoved and unaffected by my arrival and stay here

350

and it was unmoved now at my leaving. I had changed nothing.

I picked up my two small suitcases and the box that contained Cary's sailboat and started out of the room and down the stairs just as May was rushing back into the house. At first I thought something had happened to Uncle Jacob, but she was waving a big envelope at me. She signed it had come special delivery.

I put my suitcases down at the top of the stairs when she reached me, and with great curiosity I took the envelope from her. It was from Alice Morgan.

What is it? May signed. I shook my head and sat on the top step as I ripped the envelope open. How silly, I thought. She's sent me the latest *En Vogue* catalogue, a mail-order fashion company whose clothing was very expensive. I knew her mother subscribed to it and had ordered from it, but why send it to me? The top right corner of one page was folded in.

First, I read the letter she had sent with the catalogue.

Dear Melody,

I was sitting in the kitchen and eating a sandwich for lunch, when I decided to thumb through Mom's latest En Vogue. *Usually, the fashions bore me and nothing ever looks as good as it does in the catalogue. At least, that's what I always tell my mother.*

But, when I got to page 42, I noticed something I think might interest you, too. The model on the page looks so much like your mother, I couldn't resist mailing this to you as quickly as possible. Her hair is a different color, of course, but, well, look for yourself. Amazing, isn't it?

I still want to come visit, and I am waiting for you to tell me when is a good time. Let's not stop being friends just because we live far apart from each other.

What's new in your life? Boyfriends? Girlfriends? Are you doing anything fun?

Please write back as soon as you can or call. Call collect if you want.

I miss you.

Love,
Alice

I folded the letter and then opened the catalogue slowly. May watched with interest as I stared at the model on the page. It triggered a chill that started up my spine and then circled my body and froze my heart. My breath caught. I didn't realize how long I was holding it until I felt my chest constrict and May shook my hand, demanding to know what was wrong.

This woman, I explained, stuttering through my thoughts, looks so much like my mother it's scary.

May's eyes widened with interest and she peered over my shoulder.

"I've got to show this to Kenneth," I muttered. I stood up and gazed at my suitcases. "Before I go to Grandma Olivia's."

I put the suitcases back in the room and hurried down the stairs. I went to the kitchen and called the taxi company, asking for a car immediately. Then I went outside, hardly able to take my eyes from the face of the model in the latest En Vogue catalogue. She even had that little turn in her upper lip.

Uncle Jacob and Aunt Sara were sitting on the front porch. Both looked up with surprise and interest as I burst out of the house, the catalogue in my hand.

"What did you get, dear?" Aunt Sara asked. Uncle Jacob didn't want to show any interest, but couldn't help himself.

"My friend—Alice Morgan. Remember? From Sewell?"

"Oh yes."

"She sent me this catalogue because there is a model in it who looks so much like my mother," I

352

explained. Uncle Jacob's eyes widened with more interest.

"Oh. Really?" Aunt Sara said, leaning toward me as I opened the catalogue to the page Alice had marked. "Yes, there is some resemblance. Isn't there, Jacob?" she asked showing him the catalogue. He stared and then grunted.

"Some. What of it?" he muttered.

"There's more than some," I said taking the catalogue back.

"What about it?" he asked.

"I want to know more about her," I said.

"What for? When someone dies, we should let her rest in peace," he said, directing his gaze more at Aunt Sara than at me. The reference to Laura was clear. She pressed her lips together and looked away.

I saw my cab coming down our street.

"That's for me," I said as it drew closer.

"For you? What for? My mother's sending her car. No need to waste money," Uncle Jacob said, "just because you're going to be living with people that have some."

"I'm going to show this to Kenneth," I said. "I'm going back to his house."

"Now?" Uncle Jacob demanded.

"No one knows my mother's face better than Kenneth," I explained. "I'll feel better showing it to him."

"You're just wasting good time, your own and everyone else's," he said. "There's enough to do and—"

"I'm all packed. There wasn't that much to do. My bags are upstairs, ready to be brought down," I added to please him.

"Good," he said.

The cab pulled up front and I started for it.

"Melody," Aunt Sara called. I turned back. She

stared like someone who had forgotten why she had called me.

"Yes?"

"Don't you want any lunch, dear?"

"No, but thank you, Aunt Sara. I'll be back as soon as I can," I said.

"Just have Kenneth or the cab take you to Grandma Olivia's house," Uncle Jacob said. "I'll call for Raymond and he'll take your bags there while you're wasting everyone's time."

"Thank you, Uncle Jacob," I said. "I hope you get better soon and get back to the sea you love so much."

He looked surprised. I smiled as his thoughts stumbled over my words of kindness. Then I hurried into the cab, the magazine clutched tightly in my hand.

17

Out of the Ashes

Holly was just coming off the beach when the cab, the driver complaining about the beach road, pulled up in front of Kenneth's house. I paid him and he drove off swearing that if he had known where I wanted him to take me, he would never have accepted the assignment. Holly waved and hurried along, breaking into a fast walk, Ulysses barking and rushing past her to greet me.

"What's up? Why are you back?"

"I have to show Kenneth something that came special delivery to me," I replied.

"What is it?"

She followed as I walked toward the studio, explaining what it was. She looked at the pictures, even though she had never known Mommy nor seen any photographs of her.

"They say everyone has a twin someplace," Holly offered, handing the catalogue back.

Kenneth was seated on his small sofa staring at the sculpture when we entered the studio. He looked up

355

so casually I realized he hadn't even known I had left earlier.

"Lunch time, huh?" he said.

"No Kenneth. I brought you that sandwich you have wasting away on the table there," Holly said, nodding toward a plate on a tray. He gazed at it.

"Oh? You brought it to me? What about Melody?"

"I've been home and back, Kenneth," I said. "There didn't seem much for me to do here and I had to pack to move in with Grandma Olivia, remember?"

"Right, right," he said. "So. I forgot to eat lunch, huh?" He reached over and grasped the sandwich. "Looks good. What is it, Holly, sprouts, tomatoes, herbs?"

"Just eat it, Kenneth," she said. He took a bite, smiled, and chewed. Then he took his first real look at me.

"What's happening? If you went home to pack, why are you here?" He looked at Holly for some hint.

"She has something to show you, Ken."

"Oh?"

I handed him the catalogue, opened to the page Alice had folded. He gazed at it a moment, put the sandwich down, and sat up. Then he looked at me, his eyebrows dipping toward each other.

"What is this?" He turned the catalogue to the front. *"En Vogue."*

"My girlfriend in Sewell sent it to me. Her mother orders clothes from that company. She just happened to be browsing through this latest copy and saw those pictures of that model who resembles Mommy."

"Latest copy?" He narrowed his eyes suspiciously and turned to the fine print on the inside of the cover.

"Does it look like her, Ken?" Holly asked.

"It is a remarkable resemblance," he muttered. He got up and went to his tool table, shifting some things around to find his magnifying glass. Then he thumbed through the pictures. He stared ahead for a moment and shook his head gently before looking again.

"I thought if anyone knew my mother's face and could decide about those pictures, it was you," I said. He nodded. I held my breath, waiting.

"It might be something she did before the accident," he offered. "But it's Haille. No doubt about it," he concluded.

A surge of heat moved up my neck and brought a crimson flush to my cheeks. I used to wonder what it was like for the families and loved ones of actors and actresses to turn on the television set and see them on the screen. I imagined it had to be wonderful and painful at the same time.

"But if it is Mommy, why is her hair black?" I asked. "Even her eyebrows."

"It might just have been what the company or the photographer wanted for this shoot," Holly suggested. Kenneth looked at the pages again.

"I don't see why. Actually, Haille's real hair color would have worked just as well with these shots and the color of these clothes."

"Maybe she had just done something else, Kenneth. There are a dozen reasons for it, I imagine," Holly said. He nodded.

"I'm sure," he said. He stared at the magazine as if he couldn't let go of it, couldn't stop looking at the picture. He flipped to the front again and reread the fine print. "Charlie Dunn could probably find out more about this for us," he said. He looked up at me. "Charlie's a friend of mine in Boston who is big in advertising."

"What do you expect him to find out, Ken?" Holly asked. I caught the way she moved her eyes toward me to suggest he was doing something wrong, but Kenneth was intrigued on his own and not just for me. I could see it in his face and in the way his eyes continued to look at the pictures.

"Just to settle our minds about it," he replied softly. "When the pictures were done. Was this Haille?"

"I thought you said it was," Holly said.

"Nothing's for sure, but it sure looks like her to me, especially that turn in her lips, the way her cheek-bones stand out, the way she's holding her head just a little to the right."

He went quickly to a drawer in the table and riffled through some papers before coming up with a photograph. He placed it beside the pictures on the catalogue page and studied the two. I drew closer. The picture he took out of the drawer was a picture of Mommy taken on Judge Childs's dock.

"The face in this picture is about the same size," he muttered. He began to make some measurements with a thin ruler and then nodded again. Apparently, he knew Mommy's face so well, he remembered the inches between her nose and mouth or across her forehead. "If it's not her, there was a twin I never knew about," he concluded.

"When are you going to call this friend of yours in Boston?" I asked softly.

He thought a moment, looked at his sculpture and then shrugged.

"How about right now? It's time for a break," he said. "Let's go down to the Mermaid and have a brew while I call Charlie. You can have a root beer," he told me and smiled.

"What? You're actually going to set foot out of this studio during my lifetime?" Holly kidded.

"Is this still your lifetime? I thought we were already living another spiritual existence," he replied and went to change his shirt and wash his hands and face before we drove into town in his jeep.

I found myself holding my breath every time my thoughts went to the catalogue and the things Kenneth had said. Mommy had never written to tell me she had modeled for this catalogue, nor had she mentioned it the few times we had spoken on the telephone. Wouldn't she have been proud of it? Perhaps it was as Holly thought: someone who just happened to have a close resemblance.

The Mermaid was a small pub on a side street. I had never actually been inside, although I knew Kenneth went there whenever he spent any time in town. There was a short bar on the right with thick, cherry wood tables and captain's chairs on the left. Everything looked worn and weathered, presenting the illusion that this tavern had been here to greet the first pilgrims. There were whale bones on the walls, pictures of fishermen and sailors, sailboats and trawlers. A net filled with fishing gear and accessories dangled from the ceiling, and there was a large ship's bell at the far corner of the bar. There were only a half dozen customers, all of whom knew Kenneth and gave him a warm, loud greeting. He ordered a mug of amber ale for himself and Holly and told the bartender, a short man with curly light brown hair, to give me a cold root beer.

"Sure she's old enough, Kenneth? Our root beer has a bite to it, you know?"

"Just give it to her with none of your jokes, Clancy," Kenneth said and winked at us. Holly and I sat at a table in the corner as Kenneth went to the rear to use the pay phone. All of the drinks had been delivered to our table when he returned.

"Charlie's doing the research for us and promises to call back within the hour. He knows this company well," Kenneth said. He spread the catalogue before him and stared down at the pictures. "Tell me about the man your mother went off with," he asked and I described Archie Marlin and how as soon as we left Sewell, I was instructed to start calling him Richard.

Kenneth sipped his beer and listened, his eyes taking on a deep, dark glint as I spoke.

"Changing his name sounds suspicious, doesn't it,

Ken?" Holly asked. Kenneth nodded and then shook his head.

"Haille was gullible, trusting, eager to believe in fairy tales," he said, "especially if the teller of the tale made her the princess. So," he said, sitting back, "Olivia told Sara and Jacob what she wanted you to do?"

"Yes." I described what it had been like when I returned to the house. "Uncle Jacob practically salivated at the prospect," I added and Kenneth laughed.

"It sounds as if you will be better off at your grandmother's, Melody," Holly said.

"She's not really my grandmother. My real grandmother is shut up in that home. I'm sure it won't be easy living with Grandma Olivia, no matter what she promises," I added.

Kenneth and Holly exchanged looks but Kenneth said nothing. I had no reason to blame him, I thought. A teenage girl is quite a responsibility to take on at this point in his life, and he would be the first to say he wasn't stable enough for it. He was a free soul. Right now if he had the artistic impulse to drive off and stay away for days, he would do so. He couldn't if he had me to watch over.

A little over a half hour later, we heard the phone ring and the bartender called Kenneth.

"It's for you," he said. As Kenneth got up and went to the rear of the tavern, my heart started thumping again. Holly smiled at me and put her hand over mine.

"I'm sure this is all going to be easily explainable," she said.

I nodded, but my heart felt as if it had doubled in size and would soon hammer itself through my chest. We watched Kenneth as he listened. He nodded, turned his back, spoke softly, and then he cradled the receiver and just stood there without turning around.

360

When he started toward us, I knew it wasn't going to be easily explainable.

"That layout was done a little more than two months ago," he said. "The model on the page is someone called Gina Simon."

"When did you mother pass away?" Holly asked.

"It's been a little more than two months. About the same time," Kenneth said.

"So, that could be her in the catalogue," Holly said.

"But if it's my mother, why did she change her name?" I asked.

"Someone might have suggested it, told her it sounded more professional," Holly suggested. "Right, Ken?" she asked. He didn't respond and so I looked up at him. His face was pale, his eyes troubled.

"What is it, Kenneth?" I demanded.

"Charlie said the guy he spoke to in L.A. told him Gina Simon was currently doing another shoot. She got the job because of this catalogue."

"Oh," Holly said.

My heart seemed to have stopped beating. It was as if all the world, all movement, all time, had frozen.

"What else did he say, Kenneth?" I asked, my voice barely above a whisper. I wasn't sure I had even spoken. Perhaps it had just been a thought. Kenneth shook his head.

"He said her manager—"

"What?" Holly asked quickly.

"Was someone named Richard Marlin."

I shuddered as if a wave had crashed against the tavern. Someone laughed loudly and then another man entered the tavern and everyone greeted him. Kenneth gulped his ale and took a deep breath. Holly sat back, dumbfounded.

"What does it all mean, Ken?"

"I don't know. Haille supposedly died in a car fire. The remains were sent back here for the funeral and burial. The police had identification, right, Melody?"

I nodded.

"Amnesia?" Holly suggested.

"I don't know."

"That woman in the catalogue is my mother, living under a different name," I said because I had to hear the words spoken.

"Ken?"

"I don't know what to tell you, Holly."

"Well, Melody can't just be left with that," Holly said.

"I'll make some more calls, find out where this Gina Simon lives and—"

"And I'll go there," I said quickly. They both stared at me.

"Go to L.A.?" Holly asked, sitting back.

"Yes. I have to go there. Don't you see? You understand, don't you, Kenneth?"

He ran his hand through his hair.

"Why would she do this? Even after her death, she does overwhelming things. I'm right in the middle of this work. I—"

"I'm not asking you to go with me, Kenneth."

He stared at me.

"I couldn't go anyway," he said. "I couldn't get myself to go chasing after her. Not anymore."

"You're not just going to put her on an airplane and send her to Los Angeles, Kenneth Childs, are you?" Holly said.

"No. It's not my decision anyway. You had better talk to Olivia about this first, Melody," he said.

It was as if I had swallowed a rock.

"Don't look at me like that. I can't be the one who sends you off looking for your mother. I'm not one hundred percent sure it's your mother."

"It's like ninety-nine percent," Holly quipped.

"I can't just forget about it, Kenneth. I won't," I insisted. "I don't care what you or Grandma Olivia say," I shouted, tears burning under my eyelids.

"Don't get yourself upset, sweetheart," Holly said putting her arm around my shoulders. "We'll figure out what to do. Won't we, Kenneth?" she asked sharply.

Kenneth nodded.

We were all silent a long moment and then Holly sighed.

"I'll call my sister and tell her to meet you in Los Angeles if you go. She'll do me a favor and look after you. I'd go, but I have to get back to the store."

"You have a sister in Los Angeles?"

"Dorothy Littlefield is her married name. She and I get along as well as oil and water, but she's very well off. Lives in Beverly Hills, drives a Mercedes, shops on Rodeo Drive, eats nouvelle cuisine, but probably knows a lot about models and fashions. Her husband is an accountant. She's an Aries, born March twenty-second. As an Aries," Holly recited, "she has a quick temper, is inclined to hold a grudge, which she has against me for about twenty years, is aggressive, self-willed, and determined. But she's very intelligent and was always an A-plus student with little effort. She is really a good businesswoman. They have no children," Holly added. "Thank God. But I know she would do this. She likes to be needed."

"Debbie Novell is out there, too," Kenneth said. "I think she just got divorced, didn't she?"

"That was five years ago, Kenneth. Debbie Novell is a ditz anyway. I wouldn't trust my cat with her. Remember when she left her car running all night in front of the dorm? What am I talking about? That's not the worst of it. She left her four-year-old at the pharmacy and didn't realize it until they called and told her hours later."

"Yeah," Kenneth said, smiling. "I remember now, but I thought she was a big deal in California real estate."

"So?"

363

Kenneth shook his head. Then he turned to me and nodded softly.

"Okay, I'll make the call and find out what I can about this so-called Gina Simon. What do you want to do now?" he asked.

"Go see Grandma Olivia," I said. "I'm going to ask her for the money I'll need to make the trip."

"Olivia? You expect her to fork over the money?" Kenneth asked. He was about to smile.

"When she finds out what it's for, I think she might double the amount," I muttered.

Kenneth thought about this and then laughed.

"I think Melody's capable of taking care of herself, Holly," he said. Holly raised her eyebrows.

"I'll take her to Grandma Olivia's, Ken. In fact," she said, turning to me, "I'll take you to New York and get you on the plane, if you'd like."

"Would you?"

"It's the least I can do. We'll leave tonight," she added.

"I could," I said thinking about it. "I'm already packed."

Loretta nearly smiled when she opened the door this time. I wondered if that meant she had accepted the fact that I was to live in this house.

"I had your suitcases taken to your room," she said. Then she saw Holly standing just behind me and her eyes widened. Holly was wearing one of her tie-dyed dresses, a pink and yellow headband, and John Lennon sunglasses. Her lipstick was tangerine.

"Where are Grandma Olivia and Grandpa Samuel?" I asked.

"Mrs. Logan is in her garden and Mr. Logan is out back reading his papers," Loretta said, unable to take her eyes from Holly. "Would you like me to show you to your room?"

"I have to speak to my grandmother first," I said.

"We'll just go around to the garden, Loretta. Thank you."

The sight of Grandma Olivia down on her knees with a gardening fork in hand and that wide-brimmed hat on her head took Holly by surprise.

"She doesn't look so tough," she muttered. "She looks like anyone's little old grandmother."

"You haven't met her yet," I replied dryly.

Grandpa Samuel saw us from his lounge chair before Grandma Olivia did. He put down his papers and waved, standing as he did so.

"Well, hello there, my dear. Welcome," he called.

"Hello, Grandpa Samuel. This is my friend Holly Brooks. Actually, she's Kenneth's friend and now mine," I added. He widened his smile and nodded.

"Pleased to meet you, Holly. Any friend of Kenneth's is a friend of mine, and that goes double for any friend of my granddaughter here. Visiting the Cape?"

"I was," Holly said. "I'm leaving tonight."

"Oh. That's too bad. I was looking forward to getting to know you," Grandpa Samuel said.

"Somehow, I expect you'll live through the disappointment, Samuel," Grandma Olivia said. She had risen and stood wiping her hands on her apron. "Your things are up in your room," she added.

"I know. Loretta told me. This is Holly—"

"I heard all that," she snapped. "This isn't exactly the best time to be entertaining people. I would advise you to first settle yourself in, learn our schedule, including when it's proper and not proper to invite guests, and—"

"I'm not staying long, Grandma Olivia," I said quickly.

"What's that?" Grandpa Samuel said, turning to her. "I thought—"

"What does that mean? You're moving in with Kenneth Childs?" she asked.

"No. I'd like to show you something and then explain," I said.

She glared at me and then walked around the border of the garden toward the lounge chairs and table. She peeled off her gardening gloves, poured herself some iced tea and watched as I approached, the catalogue in hand.

"A friend of mine from West Virginia mailed this to me," I said, holding it out to her. Grandma Olivia gazed at it as if I were about to hand her something dirty or smelly.

"What would I want with that?" she asked.

"Just look at the woman modeling the clothes on this page," I requested.

She put her glass down slowly, reached into her apron, and came up with a pair of glasses. Grandpa Samuel moved to her side and gazed over her shoulder. They stared at the catalogue and then they both looked at us, unsure what it meant.

"That's Haille, right? What happened to her hair?" Grandpa Samuel asked.

"She obviously dyed it black," Grandma Olivia said and handed the catalogue back to me. "Are you here to tell me this proves your mother was some sort of success?"

"No, Grandma. Kenneth phoned a friend and it turns out the woman in those pictures is still alive and living under the name Gina Simon."

"Gina Simon?" Grandpa Samuel said. "Let me see that again," he said. I handed him the catalogue. "Looks like Haille to me."

"To all of us," I said. "That's why I'm leaving. I'm going to Los Angeles to find out if it is Mommy."

"Going to Los Angeles? But I don't understand," Grandpa Samuel said, once again turning to Grandma Olivia for guidance. She sat on the bench and looked from Holly to me.

"Are you taking her?" she asked Holly.

"I offered to take her to New York. She can catch a flight to Los Angeles from there. I have a sister who lives in L.A. and I'll call and ask her to meet Melody and look after her," she replied. "It's a good time for her to take a trip."

"Pardon?"

"Her astrological chart," Holly replied, "indicates that."

"What nonsense. Astrological chart, rushing clear across the country. You can't go to Los Angeles. I absolutely forbid it," Grandma said.

"No, you don't, Grandma." I smiled. "This woman could be my mother, and if she is, I have someone to live with and someplace else to live," I said.

"But how do we know this is Haille and—"

"We don't for sure, but it looks as if it might be," Holly replied. "The man with whom Haille left for L.A. is that model's manager. Kenneth found out for us."

Grandma smirked.

"Amazing," Grandpa Samuel said. "But if that's Haille and she's still alive, who did we bury in our family plot?"

"What difference does it make?" Grandma Olivia snapped at him. She sat thinking a moment and then looked up at us.

"Such a trip costs a lot of money. Where would you get it?" she asked.

"From you," I said calmly. "Call it an advance on my inheritance."

Grandpa Samuel laughed and shook his head until Grandma Olivia shot him a withering look.

"Who else knows about this—this idiotic idea?"

"Just Kenneth and my friend in Sewell," I said. How this family appeared in public was her only real concern. "Unless of course, I have to go begging for the money. I could go see my grandfather, I suppose,"

I added. She pulled her shoulders back and turned her eyes to stone.

"How dare you try to blackmail me?"

"I'm not, but I'm going and I'm going tonight," I said firmly.

She ripped the catalogue from Grandpa Samuel's hands and gazed at the photographs again, shaking her head.

"This is insane," she mumbled. "Very well." She rose. "Come with me," she ordered.

"Don't we know someone who could look into this for us, Olivia?" Grandpa Samuel asked. "Rather than send the girl, I mean."

"You think I want more people to know about this?" she spit back at him.

"Well, I just thought—"

"Don't think," she ordered. "It's a waste of time. Come along," she told Holly and me, and we followed her into the house.

She took us to the office and went behind the large, dark oak desk. Holly's presence gave me courage and I was proud not to feel even a little bit intimidated, until she raised her head and focused those eyes on me.

"You will sign this," she said, scribbling on a plain sheet of paper. I gazed at Holly, who looked amazed. Grandma Olivia turned the paper to me and handed me the pen.

The paper described my taking two thousand dollars as an advance on my inheritance. It was dated and signed by her. I signed it quickly and she folded it and put it in a small wall safe, from which she drew out money.

"Count it," she ordered. I did so. It was two thousand dollars in fifty-dollar bills. I had never seen so much money at once, much less held it in my hands. She gave me an envelope.

"If you lose that, don't come running back here for

more. Make your way on your wits," she commanded. She sat again, folding her hands and leaning forward. "I expect to hear from you as soon as you confirm something and some decision is made on your future, especially if you are coming back here."

I nodded.

"Thank you," I said.

She leaned back.

"Did it ever occur to you that even if that is your mother, she might not be worth finding? If she wanted you to know she was alive, she would have called to tell you, wouldn't she?"

"I don't know," I said. "That's why I want to go."

She smirked and then looked up at me with an expression that bordered on concern and friendliness.

"I'll give you this advice: if someone's drowning and you can't save her, you'll only drown yourself as well if you don't let go," she said.

No one was more of an expert when it came to saving herself, I thought, but I didn't say it. I held her gaze for an instant and then turned to leave.

"May I ask you when you were born? The month, day, year?" Holly asked Grandma Olivia.

"You may not. That's impertinent."

"You were born between November twenty-second and December twenty-first," Holly replied, undaunted. Grandma Olivia's eyes widened and she looked at me. She must have thought I had given Holly the correct information.

"I don't know why I care, but what is that supposed to mean if it's so?"

"That you're a Sagittarius," Holly replied.

"Whatever that may mean to you, it means nothing to me," Grandma Olivia said.

Holly smiled as if she thought that was exactly what a Sagittarius like Grandma Olivia would say.

Grandma Olivia then saw to it that my two small suitcases were brought back down.

"I had had them placed in what was your mother's room," she told me at the door. "Somehow, I think you will be back."

Holly and I put my bags in her car and drove away.

"You were right," she said after a few minutes of deep silence, "she's definitely not like everyone's little old grandmother."

I started to smile and then thought about Cary.

"I have one more good-bye before we leave, Holly," I said.

"I know. I'll drop you off at the house and go get my things. Then we'll be off."

I sucked in my breath, closed my eyes, and prayed for the right words to help Cary understand the things that I didn't understand myself.

Aunt Sara and May were surprised, but happy to see me return. They were preparing dinner. Even though Cary had not come in from the sea yet, Uncle Jacob had apparently gone back upstairs to his room.

"I had a very difficult time of it," Aunt Sara said in a loud whisper, her eyes shifting toward the ceiling. "It took nearly fifteen minutes to get him up the stairs. He had to keep catching his breath. He's very upset about it. Do you have a nice room at Olivia's?" she asked with a sad smile.

"She's giving me my mother's old room," I said.

"Oh. That's very nice. I remember that room. It's airy and the windows face the sea."

"But first I have to take a trip, Aunt Sara."

"A trip? Where?"

I told her, but instead of surprising and exciting her, the news made her sad and withdrawn. She lowered her eyes and went back to her work.

"I'll come see you as soon as I return," I promised and threw my arms around her before giving her a good-bye kiss on the cheek.

"I don't understand the things some people do. It

seems they just want to make the people who love them unhappy. Like Laura, going out to sea that day. Cary said he warned her," she mumbled, her eyes on the potatoes she was mashing. "Why did she have to go?"

She wiped her eyes and turned to me.

"You don't have to go, do you, Melody?"

"Yes, Aunt Sara. I have to go or I'll never be able to sleep one single night," I said.

She nodded, wiped away her tears, smiled, and stroked my hair before returning to her work. That was how I left her.

Outside, I sat on a bench and explained my trip to May. She wished she could come along. I promised I would write her letters and post cards every chance I got and I asked her to look after Cary for me while I was away. She promised she would and we embraced and kissed. Then she ran back into the house so I wouldn't see her cry.

I sat there for a while, just enjoying the breeze on my face and watching the thin veil of clouds move in from the sea. I hadn't lived here that long, but my experiences went so deep, it seemed I had lived most of my life by the ocean. The cry of the terns was familiar now, and the colors in the water didn't surprise me as much. In my heart I was no longer an outsider. I welcomed the salty sea air, the roar of the surf, the sand between my toes. Maybe Cary was right, maybe this really was my home, and maybe Grandma Olivia's confidence about my returning came from her intuitive knowledge about me and what was true for me.

I rose and walked out on the beach. Looking toward the dock, I saw the lobster boat had arrived. I hurried over the sand and waved as soon as I drew close enough for Cary to see me. He waved back and then watched me approach. He had his hands on his hips and I knew his sharp sea eyes were fixed on my every move. He came off the boat quickly when I reached the dock.

"What's happening now?" he asked with that tight smile and those deeply penetrating eyes.

Practically without stopping for a breath, I related the day's events and then showed him the catalogue. He was speechless. All he could do was shake his head. He looked back at the boat and then shouted to Roy.

"I'll be there in a few minutes."

"No problem," Roy called back.

Cary handed the catalogue back to me and we walked up the beach. He had his hands in his pockets and walked looking down. I had my arms folded under my breasts, my head up, waiting, wondering what words would pass between us.

"You probably won't come back," he finally said. "You'll probably end up living in California."

"That's not true, Cary. Even if—if this is my mother and she has a sensible explanation for all this, I'll still come back to see you and someday—"

"Someday, what?" he said, turning. His eyes were so full of sadness and pain, I couldn't look directly at him. I gazed out at the ocean.

"Someday you and I will have our own home and you'll design boats and—"

"And May will hear and Laura will come in from the sea and my father won't die and my mother will stop crying herself to sleep. Why stop with one pipe dream when there are so many?" he said and turned away, walking quickly back toward the dock.

"Cary!"

He kept walking.

"Cary! I swear, I'll be back. Cary!"

He turned and looked at me. I ran to him and threw my arms around him. At first he let me dangle there. Then he put his arms around my waist and sighed.

"Please, just wish me luck," I said.

He nodded.

"Good luck. I'd come with you if Dad weren't so sick."

"I know you would. I'll call you and write you and—"

He put his finger on my lips

"No promises."

"No promises," I agreed, "except just this one." I kissed him hard and long and then I smiled at him and his eyes warmed. "You can believe in that, Cary Logan, and throw your skepticism overboard."

I left him standing there, smiling at me, his shoulders gleaming in the late-afternoon sun, the sea, roaring behind him, and my heart . . .

My heart crying with the terns.

Epilogue
&

I was outside the house waiting when Holly returned. Taking one last visual gulp of the house and the beach, I got into her car and we puttered away. I didn't look back.

"You all right?" she asked.

"Yes."

"This is for you," she said, reaching beneath her seat to come up with a small bag. "Kenneth sent it along."

"What is it?"

I opened the bag and dipped my fingers in to pull out a silver heart locket on a silver chain.

"He made it himself, years and years ago," she told me.

I found the tiny lever and flipped it open to look at a picture of Mommy when she couldn't have been much older than I was now. The picture on the other side had been removed. I imagined it had been a picture of Kenneth.

"He told me to tell you he gave that to your mother and before she left with your step-father, she gave it back. I think it meant a great deal to him and it wasn't easy for him to give it away."

"Yes," I said, nodding and staring at the picture of Mommy. She was, as they say, so photogenic.

"Maybe, if she's suffering from some form of amnesia, that," Holly said, nodding toward the locket, "will help revive memories."

"You don't think just looking at me would?" I asked.

"I don't know. I've heard of strange cases where people face people they've lived with all their lives and look at them as strangers: children, parents, husbands, and wives. When the mind wants to shut something out, it slams a door of steel and it takes fingers of steel to open it again."

She laughed.

"A friend of mine," she continued, "thinks amnesia proves we have other lives. She thinks it occurs when something puts us on the border between two existences, and we can't recall either one." She shrugged. "Who knows?"

"Yes," I said as the Cape Cod scenery rushed by, "who knows?"

I looked out the window at the ocean and the tourists on the beaches. In the distance I saw the lighthouse.

"How was Kenneth when you left him?" I asked.

"Back to work." She turned, a soft smile on her face. "Did you expect less? If ever he had to escape reality, he has to now," she added.

"Mommy was always trying to do that, especially when we lived in Sewell. Actually, I shouldn't be surprised by all this," I said and then I sighed. "I forgot to call Alice Morgan to thank her."

"You can call from the motel tonight."

"I want to share all the expenses, Holly. I insist."

"No problem. I saw your grandmother give you that pile of loot." She laughed.

Provincetown fell farther and farther behind us.

Mommy had brought me here under false pretenses. Supposedly, we were just visiting Daddy's relatives after his death. She made it seem like the right thing to do, and then she surprised me by telling me arrangements had been made for me to live here until she could send for me.

Well, she never did.

Or maybe she had. Maybe, ironically, she had sent for me through these pictures in the catalogue. Perhaps fate had taken control after all, and those stars and the moon Holly talked about so much had played a role in my destiny.

I had been on a mad and desperate search to discover the identity of my father. During the course of that pursuit, I entered Cary's private world, filled with his sorrows and dreams, and we discovered each other in ways I had not expected.

I would miss our walks on the beach, our talks, our laughter and tears. I knew he would spend all of his nights in his attic workshop while I was away. He would mold his dream ships and he would stop and remember me sitting quietly beside him, watching him work. We were like two people who had been cast overboard by cruel events in their lives, two people who had found each other adrift, and we had joined hands to take each other to our own private beach; our paradise.

On it we sat and watched the twilight sun kiss the horizon and leave us night after night with promises to help us face each morning. It made us stronger, gave us courage, filled our hearts with hope.

I don't want to say good-bye, Cary, I thought, but I'm afraid of where this road leads. You were right in saying we should make no promises to each other. Too often promises were made to us that could never be kept.

I came here to unravel lies, to dig away the sand

until I reached the hidden truths about ourselves, and often, like the tide, our family pushed the sand back. Here I was on a journey to unravel more, to push away more sand.

Why bother? Your eyes asked me, Cary. Why care anymore?

The answer is if I can't find the answer to who I am, then I can't be truthful to you, and Cary, my darling, my darling Cary, if there is one thing I will never do, it's lie to you.

Lies are what we have inherited, but it's not the legacy we'll leave our children.

That's why I go on.

And why I looked toward the road west and why, as we passed the sign that read Now Leaving Province-town, Cape Cod, I smiled.

I knew I would be back, and when I returned, I would be armed with the truth.